THE GOLF CLUB
MURDER

THE GOLF CLUB
MURDER

OWEN FOX JEROME

COACHWHIP PUBLICATIONS

Greenville, Ohio

The Golf Club Murder, by Owen Fox Jerome
© 2014 Coachwhip Publications

Published 1929
No claims made on public domain material.

ISBN 1-61646-279-5
ISBN-13 978-1-61646-279-6

Cover: Golf ball © Kirill Cherezov

CoachwhipBooks.com

CONTENTS

CHAPTER 1
JOHN HARDY COMES HOME

FOR A CITY of some thirty thousand souls, it was odd that West Fork had but one main business street. True, there were numerous suburban commercial centers, a large factory district, many wholesale houses, several railroads, three or four fine bridges spanning the river, an artificial beach, and a country club. Yet all of these evidences of business and modern enterprise could not dispute the fact that West Fork had but one main artery of commerce—Wilson Avenue.

Elm Street, one block south of Wilson Avenue, boasted of the county buildings, the municipal halls of justice, the Union station, newspaper row, and, last but not least, the venerable trees which gave it name. These fine old elms, arching together overhead, and making a shady tunnel of delight of the broad street, reminded one of drives in Florida, of Massachusetts Avenue in Washington.

Along this peaceful street there came a man with journey-scarred suitcase in hand. With swinging stride he walked along, passing the administration buildings and the soldiers' and sailors' monument before taking a cross street over to Wilson Avenue.

In repose or in action the stranger's face looked hard-bitten. His clothes, while of good material and conservative business cut, could not disguise this fact. He was a full six feet in height, broad of shoulder and wiry of body. His face was tanned, his blue eyes hard, and there was a puckered, star-shaped scar on the point of his lean, fighting jaw. His light brown hair had been bleached by sun and wind until any gray was merged with the general straw color. His age might have been anywhere from twenty to forty. In reality he was twenty-nine.

Without question he looked like a hard-bitten adventurer who had lived where to be off guard for an instant meant death. He looked dangerous—until he smiled. When he operated the thirteen or fourteen muscles required for smiling, his face lost its mask of truculence, and his hard eyes would twinkle into a surprising soft blueness.

"Same old town," he murmured, as his quick eyes took in details from the wrinkled old negro's ramshackle dray to the new café which faced the depot. "Same old village—and same old mossbacks riding herd on the shekels, I can see by the general drowsiness. Ten years hasn't made much of a dent in this petrifying place.

"I wonder if 'Wolf-face' Fosdick is still president of the oldest national bank in the State," his thoughts ran on musingly. "I know he is—hale and hearty and tight as ever. I know Major 'Gas-bag' Sims still is postmaster, and controls politics so that all the ineligibles of his family have fat jobs in tax-collecting offices. I guess 'Stingy Sam' Kimball still owns half the factories, with a first mortgage on the other half. I wonder if 'Greedy' Morris has acquired any more Wilson Avenue property.

"And I'm sure they all still own the evening paper, with old 'Parrot' Grimes as editor—unless the old wart is dead. I wonder who is mayor now? One of the old guard, or some timid puppet? Ye gods! The dear old home town! Hello—what's going on?"

He halted abruptly and stared. There was nothing startlingly unusual in what he saw, but this man had the knack of seeing the unusual beneath the most ordinary external appearances.

The city and county courthouse occupied the center of a square block, looking for all the world like a puffed-up elder in a church pew. And on the extreme southeast corner of the grounds stood the white, two-storied county jail, not unlike that same pompous elder's timid wife.

Parked halfway down the shady side street, midway between the man and the jail, was a little car of popular make. A decidedly pretty young woman in a summery dress of lawn and lace was seating herself behind the wheel. Two men in white and tan linens respectively had approached the car with her, evidently talking vociferously.

In itself this was not outside of everyday occurrences. But the girl was crying, dabbing occasionally at her brimming eyes with a wisp of a handkerchief. As the man with the suitcase watched, she shook her head and reached for the ignition switch. At once the lanky gentleman in tan covered the switch with his hand, while his companion stepped around the car into the street and grabbed the steering wheel.

This white-clad individual of beefy frame and protruding waistline seemed to be insisting that the girl get out of the car, pointing with one pudgy finger toward the massive pile which constituted the hall of justice.

There was no doubt that the distressed girl was pleading to be excused. At this display of obstinacy number one caught hold of her bare, round arm and sought to remove her forcibly from the machine. The girl emitted a faint cry of surprised indignation and alarm. And the man with the suitcase put his legs in rapid motion.

The bent position of the man in tan linens as he sought to drag the girl from the car, automatically suggested the logical point of attack. Before his stout companion could more than open his mouth in dismay the lanky gentleman received a heartily delivered kick squarely on the seat of his trousers. He bounced upward, lost his footing, and slid back along the sidewalk, his face flattening against the floorboards of the car. Before he could squirm out of this painful and undignified position he was gathered up by the collar and the slack of his trousers and rudely dumped on the grass of the courthouse grounds.

"Hey! You!" yelled the portly person savagely, charging at a lumbering run and waving a pair of fat arms. "What d'you mean assaulting Mr. Brentwood? I'll have you arrested for that."

He made a wild swing at the grinning countenance above him, and found himself in the grip of a pair of muscular hands which made his shoulders ache.

"Hold up, Desperate Dave," soothed the stranger. "You didn't have to come after me. I was coming over to play on your side, too."

Almost impersonally he contemplated his captive. The fellow was no older than himself, his flesh giving him the immature look of a half-grown fat boy. The sweat was streaming down his red face, his Panama hat brim *a dance* in the faint breeze as if in sympathy with his angry emotions.

"Why—'Stubby' Mallory!" exclaimed the stranger. "And 'Slim' Brentwood, eh? A precious pair, as I live."

"You impudent scoundrel!" shouted Mr. Mallory. He jerked free and managed this time to plant a blow in his captor's midriff that brought a grunt.

"All right, Fearless Fred," gasped the tall man. "You would have it." And he brought a heavy fist down on the crown of that immaculate Panama, which made its wearer behold a goodly portion of the firmament. A swift uppercut stretched him neatly across the body of his companion, again felling that gentleman prone on his face.

For the first time the girl spoke.

"Oh!" she exclaimed. And again: "Oh-h-h!"

The victor turned back to the car and smiled as he removed his cap. He felt like gasping out a few, "ohs" himself as he gazed into her wide brown eyes, red-rimmed from weeping. Her hair, which peeped beneath her flowery hat, was of some shade of brown, just what he couldn't say, only that it was beautiful.

Two faint lines about her lips showed that she was in her twenties, and indicated that she smiled a lot as a general rule. He didn't have time to glance down at her slim young ankles and daintily arched feet. He didn't note whether she was plump or slender. All he was conscious of was the wonder and awe in her glorious eyes.

"Do you know what you've done?" she almost whispered.

"Yes, ma'am. I've rescued beauty in distress."

"Oh, you mustn't joke about it. Do you know who those men are?"

"I have that pleasure. They are Stubby Mallory and Slim Brentwood. Stubby is twenty-nine years old and has always been fat. Slim is forty-odd and has always been skinny."

"You *do* know their names," she gasped again. "And you a perfect stranger. At least I have never seen you before."

"And I don't remember you," he smiled. "Have you always lived here? You see, I've been away for ten years."

"Always," she affirmed. "My name is— Look!" she commanded swiftly, breaking off and pointing behind him.

He turned his head and observed Mallory running toward the jail building.

"Quick!" she exclaimed. "Jump in, and I'll take you wherever you want to go. Oh, do hurry! Can't you understand what you've done? Mr. Brentwood is the district attorney, and Mr. Mallory is the city attorney. And you've attacked them both."

"I don't care if they are the Siamese twins," he rejoined grimly. "They had it coming to them. They had no business annoying you."

"Come on. Let's go," she cried feverishly, flipping the switch and stepping on the starter. "You didn't understand—you shouldn't have done it. Now Mallory's gone for a policeman. You'll be arrested, too."

"Too?" the tall stranger grinned as he stooped for his suitcase. "Were you under arrest when I butted in?" he continued as he placed one foot on the running board.

"No," began the girl, "but my father—"

"You stay right here, young fellow," a harsh, cold voice interrupted her. "And you, also, young woman. You're both under arrest."

The stranger turned to observe a begrimed and irate-faced Brentwood glowering at them from the sanctity of the courthouse grounds, one long, bony finger shaking in his rage as he pointed.

"The oracle is given," chuckled the stranger as he stood his suitcase on end in the car, preparatory to getting in himself. "You've been arrested now. So, step on 'er, lady. The villain still pursues them!"

There was an authoritative shout from the rear.

"Stop! Halt, or I'll fire!"

Over his shoulder the culprit saw a burly blue-coated figure approaching at a run. At the officer's heels panted Mallory. And bringing up the reserves were two plain-clothes men. The policeman clutched a wicked-looking service revolver in his right fist and his billy in his left.

"Stubby has called out the whole force," cried the unknown knight-errant. "I can't run with you or that first fool will shoot. I wanted to ask you a lot of questions, but I'll have to wait and cover your retreat."

"If you can't leave, neither will I," she avowed, eyes flashing with excitement, tears forgotten.

"You're a stanch pardner. But don't be a goose," he snapped out almost harshly. "Get going while I renew some old acquaintances here."

His face reassumed its hard quality and his crisp voice startled her. It was obvious that this man was used to being obeyed. Automatically she threw the intermediate gear in mesh.

"Don't you move an inch!" bellowed Brentwood uglily. "Officer! Arrest them both."

"Go!" crisped the stranger sharply. "I'll meet you later."

He whirled and struck up the gun hand of the burly policeman as the car shot away from the curb. One lithe foot shot out and neatly tripped the lanky Brentwood, who, upon this advent of substantial reinforcements, was leaping after the automobile. As the district attorney sprawled into the gutter the lone champion regained his own balance and raised his right forearm high enough to block the blow of the officer's billy.

He grappled with the man just in time to prevent him from sending a bullet after the fleeing car. The gun barked twice at the sky ere he could wrest it from the policeman's grip. And then, like a pack of famished wolves, the others closed in on him.

The resulting *mêlée* was all that a rough-and-tumble fighter could have wished. While the conclusion was inevitable the attackers did not have to press forward eagerly. The energetic stranger carried the fight to them. Having tossed the revolver out into the street and appropriating the officer's stick, he was strictly impartial with his favors.

Brentwood and Mallory, having invoked the majesty of the law, would have stood aside on their dignity and allowed the three officers to subdue this turbulent character. But this latter perverse individual bent all of his efforts to bring them into the scuffle.

Despite their numbers the active stranger was working havoc in their midst. It seemed to the cursing, perspiring five that they were trying to corral a bunch of steel springs. And there was no other help at hand save the jailer, who dared not leave the building. The instant Brentwood or Mallory won free of the fight and started to withdraw to safer ground, the stranger shook himself clear of the others long enough to collar the fugitive and fling him back into the mass. It was, in all, a close-knit, loose-flung, running, standing affair with the stranger everywhere at once, and the others as slow as uncertain elephants.

Once a plain-clothes man broke free and ran out into the street after the policeman's revolver. At once the hard-faced, hard-hitting man shook loose and darted after him. He tackled the fellow in a flying dive just as the man leaned over for the gun. They went down in a heap, the detective's head thwacking against the paving with such force as to leave him out of the fight definitely. The stranger bounded to his feet and charged back so quickly as to meet his slower antagonists before they had fairly followed him into the street.

But this action of his had been too far afield. The heavy-set Mallory, linen coat torn all the way down his back, had run, or rather, staggered, in the opposite direction, and reached the nearest fire alarm box. He turned in an alarm before the fight could be carried back to him.

The girl in the car had long since vanished, turning down Elm Street. As the shrill siren of the fire chief's car from number one station, a block beyond Wilson Avenue, sounded his arrival, and as a belated patrolman came running from a point on Elm Street, the stranger succumbed to the sheer force of numbers. Handcuffed and sardonically silent, he was led by his battered captors into the jail building.

"Lock him up and chain him," commanded Mallory through thickened lips as he turned to assist Fire Chief Killore to remove the unconscious detective from the street.

Mr. Brentwood, the district attorney, dizzily forced his way through the gathering crowd and made silently for Elm Street.

Aware that he was a wreck from head to heels, heedless of the gaping stares, he walked one block beyond the courthouse and entered the building which housed the *Evening Planet*. "Parrot" Grimes, so called by the masses because he was the mouthpiece of big business, half rose from his editorial chair and stared aghast at the apparition. He followed the district attorney to the lavatory.

"Damn the scoundrel!" groaned Mr. Brentwood as he laved his bruised and battered countenance in cold water. "Oh! I think my nose is broken. Damn the troublesome whelp! Ouch! My lip! But they've got him safely in jail. Mallory didn't recognize him, but I did. I remembered him by that puckered scar he got from a broken bottle when he led the high school football team in that fight with the smelter gang. Ooh! Two teeth loosened. I'll make him sweat for this, the damned trouble breeder! I—"

"What on earth has happened, Mr. Brentwood?" gasped the smug little editor. "There were gunshots, a fire run by number one, and now you—looking like you'd been in an explosion. What happened to you? What was it?"

"Oooo!" moaned Mr. Brentwood as he straightened up and groped blindly for a towel. "Oh, my neck! What the devil did he come back for? Nobody sent for him. His people are all dead. Ouch! I—"

"What in hell?" puzzled Mr. Grimes in bewilderment.

"Oh, shut up!" snapped Brentwood. "Go sit down!"

"But, my dear Mr. Brentwood, what—"

"What? What? John Hardy's come home. That's what."

CHAPTER II
MR. WRIGHT'S PREDICAMENT

THERE ARE TWO POINTS now to be considered, one of which the heavy-fisted John Hardy had forgotten in his brief summary of the business heads of his home town, and the other he could not have known. And because of his impulsive participation in the little affair of the unknown young lady and the two attorneys, he had inextricably snarled himself in the tangled skein of both.

The first point: In recalling the financial fossils who had for years strangled and choked the natural growth and business of a young city geographically perfect, on a mighty waterway and near the meeting point of four States, he had overlooked a significant fact. This was the one rebellious factor of real importance that stood out against the old guard tyranny, which stifled the city for its own selfish ends, the ultimate aims of which were cloaked in clouds of obscurity. It was the *Morning Blade* which constituted this champion for the people.

West Fork's newspaper row consisted of one block of buildings which faced on Elm Street. Half of these were given over to the various business offices and presses of the *Evening Planet*, which was, to give Mephistopheles all merit, a modern and efficient plant. The other half of the block housed the activities of the morning paper. While operated on limited private capital, and without the powers that were to support it, the *Morning Blade* was a plant quite as up to date as its competitor and in solid favor with the masses.

Howard K. Wright, the founder and owner of this organ of the press, had settled in West Fork some twenty-six years previously.

He had come from Indiana, and was not the son of a native settler in this hidebound community. At the time he had thought he saw a great future for the town and the surrounding country. So he invested his capital, married a local belle, and involved himself inextricably, before he found that he had sat in on a sewed-up poker game. Too late to save himself, he had grimly tightened his lips, squared his shoulders, and given mighty battle, knowing that he could expect no mercy from banks and business, should his financial armor develop a vulnerable spot.

At fifty-five Wright was still the big, muscular giant that he had been in his youth, his rotundity but increasing his massive appearance and enhancing his air of power, both mental and physical. He was a brilliant man with a vast fund of humor and common sense. Perhaps it describes him fittingly to say that he was an editor who actually wrote his own editorials.

He had weathered many hardships, had struggled through numerous vicissitudes, had championed many a cause and won most of them, had been perilously near annihilation more than once, and had recovered. He had many friends among the masses, and there was no doubt that his paper greatly influenced the vote of the populace. But he had no friends in power, and therefore he was forced to step warily. He had never had the wealth openly to defy the combined capital arrayed against him, and do exactly as he pleased with his publication. He, a Hercules, had been forced into the role of a pygmy. Business has many arteries, and he had been shackled by the conventions.

All of this by way of prelude to the strike of the United Factory Workers. It was during this stressful time, a scant year previous to the return of John. Hardy, that Howard Wright made the mistake which ruined him. While not a strong advocate of unionism in its present American sense, he saw that the factory workers had justice and reason in their demands and in their trouble. The *Morning Blade* elected to champion their cause. They lost, and the financial powers decided that the *Morning Blade* had existed long enough.

Thanks to Stingy Sam Kimball and his power, the circulation of the morning paper was cut a full third. It was forbidden to every

worker in every factory in town. Greedy Morris exercised his influence along with the banks, and every worthwhile retail house
ceased advertising in the *Blade*. Stubby Mallory's father, a judge
on the Federal Bench, and Slim Brentwood proceeded to tie Wright
up in lawsuits and litigation. The result was inevitable.

Wright was forced into the arms of Wolf-face Fosdick, who had
long awaited him. He had to borrow money, a lot of money. Was
he refused? He was not. To refuse loans on first-class security was
not President Fosdick's method of doing business. He loaned and
loaned until Wright was hopelessly in his toils.

The second point which John Hardy could not have known concerned Fosdick, president of the First National Bank. Thurlowe C.
Fosdick was no longer president of the bank. He was no longer
president of anything. No longer would he clog the wheels of
progress. Never again would he lend money to a business or an
industry, which the inner clique coveted, only to close down upon
it without warning and wrest the prize from the hands of the organizer or proprietor. For Wolf-face Fosdick was dead. According to
the coroner he had been dead approximately twenty-seven hours
when John Hardy assaulted two attorneys of prominent standing
and three representatives of the law.

Two days before the advent of the troublesome Mr. Hardy one
of Howard K. Wright's notes for five thousand dollars fell due at
the bank. When the newspaperman called at the bank to pay the
interest and renew the loan President Fosdick sprang trap number one in his private banking code.

He was seated at his mahogany desk in his beautiful private
office when he deigned to see the somewhat nervous Mr. Wright.
Wright noticed the slight discourtesy offered when the other did
not acknowledge his presence for five long paragraphs in the letter he was reading. The big man's lip curled faintly, but he seated
himself silently. He hated himself because he dared not demand
Fosdick's attention. But he dared not antagonize the banker; he
was no longer master of his fate.

He studied the lean, cold face and white hair of the banker while
he waited. The piercing, calculating gray eyes did not need to rest

on him for him to visualize their sharp, wolfish expression. Fosdick was lean and wiry, active enough for his sixty-odd years. He was the sort of man who withered and shrank and dwindled down to leathery skin and stringy muscles, a sort of hard human knot that existed on little and lived on and on. Wright would have made a full two of him, but the big man was confident that the banker would far outlive him.

"Well, Wright," finally offered Fosdick coldly, "what can I do for you to-day?"

The newspaperman did not bat an eye at this curt use of his surname. He read the handwriting on the wall, but he did not falter.

"Nothing much, Mr. Fosdick," he replied easily. "A note of mine for five thousand falls due to-day, and—"

"Oh, is that so?" interrupted the banker in surprise. "It seems like it was just the other day that you renewed a note for five thousand. Time is quite ruthless with us. Wait until I send for the note case."

"That won't be necessary," remarked Wright dryly. "I did renew a five thousand-dollar loan last week. That was my third note. To-day's note is my first again. I have here a check for my interest and a renewal made out by the cashier. He would not renew it on my signature, but told me to come in for your O.K. first. Here is the whole thing."

He laid several papers on the desk before the other. Fosdick picked them up one at a time and silently scanned them. Wright waited.

"Well?" commented the banker at length, looking up.

"If you will simply O.K. the renewal that will cover the little transaction."

Fosdick appeared to cogitate. He swung partly around to stare over the green velvet draperies covering the lower half of the nearest window. He tapped lightly on his polished desk with two immaculate fingernails as he considered. At length he sighed.

"I'm sorry, Wright," he said, turning back to the waiting man, "but it is impossible. In fact, we shall have to call in your other loans. At the last directors' meeting I was ordered to retrench, as business conditions are bad just now. I'm afraid we can't carry you any longer."

"I am not asking for another loan," replied Wright steadily. "I am paying the interest, I have pledged good security, and I am worth far more than the fifteen thousand dollars I owe this bank. I merely wish to renew this note, I trust for the last time."

Fosdick slowly shook his head.

"It can't be done," he repeated softly.

"You mean you won't," stated Wright bluntly.

"My dear fellow, you put me in an unfavorable light," protested the banker smoothly. "I am not in a position to accommodate you. The board of directors—"

"—be damned!" cut in Wright tersely. "Don't hand any of that piddle to me that you use on your small fry. You are the whole cheese and we both know it. We understand conditions thoroughly. This is one of the safest securities you have in your vault. My paper alone is worth fifty thousand dollars in equipment, not to speak of its standing and circulation. My home is worth twenty thousand more. And I am not loaded down with debt except for this paper of mine you hold."

"I'm sorry," reiterated Fosdick coldly.

"Where do you stand to lose anything?" demanded Wright. "If I should die suddenly I have twenty-five thousand dollars' worth of insurance which goes to the paper alone, not to mention the insurance I carry for my daughter's sake."

"Then why don't you borrow something on your insurance?" suggested Fosdick.

Wright gritted his teeth.

"I borrowed to the limit before I came to you. I exhausted every source before you got me, and you damn well know it."

Fosdick shrugged and dropped his eyes to that important letter. Wright's face whitened. He was doomed.

"I was a fool to come to you in the first place," he declared. "I might have known—I did know, but I hoped to win out before you pinched down on me. Well—what are you going to do?"

"If you cannot pay off your notes, the bank will have to protect itself."

"And that means?"

"That I offer you ten thousand dollars over and above your notes for the paper."

"This is preposterous!"

"And that offer holds good for twenty-four hours only," went on the banker coolly, ignoring the exclamation. "If you fail to accept—I fear the *Morning Blade* will have to be sold under the hammer to the highest bidder. And I imagine that it will bring little more than enough to pay your notes."

"You would see to that," declared Wright bitingly. "And you call this—this brigandage good business."

"Threats and aspersions will get you nowhere, Mr. Wright," offered Fosdick indifferently. "I didn't ask you to come to me for money."

"Oh no," admitted Wright bitterly. "You've simply ruined me—stripped me almost clean, and I have no recourse. No wonder they call this bank the 'Suicide Club.' You leave no way out but death for your victims. And your gang has got this town frozen so tight that I can go nowhere else for help. Out-of-town aid is out of the question.

"You've frozen out every decent business and all foreign capital that ever tried to come here. You only let in small industries, allow them to grow a little and then you take them for your own. Because of the damnable tightness of this town I've had to be careful of what my paper has said and done. But now, by God, I'll tell you for once what I think of you and your blood-sucking cohorts. You—"

Fosdick, his naturally pale face going dead white, arose stiffly from his chair. One hand searched under the edge of his desk while the other pointed toward the door.

"Get out!" he commanded viciously. "Get out, you big false alarm! The *Morning Blade* will be attached within twenty-four hours. My offer is withdrawn."

"Shut up and sit down!" roared Wright. "I'm not going till I cram a little truth down your buzzard throat. To hell with your fine offer! It's worth ten thousand dollars to at last express myself. You and the others of your ilk have sucked this poor town dry of all potential business. You've petrified it. Your mind is so narrow you can't slip a piece of paper in edgewise. What this town needs is two dozen first-class funerals, beginning with yours. If I were half the man I claim to be, I'd kill you myself.

"You thought I'd come begging for mercy, and sell my soul to be allowed to hold the *Blade*. Well, that's one satisfaction you won't have. You've ruined me at last. And I saw it coming twenty-five years ago. Take the paper and be damned to you! But while you've broken me, you haven't conquered me. If I didn't have some respect for this town I'd publish in tomorrow's issue all of the facts I've been gathering about you and Kimball and Brentwood and Morris and the rest of them that would condemn West Fork forever more. You ought to drop dead—"

Wright was interrupted by a rough hand on his shoulder. He whirled to find himself facing the hard-eyed police officer who did guard duty in the bank during business hours. Behind the bluecoat stood Fosdick's private secretary and the assistant cashier.

"Put him out!" ordered Fosdick, so furious that he could not raise his voice above a whisper. "Throw him out!"

"That won't be necessary," said Wright, slowly recovering himself. "I'm leaving now in search of clean air."

He passed out with head erect and chin jutting out, brushing through the small crowd at the door of the president's office, little knowing or caring how much of his outburst had been overheard.

Fosdick watched him go with gray eyes that blazed in cold fury. Then he waved all of his subordinates out of the office and sank back into his chair, more upset than he had been for years. Wright had always had an irritating manner about him that Fosdick hated, and he always made his remarks sting when he wanted to. He didn't see the collapse of Wright when the latter was in the sanctity of his own office or hear the sobs of the big man as he faced the fact that at fifty-five he was all but penniless and on the verge of losing the thing he loved next to his only daughter—his newspaper.

Fosdick only knew that he had not broken the big man's spirit. He had been mercilessly flayed in the interview and the only balm which he had to offer himself was the knowledge that the *Morning Blade* was worth nearer a hundred thousand dollars than fifteen thousand in actual cash, and worth far more than that to his cohorts. The worst tormentor and agitator had been silenced.

Ordinarily this comforting thought would have furnished all the sedative or anodyne needed by the worthy Mr. Fosdick. But with such a man as Wright, it was different. He was thrown off his work for the rest of the day and let a loan get by him that was below his par of good security.

How Mr. Fosdick spent the night is unknown. While his enmity might have kept him awake, it is a surety that his conscience did not trouble him. But he was so off color that he did not go down to the bank at nine o'clock. Instead, he was out at the country club teeing off for the first hole at seven o'clock.

Golf was Fosdick's only hobby and only form of exercise. He played a very good game and continually dreamed of reducing his handicap. And many a financial problem and fate of a good man was threshed out and settled as he tramped along between shots.

Wright was also a member of the country club. He played a fair game, but did not participate in any of the tournaments. The morning of the day Fosdick was to set matters in motion for seizing the *Blade*, having passed a sleepless night, Wright went out to the club at eight o'clock and also started on a solitary round wherein he could think out his problem.

He returned to the clubhouse in less than an hour, his clothes muddy and torn. Without stopping for a shower and change of dress, he nervously told the attendant that he was way off his game and had quit in disgust on the third hole. Then he had driven back to town, driving furiously, according to the attendant.

At ten o'clock no word was heard from President Fosdick. By noon the bank officials were telephoning all over town for him. The morning attendant at the club now remembered that he had seen the banker start out around the course at seven o'clock and that he hadn't seen him come back in. As Fosdick was not in the habit of making uncertain moves such as this, a search was instituted.

At two o'clock his body was found in a small clump of trees to one side of the fairway between holes five and six. He was so badly mutilated that his body was hardly recognizable at first. Shattered pieces of golf club were found nearby. There was no doubt that he had been murdered, and little doubt as to the brutal method.

The club attendant made a solemn and frightened statement that no players had gone out on the course this Friday morning save Fosdick and Wright, early morning golf on weekdays being somewhat beyond the effort and inclinations of the elite. Employees of the First National Bank recalled the scene between the two men the day before and the hot words passed. The position Wright had been put in by the remorseless banker became public property.

The result was inevitable. Wright was promptly arrested and jailed without bond.

CHAPTER III
ASSAULT AND BATTERY ONLY

THE FIRST THING John Hardy did upon finding himself confined in a steel-barred cell and chained to his iron bunk, was to take stock. He had not come off scathless in the rough-and-tumble fight. One eye was slowly blackening, a beautiful knot was growing and throbbing with painful intensity above one ear, his clothing was a wreck, and he was disheveled and bloody. With his features set in that saturnine expression of his, he certainly looked the part of a dangerous criminal probably wanted for murder in half a dozen States.

His first conclusion was that he had acted a great deal on the order of a well-known beast of burden. He had never set eyes on the girl before; he knew nothing of the reason why she was being detained. She might have been a bootlegger or a shoplifter for all he knew. Within fifteen minutes of setting foot in his home town after an absence of ten years he had participated in a row, the antecedents of which he knew nothing, which had landed him in jail.

That there would be a number of charges against him and a very stiff fine, he was well aware. In fact, he would do well to escape a jail sentence of thirty or sixty days. And then, as he thought again of the fathomless eyes of the damsel in distress, he grimly decided that he would do it all over had he another choice.

This point being settled, he considered the position in which he now found himself. His wallet, containing some sixty or seventy dollars, his watch, his fountain pen and a small notebook in which he had jotted down a few addresses of people he had met and a list or two of items he had long since bought and forgotten, had been taken from his person and now reposed in the jailer's desk downstairs.

Had it not been for his name engraved on the back of the handsome watch his uncle had given him as a graduation present when he finished high school, there would have been no identification mark by which to name and place him.

John had been traveling in the fashion known as light. All of the changes of clothing, his bank books, his letters, in fact, everything, had been in the suitcase which he had placed in the car with the unknown young lady. And she had departed without leaving name or address. This was unfortunate for John. For within that suitcase reposed the necessary sesame to the door of his cell. If he didn't locate that girl immediately, he was likely to languish in durance vile until he was permitted to get in touch with certain persons in Kansas City. As to finding the young lady, it would have been a sufficiently difficult job had he possessed his freedom.

Having exhausted this avenue of speculation to no advantage, he resolutely dismissed this matter from his mind. It was not John Hardy's habit to worry about things he could not help. His thoughts turned to the conditions of West Fork, which was apparently the same single-track town it had been the day he was born here.

So old man Mallory's son, Stubby, a fellow classmate of Hardy's, had overcome his inane inertia sufficiently to follow in his crafty father's footsteps. Despite his fatty mind and bodily avoirdupois, was he developing into material proof that the coming generation was going to follow exactly in the footsteps of the old guard? If this were true, there was no help for West Fork. The town was doomed to eternal stagnation.

John's pessimistic meditations were interrupted by the approach down the corridor of the assistant jailer with a dinner tray. At the rattle of a key in the lock of the cell door he looked up. At sight of the weather-beaten old Irish face of the food bearer he grinned.

"Why, Terry Callahan, you old reprobate! Are you still playing politics?"

"Shure an' thot's me name, me bucko, but I can't say as I remember yer mug."

"The last time I saw you, Terry, you were pounding a beat on lower Wilson Avenue. Before that, a number of years before that, I used to rob your plum trees every June before the plums were quite ripe. Do you remember how you thought you stopped me when you got that bulldog? And how I fooled you by making friends with old Pat? Surely you haven't forgotten modest Johnny Hardy."

"Modest, me eye!" shouted Callahan, nearly dropping his tray. "So ye're th' demon they've got chained in number foive. Well, well, 'Scrappin' John Hardy! Where in hill have ye been fer th' last tin years?"

"I've rambled over a lot of territory since I left home, Terry. And I just got back this morning. But you malign me; I'm no scrapper."

"Oh, no," retorted Callahan dryly. "Shure an' ye've landed in jail this mornin' fer wearin' vi'let perfume. B'y, by, but 'tis wan glad sight fer sore eyes that ye be. Wot in hill possessed ye this mornin'? Shure an' I fear 'tis wan divil o' a mess that ye've got yerself into."

"Oh, that? That was just my regular morning exercise," laughed Hardy. "Where were you when the explosion took place?"

"I was in th' kitchen seem' about dinner fer th' jailbirds we're nestin' here. But ye mustn't joke, lad. 'Tis no laughin' matter. Thot's why I'm bringin' ye yer dinner first. They're gonna take ye over to th' courthouse right away an' sweat ye fer complicity in murder."

"Murder? That's an ugly word, Terry. You don't mean that I cracked that detective's skull, do you? I was just playing with him."

"No, no. 'Tis nothin' like thot. Monroe is none th' worse off fer a bit o' a headache. Shure an' it proves th' b'y has brains which I was beginnin' to doubt. 'Tis about th' murder o' Misther Fosdick thot I have reference."

"What! You don't mean Wolf-face Fosdick of the First National Bank?" cried Hardy in profound amazement.

"None other, lad," affirmed Callahan solemnly. "He was kilt entirely out on th' golf grounds yestiddy mornin'."

"Well, what do you know about that?" murmured Hardy slowly. "Who had the impulse to remove that rat from the face of the earth? It was a darned good deed and I'd like to shake hands with the man who did it. Fosdick ruined my father and hastened his death. Do you remember it, Terry?"

"Hush, lad, hush!" cried Callahan in a tense whisper. "Fer Hivin's sake, don't say thot. Shure an' it couples ye right up wid th' affair. I know 'tis idle talk on yer part an' thot ye wouldn't shake hands wid a murderer, but Brentwood would be delighted to have such a remark of yers like thot on record."

"Ah, yes," muttered Hardy, lowering his voice. "No doubt. But just how does it happen that I am linked up with the matter? I only came home this morning."

"I know it, Johnny. But there's evidence thot Misther Wright did th' job—an' ye stopped Brentwood and young Mallory from quizzin' his daughter when she came down to see her father this mornin'. Now, d'ye get th' idea? Wot in hill made ye butt in?"

"That's what this town needs, Terry. More butt-ins. So I kept the prosecutors from interviewing the daughter of the suspected man, did I? That does look bad, Terry. But, damn it, they had it coming by the way they were treating the poor girl."

"Mebbe so," admitted Callahan dubiously. "But look wot wan devil o' a fix it puts ye in."

"Wright? Wright?" mused Hardy. "What Wright is it, Terry?"

"Howard Wright, th' owner an' publisher o' th' *Mornin' Blade*. Shure ye remember him?"

"Of course! I had forgotten. Surely I remember Mr. Wright. He was the only champion of the people we had. And so she is Howard Wright's daughter. Well, who'd have thought it? I don't even re-member that he had a daughter. How old is she, Terry?"

"'Tis a leadin' question ye've th' nerve to ask. Faith, an' how should I know anything about th' *cailin*—colleen—at all, at all?"

"You shouldn't," agreed Hardy frankly. "But in this town everybody knows everybody else's business, and I'm gambling that you can tell me."

Callahan grinned sheepishly and pointed to the tray.

"Eat yer dinner, ye spalpeen," he directed. "Shure an' I'll lose me job tellin' ye th' least bit. I must be feedin' th' rest o' th' guests."

"Tell me that before you leave, Terry. Please. I'll be good," begged Hardy.

"If ye must know, Zoe Ann Wright has just turned twenty-foive. She's heart-whole an' fancy-free, her father's in wan hill o' a fix, an' she's not fer th' likes o' ye. Young Mallory an' young Wilson, whose father is president o' th' Farmers' National Bank, seem to be castin' sheep's eyes after her."

"Well, it was a damn poor play Mallory made this morning then," growled Hardy savagely. "Further more I can see that West Fork needs me, Terry. I hadn't made up my mind this morning when I got off the train whether I was staying here for two hours or two weeks. I can see that I'm going to stay here indefinitely."

"Without doubt," agreed Callahan sarcastically, evening up the score with Hardy for his comment on gossip. "Ye'll likely spend thirty days here wid me. Brentwood an' Mallory'll be holdin' ye fast fer assault if they don't pin bigger trouble onto ye."

"They'll be anxious to let me go before I'm done with them," prophesied Hardy ominously, his eyes losing their softness and fixing Callahan as though he were partly responsible for the attitude of the two attorneys.

"Domned if ye don't look like th' father o' trouble. Don't eye me like thot, ye rascal," declared Callahan hastily. "Shure an' ole Terence Callahan ain't mixed up wid this business."

"Not yet, but you're going to be," stated Hardy. "Wait! Come here! Come over here—I'm not going to grapple with you," he said, as the wary jailer hesitated. "Come here, I want to tell you something. Is Mr. Wright confined in this building?"

"Shure," nodded Callahan. "He's up at th' end o' th' corridor on this floor. They won't let th' poor man see any wan but his daughter an' his lawyer."

"I see. Now, listen to me, Terry Callahan. You've worked hard all your life here in West Fork and you've never got anywhere. Don't interrupt, and don't argue. I know you. Terry, a comfortable income and a cheery old age is staring you in the face at this very minute. It beams upon you under the guise popularly called opportunity. Do you understand? And there is mighty little effort you have to expend in order to grasp it. But you must not err in what you are to do.

"In the first place, see that I am put, not in this cell, but in the cell next that of Mr. Wright when I am returned from the chamber of investigation over yonder. I don't care how you do it. See that it is done if you have to shuffle every prisoner about on this floor."

"'Tis impossible!" gasped the assistant jailer, aghast at his commission. "Ye're loony, me b'y. Ye—I can't do it, Johnny. Shure an' I'd lose me job immediate if I done it. Why—"

"You'll lose more than your job if you don't," warned Hardy crisply. "Now, get out! I hear somebody coming up the stairs."

Callahan got out. And John Hardy fell to musing as he munched the rather insipid and tasteless meal before him.

"So her name is Zoe Ann. Zoe Ann! Zoe Ann Wright! A euphonious name, certainly. Zoe Ann! An unusual name, a pretty name—a melody in two simple syllables. And she is twenty-five. Twenty-five—she must have been graduating from eighth grade the June I graduated from high school.

"I tried to make good for a strenuous year during what would have been her freshman ordeal—if she went to school here. By the time she hit the society columns I was gone. So I guess there's nothing unusual in the fact that I don't remember hearing of her before. And now I know how to find my suitcase."

IT WAS A TALL-CEILINGED but nevertheless stuffy box of a room in which John Hardy was seated for a rigid examination. He found himself surrounded by the deputy sheriff who had accompanied him from the jail, a court stenographer, a patched and sore Mallory, and a wooden-faced individual of numerous years and grafts who was the present incumbent of the office of municipal judge.

"This is the prisoner to be arraigned, your honor," announced Stubby Mallory through painful but dignified lips, as Hardy seated himself facing the judge. "He answers to the name of John Hardy."

Hardy grinned faintly at the legal phrasing of the other. Swiftly taking in the details about him he gathered that this was a private hearing. He lifted his voice in a familiar cant:

"Oyez! Oyez! Oyez! Comes now the defendant, one Jonathan Davidicus Hardybus, produced without writ of habeas corpus, to answer to divers charges which border on high treason," he mimicked. "Carry on, gentlemen. The prisoner sits handcuffed, humble and impotent in thy august presence."

"Silence, young man!" rapped out the judge sharply. "I'll fine you for contempt of court."

"Wouldn't that be rather difficult, your honor?" rejoined Hardy cheerfully. "Especially at a private hearing where court has not been convened? Jot that down, Mr. Stenographer, as an able rejoinder, even though the papers wouldn't dare print such an evidence of *lese majesty* if you dared offer it to them."

The deputy grinned as Judge Melguard frowned. Mallory spoke.

"John Hardy," he said, "this may be a private examination, but I advise you to talk mighty straight because a serious charge is pending over you."

"What charge?" demanded Hardy at once.

"Er—you will be informed in good time," put in Melguard.

"I'll be informed now or I won't submit to this cross-examination," corrected the prisoner firmly. "What kind of high-handed monkey business do you think you're running here? Whoever heard of a prisoner not being informed of the charge against him?"

"There is no charge against you as yet except that of assault and battery," stated Mallory ominously. "And if—"

"Very well, examine me on that count only," interrupted Hardy crisply. "I'll submit to a private hearing on that count and a private sentence."

Melguard seemed in somewhat of a quandary. Hardy intercepted a gesture of assent which Mallory made toward the judge. The latter official cleared his throat and frowned heavily at the prisoner.

"You are held for assaulting the district and the city attorneys," he stated pompously. "What have you to say?"

"How about the three policemen?" prompted Hardy.

"They—they are included in the charge."

"Then you are waiving a charge of resisting arrest?"

"Er—"

"Yes," decided Mallory, answering for the judge.

"There are no other charges to be brought against me?" insisted Hardy. "Disturbance of the peace? Any technicality? Anything concerning my little activities this morning? In brief, you prefer a blanket charge of assault and battery on two citizens—two attorneys, I mean? Whatever the decision in the case covers the entire affair?"

"Never mind the sarcasm," growled Mallory viciously. "Yes, you may consider the matter as a blanket charge—regarding your acts this morning," he concluded with a sinister smile.

"Make a note of that, Mr. Stenographer," directed Hardy. "Mr. Deputy, you are a witness to that statement."

"You act like a shyster lawyer who is afraid of the word of his betters," sneered Mallory. "What have you been doing since you left home? Were you an ambulance-chasing lawyer?"

This was Mallory's first acknowledgment of Hardy's identity.

"I am afraid," admitted Hardy frankly. "You ask what I've been doing? I've been tied up in litigation over range water rights for cattle and then over deeds and leases for the same land after oil was found under it. I've learned enough about sharp lawyers to keep you from sewing me up, Stubby."

Mallory flushed furiously.

"Don't address me so familiarly," he fumed. "And don't call me 'Stubby.' My name is Mr. Mallory."

"Not to me," announced Hardy contemptuously. "I knew you as Stubby, and Stubby you shall remain to the end of the chapter."

The attorney sprang angrily to his feet and raised one clenched fist.

"Please take things easy, Mr. Mallory," soothed the deputy. "I can't let you hit a handcuffed prisoner, you know."

"Let him hit me," taunted Hardy. "That will give me grounds for a countercharge. We'll have this whole thing thrown out of court before it can come up."

It was obvious to every one present that the prisoner had the best of the legal arguments by far. Mallory realized that he was letting a layman make a legal donkey out of him, and he controlled his emotions with an effort. He subsided into his seat and nodded to Judge Melguard.

"Proceed with your examination, your honor," he said. "I will restrain myself."

"What is your name, your age, your occupation, and your residence?" Judge Melguard demanded of the prisoner.

"John David Hardy—twenty-nine—rejuvenator—West Fork," stated the latter.

"You will kindly drop that jocose or sarcastic manner," frowned the judge, disapprovingly. "Answer the last two questions properly."

"I never was more serious in my life. My residence is West Fork, both now and formerly. And my task is to rejuvenate this city."

"Humph!" the judge cleared his throat, while Mallory openly sneered. "I understand that you really were a former resident of this city. Is this true?"

"It is, your honor."

"Where have you been in the intervening time—ten years, I believe?"

"I must decline to answer that question as it is none of the court's business. It is an immaterial matter on such a trivial charge."

"You are well on the way to indictment on a far more serious charge than you imagine," stated the judge grimly.

"So you hinted before," returned Hardy dryly. "When that moment arrives, and it becomes necessary, I will reply to your question."

"Hummmm. You will please give your true occupation."

"I have done so."

"Such a profession is not recognized in law. By what occupation do you earn your livelihood?"

"None, your honor."

"Ha!" exclaimed Mallory triumphantly. "You admit that you are not working?"

"I admit that I am not working in the accepted ways to which you are trying to pin me down. I deny that I am not working, however."

"Where is your source of income?" demanded Mallory.

"I decline to answer on the same grounds as I refused to answer the judge's question—Stubby."

Mallory colored, but he held his temper admirably. He turned to the judge.

"Note, your honor, that the prisoner refuses to answer that particular question."

Melguard nodded judiciously. He fixed the prisoner, who sat at such nonchalant ease, with hard eyes.

"Give an account of your actions for the past forty-eight hours," he ordered.

"I fail to see what that has to do with the charge of assault," replied Hardy coldly, "but I will reply to that question. The day before yesterday and yesterday I spent in Kansas City—the closest I have been to West Fork since I left here ten years ago. If you will get in touch with President Lyons of the Industrial National Bank of that city you will learn that I was in his office with him on both days in question.

"I took the night train out of Kansas City and arrived here just a few moments before the little street-brawl. As this is a junction point for the Kansas-Pacific Railroad you can verify my statement that I was on this train by interviewing both conductor and Pullman porter of the train that came in this morning."

The judge turned his gaze dubiously toward Mallory.

"If this man's statement is true, Mr. Mallory," he said, "I fail to see how we can find an indictment on that other charge."

"If it is true, we can't," admitted Mallory savagely. "But I know this man's shady reputation of the past, and we're going to hold him until we check up on him. In the meantime, I'll press that charge of assault."

"Shady reputation!" ejaculated Hardy, stiffening. "That's a libelous remark, my fat friend, and unless you retract it right now, I'll see that you are put to the expense and trouble of proving it."

Hardy's face settled into that grim mask of forbidding aspect as his eyes glinted dangerously. Mallory saw that discretion was the better course. No telling how much money this fellow might have to fight a libel suit with.

"Very well, I withdraw that exact statement," he said lamely.

"What have you to say for yourself anent the charge of assault?" demanded Judge Melguard severely. It began to look to the judge as though this wily culprit were going to win all points.

"If you have reference to that fight this morning," replied Hardy sturdily, "I plead guilty to assaulting a pair of precious rascals who were molesting an unknown young lady."

Mallory checked an exclamation of anger at the phrasing. Melguard went on with his questioning.

"If this young lady was unknown to you, how do you know she was being molested?"

"I could tell by the actions of the three."

"Were you near enough to overhear the conversation?" demanded the judge shrewdly, while Mallory's face sharpened in faint hope that the prisoner would fall into this trap.

"I was not," admitted Hardy truthfully, knowing that this admission cinched the charge against him, but left him clear of any complicity in murder by interfering, with knowledge in what he was doing, between the law and the daughter of the man held for manslaughter.

The judge turned back to the younger attorney for counsel at this point. Mallory's face fell, but he arose and whispered in the judge's ear. The latter nodded and made known his decision.

"Very well, your own admission finds you guilty of the charge. I fine you one hundred dollars for assault and battery, or ninety days in jail. If you are not satisfied with this private hearing you may make known your protest and I will try your case in the municipal court the first thing Monday morning, to-morrow being Sunday."

"I am perfectly satisfied, your honor, irregular though the proceedings have been," announced Hardy. "It was worth a hundred dollars to ruin two linen suits, although I didn't do half enough to the wearers. In suggesting the amount of the fine to Judge Melguard, Stubby," he went on, grinning devilishly at Mallory, "you neatly calculated to top the cash I carry by twenty-odd dollars, so that I would be sure to remain in jail for a few days at least.

"But you forgot my watch, didn't you? I can pawn it for thirty or forty dollars, put all the money together, pay my fine, and be free before sundown this afternoon. That's the trouble with this town, Stubby. Vision entirely too narrow. You can't see ahead beyond the end of your nose."

Mallory's face expressed such chagrin that Hardy laughed aloud.

"Never mind, Stubby," he consoled, "I am not going to pawn my watch. I'm going back to jail like a good little boy with my friend the deputy here. When you run along to see Slim Brentwood, present him with my compliments and tell him that I have been properly subdued on the meager charge you had against me.

"And say, Stubby," he added keenly. "When I do pay my fine or the balance of my fine which I don't serve in jail, and you see me walking free on the streets, don't have me arrested on that second count of vagabondage you are considering without first looking me up carefully. Let's go, Mr. Deputy. I'm tired of associating with my betters."

CHAPTER IV
WRIGHT MAKES A STATEMENT

THE FUTURE LOOKED very black indeed to Mr. Howard K. Wright as he sat brooding in his cell. Fosdick's body had been found at two o'clock Friday; he had been arrested an hour later at his office at the *Morning Blade* plant, where he had been putting his affairs in order. This very fact had been contorted into evidence of his intentions of fleeing the country. It was now something after three o'clock Saturday afternoon. He had been confined for more than twenty-four hours—nor was this the end.

He was practically penniless, his lawyer was not the most brilliant man at the bar, the evidence against him was overwhelming, the powers were against him. The course of suicide to save his daughter from poverty and his newspaper from disaster was no longer open for his consideration; he had lost the power to control his own actions.

The only kind words he had heard since his arrest had been the brief phrases of Terry Callahan. Despite himself, the big man's nerve was weakening. He wondered how long it would take them to convict him of murder in the first degree. With a sort of impersonal detachment he wondered how it felt to be electrocuted.

This legalized killing over, he wondered what would become of his daughter. This trend of thought led naturally to his life insurance. He carried fifty thousand dollars' worth, twenty-five payable to his daughter and twenty-five payable to the newspaper. Although the executive head was gone, there was little doubt that the bank would confiscate the *Blade* before Wright died.

This being the case, he speculated on whether his daughter would become the beneficiary of that second twenty-five thousand or whether it would go to the paper, which would no longer belong to him. He wondered if, by any technicality of the law, the bank could grab this sum of money and keep it. He must discuss this matter with his lawyer and change the name of his beneficiary as soon as the paper passed out of his hands.

This brought up another point. Regardless of the amount of life insurance carried by a man, was it collectable by the beneficiary if the endower were executed by the State? Some policies were not paid off on suicides, he knew. How did they stand as regarded death by the law? Wright had to admit that this was a point he had never dreamed of investigating and that he was utterly ignorant upon this question. All of which added greatly to his worry. He would have broken down under this increased torture had it not been for Zoe Ann.

Immediately upon his seizure by the sheriff and chief of police, upon being apprised of the bare facts surrounding his arrest, he had written a concise letter to his daughter, setting forth the entire matter, and forbidding her to come to him until the morrow, when she would have had sufficient time to compose herself and her emotions. Zoe Ann had obeyed implicitly his instructions. She had come down to the prison and spent all of Saturday morning with him after spending the night digesting the meager facts set forth in his letter.

And she had come ready to fight. She had given him new hope, new incentive. She had not even asked him if he were guilty, evidently taking it for granted that he was, and taking the position that, guilty or innocent, he had been in the right, that right or wrong, he was the one person in the world worth championing. And she had left him at length to take over the reins and editorship of the *Blade* until dispossessed, and to consult with Barbington the lawyer.

But, despite her high spirit, what did the future hold?

Wright was roused from his somber reverie by the clang of the iron door to the cell next his own. He gazed indifferently at the hardy looking specimen who was to be his closest associate for the present. Some bum picked up in a boarding-house fight, doubtless, judging by appearances. At no time in his life would he have shrunk fastidiously from contact with such a being and now, with the supreme punishment staring him in the face, he was even less concerned. He merely turned his eyes away.

No hint of the street brawl which had revolved about his daughter had reached his ears. No one but the loquacious Callahan would have mentioned the matter to him and Callahan, after his interview with John Hardy, deemed it wiser not to mention anything to anybody for some time. Wright's thoughts drifted off on the sea of his own troubles until his attention was recalled to his neighbor by a pleasant, whimsical voice which was at variance with the man's battered appearance.

"It seems that the clientele of this delightful establishment is reaching a higher plane. According to the Egyptians and subsequent propounders of geometric laws, a plane has but two dimensions. To mention a higher plane indisputably infers a necessary third. In brief, there seems to be a tendency to rise above the usual run of flatheads found around municipal buildings such as this, and to introduce brain pans of three dimensions—with all due respect to our unfortunate fellow prisoners. Witness—the sole champion of the people and the champion of beauty in distress occupying adjoining cells."

Wright eyed the speaker who faced him through the steel bars. He silently turned back to the restricted view from his window, mentally cataloguing the other as a tiresome and garrulous creature that had fallen low on whisky or dope and who retained nothing of his no doubt excellent education and teachings except a verbose vocabulary.

"Come, good sir," smiled John Hardy invitingly. "Whate'er the penalty for speech in our modern penitentiaries, verbal restraint has not yet penetrated to county jails. An expression from you."

"I fail to see anything brief about your lengthy harangue," responded Wright shortly. "Please keep your cheap philosophy to yourself."

"What! You an advocate of brevity? And at your age? You have fallen on sad days, my friend. I well remember many a long-winded editorial by you."

"Who the devil are you?" curiosity compelled Wright to ask.

"Ah! I have aroused your curiosity, the first step toward arousing your interest. Wait! Before you force me to a dramatic disclosure of my identity, I have something to say to you."

"Keep it to yourself," rejoined the newspaperman, coldly polite. "I have never seen you before and I am powerless to help you out of jail."

"You are mistaken and you wrong me," said Hardy reproachfully. "I have no ax to grind, although you are indirectly responsible for my sojourn here."

Wright started slightly.

"If this is a gag of Brentwood's to trick me into talking about my affairs, it has failed," he stated coldly. "Don't waste any more of my time, but call the jailer to come and let you out."

Hardy dropped his guise of humorous raillery. His clean-cut face became forbidding in aspect as he gripped a pair of bars before him and spoke crisply.

"Brentwood is doctoring himself with arnica just now," he stated tersely. "I had the pleasure of messing up his features because he was attempting to detain your daughter just after she left you this morning. I only came to West Fork this morning and I do not know anything about your affairs beyond the bald statement that Wolf-face Fosdick is dead and you are suspected of killing him out on the golf course yesterday morning.

"Naturally there was a motive by which to couple you up with the deed. I haven't heard a word on the matter, but I am willing to gamble that Fosdick had the *Blade* by the throat and was either about to or had pinched down. Just answer yes or no."

"Yes," almost whispered the big man, slowly approaching the dividing bars and staring into the younger man's face. "You stopped Brentwood from annoying my daughter? Wolf-face? You knew Fosdick's nickname? You are no stranger here, and yet—and yet—

Yes, your features are vaguely familiar. Tell me, man, in God's name, who are you?"

"The bad penny has turned up," said Hardy in faint cynicism. "I'm young John Hardy, the disgrace and bane of West Fork."

"John Hardy? Hardy? Not the son of Hardy the contractor who put in so much of the city's cement work?"

"The same," nodded Hardy grimly. "And you might have finished your sketch by saying: 'Hardy, the man who was ruined by Wolf-face Fosdick and who died as a result of his failure before his son got out of school.'"

"Why—why, I remember you now. 'Scrapping John' they called you, wasn't it? You were always in trouble with one element or another. I believe I prophesied once that you would either land in the penitentiary or else make a name for yourself."

"And the best I could do was to land in my home town jail," lamented Hardy in mock sorrow. "How I have failed, even your broad prognostication."

Wright laughed faintly, his first laugh in forty-eight hours.

"Where have you been, John, and what have you been doing?" he asked in interest. "What brings you back to West Fork?"

"I came home with a half-formed idea of walking into the First National Bank and publicly horsewhipping Wolf-face in partial payment of the debt I owed him," said Hardy seriously. "That was a childish idea of revenge that I might have been fool enough to carry out. Since I've been here these few hours I have found a far more worthy deed to render for the public good. I am going to save your life in this murder trial if it takes every cent I possess to do it."

Recalled to his own grave predicament, Wright sobered instantly. He scrutinized the younger man with solemn eyes.

"You certainly show signs of having been in a stiff fight," he remarked. "You say that Brentwood was bent on quizzing Zoe Ann—my daughter? Tell me about it."

Hardy complied with a brief account of the affair which was accurate despite its brevity. When he concluded Wright solemnly thrust his big hand through the bars between them.

"You are a gentleman," he stated gravely. "May I thank you and shake your hand?"

Hardy grasped the extended hand, his face melting into softness again with one of his winning smiles.

"The pleasure was mine, Mr. Wright," he grinned.

"You have placed me under an obligation that I am powerless to repay I fear," went on Wright slowly. "The least I can do right now is to pay your fine and see that you regain your freedom. Do you know how much it will be? I'll send word to my daughter to bring a check over from the paper office."

"Thank you, Mr. Wright, but the fine has already been assessed and the case is clear. I was given the honor of a private hearing right after dinner, because Stubby Mallory had the bright idea that he might slap a charge against me for complicity in Fosdick's murder."

"Then, why are you still in jail?"

"Because I didn't have the amount necessary to pay the hundred-dollar fine on my person. Your daughter, fortunately, had taken my suitcase with her and our friends were unable to go through any of my effects except my pockets. Now I am waiting to get in touch with Miss Zoe Ann so as to get the difference out of my traveling bag."

"Indeed, I cannot allow that," said Wright emphatically. "You haven't any too much cash, I'll warrant, and you'll need all you have. I'll send a messenger over to the newspaper for the amount of your fine. Oh, Callahan!"

"Wait just a moment, Mr. Wright," Hardy cut in quickly. "If you insist on paying my fine, well and good. But you mustn't remain under any misapprehensions regarding my position. Besides which, there are a number of matters I want to take up with you."

"Well?" Wright was polite.

"In the first place, you asked me where I'd been and what I'd been doing the past ten years. Mallory wanted the same information. However, I'm going to tell you somewhat about myself. I roamed about for two years, drifting from one part of the country to another until I landed down in the Southwest. I must have been drunk when I did it, but I took an option on a section of the poorest, sorriest range land down there, paying all the cash I happened to have on me, and pledging my very soul for the balance.

"There were two or three hundred tough and scrawny cattle on that strip of desert and mesquite, that they called a ranch. Think of it! A mere section of land—between six and seven hundred acres, and me—a tenderfoot who could hardly tell a cow from a bull. I learned that that sale to me was a regular graft worked on newcomers to get all their ready cash. The sale was always straight enough all right, but the new owner could never make a go of the thing if he tried—which wasn't often—and the property would fall back into the grafters' hands.

"Well, somehow they must have angered me. Anyway, I decided to stick. At once I had all kinds of trouble on my hands, from fights to frame-ups. It was a good thing I frittered away my youth in learning to play tag with trouble. I got so mad that I vowed I'd make good or die. I made a friend out of an old cowhand who knew the business and he proceeded to help me. He said it wasn't worth the effort, but that I was the stubbornest critter he ever saw.

"Anyway, we fought it for two or three years. I paid the original owners their stiff price. And, Mr. Wright, by sinking wells and doing other things we made the darned place pay big dividends. Then, as soon as it developed that I was making money out of my investment, the crooks took me into court to get the property back. We had land fights and water fights, lease fights and deed fights. I learned enough about law to start a correspondence school. But I kept the ranchlet!

"And then, some nosey geologist made the discovery that there was an underground reservoir of oil beneath my land which I hadn't tapped at all in drilling for water. I had already made several thousand dollars above the improvements I had put on the place. So after he convinced me that he knew what he was talking about, I sold all the cattle and ranch equipment and turned the whole six hundred and forty acres into an oil field.

"Well, the oil was there. And I had the stiffest legal trouble of all in keeping it. But I managed to keep it. And after collecting royalties until I was almost ashamed to accept the checks, I leased every acre of that place at a terrific price and then sold the land piece by piece to folks who wanted to collect the royalties from the wells. When I got through Shylocking everybody, I didn't own a dime's worth of property. I don't own any now except for the dust and dirt that soil my clothing, but there are—don't gasp for breath because I am disgustingly wealthy—twenty million cold iron men at my command right now. I have spent ten years getting that money together, fighting for it nearly every step of the way. And I have found a fighting way of spending it.

"Pay my fine if you want to, but as soon as I get out I shall set some private machinery in motion. You have just done a deed for which posterity will thank you. And, if necessary, I'm going to spend every nickel I own to save you from the consequences of your act."

"Just—just what do you mean?" demanded the dazed Wright queerly.

"I mean that you shall not die for the murder of Wolf-face Fosdick," declared John Hardy, squaring his jaw.

"I don't want to," admitted Wright truthfully. "And why should I? I am not guilty!"

CHAPTER V
THE *BLADE* CHANGES HANDS

THIS SIMPLY DELIVERED STATEMENT was so at variance with Hardy's preconceived idea about the matter that he stared with slack jaw. Finally his brows drew down in an astounded frown.

"What!" he ejaculated.

"I am not guilty of Thurlowe Fosdick's death," reiterated his fellow prisoner in quiet dignity. "However, Fosdick closed down on me the day before, when I all but threatened his life. And yesterday morning we were the only two persons out on the golf course; his body was found and the shattered golf club showed that a heavy man had beaten him to death—the conclusion was obviously simple. I am condemned before I am tried. I see very little hope for me."

John Hardy reached through the intervening bars and caught the newspaperman's wrists in a crushing grip. He almost shook the man in his earnestness.

"What are you saying, man?" he ripped out crisply. "Why do you deny the deed to me? I know you are not a cold-blooded murderer—it was a flare-up of temper. And I have just sworn that, guilty or not guilty, you shall be saved. Why do you deny it to me?"

Wright shrugged his shoulders hopelessly.

"It seems a waste of words to deny anything," he said. "And it really makes little difference, because I am sure as I stand here now, that if I had met Fosdick out there that morning, if he had opened his ugly mouth, I would have killed him. I was in a black mood. But the fact remains that I didn't even know he was on the links. Had I known he was out there, I wouldn't have gone near the place. I am innocent."

"You profess innocence, and at the same time admit that you would doubtless have committed the deed exactly as it occurred, if you had met Fosdick!"

"Yes," admitted Wright. "I can readily see how the prosecutors are positive of my guilt."

"This is ridiculous! Think, man, think! In the frame of mind you have been, and in the light of the admitted possibility or probability you have mentioned, was it possible for you to have met Fosdick and killed him without actually being aware that you did so? Could you have been so insanely angry that the entire tragedy is a blank to you? You have practically admitted that such could be the case. Consider it well. Could you have gone out of your mind at first glimpse of that thin form of your enemy ahead of you?"

Wright made answer slowly.

"I see what you're driving at," he commented. "While temporary insanity is an indisputable fact, it has been done to death in murder defenses. We couldn't build up a case on such flimsy material. On the other hand, no man living can guarantee his continued sanity or future course of action for ten minutes. One can't always even be positive about incidents of the past. In fact, it is all a morass, and I can't express myself any clearer. Only, admitting the ever-present possibility of error, I am positive before God that I did not meet Thurlowe Fosdick yesterday at any time, either consciously or unconsciously."

Like a madman Hardy released the other's numbed wrists and rushed to the door of his own cell. With a strength that was astonishing, he shook the sturdy barrier until the whole building seemed to resound to the clamor.

"Callahan!" he shouted lustily, *"Callahan! Quick!"*

The assistant jailer came at a faster gait than he had used since he had retired from the police force. Before he could open his mouth Hardy fired an instruction at him.

"Bring my notebook and fountain pen from the desk downstairs, Terry," he commanded. "Make it snappy!"

"Just what is the cause for all the—the excitement?" puzzled Wright while they waited.

"What you have said changes the entire aspect," growled Hardy, impatiently pacing up and down his allotted floor space. "You say you are innocent. In that case I haven't time to loiter around here for another instant. I've got to get out and get busy in your behalf. Oh, why didn't I know all about it yesterday? A murder mystery right under everybody's nose and they shut their eyes, smugly declare it no mystery, and pin it on the nearest handy person.

"A life-size picture of West Fork, all right! Great God, why don't that jailer hurry? Can't you see, man? The whole complexion of things is changed. I'm not going to buy your way to freedom—now. I'm going to fight your way out."

Wright was deeply thrilled in spite of himself. Hardy glanced at him in time to see a yearning hope in his eyes. It plucked at the young fighter's heart. As he took his pen and notebook from the vaguely alarmed Callahan there was a faint ache in his throat.

"Here," he said, thrusting the articles at Wright. "Take a clean page and write out a concise note to your daughter, telling her to come here at once with my suitcase and your lawyer. Say that the lawyer is to come prepared to draw up legal documents which we may want witnessed or executed to-night and so he'd better bring a complete assortment of blank forms covering everything from the cradle to the grave."

The newspaperman had caught the spirit of hope fast. He nodded briefly without replying and began writing furiously. Hardy turned back to the uncertain man in the corridor.

"Terry," he commanded, "you are to take this note over to the *Morning Blade* yourself. If Miss Zoe Ann Wright is not there, find her and deliver this paper to her alone. Then you escort her back to this spot and see that no person lays hands on her or my valise. *And get them here safely.* Do you understand?"

"But—but—" stammered Callahan. "Shure an' ye're askin' too much o' me this time, John. I can't go right now. Gilhatch, th' head jailer, has jus' come back from dinner an' ye see he—"

"—Wants to take his afternoon nap!" snapped Hardy savagely. "Well, he can't do it to-day. You get out of this building and do exactly what I told you. This is a matter of life and death."

"Shure an' I'm fired th' minute thot I set foot outside th' door," stated Callahan positively.

"You are hired at double your salary at that minute. In fact, you're working for me right now whether you're fired or not. And to offer you material and concrete evidence of where you stand I shall pay you your first month's salary as soon as you come back with Miss Wright. And if you want to see an innocent man cleared of suspicion, please hurry."

He transferred the message from Wright's hands to the man at the door of the cell.

"Ye ain't meanin' thot—thot Misther Wright ain't guilty?" stammered the old ex-patrolman.

"Before God I am innocent, Callahan," averred Wright solemnly.

The jailer's face lighted up. He straightened and snapped into a very creditable salute.

"Shure an' fer th' *cailin's* sake I'm glad to hear ye say thot," he cried. "I'm on me way."

John Hardy turned back to Wright and accepted his pen and notebook through the bars.

"If you'll tell me all about it now?" he prompted gently.

Wright did so, omitting nothing.

From time to time Hardy jotted down a memorandum or interrupted the narrator with a keen question. At length the story reached the point where Wright had been on the golf course.

"You say you quit at the third hole and came back to the clubhouse?" interrogated Hardy.

"Yes. My game was rotten."

"How did your clothes come to be muddy and torn?"

"I dropped a shot into the water hazard between the second and third hole. If you don't remember the course, there is a small ravine about twenty feet wide and fully as deep which cuts through there. I got wet and muddy trying to drive or lift out of the ditch with a mashie shot, instead of tossing the ball out and counting a stroke. It was a ridiculous play. After I broke my favorite mashie I quit in disgust. I must have torn my garments as I scrambled out of the ravine."

"You broke a club? Uuummm—that's bad. What did you do with it?"

"I stuck it in my bag with my others."

"Then you never got as far as the third green?"

"No."

"And Fosdick's body was found somewhere between the fifth and sixth holes?"

"So I was told. I didn't see it."

"Just how is the course laid off—no, never mind. Don't tell me any more about that. I'll go look it over for myself."

"You play golf?"

"I begin to-day," replied Hardy. "I've played hockey and shinny."

"There is a difference."

"That's what I am going to study. Now, about Fosdick. He was killed with a golf club. Whose? You say you brought your own back with you."

"I don't know," admitted Wright. "They penned me up here without telling me any more than they could help. Chief of Police Roland grabbed my golf bag at once and jerked out the broken club."

"What did he say? How did he look and act?"

"Rather noncommittal, I should say. They hustled me off as soon as I had written a note to my daughter. They sweated me yesterday afternoon and this morning, but I could tell them no more than I have told you. From what you have told me they evidently thought to get something out of my daughter after she left me."

"I see," frowned Hardy. "We're not going to be able to keep them from interviewing her, either."

"Who wants to?" rapped out Wright. "Besides, she knows less about the matter than they do."

"I know, I know, but I was thinking that we are not going to let them molest and annoy her. One interview is all they get. And then I'll warn Brentwood to keep away from her."

"What will be your first move?" Wright asked. "I have already turned my hopeless case over to Barbington—my lawyer."

"You are to stop considering it hopeless," announced Hardy tersely, shooting out his jaw. "I thought you were a fighter."

Wright stiffened slightly.

"There. That's better," approved Hardy. "Let this Barbington handle the legal end of the matter and go on preparing his case. Have you been indicted yet?"

"No. I waived examination in the municipal court because the grand jury convenes the first of the week and they'd have held me anyhow. So I am in jail without bond until Monday or Tuesday."

"Very well. We won't make it public that I am working on your case from another angle just yet. We'll let Barbington fight it up through every court if necessary. My first move is a business deal which can be consummated between you and me right here."

"What do you mean?"

"You told me that you have lost your newspaper, that it passes out of your hands as soon as the bank recovers from the shock of Fosdick's death and forecloses, didn't you?"

"I did."

"Well, if you were not in a financial jam and you were asked to sell the *Blade*, what would you ask for it?"

"I wouldn't sell—after all these years."

"Uumm. Well, tell me what it is worth, then."

"Well," Wright hesitated. "I know that it is worth closer to a hundred thousand than it is fifteen. Of course, it would be worth more than that to me."

"I see. And yet you stand to collect less than ten thousand dollars above its indebtedness?"

"Exactly."

"Very well. Mr. Wright, I offer you one hundred thousand dollars for the *Morning Blade* right now, purchaser to assume all outstanding liabilities, payment to be made by check this afternoon on the Industrial National Bank of Kansas City as soon as Barbington makes out a proper bill of sale which same is to be duly registered at once. What do you say?"

Wright gasped audibly.

"Oh, yes," added Hardy. "You may wire for identification of my check at my expense. Sorry I can't offer you cash, but I haven't brought that much with me in my suitcase."

"But—but, why do you want to do this? If you want to help me, why don't you simply lend me fifteen thousand dollars to pay off the bank, and take a first mortgage on the plant?"

"I'll tell you why," stated Hardy crisply. "Because I will use the paper to say things that you haven't the capital to say. I'm going to bust this town wide open from end to end. For one thing, I will use the *Blade* to fight for you, and they can't say it's because it is your paper."

Wright simply stood and stared. It was hard for him to believe that this hard-looking man with a blackened eye and torn, soiled garments was in a position to talk in the thousands—nay, millions if he would.

"We'll have it drawn up in the agreement," Hardy continued suddenly, "that after the *Blade* has served my purpose—we'll fix the time as one year or less—you have the option of buying the paper back, unencumbered of any debt, for the one hundred thousand that I now pay you for it. How's that?"

Wright strove to grasp this detail.

"You mean that—that you would pay off all debts and not subtract them from this second sale price? In other words, you are willing to fling away fifteen or twenty thousand dollars just for the use of the paper for a year?"

"It won't be money flung away. It will be well worth it." John Hardy laughed.

Wright, upon hearing that vibrant sound, was glad that he was not one of the eight or ten men who controlled the town. Perhaps Fosdick was well off, after all.

"I might make more than I spend," went on Hardy. "Or, on the other hand, I may ruin the paper so that you wouldn't want it at one thousand dollars by the end of the year. That, of course, will be at your option."

Wright clasped his hands before him and spoke aloud without directly addressing the younger man.

"After all these years!" he murmured. "At last, is the *Blade* to be a free and fearless organ unhampered by local politics?"

"Men like you were burned at the stake in the Middle Ages," commented Hardy.

"How about men like *you?*" cried Wright, eyes shining.

Hardy shrugged and laughed.

"Men like me," he said, "were killed in street brawls. They are too quarrelsome to stay out of trouble."

"I have my own opinion on that," declared Wright firmly. "But say, I want to be in on this. Don't freeze me out of the game. Let me sell you a half partnership in the paper for fifteen thousand dollars. This has been my dream for years—to save West Fork from oblivion."

"You're certainly a four-square sport," said Hardy. "For a man your age and with a family to consider, I'll say you are game all the way through. But, my friend, you have forgotten a significant item in your enthusiasm. You are not in a position to direct the activities of a paper just now."

Wright blinked and stared without expression for a long moment. Then, as realization of his own dangerous predicament came back to him, he flung his arms about his face with a deep groan.

"Forgive me," murmured the younger man contritely, "but you see what I mean. I tell you what, close the deal with me, as I have suggested, and as soon as we have won your personal fight and you are free we'll talk about a partnership. Maybe I will turn the paper back over to you altogether and just stand by to see that they don't break you. Come! What is your answer?"

They were shaking hands when Callahan conducted a gray-haired gentleman with close-clipped imperial and Hardy's vision of the morning down the corridor. Callahan set down the suitcase with a bang of importance and produced his keys. The girl fairly flew into her father's cell and embraced him with a tender cry. In that moment John Hardy envied the other man.

"My dear," murmured Wright, stroking her hair, which Hardy could now see was a beautiful coppery brown. "My dear, let me introduce an acquaintance of yours. This is Mr. John Hardy, the new owner of the *Morning Blade.*"

Zoe Ann turned and looked at her erstwhile companion and defender. She stifled all impulse to laugh at that ludicrous black eye, and pity for his plight, all on her account, caused tears to well up in her eyes. But Hardy himself destroyed all tender romance that was contained in that fleeting moment.

He thrust his hand through the dividing bars and grasped her cool, slim fingers.

"Well," he grinned, "it seems like we are fated to meet in jail, after all."

CHAPTER VI
ON THE GOLF COURSE

LEGALLY AND OFFICIALLY DISCHARGED from jail, John Hardy stood beside the jailer's desk stowing away his watch and other little trinkets as Gilhatch took them out of the drawer.

"You're a lucky guy," volunteered the latter grudgingly. "As a rule Judge Melguard would of made you wait until he come down this evening to see about your release. An' one hundred dollars ain't no fine at all for assaulting two prominent citizens."

"I think Judge Melguard has begun to see the light," replied Hardy grimly. "As for the amount of my fine—they didn't know I had any more money or they would have soaked me heavily. And, by the way, my friend, we're choosing sides and getting ready to play ball. You have already noticed that Callahan has been doing some pinch hitting for me.

"You needn't go to the trouble of firing him, because he is quitting right now. Now, as for you—play with either team you wish, but see that you treat Mr. Wright exceptionally nice for the short time he remains here and you will be here when the old home team retires. Let's go, Terry."

"Here—say," spluttered Mr. Gilhatch. "I didn't fire you, Terry. You can't leave like this. Why—I—"

Fortified with one hundred and fifty dollars in travelers' checks indorsed to him, in his pocket, Callahan made reply in no uncertain manner.

"Go chase yerself!" he suggested shortly. "Shure an' I'm through lickin' boots fer all th' cheap politicians who pollute West Fork. Where are we going, Mr. Hardy? 'Tis after four o'clock."

53

"Do the banks open here Saturday evening?"

"Yes, sir. At foive o'clock," said Callahan, picking up his new employer's suitcase. "Don't ye want to go to a hotel an' change yer clothes?"

"We haven't time, Terry. Take me to the nearest photographers' supply house."

They departed without another word to the discomfited jailer, whose mental processes found it hard to digest such *outré* actions.

"Well, I'll be damned!" was all he could offer to the four walls of his office.

Indifferent to the worthy Mr. Gilhatch's bewilderment, Hardy and his companion made their way to a photo supply company just off Wilson Avenue.

"Now, Terry, while I do a little shopping I want you to take a piece of paper and write down the names of every city employee you can think of and the department in which he or she works. Don't overlook anybody. Remember we are choosing our ball team, and we need all the help we can get."

Callahan borrowed paper and pencil from a clerk and proceeded to comply without comment. Hardy turned his attention to the camera stock.

"I want to buy or rent the best camera you have," he said to the clerk.

The said young gentleman eyed his disheveled customer askance.

"Do you wish a plate or film machine?" he queried, somewhat loftily.

"Film," returned Hardy briefly, having no time to waste on the youth.

"That will be a Rayflex then," stated the salesman. "The best machine to the amateur trade sells for one hundred and seventy-five dollars."

"Get it out!" commanded Hardy. "Load it with a roll of films and show me how it works."

The youth's sagging jaw told that he was completely taken aback.

"You—you mean you want to spend one hundred and seventy-five dollars for a *camera?*" he gasped.

For answer Hardy produced his wallet.

"I am in a hurry, young man," he stated.

The young man glanced wildly about the store. He was caught in his own trap.

"I—I'm sorry, sir," he stammered, "but we haven't such an expensive machine in stock. We would have to order that particular model for you. We can have it here from Kansas City in two days—"

"I must have it now," snapped Hardy briskly, not even enjoying the youth's discomfiture. "What other machine have you that will do accurate detail work?"

"That—that machine is the best, sir. Mr. Kertz has a Rayflex for his own use. He might—might rent it to you if you put up a deposit."

"Find out, and name the deposit."

The clerk hurried toward the rear of the store while Callahan chuckled silently to himself.

Ten minutes later, having put up a one hundred dollar deposit for the use of the camera, Hardy led the way to the street.

"A taxicab now, Terry," he commanded. "Get us to the Country Club as quickly as you can."

While his employer's actions seemed foreign and strange to the old Irishman, nevertheless Callahan knew how to take orders and execute them. Thirty minutes later they were entering the grounds of the clubhouse. At once they sought the attendant who had been in the search party that found the murdered banker.

"Were you among the first to see the body of Mr. Fosdick?" queried Hardy.

"Yes, sir," admitted the attendant, looking from his hard appearing interrogator to the old ex-jailer. "I helped carry him back here after the detectives looked him over."

"Detectives? What detectives?" queried Hardy sharply.

"Colter and Preston," stated the surprised attendant.

"Shure an' ye remember th' b'ys, Johnny," put in Callahan. "Harry Colter an' Freddie Preston. I have them on me list here."

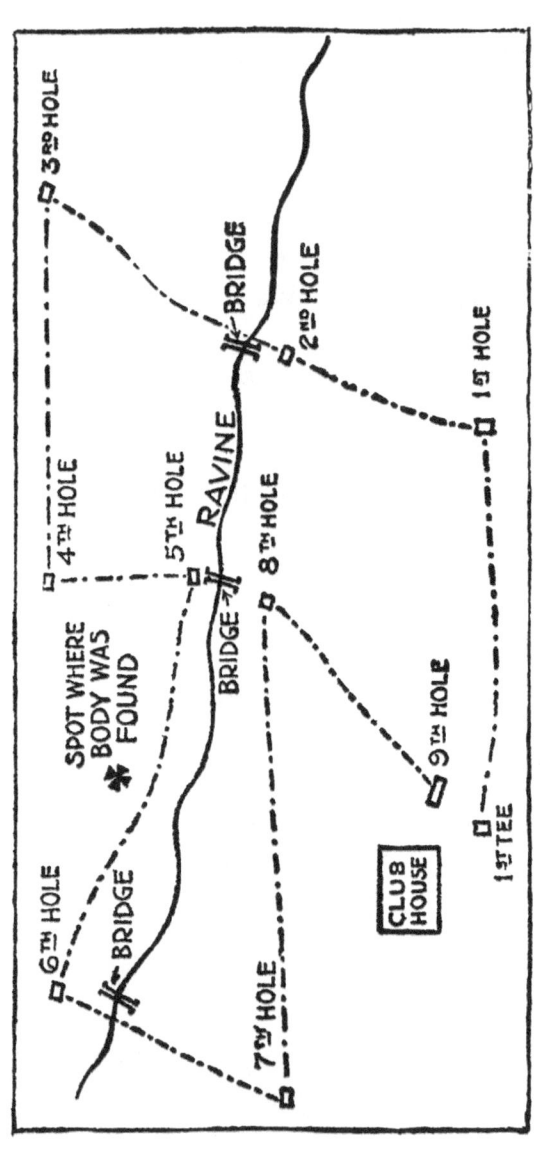

Hardy nodded.

"All right," he said, turning back to the attendant. "What's your name, friend?"

"Jenkins, sir," responded the man, highly impressed with the manner if not the appearance of the disreputable one.

"Very well, Jenkins. Here's a flyer for your trouble. Now take us out to the spot where Fosdick was found and explain the position of the body as accurately as you remember it."

The three of them walked out across the rolling course, Callahan still clutching the handle of the valuable suitcase and Hardy carrying the big camera. A few golfers were scattered about on the links, but they did not pass near enough to hail any of them. As they crossed a handbridge over a fairly deep ravine Hardy spoke:

"Is this the water hazard which runs between the second and third holes?"

"Yes, sir," replied Jenkins. "It angles down across the grounds so that it cuts between the sixth and seventh holes, too."

"Then this is the bridge which crosses the ravine between the second and third greens?"

"No, sir. This is the bridge between the fifth and eighth. That was the eighth hole we passed back there over the hill."

"Why is there a bridge here, then?"

"So any one wishing to quit at the fifth hole or wishing to start there doesn't have to go away out of his way to cross this gulley. Here is a chart of the course, sir, if you care to see it. Of course, the traps and bunkers and rolling ground and trees are not shown. I made this for the police."

Hardy stopped and examined the diagram.

"Uummm—the outline of the course looks like a big airplane," commented Hardy thoughtfully. "Then roughly, according to this, the bridge across this ravine between the second and third holes should be three hundred yards to our right."

"It is, sir," announced Jenkins promptly. "You've a good eye for yardage."

"You've a good hand for drawing maps to scale, rather," replied Hardy. "May I keep this diagram, Jenkins?"

"Certainly, sir. I'll make you a much better one if you wish."

"No, this will do. We'll go over the course to check it just for my own satisfaction, however, if you don't mind."

It was about midway between the fifth and sixth holes, and at the very edge of the rough to the right side, which was farthest from the ravine, that the banker had been found. Jenkins indicated the exact spot where the body had lain, almost hidden by the engulfing shrubbery.

Hardy proceeded to examine the spot carefully, circling it on hands and knees.

"I'm afraid that all substantial clews have been destroyed, but we'll go over it thoroughly," he said. "How was the body lying, Jenkins? On back or face?"

"On its back, sir. And in the left hand was the leather-wrapped hilt of the shaft of a golf club. The features were so battered and bloody we had difficulty in recognizing him. The thumb and forefinger on the right hand had been knocked off. His clothing was torn and soiled, and there was blood all over him and under his head. I guess the ground has soaked up all that wasn't on him."

"Hello—what's that? He held part of a golf stick in his hand? I hadn't heard that. Then it was a fight and not a defenseless murder? Do you know whether or not it was the handle of Fosdick's own club?"

"I think so, sir," remarked Jenkins slowly. "Of course I couldn't swear to it. We didn't disturb the shaft. Preston thought it was his own club all right enough, and that he'd raised his club to strike his assailant when the latter struck first and shattered his club, at the same time shearing off the right thumb and forefinger, which would have been farthest down the shaft toward the head. You know how a club is held, don't you?"

"In a general way," admitted Hardy. "Go on with your explanation."

"Well, after breaking Fosdick's club, the man beat him to death and flung his body under this shrubbery here so that it wouldn't be seen so readily."

"Uumm—what became of the rest of the splintered club?"

"The detectives supposed that Mr. Wright carried it off with him in his excitement."

"I see. That's one reason they wanted to examine his golf bag. Well, there's no use looking for the assailant's footprints now after all you men have trampled over the ground. It looks like a herd of cattle had milled around here."

"That's the way it looked when we got here," said Jenkins quickly. "That's why I can't agree with Preston. It looks like there was a regular fight here. I can't understand how Mr. Wright got off without any blows."

"The first thing you want to do, Jenkins, is to get the idea that Mr. Wright is guilty out of your mind. Mr. Wright is as innocent as you are, and I think you have suggested one of the points by which we're going to prove it."

"Who are you, anyhow?" demanded Jenkins curiously.

Callahan answered for Hardy.

"Shure an' this is Scrappin' John Hardy, th' new owner o' th' *Mornin' Blade*," he announced proudly. "Ye'll probably learn somethin' about him in th' mornin' paper."

Jenkins's eyes bulged. He smiled a trifle uncertainly.

"I hope I haven't said anything to offend you, sir," he began. "I—"

"On the other hand," smiled Hardy, "you have helped wonderfully. Without doubt there was a most terrific fight here, and the victor did not get off unscathed. You and the detectives are witnesses to the condition of the ground. Mr. Wright shall be examined by a board of physicians, and I can prophesy right now that there won't be a scratch on him.

"I see already where Preston was wrong in one surmise. Fosdick wasn't flung under this shrubbery to be hidden. He was flung squarely on top of it. Look at the broken twigs and dying leaves which prove the passage of his body from the top of the bushes to the ground. It doesn't look like a very good attempt at concealment, does it?"

"Merciful Heavens!" gasped Jenkins. "You are certainly right about that, Mr. Hardy. I never thought of that."

"Still, you have proven that you use your mind. Keep on thinking while I photograph every inch of this ground."

After a space he finished his work. He turned to Callahan.

"Terry, there is a newspaper in my suitcase. Take it out and tear off about six single sheets. Dig up a double handful of dirt from these spots I have marked and wrap each handful separately, marking the packages from one to six, beginning here below where the feet were found. Jenkins, do you mind looking around for bits of that shattered golf club?"

"Not at all, sir," responded Jenkins, "but it won't be much use. Colter went over the spot by inches for the same thing, sir."

"Did he have any luck?"

"I think he found two or three small slivers."

"All right. Never mind that. We'll go back to the second hole and start over the course from there."

"Sure an' what's th' idea o' all this gardenin', Johnny," complained Callahan as he finished his labors.

"Terry, if I'm not badly mistaken, you've gathered up earth which contains human blood, especially the bit of ground which was under the head. If there is a good chemist in West Fork we'll know, before morning whether there is any other blood besides that of Fosdick on this spot. By the way, were the missing fingers found?"

"No, sir," stated Jenkins. "They looked hard for them."

"That's funny," mused Hardy. "I've looked hard, too, and I haven't found anything—much. Let's get back to the second green."

They returned to the fifth hole, where Hardy insisted on crossing the bridge here instead of following the ravine on that side. When they reached the first bridge which spanned the ravine he halted.

"Now, within one hundred feet of this spot is where Mr. Wright dropped his ball into this ditch from the tee at the second hole," he said. "We're going to search here until we find the spot where he scrambled down into the ravine. Watch for distinct footprints. If no golfer has lost a ball here since yesterday morning we'll find plenty of signs. Mr. Wright is a big man, and his clothing showed a severe strain I understand."

They combed the bank of the ravine for some time before Callahan announced a discovery. He had found a shred of tweed cloth on a brier bush just below the lip of the ditch. Hardy carefully took charge of the tiny bit of evidence and led the way down to the bottom of the crevice which bisected the course. Here, after some further delay, they found the spot where Wright had broken his mashie. A water-soaked sliver of second-growth hickory and one perfect footprint were their rewards.

Hardy photographed the spot and put the bit of wood in his pocket with the shred of cloth. It was easy to trace the newspaperman's ascent from the bottom. After the incident of the broken club he had plowed up the wall of the ravine like a mad elephant. A larger shred of tweed was the harvest here and another picture. There was no evidence that Wright had passed beyond the middle of the ditch in the direction of the third hole. If he had done so it was by way of the handbridge before or after his adventure in the bottom of the ravine.

They passed across the bridge and tramped around the course, overtaking a lone golfer between the sixth and seventh holes. As they approached the bridge over the ravine, Hardy slowed down and accosted the young fellow.

"Say, my friend," he smiled winningly, "do you play much on this course?"

"Quite a bit. Why?"

"I noticed how easily you cleared the ravine when you teed off at the sixth hole back there. It looks like it's just about the same distance from the coulee—the ditch, I mean—as the tee at the second hole."

"Number six is ten yards farther from the hazard," offered Jenkins quickly.

"And you seemed to drive about a hundred and fifty yards— fully a hundred yards on the other side of the ditch," went on Hardy to the golfer.

"Well, yes," admitted the latter modestly. "That one was a moderately fair shot."

"What I want to know," continued Hardy, "is this: is it possible for a good golfer to drop a ball in the ditch from either the second or sixth holes?"

"Why, yes," answered the player readily. "If you slice your ball you can drive it a hundred yards to left or right. Or, if you drive straight and loft the ball you can drop a pot shot straight in the ravine. I guess a hard-driven grounder could make it, too, although that never happened to me as the grass in the fairway slows the ball so quickly."

"Thank you," said Hardy. "You have assisted in relieving my mind. What time is it, Jenkins? Is my watch right?"

"Yes, sir. Ten minutes to five."

"Good. We must hurry back to town, Terry. One thing more, friend. Would you mind showing me how you hold a golf club?"

"Not at all," obliged the golfer, drawing a club from his bag and demonstrating the grip for a right-handed man. "There are many different ways of gripping a club and interlocking the fingers, but this is the general way."

"I see. The right hand is always forward."

"Yes."

"How long does it take a single player to go around the course?"

"A good player can make it in an hour without hurrying. The poorest player shouldn't take more than an hour and a half."

"Thank you for your kindness."

"Not at all."

Hardy parted from Jenkins at the clubhouse.

"You've been a great help, Jenkins," he said. "Don't forget what you've thought out and what you know to be the actual truth. And here's the mate to that bill I slipped you before we went out."

"I won't, sir, and thank you."

On the way to town Hardy drew forth the map of the course and began studying it. Callahan leaned over his shoulder and matched his old eyes against the springs of the taxi.

"Jenkins drew a fairly good diagram of the grounds," mused Hardy aloud. "Does this chart tell you anything, Terry? You may add to it what we discovered this afternoon."

"No, sir," admitted Callahan blankly. "It looks like a map o' th' course is all, Johnny."

"You must use your brain at the same time that you use your eyes," remarked Hardy. "Look here. We saw beyond the shadow of a doubt where Wright was in the ditch near the first bridge—that is, if his clothes match these two shreds I have and if this sliver fits his broken mashie."

"Yes, sir, thot's so."

"Hence, if he did return to the clubhouse in less than an hour after he started, he didn't have time to play two holes, get tangled up in the ravine, and then go kill Fosdick between five and six and get back to the club-house. You can see that it is between six and eight hundred yards from where Wright admitted being and where Fosdick was found dead—nearly half a mile."

"Sure, but 'tis true thot Wright could of gone straight out an' killt Fosdick an' then come back to th' ravine an' broke his club as an alibi, an' thot's what th' prosecution will claim if ye bring up this point," sagely offered Callahan.

"You're right, Terry, but you are overlooking one point which is up to us to prove. That golfer said that a good player should make the course in an hour. According to that, Fosdick should have been playing the ninth hole before Wright even teed off on the first. Remember that he started an hour earlier. Now, why didn't things work out like this? I'll answer that question for you. *The man was dead before Wright started to play.*"

"Good Salem!" ejaculated Callahan. "Shure any ye're right, Johnny. But—but, th' prosecution will be claimin' thot somethin' detained Fosdick like a lost ball or so, until Wright could walk out there to him," he finished, his face falling.

"Surely they will," agreed Hardy calmly. "They aren't trying to clear up the mystery; they are trying to convict Wright. And it's up to you and me to fool 'em. That's why you are to take the city doctor and a couple of others over to the jail and see that Mr. Wright is given a thorough physical examination to prove that he is un-hurt and has lost no blood, while I find a chemist who will test these dirt samples for traces of the unknown assailant's blood. Better tell them to test Mr. Wright's blood, too, so we can compare the specimens. What did you do with that list of city employees?"

"Here it is, Johnny. But ye go to Professor Walker at th' high school fer yer test."

"What? Is Professor Walker still head of the chemistry department there?"

"He shure is."

"I'll go right to his house. I wonder if he remembers the day I blew out one wall of the laboratory in making nitroglycerin that we were just supposed to read about?"

"Shure an' I don't think anybody whoever met ye could forget ye," offered Callahan. "Nor anythin' ye did."

"Never mind the personalities," grinned Hardy. "You get an affidavit of that examination and turn it over to Mr. Barbington for safe-keeping. You can find me at the office of the *Blade* later this evening."

CHAPTER VII
CROSSING BLADES WITH KIMBALL

SAMUEL B. KIMBALL was seventy-eight years of age. His wife, the sister of Fosdick's wife, had been dead some twenty years. Kimball had waited until he reached the ripe or over-ripe age of forty before marrying and then he had married the older Mallory girl, sister to Judge Mallory. Nancy Mallory had been but twenty when she married Sam Kimball. Thus the faintest bit of mental arithmetic brings forth the fact that she died at the premature age of thirty-eight, eighteen years being all she could endure of Sam's constant society.

Before giving up the attempt to live longer with her husband Mrs. Kimball left him one daughter and two sons. Since her death the girl had married Brentwood, the district attorney. One of the sons, Thomas, had married and brought his wife to live on his father's estate. The youngest member of the family, Robert was nearly thirty and a bachelor. He also lived at home. Both sons were employed by their father in his factory interests.

At seventy-eight Sam Kimball was as hard and unyielding as he had been the day poor Nancy Mallory put her life in his keeping. He had hard blue eyes, a square head which was flat on top and behind the ears, and the belief that wife and family should remain in utter bondage to their lord and master. He had succeeded in crushing the spirit out of his wife. He succeeded in ruling his sons, not because of love for him, but for love of his money.

Sam was a financial success as much by accident of birth as by any other method. His father had established the first two factories at West Fork and Sam had inherited them. He was not a worshiper of the almighty dollar; he was a devotee of the elusive penny. He superintended his business from the daily purchase of a nickel's worth of ice for the office cooler to the largest contract the amalgamated factories put out.

Despite the existence of other stockholders and other heads Sam Kimball was the soul of the factories. It was a one-man business; Sam had crushed all other initiative. As West Fork was mainly a manufacturing town, despite the existence of other interests and wheels within wheels, it was easy to foresee that Sam Kimball was the biggest figure with which John Hardy had to contend.

It is not to be presumed that this condition made a probable conquest easy for the young millionaire, On the contrary. At the age when he should have been showing signs of senility Sam Kimball was the hardest, most ruthless dictator who ever ruled a small town. The only indication the man gave of advancing age was his attention to the church.

He was the sternest deacon and the strongest advocate of blue laws, he gave the largest financial support and he dictated the policies of the strongest sect in West Fork. He was sincere in his attention to blue laws; he was too old to enjoy any of the pleasures and frivolities of youth whether dangerous or harmless. Yet, how he reconciled his religion with his conscience is a matter of speculation for the enterprising psychologist. That he was successful was obvious in his smug complacency.

The home of the Kimballs was the only beautiful thing about the family.

Occupying two acres of ground on the choicest heights fronting on River Road, with the shrubbery, flowerbeds, walks, cozy nooks, and winding drive, the big house of tapestry brick was little short of a mansion. Whether or not Sam himself possessed the faculty, the landscape gardener at least had splendid taste. The estate was worthy of a gracious master and a charming hostess. The charge, however, of being *nouveau riche* because he didn't fit, could not apply to Sam Kimball; he had been rich all his life.

In spite of his eminence Sam Kimball was not a figure of national importance. Thus, as the family sat at dinner Saturday
evening, it was no feat of legerdemain which permitted the figure of a
man to hide in the clustered rosebushes just outside the opened French
doors which gave on a small balcony. His presence unsuspected and
undetected, the skulker surveyed and overheard the family off guard.

"When is Mr. Fosdick's funeral to be?" asked Ruth, the wife of
Thomas Kimball. "In the morning or in the afternoon? I haven't
heard."

"To-morrow afternoon at two o'clock," answered Sam Kimball
from the head of the table.

"The body is still at Greenwald's mortuary, isn't it?" murmured
Kimball's daughter, Mrs. Cyrus Brentwood.

"It lies there in state until to-morrow morning," announced
Sam. "That was my suggestion to his bereaved family. Poor
Thurlowe will be laid away in the family vault after funeral ser-
vices at the church."

"With all due pomp and glory, eh?" murmured Robert in faint
sarcasm.

The old man glowered at his younger son. He clenched his right
fist preparatory to delivering an ultimatum.

"That is no way to speak of your uncle," he stated coldly. "Don't
let me hear you make such a remark again."

Brentwood interposed at this juncture.

"This tragedy has been quite a shock and a blow to our city," he
murmured. "It was revolting from a mere human standpoint."

"You look as though you have been up against quite a shock
and a blow, yourself," offered Thomas, who had not been informed
of the events of the morning. "What did you do, Cy? Run up against
a door in the dark?"

Brentwood bridled angrily. But Kimball tabled the persiflage
at once. His clenched fist rose and fell, delivering the said ultimatum. Bang! The chinaware rattled in terror. This ruling blow was a
favorite gesture with Sam. His little finger and the edge of his hand
were used to it. But what Sam needed was a gavel.

"That will do for you, Thomas," he commanded finally. "Cyrus was viciously assaulted this morning, but the culprit is in jail."

Kimball turned from his squelching of Thomas and surveyed his rather battered son-in-law.

"It certainly was a horrible crime," he agreed. "It rests on your shoulders, Cyrus, to see that the murderer gets all the punishment the law can mete out. With Mallory's influence on the Federal bench it should not be difficult to send that ruffian Wright to the chair."

Brentwood's lean features assumed a savage expression. For an instant he looked more wolf-like than the departed banker had ever looked.

"Don't worry about that," he uttered vindictively. "That blowhard is done. And I shall try to send that roughneck, Hardy, to the penitentiary for a long stretch as an accessory either before or after the fact. Raymond Mallory had him fined more than he had on his person. So he'll stay in jail for a few days until we gather evidence enough to implicate him. He'll pay dearly for that assault."

"But—but are you sure that poor Mr. Wright is the murderer?" put in Ruth hesitantly. She had not been a member of Sam Kimball's household long enough to be utterly subdued. "He doesn't appear to be just that—that kind of man. I can scarcely believe it."

Bang! Another ultimatum. Another dance of dishes.

"You shut up, young woman," commanded Sam. "You don't know anything about the world with its snares and pitfalls. Wright killed Thurlowe Fosdick simply because Thurlowe refused to lend him more money to squander on the *Blade*. Is that reason for murder?"

"I understand that Fosdick was pinching him down on the *Blade* and getting ready to throw Wright out into the street," remarked Robert with a faint smile. "That gives Wright something like a real motive. If he did it, he had enough reason to do it."

Bang! Bang! The heavy table itself shivered in apprehension.

"Silence!" roared the father in anger. "He had no reason."

Robert flushed angrily.

"What are you mad about?" he retorted. "It was your scheme, too. You haven't lost anything. Fosdick was the goat."

Sam became almost speechless in his rage.

"Another comment like that out of you," he snarled, "and I'll disinherit you. You have no respect for your elders. You have lost sight of your God. See that you attend church in the morning or—or—"

Brentwood was always the most diplomatic and suave of the three younger men.

"How about the newspaper, Mr. Kimball?" he put in smoothly. "Nothing has been done since the sudden death of Fosdick. Wright's note for five thousand was due Thursday. It's still unpaid."

"We'll go down to the bank at once," rasped the old man, arising from his chair with decision. "We won't wait until we appoint a new president at our directors' meeting. I can carry it through as well as Fosdick. Have you finished, Cyrus?"

Brentwood patted his bruised mouth gently with his napkin and got up with a murmured excuse to the others. The two of them left immediately and almost at once the sound of their car going down the driveway was heard.

The four people left at the table did not at once arise. Robert began molding a bit of bread between his fingers. Without looking at the others he voiced a very frank and brutal statement.

"Sam is the blackest and dirtiest penny grubber I ever knew," he said. "And Brentwood always manages to curry him the right way."

"Why not?" laughed Mrs. Brentwood shortly. "He can't afford to antagonize Father. Cyrus is not his son."

"What's the difference?" shrugged Robert callously. "He'll get his share through you."

"Really, you shouldn't talk about him that way," said Ruth Kimball uncertainly. "Remember that he is your father."

"A hell of a father!" said Thomas viciously at this. "I let him talk to you like a dog. He holds the purse strings so tight that I—a man of thirty-six—have to ask him if I may buy you a car."

"If you were half the man you ought to be," averred Robert, "you'd pack up and leave the old reprobate."

"And let you and Sis inherit my share of the estate, eh?" sneered Thomas. "Fat chance."

"Stick around then," shrugged Robert. "Ruth isn't my wife."

"You're single," suggested Thomas. "Why don't you leave?"

"Why should I?" returned Robert airily. "I can stand his insults the rest of his natural life, having survived his brow-beating this long."

"How old is he now?" mused Mrs. Brentwood, calculating.

"Seventy-eight," replied Thomas. "The old devil ought to have been in his grave ten years ago."

As they toyed with their dessert and the two brothers lit cigars the skulker in the flowerbed without smiled sardonically and glanced at his cheap watch.

"A happy family," he murmured as he withdrew. "And you needn't worry about your fine father's health. He'll be rotting along with Fosdick very shortly."

IF SAM KIMBALL was at all aware of the repute in which he was held by his children, he was supremely indifferent to it. What actual joy he got out of living no one but a man like Sam Kimball could answer. He had already dismissed his family from his mind and was listening to Brentwood's discussion on John Hardy.

"I can't say that I remember the fellow at all," he frowned. "What is he doing here in West Fork?"

"I suppose he came back to breed trouble and sponge off of every old acquaintance he can find," growled Brentwood. "Surely you remember his father—the cement contractor?"

"Oh—that Hardy. Yes, I remember that he took a lot of unimproved property from the city for lots of his work. He borrowed some money from Fosdick to pay taxes and improve it. He couldn't carry the load and lost his health. The bank had to take the property. Strange I can't recall the son."

"It isn't likely that you ever met him," remarked Brentwood. "I expect Robert knows who he is—they're about the same age. I remember him as a young trouble maker."

"In what way?"

"In every way," snapped Brentwood. "For one thing, he led the high school rowdies in a fight that broke up the Gearshong smelter gang; he blew out one wall of the chemistry laboratory making a forbidden explosive, he—"

"I don't see anything wrong with the breaking up of the smelter hoodlums," interrupted Kimball.

"Perhaps not, but that was just one item of his activities," Brentwood returned shortly. "He led the students on a strike when the school board tried to compel them to eat lunch in the school cafeteria. He was always in private brawls and fights. Look at me now for an example."

Kimball snorted like an old billy goat as Brentwood pulled up and parked the Kimball family car as near as possible to the bank building.

"I was on the school board during that affair," he growled. "It was my idea to install that cafeteria."

Then, as they ascended the steps of the bank:

"You crush him like a bug, Cyrus," he instructed. "West Fork hasn't any room for black sheep."

"Watch me," smiled Cyrus thinly.

It was the rush hour at the bank with pay checks and small deposits and they were forced to wait before they could get to the ear of the vice-president, one Smythe who was closeted with a small merchant desiring financial succor. It was nearly closing time when Sam Kimball was giving Mr. Smythe some very emphatic instructions regarding the action of the bank the first thing Monday morning. Cyrus Brentwood offered a few words of advice as Mr. Smythe sagely looked at the three notes in his hands and nodded slowly.

They were interrupted by the entrance of the assistant cashier.

"I beg your pardon," murmured this gentleman, "but I am looking for the note case. Ah, I see you have it here. Excuse me just a moment."

The man pulled open a certain drawer and ran rapidly through the index therein. Then he started again and went through the file more slowly.

The three men were silently awaiting his departure before re-
suming their conversation.

"What are you hunting for, Roland?" asked Smythe impatiently.

"The notes against Howard Wright, sir."

"What for?" shot out Sam Kimball.

"Why, there is a man here to pay them, sir," responded Roland
in surprise.

"To pay them?" Mr. Smythe quavered uncertainly, weakly waving
the three bits of paper about in the air.

"What's his name? Who is he? Where is he from?" fired Brentwood quickly.

"Why—why, he didn't give his name. He's a hard looking customer, but he has a roll of bills on him that would choke an elephant," said Roland in bewilderment.

"What license does that give you to paw over the note case?"
ripped out Kimball uglily. "You know this bank doesn't sell its
paper to every Tom, Dick, and Harry who comes along. Such a business would put our customers in a nice fix."

"Oh, but he has the authority of Mr. Wright," began Roland.
"It's perfectly regular—"

"It's perfectly irregular," snapped Sam Kimball. "Those notes
were forfeited Thursday. He can't redeem them now."

Brentwood was already at the door to get a glimpse of the mysterious man of money. He saw the profile of a man he would never
forget, a man with a blackened eye and begrimed clothing.

"Good geemany!" he whispered. "That fellow Hardy is out of
jail."

The others crowded to the door behind him to peer out on the
main floor.

"Why, that's the man who wants to redeem the notes," announced Roland.

Brentwood and Kimball eyed each other aghast. Bewilderment
became anger, and anger slowly turned to suspicion. Smythe looked
rather helpless.

"So that's John Hardy!" snorted Kimball. "Well, Roland, you
go right back and tell him to get out. There's nothing doing with

these notes. We'll put the thumbscrews on him if he starts a ruckus."

"Wait!" commanded the forensic Mr. Brentwood. "That's not the way to handle that fellow. Besides, it's illegal. Roland, you tell him that the bank officials are too busy to transact business with him to-night. Tell him to come back Monday morning at nine o'clock sharp and he will be properly cared for. Go on. You see, Mr. Kimball," he went on, turning to his father-in-law, "there is some sinister connection between this fellow and Wright."

"He'll come back Monday and then we'll be sold out," snapped Kimball. "What did you tell him to say that for?"

"Before the bank opens Monday we shall have the paper attached," stated Brentwood. "That is the easiest way out. But I wonder where the mischief he got hold of that money. Mr. Smythe, try to get in touch with Mallory by phone. He's made a mess of things somehow."

They drifted back to their chairs and resumed their discussion stiltedly and in some trepidation, awaiting the return of Roland with the assurance that all was well. They reckoned without the energetic Mr. Hardy.

There was a faint cry from without, a vast shadow looming on the other side of the frosted glass of the door, and the barrier was flung open suddenly by a commanding hand. John Hardy stood framed in the opening, the necktie of Mr. Roland still clutched in one hand.

He surveyed the three men grimly without speaking. They, in turn, were too astonished to say a word. Then Mr. Hardy whirled and contemptuously tossed the scarf he held out through the door and slammed the barrier shut in the face of the advancing policeman who was on duty in the establishment.

"So!" he exclaimed, facing the silent trio. "So; I thought I recognized your Latin touch, Slim Brentwood. It looks like I got here just in time. Produce the three notes against Howard K. Wright which this bank holds, and do it quick."

"Who are you and what do you want?" rumbled Sam Kimball ominously.

"Cut the monkey business," ripped out Hardy. "Slim Brentwood has already told you who I am and your tieless tiler without the door has told you what I want."

"Get out!" was Mr. Kimball's irate reply. "I'll have you arrested for intrusion."

Hardy shot the old man a hard glance.

"You're Stingy Sam, aren't you? I had almost forgotten what you looked like. You're the biggest stockholder in this bank, I believe. You own a lot of factories and more first-class mortgages. In fact, you've got the town pretty well lassoed. But let me tell you one thing—flat. You're not going into the newspaper business just yet.

"Now, figure out the interest Wright owes you for three days and figure out how much interest he has coming back on the two notes which are not due. Deduct the difference from the face value of the sum of all three notes and I'll pay you cash right now."

Brentwood edged toward the door. Hardy glared at him.

"I wouldn't do it, Slim," he warned. "That copper had the good sense to stay out. You better have the good sense to stay in."

"But—but, Mr.—er—Mr. Hardy," faltered Smythe. "We can't sell our paper like this. It is against our principles; we must protect our customers' interests."

Hardy laughed shortly.

"Now I'll tell one. You bloodsuckers first get your customers' interests and then you get their principals. Start figuring—*now!*"

Mr. Smythe had been in a near state of collapse ever since seeing the awful face of this Hardy person. But the face was mild compared to the unmentionable terrors he could put in his voice. Mr. Smythe bent his attention to his desk.

"Young man," bellowed Kimball, "what authority have you for this proceeding?"

"The best in the world—protection of my own interests. Read this!"

Hardy thrust a sheet of paper before the nose of the shouter. It was a note signed by Wright and witnessed by the latter's lawyer. With bulging eyes the manufacturer read:

This is to certify that John D. Hardy has this day purchased from me the *Morning Blade* for the sum of one hundred thousand dollars, certified check for the entire sum in hand. This paper is his authority to take up fifteen thousand dollars in paper against my name at the First National Bank of West Fork.

Howard K. Wright.

Witness: Edward Barbington.

"Suppose we refuse to let you redeem this paper?" Kimball growled.

"If you even make a motion to try any such stunt, I'll first take all three of you apart to see what makes you go—wrong. Then, I'll sue you individually and collectively. Next, I'll break this bank so flat it'll look like a dent. And last but not least, I'll send all three of you to the penitentiary for fraudulent banking."

Kimball looked at his son-in-law expectantly. Brentwood eyed the roll of bills in Hardy's hand and slowly shook his head.

"This chap is a crude bluffer," he stated with a cold sneer. "I have no doubt that he stole the money he has on him. But he has us as far as the notes are concerned. We can't refuse to surrender the paper."

"Can't! Can't?" roared Kimball, his wicked old eyes glittering viciously. "We lose our hold on the *Blade* if you give up those notes. You've got to. Fix it so Smythe can keep them. Is there no law you can employ? Is there no justice for capital which has been abused? Is there no way of stopping the murderer of Thurlowe Fosdick from reaping the profit of his deed? Jail this young upstart for complicity."

"Before you lay a finger on me," warned Hardy very grimly, "be sure that you carry all the accident insurance you want. And before you invoke the law in any way against me be prepared to spend all you are worth to fight your case. Bluffer, am I? Suppose you wire the Industrial National Bank of Kansas City for my standing. And, one thing further—from this moment on corral your tongues and stop all that loose talk about Mr. Wright or me until the case has been proven. Otherwise, I'll institute suit for libel. What is the answer, Smythe?"

"Mr. Wright has three weeks' interest coming to him on the first note and two weeks' on the second," announced Smythe.

"Give me the amounts so I can check them," snapped Hardy.

The vice-president did so. After a brief appraisal of the figures Hardy counted out fifteen thousand dollars onto the desk.

"My change and a receipt for this payment," he commanded curtly as he stowed away the three notes.

Smythe glanced toward Sam Kimball for guidance. The old man glanced at Brentwood. Brentwood glanced at Hardy and then nodded. Kimball nodded to Smythe, and Smythe nodded to Hardy as he disappeared to see about the exchange.

Sam Kimball was thinking rapidly. The threats of John Hardy had a very realistic ring. Then again, Wright was not the man to pretend to sell his paper. There was no doubt that Hardy had purchased the newspaper. There was also the substantial evidence of the fifteen thousand dollars in cash.

Whether all of this money emanated from John Hardy or not, it was perfectly clear that not less than one hundred and fifteen thousand dollars was in operation and that John Hardy controlled it. One hundred and fifteen thousand dollars was a lot of money to be set so casually in motion in one afternoon. This young man was worth more than a passing thought.

As Hardy pocketed his change and his receipt Sam Kimball spoke.

"You will regret your hasty actions in this affair, young man," he remarked in a sanctimonious tone. "If your intentions are right, if your heart is honest, you are digging a pitfall of evil before your feet by consorting with a murderer. You are aiding and abetting crime.

"Think, young man, think! Do you want to be eternally damned? You know nothing of this tragedy. Sever your connection with sin and we will see that you are enlightened and your feet placed on the road to salvation. Young man, do you ever think of the future?"

John Hardy's reply to this rather sickening harangue was quite terse and to the point. He said nothing until he stood with his hand on the doorknob. Then:

"Speaking of salvation—old man, do you ever try to cover up the past?"

The door slammed behind him, terminating the brief theological discussion. In some remarkable manner this bit of bitter repartee scored. In the silence which followed the belligerent Mr. Hardy's departure, Sam Kimball, staring at nothing, sank slowly into his chair.

CHAPTER VIII
MR. PRESLEY IS WILLING

THE THUNDER OF THE BIG PRESS, the shouts of paper boys, the blasts of heat from the casting room where the half-cylinder forms of a whole page at a time were made for the press, the tinkle and clatter of the linotype machines in the composing room, the smell of warm paper and fresh ink, all combined to give one who shut his eyes for a moment the illusion that the *Morning Blade* was a big metropolitan daily. In its own way it was.

The first edition of Sunday's paper for the mail trains was feeding into the great press in the form of three rolls of blank paper at one end and coming out, a twelve-page paper, cut and folded, at the other end. Frantic press boys were rushing with bundle after bundle to the circulation department where papers were individually tagged with the little yellow address label for out-of-town readers or done up in groups for out-of-town news stands. At eight o'clock Saturday night activity was at its height in the building. It was no time for an inquisitive stranger to be strolling through the plant.

Nevertheless, it was the first moment since his arrival in West Fork that John Hardy found time to inspect his new possession. The first intimation of his presence came when an anxious pressman, in stepping around to see if the folding blades were functioning properly, discovered a begrimed young giant with a blackened eye calmly picking up one of the fresh copies to examine it.

"Hey! Wotinell!" bellowed the pressman above the roar of the machine. "Leave them papers alone! Wot d'yuh want in here?"

John Hardy merely glanced at the other and quickly shook open the copy of the *Blade*. His eyes sought the headlines on the front page.

NO HOPE FOR WRIGHT, STATES
DISTRICT ATTORNEY
Confession Expected Hourly from Prisoner

And then in the same screaming-faced type:

TWO PROMINENT CITIZENS ASSAULTED
IN BROAD DAYLIGHT

Hardy did not take time to read the smaller type or sub-heads. He whirled on the belligerent pressman. "How long has this edition been in the press?" he shouted.

"About half an hour," yelled the other. "Yuh can buy it on th' street in another hour. What business yuh got here?"

"Plenty," replied Hardy. "Shut down that machine!"

"Huh?" gaped the press tender.

"Shut down that press!" roared Hardy. "Quick!" The pressman slowly closed his sagging jaws. He wasn't sure whether to laugh or become angry. Because of that hard face he chose an intermediate course.

"Get out before yuh get throwed out," he advised. "Who let yuh in, anyway?"

Hardy's hand shot out and crushed down on the speaker's greasy shoulder. He thrust his lean face within six inches of the other's.

"I said to stop that press," he bellowed.

"Yuh're crazy!" informed the other rudely. "Get out or I'll throw yuh out!"

The appearance of a paper boy with a small truck to cart away the accumulated pile of papers stirred Hardy into action. He released the fellow and darted around to the rear of the press. With an alarmed cry the other followed him. Before he could be stopped

John Hardy opened his pocket knife and slashed across the top-most roll of paper.

It was an imperfect job and the mutilated ribbon possessed enough tensile strength which, with the momentum of the turning roll, permitted it to carry the break as far as the plates. Hardy braced himself to meet the onslaught of the irate press tender. But just at that instant the paper parted under the stress of printing and the resultant sound forced the attacker to leap for the lever controlling the machine.

As the noise of the press died away and human voices resumed their normal carrying power, John Hardy found a gathering crowd of workers before him and a babble of voices arising.

"Shut up!" he commanded harshly. "Where are all the papers already run off in this edition? Has a single copy gone out of this building? Any of you men know?"

"They oughta be in the mailing department," volunteered one from the composing room who had not learned the exact trouble with the silent press.

"This guy is a nut!" shouted the pressman. "He stopped th' press by cuttin' a roll of paper. Call a cop! Grab 'im, Mike!"

"Be careful, Mike," warned Hardy. "Stay where you are. One of you men go get the foreman or the editor. Another go and see that no paper goes out of this house. If a single copy of that paper gets out every man on this paper is fired to-night. Make it snappy! Pronto!"

"Who in hell are you?" demanded the man called Mike.

"Are you dependent on your job here for a living?" shot out Hardy.

"Yeah. What—"

"Then, as far as you are concerned, I'm Santa Claus."

There were two or three smiles, and the group grew larger as work was dropped in other parts of the mechanical end of the *Blade* and newcomers came nearer to listen. But something about this hard-eyed stranger carried conviction. Footsteps sounded on the stairs leading from the first floor to the sacred precincts above, and a man with a green eyeshade across his worried forehead pushed his way to confront Hardy.

"What's all this? Why this disturbance? Who are you?" he fired at the begrimed individual.

"Who are you?" demanded Hardy.

"Managing editor—news editor," barked the other. "What's this about you stopping this press?"

"I did, and you are the man I want to see." He shoved the copy of the *Blade* under the other's tiny mustache. "Who wrote these two articles and who gave them authority to do so?"

The news editor barely glanced at them.

"What about them?" he crisped out.

"Just this—the reporter or reporters who did it are fired unless they can prove somebody over them is guilty."

The gentleman with the hirsute trinket on the upper lip bristled at once.

"Who are you?"

"My name is John Hardy and I am the new owner of the *Morning Blade*. This note of Howard Wright's may aid you in making up your mind."

The editor accepted the note and read it. Visibly he smoothed down. He eyed Hardy appraisingly.

"This seems to be authentic, Mr. Hardy," he murmured. "Er—just what are your objections to the two articles in the paper?" he asked carefully.

"Who gave you authority to write up Mr. Wright in that libelous manner?"

"Er—Cyrus Brentwood. The paper was to be attached by the First National Bank, you know. Brentwood was practically an arbiter, you know. He—"

"Did he show you any legal writ giving him permission to dictate to you?" ripped out Hardy.

"N-no," admitted the editor slowly. "You see—"

"No, I don't see," cut in Hardy savagely. "That's what's the matter with this town. You are all afraid of the old fossils who have a little legal power or money. What's your name and how long have you been on this paper?"

"George Presley—two years," smiled the news editor.

"And you want to know how the new owner stands, eh?" added Hardy. "Well, this is it. This paper belongs to me and not to Mr. Wright or to the First National Bank. One of the first policies will be to prove the innocence of Howard K. Wright. Mr. Wright is not guilty of enriching the soil with the carcass of Fosdick. Any person in the pay of this paper who thinks that he is, can draw their time to-night. Pass the good word along."

There was a confusion of murmuring which slowly rose to the heights of a shout. A beatific smile lit up the countenance of Mr. Presley. The habitual harassed expression in his eyes lifted for a moment.

"May I shake your hand, Mr. Hardy?" he said.

Hardy gripped his hand so fiercely that Presley winced.

"Now kill every copy of that first edition and destroy the forms for the first page," directed Hardy. "I'll write the headlines about Wright myself."

Mr. Presley's face became woebegone. He was again the harassed newspaper editor.

"But, Mr. Hardy, that will put us in a bad hole," he said. "We'll lose several hours and miss the mails."

"Are you working for me or for the First National Bank?" snapped Hardy.

"For you, of course."

"Then get busy. We'll send the first edition out by special delivery. Get me a first class reporter to take down what I have to say about Wright and then put it into printable shape."

"Come upstairs," invited Presley. He shouted several quick instructions to various employees, and the place again assumed the hum of industry. Mike and the first pressman methodically started to dismantle the press and remove the offending first page forms.

"What is wrong with the other news item?" demanded Presley.

"Everything! I am the man who assaulted the two prominent citizens, so I know all about it. That article is going to be condensed into a short paragraph and put on the back page with the obituaries. The small lead will read like this: 'Home-coming citizen chastises two ruffians for forcing attention onto young lady.'"

"Wow!" cried Presley. "Are you crazy?"

"If I am the whole town is going to be before I am through."

"But, man, Brentwood and Mallory will sue you."

"Let 'em sue—if they dare. I already have a little something on Slim Brentwood without trying to get it. Wright told me that you have a morgue of good stuff which was killed from time to time. We're going over it as soon as I have the slightest breathing spell and see if we can't print most of it."

"My God!" breathed Presley in awe. "Why—why, they'll break you. You're insane!"

"Do you want to resign before the fire-works begin?"

"Hell, no!" shouted Presley. "I am just warning you before you start. You don't know this town."

"How long have you lived here?" demanded Hardy curiously.

"Just two years. I came here from St. Louis to take my job under Mr. Wright. If I hadn't thought so much of him I'd have pulled out long ago."

"It's you who don't know this town. I've come home either to wake it up or to bury it."

"My boy," said Mr. Presley solemnly, "that sort of idea is what ruined Mr. Wright. I predict your speedy downfall. But you sure have found a willing little playmate. Just give me time to verify your ownership and then all you have to do is to tell me what you want done."

Hardy sat down in the chair opposite Presley's desk and studied that gentleman curiously. He liked the other's slender face and pointed chin. The little mustache no longer looked obnoxious, and Presley's nervous, fluttering little smile made an instant appeal to his sympathy.

"Get Wright's lawyer on the phone and ask him to come over here," he directed. "I want to see him anyway."

After Presley complied he produced the three notes he had redeemed from the bank. He spread them out for the news editor's surveyal.

"Now then," he said briefly, "I take it that nobody in town has any strings on you."

"Not a soul," informed Presley.

"And I further take it that you know how to run a newspaper from top to bottom."

"I harbor that delusion myself," admitted the other promptly.

"In fact, you are managing editor with Mr. Wright as editor-in-chief?"

"Precisely."

"Very well," decided Hardy. "From now on you are the editor of this paper with your salary doubled. The first thing you are to do is to weed out all inefficients and sympathizers with the old guard. Then raise everybody's salary ten per cent. I didn't see any comic section with that Sunday edition. Don't you have one?"

"Yes—four pages. We get them from the syndicate and put them with the paper in the circulation department."

"How about the *Evening Planet?*"

"They do the same."

"Beginning next Sunday, if you can put the order through quick enough, add to our Sunday issue the same four pages of comics that the *Evening Planet* has. Write a smashing—"

"What for? They can retaliate by adding the comics we use."

"That's all right. The minute they do you add another four more pages. If they drop the comics we take and change to another set, you simply add whatever they pick up. Write a smashing editorial that tells the public the *Morning Blade* is not only the best newspaper in West Fork—it is the only newspaper in West Fork. You are to see that we have everything the *Planet* has—and a whole lot more. Tell 'em the paper has changed hands, but that we are going to carry out Wright's ideals and carry 'em to a finish."

"There's going to be a newspaper war," prophesied Presley. "Why do you want to do this? West Fork is big enough for two good dailies."

"True enough, but we're going to make 'em holler calf rope first, if we have to get out an evening edition to do it."

"Have you got enough money?" demanded the practical Mr. Presley.

"How much do you need?"

"Well," hesitated the other, "to carry out your plan might cost us two or three hundred thousand dollars."

"Half a million will be placed to the credit of the *Blade* next week. See that you can account for every penny. What do you think I raised your salary for? I expect work for it."

"You'll get it—and plenty of trouble, too," promised Mr. Presley.

"That's what I'm looking for," Hardy stated. "Have these three notes photographed and a plate made, or whatever is necessary to print them, and get them ready to run right away with a story exposing the rotten banking methods of the First National Bank. The caption of that article will be, 'Exposé of the Suicide Club.' Have it ready to break this coming week. Follow it up with facts on my father's case the next day.

"Then send out your best reporters and get the story of how the bank broke these people whose names I put down here. If they can't or refuse to tell anything, find out what roundabout hold the fossils have on them and we'll break it. By the way, what sort of an institution is the Farmers' National Bank?"

"Conservative and solid, but they are in the private ring."

"Um—we'll look into that later. Look up everything you can find on Sam Kimball and have it ready for me to-morrow."

"I can tell you about his latest exploit now. Chain Brothers tried to put in a preserving plant here last year. The Chamber of Commerce blew a loud horn and made a drive, collecting twenty thousand dollars from the retail merchants to offer them something in the way of a factory site. The deal mysteriously fell through, but it is understood that Kimball is responsible. The twenty thousand hasn't been returned to the donors."

"I don't like the way you add that last sentence."

"I don't like the looks of the deal," declared Presley.

"Who is on the Chamber of Commerce?" demanded Hardy.

Presley rattled off a string of names which needed not his explanatory remarks to show Hardy who owned the board.

"All right, I see," he interrupted. "Add another sheet to this present issue and agitate the question of a new Chamber of

Commerce composed solely of small merchants and business men whose interests will be more or less unselfish."

"But—but, man, you hand out orders as though I were a magician," protested Presley. "I can't do all this for to-morrow's paper. We won't get an edition out before noon."

"I don't care if it's black night. This is a very special edition. Round up everybody who's off the job and put 'em back to work until this rush is over. We'll pay 'em for everything, and I am personally responsible for any and all trouble accruing from my actions."

Presley mopped his sweating brow with his handkerchief and turned to greet Barbington in something akin to relief. Hardy arose and gravely shook hands with the incoming lawyer.

"I'm afraid my plans are a little heavy for Presley to digest at once, Mr. Barbington," he smiled. "Please assure him that I have the wherewithal and authority to back my insanity."

Barbington smiled faintly.

"All I can say, Presley," he advised, "is for you to do exactly as he tells you."

"Then this is no dream?" demanded Presley.

"If it is, you are not likely to be awakened until a number of millions have been spent," assured Barbington.

Presley came to himself. An unholy gleam of joy entered his eye.

"Get out of my office," he snapped. "I have work to do. Do your loafing in Mr. Wright's office. Here! Copy boy!"

Hardy and the lawyer withdrew smiling.

In Wright's office Hardy picked up the receiver to the desk telephone and called the photographing firm.

"Hello," he said. "This is John Hardy. About those pictures I took with your camera this afternoon—you promised them to me to-night. What? Yes, yes, I know it's Saturday, but you promised to send them over to the *Morning Blade*. Right away. All right."

He turned toward the elderly lawyer.

"The papers all filed?" he asked.

"Everything that you told me to do this afternoon," nodded Barbington.

"How about Mr. Wright?"

"His case will be the first one before the grand jury when it convenes Monday morning. They will not deny him bail, but it will be fixed at a figure which he cannot meet."

"How much?"

"Not less than half a million, I fear."

"Beat them down all you can," instructed Hardy. "The amount of the bail will be forthcoming." The lawyer's eyes glistened.

"Young man," he said, "you are truly a flaming sword. May I shake your hand?"

"I guess so," responded Hardy wearily, "but I'd rather have more results and less handshaking. What I want is action."

The doorknob rattled and a wild-eyed Terence Callahan burst into the room.

"Mister Hardy! Mister Hardy," he cried. "Shure an' I've been lookin' fer ye all over th' buildin'."

"Did you get that affidavit proving Wright hasn't a scratch on his body?" rapped out Hardy.

"Yes, sir," gulped Callahan, flinging down the document onto the desk. "But what I've come to tell ye is thot Brentwood an' young Mallory have got Miss Zoe Ann in Brentwood's office at th' courthouse right now givin' her th' third degree over this affair an' her fayther's connection with ye."

The door slammed, and Callahan and Barbington blinked to find themselves alone.

CHAPTER IX
THE INQUISITION

THE SOCIAL CIRCLES in West Fork were emphatically concentric. Prestige and standing were at a greater premium than at the national capital. While it was easier for the young men of the town to gravitate from circle number three to, say, circle number one for dates and entertainments, it was well-nigh impossible to climb out of the orbit of their own caste for good. Occasionally this did happen. But for the girls it was beyond the bounds of possibility. The conventions of the small town are unyielding.

While the ancestry of those composing the innermost circle was nothing startlingly patrician, the bounds circumscribed by each ring were rigidly fixed. Just where to classify Zoe Ann Wright would be puzzling. From the crown of her glorious little head to the soles of her delicately arched feet she was decidedly the most patrician person who graced West Fork with her presence. Yet she did not rotate within the limits prescribed by circle number one.

Zoe Ann simply did not like the insipid girls of that set, with their silly chatter and risqué anecdotes. The idle life they led and their uselessness in general she could not tolerate. Had she been a snob she might have been the unenviable and unapproachable center of the entire system. But Zoe Ann was far from being a disagreeable person. She was friendly, warmly sympathetic, she was democratic, she was her father's housekeeper by choice. For want of a more exact classification, she was relegated to the ranks of circle number two.

This did not render her *déclassé* exactly, because, for business reasons or political reasons, it was possible for women of circle number one to associate at times with women of circle number two. This suited Zoe Ann precisely. It hurts any woman to feel that she is absolutely barred from the best of society regardless of what she may think of that best. So Zoe Ann moved in the greater friendliness of circle number two with free access to circle number one and with many friends in circles from three on down the scale.

She could attend operas without boredom and play bridge in circle number one without giving or receiving a dirty look across the table for poor cardship. And she could play golf or go swimming with either circle one or circle two. And, transcending this, she could enjoy chatting about babies or housework with Mrs. Wadler and Mrs. Boardman of circles three and four, respectively.

At twenty-five it was high time Zoe Ann was married. She had had plenty of chances to marry Herbert Wilson or Raymond Mallory of the elite and keep her life in the same state of flexibility, or she could have married more than one ardent admirer and forever fixed the bounds of her caste in three, four or five. Just why she had not married Zoe Ann herself did not know. That she did not want to be a spinster was certain.

If she was waiting for any one thing in particular she did not know it. Life moved on in a relentless stream without the necessity of sharp analysis. Until the death of Thurlowe Fosdick.

This brutal murder shocked the hidebound little city greatly. From a deadened town of subdued industry in the back waters of national life, it leaped into stark, ugly prominence. The front-page altercations between the mayor and one of the commissioners, or between a commissioner and the chief of police, which petty squabbling was back-yard gossip and which the *Planet* saw fit to spread on the front page and make West Fork the laughing-stock of all other towns that saw the paper, had suddenly changed into a murder which aroused national interest.

The easy-going, ridiculous air of the town changed in one stroke from petty tyranny and petty affairs to a lethal atmosphere. And

Zoe Ann Wright lost her privilege to move in circle number one. While events had moved too swiftly for this barring of the sanctum sanctorum to become apparent, Zoe Ann knew it was a reality as surely as if she had been sent a legal writ.

Regardless of the outcome of her father's trial she would henceforth find the magic door closed. There was a spark of sardonic laughter at the back of her mind because of this observance of the proper conventions which shuddered at notoriety, but she had no time to worry about society. She had to fight for her father's life.

Facing the keen-faced, albeit battered, Brentwood across the table in the latter's office, she fought gloriously.

"Now, Miss Wright," went on the district attorney in a smooth voice, "we know that we cannot compel you to testify against your father, but we already have sufficient facts to condemn him. All we want you to do is to plead with your father to sign a confession to the deed. This will save us time and trouble and will gain for him as much leniency from the court as can be granted for murder committed under the stress of emotion."

"This—this is outrageous!" cried Zoe Ann, drawing herself up furiously. "You decoy me here under pretense of gathering all possible evidence which will shed light on this affair, and when you get me here you want me to make my father confess to a crime."

"My dear girl, can't you see that I am suggesting Mr. Wright's only sane course? We have the case in a nutshell. He will go to the chair unless he pleads guilty. In this event, he will get off with a life sentence."

Was this smooth, cruel prosecutor the same man with whom she had danced and played bridge? It didn't seem possible. How ruthless and remote he seemed now.

"Why should my father plead guilty to a crime he did not commit?" Zoe Ann cried out passionately. "Aren't things black enough against him without asking him to disgrace his name forever?"

"A crime he did not commit?" repeated Brentwood softly. He glanced from the girl to Mallory in faint amusement. Then he looked at the two detectives seated on the other side of the table.

"Come, come," he said. "Please be reasonable. I am trying to make this painful matter as easy for you as possible."

"If this is all you want with me the interview is closed," declared Zoe Ann frigidly, rising to her feet.

"Oh, come now, Zoe Ann," protested Mallory. "Your father killed Fosdick, my aunt's husband. Everybody knows that. There is no question about that part of it. No doubt Fosdick was too hard on Mr. Wright. I'm sorry about it—we are all sorry about it. I guess Fosdick is the most sorry of all—if his spirit still exists. We don't think any the less of you because of this unfortunate tragedy. We don't hold any hard feelings against Wright himself personally. But you know justice has got to be administered. Let's make it as light as possible on your father."

"In the first place," stated Zoe Ann very distinctly, "I couldn't get my father to sign such a confession if I tried, because he isn't guilty. He isn't! He isn't! Can't you understand? I don't care how black things look, he isn't guilty. Instead of spending your time trying to convict him, won't you please try to unravel the mystery?"

She turned appealingly toward the two plain-clothes men, Colter and Preston, the tears welling up in her eyes. The two men shifted in their seats and looked uncomfortable.

"I'm sorry, Miss Wright," murmured Preston, "but it certainly is a plain case."

"There you are," interjected Brentwood smoothly. "We've covered the ground thoroughly, motive and all. It was no cold-blooded affair; your father is no criminal. But he is guilty and we are trying to make the best of it. This was all we wanted to talk with you about this morning down town when that scoundrel and ruffian intervened."

"This was all?" cried the girl scornfully, her eyes flashing disdainfully. She turned toward Mallory. "Take me home, please, Raymond," she said.

"Stop!" Brentwood's soft voice became hard and commanding as Zoe Ann started toward the door. She halted and quivered as under the lash, at the tone he used. "It is hard not to lose one's patience when a person will not listen to reason," went on Brentwood in a milder voice. "I know this is trying for a girl like you, but we must serve the ends of justice. Please reconsider. It won't hurt anything for you to talk with your father. He will not listen to Mallory or to me."

"But my father is not guilty," protested Zoe Ann.

"Perhaps he has told you that," snorted Brentwood impatiently. "We will grant that you believed him when he denied the deed. But we know that he killed Thurlowe Fosdick."

"In that case," Zoe Ann said bitingly, "you do not need my aid to convict my father. Are you going to take me home, Mr. Mallory? You brought me down in your car."

"No," stated Brentwood; "he isn't. And you are not going home just yet, either, young lady. Sit down while I tell you a few bald facts."

The color flamed high in the girl's cheeks and she drew herself up proudly.

"Good-night," she said distinctly, and with three indignant steps she was at the door.

Brentwood motioned quickly at one of the detectives. The fellow sprang up and caught the girl's arm just as she was passing out through the doorway. She became rigid at his profaning touch.

"I'm sorry, miss," he mumbled apologetically, "but Mr. Brentwood doesn't want you to leave."

As gently as possible he drew her aside and closed and locked the door. Zoe Ann whirled and faced the thin-lipped attorney.

"You would detain me by force?" she flashed ominously.

"I would," he snarled grimly.

Zoe Ann looked at the uncomfortable Mallory. "And do you sanction such an outrageous action, Raymond Mallory?" she demanded.

The heavy-set young lawyer dropped his eyes under her accusing gaze.

"Zoe Ann, I'm sorry, but you are a material witness. You—"

"And to think that I was sorry John Hardy dealt roughly with such as you two," she scorned. "Let me go," she cried, stamping her foot. "You have no right to hold me."

"Young woman, we have tried to deal kindly with you," snapped Brentwood, "but I see that it will not work. Now you sit down and answer a few questions."

"I prefer to stand, and I will answer no questions," she flamed.

Brentwood's bruised mouth twisted into a sneering smile. He shrugged.

"Very well. Answer them or not, as you please. You were at your father's office Friday morning after he came back from the golf course, were you not?"

No answer. She surveyed him as some loathsome creature far beneath her.

"Your answer is immaterial," went on Brentwood's hateful voice. "We know that you were. You were in the room alone with his golf bag for at least five minutes."

Still no answer.

"What did your father instruct you to do when he came back in?" said Brentwood suddenly.

"I didn't see my father," she burst out involuntarily, and bit her lip in vexation at having spoken. At the sneering expression on her questioner's face in having trapped her into speech, she decided to finish her statement.

"I was down town to do some shopping before the heat of the day and I went in to see Papa for just a minute. One of the reporters told me that he thought he had just come in from golfing a few moments before. I went to his office, but he wasn't there. If he was in the building, he must have been downstairs in the printing department, for after waiting a minute I went back and looked into the news room and he wasn't in there. So I left."

"You say that you did not see your father!" demanded Brentwood in surprise.

"I did not."

"You had better be careful, young woman," warned the attorney. "Your answer to this question means a lot to you."

"I did not see him. Why should I lie about the truth?"

"To save yourself trouble," answered Brentwood grimly. "You—"

"For God's sake, Zoe Ann," cried out Mallory in anguish, "say that you saw him and explain what he told you to do."

"I did not see him," repeated Zoe Ann stonily, not even glancing at the paling city attorney.

"In that case, I shall have to put you under arrest as accessory before the fact," announced Brentwood. "You knew when and how the murder was to be committed. What did you do with the shattered half of Fosdick's golf club which your father took into the office in his golf bag?" he thundered.

"Oh, what do you say?" faltered the poor girl. Her knees began to tremble and she felt that they were going to give way beneath her. Fearing that this natural act would be interpreted as evidence of guilt by this ruthless crew, she fought with all of her will power to hold herself erect.

"I say that you removed the lower part of a golf club from your father's golf bag for some obscure reason. Why did you do this and what did you do with it?"

"Oh, oh, I didn't do it," she cried. "What are you trying to prove?"

"Simply this: Howard Wright picked up all slivers and pieces of the club he could find, overlooking the section of handle in his victim's left hand, and took them with him—intending to get rid of them later. The golf course has been searched for the missing club and so also has every inch of the road he took coming back to town. The only moment he could have got rid of the pieces was when you were at the *Blade* Friday morning.

"The pieces are not to be found in the *Blade* building, and while you are here your home is being thoroughly searched right now. Come clean, my girl. Tell the truth while there is time. You couldn't destroy that club head by any method known to you, as that brassie of Fosdick's had a plate of brass across the sole. It will be found in the ashes if you burned the stick. Now, will you talk?"

"Oh, you are wrong—horribly wrong," she cried hysterically. "I didn't even see my father's golf bag in his office. It may have been in its customary corner, but I didn't look. Anyway, no club of Mr. Fosdick's was in it. My father isn't guilty, I tell you. He is not guilty. He—is—not—"

Her voice trailed off and she would have fallen if Preston hadn't sprung forward to catch her. At Brentwood's command he placed the half-fainting girl in the chair she had previously occupied and let her head rest on the table.

"Get a glass of water quickly!" commanded the agitated Mallory to Colter as he began chafing one slim hand.

"Now," Brentwood smiled thinly, "we are about to get down to facts. Her resistance has given way. We shall have a confession out of her that will send her murderous father to the chair and implicate that devil Hardy so that he will get a long sentence."

His words penetrated Zoe Ann's understanding and she struggled to sit up.

"Whatever you do," she whispered, "you leave John Hardy out of this. He knows nothing about it—nothing. He merely acted a gentleman when a gentleman was needed this morning."

Brentwood was too inured to the cutting repartee of the courtroom even to feel this barb. But he had a further point to make.

"Is that so, my dear?" he snarled. "He knows nothing about this mess, but he protects you from this fruitful interview, he buys Wright's paper and saves it, he spends all afternoon out on the golf links to make sure no clew was left by the murderer, and—"

"You lie!" cried Zoe Ann in a clear voice.

"She doesn't need water to revive her," sneered Brentwood at the man who offered the glass. "John Hardy has been in touch with these people, perhaps he was here when the brutal deed was done, and we are going to land him for complicity."

At this tense instant the doorknob turned and the door creaked against the weight of a person who had not, evidently, expected the barrier to be locked. Then the knob rattled noisily.

"Who is it? What do you want?" shouted Mallory.

"In, and that quickly," answered a very determined voice, the accents of which made Mallory start in recognition.

Brentwood had no difficulty in recognizing the timbre of that voice either. His eyes narrowed and he shot keen glances at the two detectives. "This is an important conference," he rapped out. "Go away from there. No admittance."

Zoe Ann opened her mouth to cry out. Instantly the long, bony hand of the district attorney shot across the table and clamped across her jaws, sinking cruelly into the flesh.

"If that fellow attempts to come in," he warned to the two officers, "get him!"

All eyes were on the vague shadow which blurred the frosted plateglass at the top of the door, the shadow made by the intruder's body. At Brentwood's words the rattling of the doorknob ceased. And as they watched the shadow drew away. Before Mallory could wheeze in relief, there was a terrific crash of glass. The frosted upper half of the door shivered into many fragments. A heavy foot vanished from sight and framed in the opening was the fierce countenance of John Hardy.

He took in the situation at a glance. Without pausing to reach in and unlock the door, reckless of sharp edges of glass, with one mighty leap that was half dive John Hardy sprang into the room. Out of the corner of her eye, over the tip of Brentwood's restraining forefinger, Zoe Ann caught the flash of that lithe figure. In that instant, without process of reasoning, Zoe Ann realized that all her life she had been waiting for this man.

CHAPTER X
PRIMA FACIE EVIDENCE

THE PROSECUTING ATTORNEY released the girl and drew back across the table for all the world like a turtle withdrawing into his shell. Then, while John Hardy steadied himself on his feet, no one else moved.

Hardy's blue eyes took in the disarranged hair of Zoe Ann, the marks where Brentwood's fingers had bruised her cheeks, her wan appearance in general, and they became like glittering points of steel.

"Slim Brentwood, you cur!" he exclaimed. "This is the third time you've clashed with me to-day, and the second over the same fair cause. Out in the country I've been living in, that's two too many. This time you're going to the hospital."

He leaped forward and put out one hand to vault over the table. The exclamation to which Brentwood gave vent sounded like the yelp of a frightened terrier.

"Shoot him down!" he shouted desperately as he recoiled.

Before the dazed and uncertain minions of the law could respond in any manner, Zoe Ann's hand flashed out and rested lightly on that muscular forearm reaching down to the table.

"No, John, no!" she cried. "Don't touch him! Don't you see that it will just make us more trouble? He has the law on his side."

Her tone, and her use of his Christian name as well as the touch of her hand exerted a powerful restraining influence on Hardy. He hesitated and glanced down at her curiously. He slowly relaxed and his hard eyes softened in bewilderment.

97

"That's funny," he said aloud. "That's the first time since my mother's death that anyone's voice took the desire to fight out of me."

Zoe Ann laughed tremulously. She was at a loss to answer this. She thrilled at the thought that her small hand and her girlish voice had the power to check the dynamic energy which flowed all through this man like a vast current. There could be a hundred explanations why she had been able to exert this control, but she feared that her eyes showed the one reason she thought might be the answer. So she looked down and laughed tremulously.

Mallory was kind enough to bridge the embarrassment of the moment.

"What the devil do you want here, Hardy?" he growled. "You fool, can't you understand that every action you are making is pulling you deeper into this mire?"

"Mire is right," agreed Hardy. "You certainly don't know how to treat a lady."

"I give you my word that no hand has been laid on Miss Wright in violence," said Mallory quickly, apologizing not so much to Hardy as to his own ears. "What you saw was just to keep her from crying out—" He checked himself too late.

"So!" breathed Hardy, baring his teeth. "You were keeping her here against her will."

"Yes, we were," ripped out Brentwood angrily. "We merely want the truth of this matter, and we want to hear what she has to say."

"And holding her by force is your method of extracting the truth?" queried Hardy in grim irony.

"Think what you please," snapped Brentwood. "I am going to prosecute this case. I'm going to resume my quizzing of this girl now. If you interfere, I'll have you thrown into jail without bond until I clear up this matter."

It was obvious that the attorney meant what he said. That he was no coward, Hardy was certain. The fighting man changed his tactics.

"Words and tones such as you use, Slim, have always made me fight first and argue later," he said slowly. "But I realize, thanks to this little lady, that you can't fight your way satisfactorily through layers of misunderstanding. Fight with your fists, I mean. So I'm going to try to reason with you. It isn't your zeal in invoking the law, regardless of whether or not you're disinterested, that I am quarreling with. It's your method of going about it. Now—"

"If you will keep out of my way for forty-eight hours I'll have the business finished," interrupted Brentwood savagely.

"I believe you," agreed Hardy. "But you'd have it finished the way you want it finished, and not according to justice. I haven't been getting in your way, I've been driving ahead on a straight course since I got here this morning. It's because you are as crooked as a dog's hind leg that you have been crossing my trail back and forth all day."

Brentwood's fingers played an impatient tattoo on the edge of the table. He essayed a smile.

"If you have done with your insults," he said with an ironic bow, "I will ask you to withdraw from this legal conference. The city will render you a bill for that door glass, and I would suggest that you attend your own business long enough to cleanse yourself from that disgraceful affray of this morning."

"Thank you," bit out Hardy. "You surely are hard to reason with. You don't give me any chance of showing you how you're wrong except by way of fist. Instead of leaving, I'm staying right here. As an officer of justice you are entitled to an interview with Miss Wright, and she, as a good citizen, should tell you all of the truth that she knows.

"If you really want the truth, I, as a supreme arbiter, will see that you ask for it in the proper way. Further than that, I'll see that you get a lot of truth you are not expecting. Hurry up now and start your questions. Miss Wright wants to go home."

Zoe Ann flashed Hardy a grateful smile, and he reciprocated by patting her gently on the shoulder. But Brentwood would admit of no such solution to the situation. He lost his suavity as he lost his patience.

"Get out!" he roared. "Get out before I go mad. I'll attend to your case later."

"May I see you home, Miss Wright?" asked Hardy, bowing to the girl.

"Thank you," she accepted, rising to her feet and almost clinging to her champion's arm.

"Stop this monkey business!" rasped Brentwood. "You go, but she stays."

"Either we both stay or we both go," stated Hardy firmly.

"Hell!" said Mallory. "This is ridiculous."

"Right you are, Gallant Gerald," agreed Hardy. "It's worse than a stalemate—it's plumb stale, isn't it? What are they trying to get out of you, Miss Zoe Ann?"

"They want me to beg my father to plead guilty," she replied in a level voice.

"Is that so?" demanded Hardy.

"It is," agreed Brentwood sharply. "It will save the State time and money, and it may save Wright's life."

"And what is the idea in this stunt?"

"Because we'll send him to the chair if he doesn't confess."

"Then, why do you crave a confession? Your outfit is out to get Wright, isn't it? Why halt the good work?"

"None of your damned business!" ejaculated Brentwood in exasperation.

"I'll tell you why," Hardy said crisply. "First, you and Mallory can both leave the expletives out of your speech. The reason you want a confession is because there is a weak link in your chain of evidence. What is it?"

"I think I know what it is," said Zoe Ann quickly. "They can't find the rest of Mr. Fosdick's brassie, and they are trying to prove that Papa took it."

"Ah, ha! And they haven't been able to find it on him or on his property, eh? They have the chain of circumstances, but they haven't the slightest shred of material evidence to prove their case completely."

"And they have searched the newspaper plant, and they are searching our home right now for the golf club," added Zoe feverishly. "Mr. Brentwood told me that just before you came in."

"Well, well, isn't that nice?" Hardy said in grim humor. "Your men won't find a thing, Slim. Shall I tell you why?"

"Why?" demanded Mallory, while all the others eyed Hardy in interest.

"Because Wright never saw the missing club," announced Hardy calmly. "You are as wide of the real trail as this town is of life."

"We've listened to you long enough," decided Brentwood. "You talk in circles."

"I don't even commit myself, do I?" asked Hardy maliciously. "And my metaphors carry too strong a ring of truth for comfort."

"You don't know what you're talking about," corrected Mallory wearily. "We know what we know."

"But you don't know all you think you know. If I give you some proof on this matter, will you listen to reason?"

"What do *you* know?" asked Brentwood, interested or feigning interest for the first time.

"I know that Wright could not have killed Fosdick by a wide margin," stated Hardy. "I know that Fosdick started to play at seven o'clock. I know that he was a good golfer, and should have played the course in one hour. I know that he should have been playing the ninth hole within sight of the clubhouse, as Wright drove off the first tee at eight o'clock. Why wasn't he? Think that over!

"I know that Wright actually played around as far as the ravine between the second and third holes. I know that he broke his mashie in the ditch, and not over Fosdick's head. I know that—"

"How do you know this?" asked Colter quickly, speaking for the first time.

Hardy glanced from the speaker toward the corner of the room. "Is that Mr. Wright's golf bag over there?" he asked.

Colter nodded.

"Is the broken mashie still in it?"

"It is."

"Bring the bag here to the table," directed Hardy.

Colter looked at Brentwood for sanction of this move. The lawyer eyed Hardy keenly for a moment and then nodded briefly. Zoe

Ann, sensing a *dénouement*, cupped her hands under her heart and gazed at the disheveled Hardy in fascination.

"Take out the broken club and fit the pieces together," commanded Hardy. "I won't touch it."

Preston did so in silence, and all four of the men bent over to reexamine the club they had examined a hundred times.

"Well?" demanded Brentwood, looking up.

"A good-sized sliver is missing from the club shaft, isn't it? Perhaps two or three?"

"Yes," admitted Mallory.

Hardy drew his thumb and forefinger from his breast pocket and, leaning over, lightly dropped a sliver of wood beside the club.

"See how that fits," he suggested.

There was silence for a space while the experiment was made.

One of the detectives whispered under his breath: "It fits perfectly."

"Where did you get this splinter of wood, and what does it prove?" demanded Brentwood.

"I got it from the stream in the ravine just where Wright claimed to have been. It was water-soaked when I got it, as any chemist can tell you. And Terry Callahan and Jenkins, the club attendant, were my witnesses when I picked it up. Do you get the significance of that?

"Exhibit B. Shreds of cloth from Wright's tweeds, gathered from the bushes at the same place. Take them and match them with his golfing togs. Over at the office of the *Blade* I now have photographs of the spot where these things were found, and one picture of Wright's footprint—a fresh footprint, by the way. He made it Friday morning.

"I have among those pictures a complete map of the ground where the body of Fosdick was found. When I piece them together it will give the ground spread out like a carpet. The spot looks like a couple of bull elephants had a wrestling match there. Which brings us to Exhibit C.

"I haven't had time to see the body of the murdered man, but I've seen the ground, and I've heard about the broken golf club. He didn't smash that club on empty air, did he? And the ground showed there had been a terrific struggle, didn't it? And you are smart enough to realize that the assassin couldn't get away from a fight where a club was broken against him without a wound of some sort, aren't you?

"Well, here is an affidavit made this afternoon by your county physician and two of his medical brethren swearing that Wright hasn't a scratch or bruise on him. Now, go ahead and question his daughter. Go ahead and search for your missing golf club. Go ahead and try to convict Wright. And go ahead and make some more libelous cracks about both of us, Slim, like you tried to put over in the *Blade* before you fairly had your hooks securely in it. My dear fellow, you'll sweat blood before you send Howard Wright to the chair for this crime, and West Fork will have to have some real detectives.

"Furthermore, I've just begun to unearth evidence about Wright and about the town in general. If what I have offered you to-night is only negative proof, I'll add that I have specimens of blood-soaked dirt from the spot of the murder being tested right now for the two different kinds of blood which will be there. Wright's blood was tested this afternoon by your city chemist under the direction of the county physician.

"Fosdick's blood was tested at the morgue. When I show you that another's and not Wright's blood was mingled with the dead man's out there on the fatal battleground, I'll have given you positive proof and also a clew in the form of knowledge of the exact composition of the assassin's blood."

Hardy ceased, out of breath and carried away with himself. Not a one of the four men said a word for a long moment as they endeavored to assimilate all they had heard. Zoe Ann was crying unrestrainedly now. Emotion after emotion had racked her to-night until the simple feeling of joyous relief brought the tears of happiness.

At sight of her bowed head Hardy's rage rekindled. He raised his clenched hand angrily.

"For no reason at all you thick wits have caused a good man to be detained overlong in prison, while you criminally neglect clews. You've caused infinite anguish to a good woman's heart, and have

sought to blacken her name. You're a bunch of misfits and ineffi-
cient meddlers, who have no right to be in control of the govern-
ment and safety of thirty thousand people.

"You haven't anything worth while to do, and if you had, you
couldn't do it. Well, I'm going to give you something to worry about
that will mean more to you than the hounding of Howard Wright,
because he is a champion of the people. Slim and Stubby, read the
Morning Blade to-morrow. Read the whole of it from front to back.
You'll find plenty of food for thought.

"And remember when you read it, that the *Blade* belongs to
me, and that I am responsible for everything in it. You won't have
any trouble finding me when you want me. Good night!"

The telephone, tinkling sharply, aroused them with a start.
Hardy bent over the girl in clumsy solicitude as Brentwood answered the instrument.

"Don't cry, little lady," he murmured gently. "It's all right now.
Come on, let's be going. I am sure that you will not be bothered again."

"Oh, oh, it isn't that, John Hardy," she whispered, raising those
fathomless eyes to his. "It's—it's just that you are simply wonderful. I shall never live long enough to thank you for what you've
done this day."

"On the other hand, I'm thinking that you will," said Hardy
before he could curb the strange impulse.

Again Mallory covered confusion.

"Brentwood says the call is for you, Hardy," he called loudly in
the latter's ear.

Hardy looked up in undisguised annoyance. Impatiently he
stepped around to the phone.

"Are you through questioning Miss Wright, Slim?" he demanded as he picked up the instrument.

"For the present," admitted Brentwood ungraciously.

"All right. Hello? Hello? Who? Oh, Presley. Oh, the council of
war has decided on disarmament for the present."

"That's bearding the lion in his own den, then," chuckled the
editor of the *Blade* over the wire. "I called to tell you that Professor Walker called up here for you and wants to see you right away."

CHAPTER XI
PIPES OF PAN

ELM STREET WAS QUIET when John and Zoe Ann left the courthouse. The street lamps were partially hidden by the dense foliage of the old trees so that the walks were darkened except in small circles directly under the lights at each corner. There was little nearby sound as John assisted his companion down the lonely sweep of steps. It was true that West Fork was a Saturday night town, but all of the noise and traffic pulsed up and down Wilson Avenue save for the occasional hum of an automobile and its piercing double lance of light when a motorist sought the deserted Elm Street in his desire to make haste.

It was a scant two blocks from the administrative building to that of the *Morning Blade*. They walked along in silence, the man taking it for granted that she would wish to go to the newspaper offices with him. For the first moment since he had come home he felt like he was enjoying a calm spell. He had leaped from one action to another with such rapidity that he felt he had earned a breathing spell. A faint void within informed him that he had as yet eaten no evening meal, and it was after nine o'clock.

The girl's voice recalled him.

"If you are to be busy, I can take a streetcar or a taxi home," she said. "As Raymond Mallory brought me down I left my own car, you know."

"Oh, pardon me, I had forgotten," said Hardy. "I must speak to Presley a moment, if you please, and then we will go."

"I don't mind going home alone."

"Please, I'd like to take you."

"Thank you, John Hardy," she made answer as they paused before the entrance. "And when will you get that report on the last blood tests? Surely that will clear Papa's name completely."

"Oh, that? Yes, that was Presley who called me on the phone. That's why I want to see him. Professor Walker is calling for me."

"Professor Walker? Is he making the test for you?"

"Yes. That is, I think so. He hadn't come in for supper when I went by his house, but I left my suitcase there with the packages of soil to be examined. I left a note explaining exactly what I wanted him to do. I didn't have time to wait to see him personally. I thought it best to let different men analyze the different specimens and Callahan suggested Walker."

"I see. You think of everything. May I—do you think it will be all right for me to go with you? I'm so anxious to hear about it."

"Why, certainly," he agreed heartily. "Wait until I see if the photographer has delivered those prints for me and see how Presley is coming along with the revised edition he is putting out. I won't be half a minute. Do you care to come upstairs?"

She declined and turned to stare through the big windows at the linotype machines and their nimble-fingered operators. It was hard for her to view with a sense of detachment the familiar scene which she had always associated with her father. The monotonous buzzing of the ventilator fans, circulating the humid air of the hot night, had a sort of hypnotic effect on her.

All that she surveyed now belonged to a stranger. Her father had lost the slight purchase he had had on power to fight for the people. Instantly she rebelled against that thought. It was unjust to think that the *Blade* belonged to a stranger. Rather, it belonged to a powerful friend. It was an effort to realize that she had known John Hardy less than twenty-four hours. It seemed weeks almost since that brief encounter of the morning.

"Are you ready?" his voice sounded in her ear. "Professor Walker is waiting for me at the high school laboratory. We can walk over to Wilson Avenue and get a taxi."

"Let's walk," she suggested. "It's only twelve or fourteen blocks. We can go up Elm Street and cross over by the Catholic church. I want to talk to you."

"All right," he agreed readily. "I'm sorry it's so warm to-night."

They traversed the first block in silence. The subdued roar from Wilson Avenue reached their ears faintly across the intervening buildings. A slight breeze set the leaves and boughs overhead to whispering and murmuring. A metallic click sounded occasionally as some hard-shelled nocturnal insect had a head-on collision with a light globe. Zoe Ann shuddered as she saw the lights of the county jail and thought of her confined father who could do nothing but wait. If her companion noticed this involuntary action he gave no sign.

"John, what did you mean by telling Brentwood and Mallory to read to-morrow's *Blade* to give them something to do?" she finally broke the silence.

"Just what I said," he responded gravely. "In that fight we had this morning they are called a pair of ruffians instead of prominent citizens. The *Blade* today has ceased printing insignificant news items for the personal aggrandizement of private individuals who deserve no such publicity. Then, there will be other news of interest. The Chamber of Commerce belongs to the monied interests. The *Blade* devotes an entire page to this sad condition and begins to agitate plans for a new organization composed of disinterested merchants. And this week we begin to expose the Suicide Club."

"Suicide Club? What is that?"

"The First National Bank. They killed my father, they are trying to kill yours. Do you remember Mr. Gregg, the president of the Gregg Grocery Company? Well, that was a big wholesale house which was not run by the greedy wolves of West Fork. They couldn't dictate to Gregg, so they broke him. He killed himself so that his family could collect his life insurance to keep from being penniless."

"Oh, that is horrible. I remember dimly that he shot himself some fifteen years ago, but I didn't know that was the reason. Are you sure about it?"

"You were a little girl then and I wasn't much bigger. But I remember what my father said about it. I have Presley digging up the facts. Do you remember Grottshein? He was the biggest retail clothier here when I was a boy. The bank pinched in on him and he killed himself in despair. But he was so involved that this act didn't save his business."

"But, John, how did the bank get him into that condition, and why did they close down on him?" Zoe Ann cried.

"How? That's easy. He banked with them, he borrowed money from them. When they caught him long on merchandise and short of cash they demanded their loan back just like they did with your father. They are as cunning and patient as spiders, and when they spring their traps there is no escape. To bank with them is to sign your own death warrant. That's why I have called that bank the Suicide Club. And I'm going to prove it in the *Blade*. You are asking why they broke Grottshein? Because Trundham wanted to be the biggest clothier in West Fork, and Trundham is the brother of Judge Mallory's wife."

"Why didn't Grottshein borrow money elsewhere?"

"Where could he have got it? The Farmers' National is in the ring. They wouldn't have saved him. Both banks have fattened off the small individual. Look at their system of handling these little industries organized here at home. After Mr. Citizen buys stock enough to put the industry in operation the banks wait until it gets on its feet and then break it. They buy in the company for next to nothing, reorganize, and go blithely on with the money donated by private citizens who now have nothing to show for their funds except worthless and defunct stock certificates.

"Do you want me to tell you more? Well then, what does West Fork offer to the laboring man when he is at leisure on Sunday? Nothing! On top of their stifling of this town they have piled up adverse legislation at the State capitol until it is no longer a pleasure to live in the State. Blue laws are killing this section of the country. No wonder people flock to the big cities like Chicago and New York. How old is West Fork? Anyway, thirty years ago it had a population of nearly twenty-five thousand. And now it has but thirty thousand. Six or seven thousand increase in thirty years! Why, there have been far more births than that. We haven't even kept our natural increase.

"And why should we? People want opportunity to get ahead. There is nothing for a home-town boy to do. Besides, folks want more than mere bread and butter to-day. They want to live, to enjoy themselves. After working hard all week in Sam Kimball's factories they want a place to take their families on Sunday besides church where Kimball orders even their religion for them. There should be band concerts on Sunday, baseball, picture shows, public contests and meetings. Yet, what is there going to be open for the public to-morrow? Why, it's against the law to play cards in your own home on Sunday."

"What is the way to correct this condition, do you think?" she asked eagerly. "Papa has said those very things many times."

"Well," said Hardy slowly, pondering on the matter, "the evils which may be attributed to State laws are going to be hard to combat. Before we can get the people to vote for certain measures we have to educate them up to the desire for the good things of life. How can we expect the farmers and villagers scattered over this state to demand something they have never had? Not having the taste for these things, they simply do not comprehend what they are doing without. They don't even want good roads. They never had them; they can't see the advantages therein. The automobile has been a blessing to the eastern states by educating the farmer. Ask any hillbilly of Ohio or Pennsylvania if he would like to get rid of the fine roads with their cost of upkeep. Not on your life He has tasted the benefits and he won't give them up. Texas, way off there in the southwest, is outstripping this State in modernity. Dallas is the livest town in that section of the country. I reckon I should have stayed there."

"How would you go about educating the people to demand the comforts they should have?"

"Well, there's the automobile and the motion picture. There are the many magazines. In time these things will have weight. What is needed is a fearless group of ministers who will preach to the people what they ought to hear and not what they think they want to hear. Get men who are not afraid of being thrown out of their churches and turn them loose. Open the church all day every day as well as on Sunday and prayer meeting night. Let 'em get away from this smirking, sanctimonious hell-fire and get interested in life as it is and as it should be lived on earth. That will start things quicker. If I had national authority I'd close up the big towns tighter than drums and open up the amusements of the little towns. That would soon balance the center of population. All of these things take time and many willing workers. As for the trouble with West Fork personally—well, I'm going to see what I can do for it."

"And did you come home just with that intention?" Zoe Ann asked breathlessly.

"No," he admitted frankly. "I came home to lick Fosdick. After meeting your father and you I decided to stay and lick the town."

"But, John," she ventured, "don't you think that it is a terribly big job?"

"Yes, I do. But it's one to my liking."

"I'm afraid you are going to find yourself tied up in all sorts of libel suits and trouble through the *Blade* if you carry out your plans."

"Trouble, doubtless, but not libel suits. The truth isn't libel. And I'm not dependant on local business to have to be afraid to print it."

Silence fell again as they passed by the church and turned up Maple Avenue. Here the street lamps were spaced farther apart where the residences of the middle class began. Cigar or cigarette tips glowed from the darkness of front porches, an occasional voice sounded, the appearance of some figure in white who passed like a ghost in the night. The singing of belated crickets, the earthly smell of a garden freshly sprinkled, the mingled odors of growing flowers, the murmuring laughter of a young couple in a car parked without lights. Under cover of the dark which hid any changes of time John Hardy felt himself being carried back across the span of years to his school days.

He had been so busy during the years of his absence that he hadn't had much time to think of home. Now, a queer ache seized him. In spite of all West Fork was home to him. Many times had he walked along this same Maple Avenue. He had trod the way before his father laid the first curb and gutter which marked the era of paved streets. Thought of his father brought a lump to his throat.

At the next corner which was without a street lamp he silently took the girl's arm to assist her across the side street. Safely over the second curb, he released her. His fingers slipped down the length of her soft, young arm to hang at his side. Their fingers met, and Zoe Ann clasped his strong hand in an impulsive little squeeze. John returned the pressure, and neither loosened their grip. So they walked along under the whispering maples hand in hand.

It was just a hot night in a more or less modern town which was afflicted with its traffic and radio troubles. Their fingers became moist and sticky because of the heat of contact. There was nothing romantic in the situation or under the circumstances surrounding this walk to the high school, but somehow Hardy felt borne out of himself by the mere touch of this girl's hand. Without warning something clicked within his brain. This was the very first time he had ever taken a walk with her. In fact, it was the first day he had ever set eyes upon her. But there was something startlingly familiar in this stroll.

John Hardy was experiencing that queer feeling like a flashback to a previous existence. He felt that this incident had occurred before. Perhaps an incident in his childhood, a picture he had once seen and forgotten, or the unrelated fragments of dreams was responsible for this queer pseudo-memory which psychologists and scientists have tried in vain to explain satisfactorily to us of lesser brilliance. Whatever the cause, John knew syllable for syllable what her first words were going to be when she broke the magical silence.

"You have made me happier than I ever was in my life," finally came her soft tones, voicing the expected phrase.

"I am glad," he answered simply, wondering how he had known what she was going to say and wondering how he knew exactly what her next words would be.

"I think I have lived all my life passively awaiting this day," she said.

Every step he took, everything he could discern of the trees and the soft grass of the parking carried him back to some dim pastoral age when he had walked hand in hand with this same girl before. He knew such a thought to be the rankest kind of folly, but how had he known what she was going to say before she said it and why did it awake a yearning in his breast that was almost an ache?

This was all. There was nothing more to be said by either of them that would seem familiar to him; the clairvoyant moment was lived. But the tingling illusion persisted, baffling him by its vividness. Across his mind flashed the lines of a poem which had struck him with such similar force that he had memorized it. He had never fully understood the meaning until now.

> "The poignant yearn of manhood and of age
>   For moments of almost forgotten youth
>   Assails me not alone with mem'ry's gauge
>   Of childhood days which I recall as truth.
>
> "Profound the depths of the subconscious mind.
>   As I reflect upon the years gone by,
>   I see a lad who is to reader blind;
>   His lesson's text had caught his fancy's eye.
>
> "'Twas naught but tale of buckwheat and of storm,
>   Of spreading fields of green stalks and sunshine,
>   Of gath'ring clouds, of rain which did no harm,
>   And buckwheat bowing 'neath the rushing wind.
>
> "Somehow, the vision had enthralled his heart.
>   Perhaps his soul glimpsed past of joyous mirth—
>   The Golden Age! Fresh soil! Man's humble start!
>   Pure instinct told him, God, he loved Thy earth.
>
> "What was this urge, this unrest, in his soul,
>   This yearning caused but unassuaged by text?

I knew not then; to-day I've reached no goal.
The answer may be learned in life that's next.

"Nostalgia of time which grips men grown,
The wistful longing for the used-to-be,
Engenders wish not for the past alone;
But waving buckwheat field again I see."

"Why, that's *Yearning Unassuaged* by Frederick William Fitzhugh," cried Zoe Ann in wonder. "How did you happen to know it, and what made you say it now?"

He had recited the poem aloud without being conscious of the act.

"I—I don't know," he stammered. "I know I've just caught the full meaning. I didn't know I was speaking aloud."

"But what made you think of it at the moment?" she insisted. "Tell me."

"I can't explain," he said helplessly. "Just walking along here with you reminded me of something I couldn't place and made me long for it in an unaccountable manner. I guess my empty stomach is making me light-headed."

But Zoe Ann refused to laugh.

"Was it because—did it seem like an experience which has happened before?" she queried in a frightened voice. "Was what I said familiar to you?"

So this was the answer. She had experienced the same thing. And the psychic rapport between them had established a sort of mental telepathy. But, as he seized upon it, this solution did not satisfy.

"I mean as I was thanking you for all you have done did it seem as though you had heard me thank you in the same words—"

"Please don't," he said in a strained manner. "You mustn't feel under any great obligation to me. It sounds all wrong for a queen to be too grateful to a subject."

Zoe Ann released his hand and drew away, repulsed and hurt by his words. Her usual calm dignity and reserve recloaked her emotions. Again the queer spell of a priceless moment was shattered.

"Oh, I didn't mean it that way, Zoe Ann," he hastened to assure her. "Please, I didn't mean to reject your thanks. I appreciate your gratitude more than anything else I can think of. But I meant that it isn't right for you to be as grateful as—as a befriended pup. Er— I didn't mean that, either. I mean that I—that anyone should— would do things for you and your father. I mean that you have the right to expect it. I—oh, I don't know just what I do mean," he finished lamely, angry because he couldn't express the exact thoughts that possessed him.

"I don't believe you do, either," agreed Zoe Ann a trifle coolly. Then she laughed softly and in a friendly way. "Anyway, I'm deeply grateful to you. Papa and I shall never forget your kindness."

As they waited for the night watchman of the school building to respond to their knock and admit them she held out her hand frankly. He clasped it warmly, and their friendship was sealed for all time. But that brief moment of intimate contact, that intangible essence of something rare and beyond everyday life was lost.

John Hardy was not given to ethereal wanderings of the spirit. He disliked vague emotions, fanciful vagaries, or queer half-thoughts which couldn't be classified. Hence, this material and more normal plane upon which he now found himself with this woman was more to his taste. Yet, there had been something oddly disturbing in that flash of the subconscious mind akin to memory. While glad to withdraw from that uncharted morass of the unexplored soul, he was vaguely disappointed in the loss of that mystic moment he could not understand.

Yet, he could not have retained or plumbed the depths of that queer moment had he willed. For, at the attempted probing of the odd incident by Zoe Ann, a strange, unreasoning fear had gripped him. This was the first time in the life of the prosaic, hard-fisted and hard-headed John Hardy that he had heard the pipes of Pan, and he was afraid.

CHAPTER XII
PROFESSOR WALKER'S ANALYSIS

JOHN HARDY WAS NOT GIVEN to philosophy; he was a man of action. Yet, when he pondered on the matter at all, it seemed to him that life was a swiftly flowing stream which flashed across a brief open space of sunshine between two grim and forbidding cliffs. It was an unknown underground river which burst without warning from the black depths preceding the cradle, ran swiftly across the sunlit space and plunged again into darkness through the opaque clouds of mist which obscured the opening in the cliff of death.

From whence it came and whither it went no one knew. Man was conscious only of that fleeting moment of sunshine between birth and death. Like a voyager borne along in a skiff without oars, he was helpless to stay the rush of the stream. All he could do was to note the snags and try to avoid them, note the rocks and eddies and trees which served as landmarks of time and try to remember them if he could.

Of his voyage past the quiet eddy which composed the life of Professor Thomas Walker he could recall but three little snags or rocks which stood out in a row across the mouth of the chemist's little bay of existence as Hardy saw it. To others whose life stream mingled or came into contact with that of the professor, there might be other marks of identification, but to Hardy there remained just these three.

His first outstanding recollection of Professor Walker came to him the first week he became a student of chemistry. Because of the necessary freedom of speech and action in the laboratory there was less discipline in Walker's classes than in others. Unruly or exuberant spirited students took advantage of this opportunity to carry on conversations or flirtations foreign to the business of atoms and their valences. Just so much of this would Walker tolerate before he would bring the culprits to order with a favorite sharp remark. The first time John Hardy heard it he found that he himself was being addressed.

"Mr. Hardy, I am running this circus," rapped out the professor. "If you want to put on a show, get a tent of your own."

Slang! Argot of the street! This crude, but succinct phrase falling from the lips of an otherwise cultured professor! John Hardy never forgot it.

The second episode anent Walker he recalled with something of chagrin. In some manner, perhaps through discussion of Mendel's law of heredity, the matter of mixed blood arose. Was America sufficiently a melting pot to absorb the Negro and the Indian? Examples were discussed. Professor Walker vetoed the suggestion that the Negro blood would successfully mingle with white, but, as the Indian was of a disappearing race, numbering considerably less than half a million, and there being a number of conditions to consider, an amalgamation of Indian and white blood was more or less probable.

Hardy, ever positive in his beliefs and convictions, took issue with the speaker.

"An amalgamation between white and red men is intolerable," he declared vehemently. "It is no more to be thought of than mixing with the Negro."

"And why, may I ask?" demanded Walker with some asperity.

"Why? Because the Indian is not white," stated John proudly.

Walker merely looked at him without reply. A faint flush rose to the chemist's cheeks. A chill fell upon the subject and it was dropped. It was some time after this that Hardy learned there was Cherokee blood flowing in Walker's veins from his mother's side of the house. He thought of the professor's high cheekbones, the queer expression in the man's eyes as his pupil proudly disdained Indian blood.

Regardless of the permissible difference of opinion on the subject, Hardy would never have intentionally hurt the older man's feelings. And, having learned this bit of Walker's family history in an indirect manner, it was not a point upon which he could apologize to the professor. The matter was never mentioned again. After all these years it was to be doubted if Walker would remember it. But John Hardy never forgot it.

The third and most significant landmark by which he remembered the chemist was something in the nature of an epochal event. It concerned Hardy's experiment with nitroglycerin. When the class came to that section of the work dealing with explosives Walker furnished guncotton in minute particles and a tube gun with which to explode it. He produced pure sodium and demonstrated the theory of spontaneous combustion.

All of this led to discussions of fire and insurance bugs and their methods. The class enjoyed a two weeks' sojourn in the giant land of explosive power, carefully guarded by their instructor. When the subject of glyceryl trinitrate, more popularly termed nitroglycerin, was reached the class was bidden to read the lesson, learn to distinguish the properties of the explosive, and forget it.

Because of the danger surrounding this high explosive, its manufacture was forbidden. Not so to hardheaded John Hardy. He had already survived a mixture of potassium chlorate and sulphuric acid. He desired to read the riddle of the heavy, sweetish, innocuous glycerin which his mother had mixed with rose water for his chapped hands as a child. Withdrawing to a workbench against the wall, well away from the other pupils, he proceeded to follow instructions concerning the mixture of nitric acid with glycerin.

He added the necessary sulphuric acid to take up the water formed in the mixture, placed a rubber stopper in the test tube, and carefully set the little phial in a rack against the wall. Unfortunately he had a Bunsen burner going within a few inches of this product. He paused to consider how he was to test the efficacy of this new compound and how he was to dispose of it safely thereafter.

The Bunsen burner acted as the judge in this question. Heated under pressure, the nitroglycerin reacted true to form. There was sudden ominous thunder. John Hardy came to himself on the floor with Professor Walker bending anxiously over him. His wandering eyes observed an expanse of blue sky where a moment before had been a thick wall.

"Wha—what happened?" he quavered.

"That's precisely what I want to know," answered Walker. "What were you doing, and where are you hurt?"

"I—I just made a little nitroglycerin, Professor," he answered weakly. "I put it in the rack while I was deciding what to do with it. Did I blow that hole in the wall?" he asked, as he got haltingly to his feet.

The semicircle of students about them began to laugh nervously.

"You did," agreed Walker grimly. "The only thing that saved your life is the fact that nitroglycerin does not explode away from resistance, but toward the point of nearest resistance. The proximity of your mixture to that wall saved your neck. You certainly fit your surname, young man."

The questionable fame he bore for some weeks, the irate school board, the matter of repairing the damaged wall, all faded into the forgotten things of the past before the memory of the chemist kneeling over him with anxious face, which was at variance with his angry words.

All of this had been some twelve years ago. Hardy had seen and talked with Walker many times in the two years that followed ere he left home. But nothing stood out in his mind as he and Zoe Ann climbed the stairs of the deserted school building except these three lone markers of remembrance.

"Doesn't it seem queer to be passing through these familiar old halls again?" murmured the girl almost wistfully. "The building is alive with memories and the faces of chums of school days. Can't you just see society nights, reception nights, graduation—senior plays—debates on Thanksgiving after a close football game with Dansville or Piney Grove? Those things still go on, yet how deserted the old place is, just because we know it is vacation time, I guess."

Hardy's nostrils twitched at mention of football.

"Yes," he sighed. "I can see the beribboned section of the auditorium set aside for the football squad who came to see if their debaters and orators would win the cup after they won the football game. The noise and the cheers, the music and smell of cut flowers, and a fellow's best girl he could walk home with afterward. How short those days were."

"And how long they seemed to be then," she smiled. "Did you have a best girl, John?"

"A new one every year," laughed Hardy. "Sometimes three or four."

"But wasn't there one particular shy mouse of a girl, or perhaps a regular belle of the school, that you felt you were going to marry when you finished growing up?" persisted Zoe Ann. "Wasn't there one girl you liked above all others?"

"No, there wasn't," said Hardy soberly. "I have always been too busy getting into trouble to think of marrying. To tell you the truth I can't do any more than recall the names of some of the girls I knew. Here we are, and Professor Walker is probably tired of waiting."

Ten years had not changed the chemistry instructor more than might be expected. At fifty he looked very like the man Hardy had known at forty. It was true that his black eyes seemed more tired, his high cheek bones higher, the lines in his face deeper, and the mole on his chin more hairy. But then Hardy had himself reached an age where he was far more observant than a thoughtless, careless youth. Perhaps Professor Walker's shoulder stoop was a trifle more pronounced, but his step still had the active spring and resiliency of yore. And his handshake and his voice were firm and steady.

"Well, well, so you've come home, John Hardy. We had begun to think West Fork had lost you for all time; your name was rarely mentioned any more. I might say that nothing has surprised me more in recent years than the note you left with Mrs. Whitlowe. That was the first inkling I had of your return. I am sorry I wasn't at home, but I was out in the woods for the afternoon. Of course, you ran true to form and got tangled up with trouble the moment you landed."

"Yes," agreed Hardy soberly. "Big trouble this time, Professor. You know this young lady, don't you?"

"Certainly," Zoe Ann answered for the chemist. "We meet each other on the streets frequently."

"My dear girl," said Walker, holding out his hand sympathetically, "you don't know how sorry I am that your father has been brought into this affair. Who would have dreamed that they would dare draw his name into it on such flimsy evidence?"

"Oh, it's simply awful," she made answer, trying to smile bravely.

"I cannot understand the workings of Fate," murmured the scientist, shaking his head slowly. "In death, as in life, Fosdick causes trouble and agony for better men than he."

"Oh, I wouldn't say that, Professor Walker," exclaimed the girl. "Poor man! I am sorry for him. Think how he must have suffered."

"Yes, yes," agreed Walker thoughtfully. "I, too, am sorry—for your father."

Evidently Walker had not held the deceased banker in very high esteem. Hardy covered the awkward pause.

"Did you analyze that soil for us, Professor?" he asked. "I judge that you did, from what Presley told me."

"Yes, I did. I have all the figures here on my desk," replied Walker, leading the way into the laboratory. "I am glad I was here to do the work for you. I generally go up into the mountains for the summer, but things haven't been going smoothly for my finances the last two or three years. So I've been staying in West Fork."

"You won't have to this summer," promised Hardy generously.

Walker smiled faintly.

"If you mean that you intend sending me on a vacation for telling you what you want to know, I fear that I will remain in West Fork," he answered gently.

"What do you mean?" cried Hardy quickly.

Zoe Ann merely looked her distress.

"You specifically asked me to test these specimens of soil for two different kinds of human blood, did you not?" asked the chemist, waving his hand toward a table upon which were the several newspapers holding little mounds of dirt.

"Yes."

"I have done so. I have been two or three hours at it for you. That was a clever thought of yours, John Hardy, and I am proud of you. Out of several hundred people it would be well-nigh impossible to identify the blood of each, but out of two or three individuals there should be all the chance in the world of separating and identifying specimens.

"You know that the general composition of human blood is the same, being composed of liquor sanguinis—liquid of blood— water, proteids, salts, nutritive and excrementitious matter. The red corpuscles are one thirty-two-hundredths in diameter and the white are one twenty-five-hundredths. The white corpuscles exist in the proportion of one to three hundred reds, sometimes as high as four hundred reds to one white. They will vary in size a fraction with individuals, also. Then there are disease germs and varying quantities of salts in individuals. Following Ehrlich's side chain theory regarding amboceptoids—"

"But, Professor Walker," cut in Hardy worriedly, "aside from the laboratory method of doing the work, what did you find out?"

"I was just trying to tell you that while such a test as you wanted was delicate, still it could be done," remarked Walker in disapproval of the interruption. "And the chances should have been ten to one that the two different kinds of blood offered for analysis would be sufficiently different to be distinguishable from each other. This, I regret to say, is not the case. The soil you brought me most certainly contained human blood. However, it was every drop from the same individual—or else the two persons had blood that was identical in character so far as I could determine."

Hardy and Zoe Ann looked at each other in dumb misery. The hope which they held had faded.

"Are—are you sure of that?" demanded Hardy earnestly. "This is a mighty important thing, Professor Walker."

"Positive. Here are my figures. There is your soil. Have it done over by someone else," suggested the chemist stiffly.

"No, I didn't mean to doubt your ability, sir. But you don't understand what this means. If Wright's blood should happen to test out the same as this—but it couldn't! There is no question that part of this is Fosdick's blood, and Wright's tests out differently."

"Isn't—isn't it queer that the assassin should have blood exactly like that of Mr. Fosdick?" Zoe Ann managed to utter.

Walker eyed her white face keenly. His features softened a trifle at the suffering depicted in her countenance.

"If I may venture an opinion," he said softly, "I should say that there is no blood here save Fosdick's."

"Then—then you think that the murderer got off from the fight without losing any blood—without getting hurt in the encounter?" she murmured.

"Without question," agreed Walker.

"But—from the description of the body's condition there must have been a regular battle," protested Hardy. "How would you account for that, Professor?"

"I should say," replied Walker shrugging slightly, "that Fosdick at last ran into something he couldn't browbeat."

There was silence for a moment. Then:

"If Mr. Brentwood learns of this result, he'll try to lay the blame on Papa again," murmured Zoe Ann. "The fact that there are no marks on him will but bear out this analysis. Being such a big, strong man, Brentwood will say that he was able to beat down Mr. Fosdick without receiving a blow in return."

"If they learn of it?" muttered Hardy. "When they learn of it, you man. I promised them to-night to let them have proof of the blood test. I guess I talked a little fast, Zoe Ann. I—I'm awfully sorry. But I was too sure of the results of this analysis."

"Don't," protested Zoe Ann, the tears coming to her eyes. "Don't try to blame yourself, John. You have more than overbalanced this slip—if slip you call it—by all else that you've done."

"Well, I guess we'll have to begin all over for a clew," said Hardy.

"Maybe they won't be so anxious to push things after what you said about the time limit involved," offered the girl hopefully.

"I'm sorry," murmured Professor Walker. "Here are the notes, John. And your suitcase is there by the table."

"You didn't find anything else in the soil?" queried Hardy desperately, clutching for a last straw.

"Not a thing," said Walker. "Of course, there is some grass and perhaps a twig or two. I didn't sift the dirt for any articles."

"I didn't mean that," said Hardy wearily, shaking his head. "Still," he went on as he picked up his handbag, "there might be something in that. I'll just take these packages of dirt with me, too."

"I'm sorry I couldn't earn that vacation," Walker offered, essaying a smile meant to be cheerful.

Hardy looked up from the bundles he was making.

"You have, Professor Walker, just the same," he said. "Where do you want to go, and how much will it cost you?"

The chemist raised a protesting hand.

"I was just trying to be cheerful," he said. "I do not care to go anywhere this summer."

"Come now," Hardy said. "You've worked hard enough on me in the past to earn a dozen vacations. How much do you need?"

"I couldn't think of taking a dime from you," declined Walker firmly.

"Perhaps not for a vacation," agreed Hardy, "but you shall for this analysis work. It is worth five hundred dollars to me to find out that I haven't anything to depend on. You've got to know exactly where you stand before you tangle with the law enforcement league here. Will five hundred dollars be enough?"

"Five hundred dollars? My dear boy, you—you are generous, to say the least," gasped Walker. "I'm sorry, but I cannot accept a penny of your money."

"But I insist. I don't like to rest under obligation to anybody when money will lessen my debt. You must be paid for what you've done at any rate."

The chemist eyed the speaker rather queerly.

"Very well," he said. "Five dollars will cover everything."

"That won't pay you for your time," snorted Hardy. "You have earned a vacation this summer."

Walker drew himself erect. His dignity was impenetrable.

"I am sorry, but I cannot accept your generosity. I beg of you to desist."

Further urging would have been extremely distasteful to the man. As unostentatiously as possible Hardy laid a five-dollar bill on the desk. The chemist folded and handed to him the paper containing the results of the analysis.

"Do you play golf, Professor Walker?" Zoe Ann asked irrelevantly as they bade the elderly man good night.

Walker's black eyes were almost piercing in their intensity as he looked at her.

"I do not," he stated distinctly. "Such amusements are not for poor professors."

On the way to the Wright home Hardy tried to shake off the depression which was settling upon his shoulders because of the astonishing result of the analysis.

"Anyway, I'll have time at last to care for my black eye," he endeavored to speak lightly. "I'll change this ruined suit for a suit of pyjamas. Good Lord! I haven't registered at any of the hotels. I forgot it. Do you think I can get a room at the Marlton at this time of night?"

"I suppose one could," Zoe Ann replied almost indifferently.

"Thank you for your interest," Hardy rejoined, faintly sarcastic.

"Oh, excuse me," she said, rousing herself. "I was thinking about Professor Walker. Hotel? You're not going to any hotel. You're going home with me."

"But—but, isn't such a proceeding a bit unusual?" he queried. "I appreciate your kindness, but there is something else I have to do yet to-night. And then, I've just come to town, and it is rather late at night to be walking in with you. And then your father isn't home—"

"I wish everybody wouldn't remind me that my father is in jail," she declared, bursting into tears.

"I'm sorry. I didn't mean to recall that to you," he said helplessly. "I—"

"I—I guess I'm buckling under the strain," she tried to smile. "Excuse my childishness. But we have a big house and two or three servants. There's lots and lots of room for you. It seems like an age since—since yesterday morning."

"There, there," soothed Hardy. "You're just getting tired, that's all. You're a brick to stand up under what you've been through. I'd be glad to accept your invitation, but there's one more thing I've simply got to do to-night."

"What?"

He studied her features for an instant. Should he tell her? If she were becoming hysterical it was hardly the right thing to discuss at the moment. Yet, it was either tell her or accept her hospitality.

"Well," he hesitated, "you see, to-night is the only chance I'll have to see Fosdick's body for myself. I don't know whether that can do me much good now, but I don't want to overlook anything. That's why I can't accept—"

"All right," she agreed, "I hadn't thought of that, but you are right. Let us hurry. I shall go with you."

"You? Why, Zoe Ann, I wouldn't think of taking you to such a place. Why—"

The tears were gone. Her expression was grim and her rounded young jaw was squared and hardened in a delicious manner.

"We are fighting for my father's life," she declared. "I'll go any-where and do anything."

"You are simply immense!" he stated slowly. "I didn't know there were any young women like you."

"I didn't think there were any men like you," she answered.

Her frankness was disconcerting. Abruptly Hardy changed the subject.

"What made you ask Walker if he played golf?" he inquired.

"Oh, yes, that was queer. I asked him that because I saw among the other bottles and things on his desk a freshly opened bottle of Permanex."

"Permanex? And what is Permanex?"

"It is a white enamel for recoating old golf balls. I thought it queer that he should have a bottle of the stuff up there at the school building during vacation time."

CHAPTER XIII
THE SILENT WITNESS

SILENCE! SILENCE AND MIDNIGHT! Too late for the hum of traffic to sound from the deadened street without. Too late for trolley cars, too late for automobiles, too late for revelers in West Fork—too late for all this noise, had it existed, to penetrate this silence. A subdued glow from the dome light in the ceiling—the sickening, cloying odor of mingled flowers—banks of floral designs around and over the gray casket in the alcove—soldierly array of folding chairs with the name "Greenwald" stenciled on the back—a peaceful sleeper whom noise will ne'er awaken—brooding solitude—silence. And midnight.

The last candle gutters in its socket. The vain display is o'er, and life turns to witness the antics of a newer puppet. Gather ye young buds and old bloods while ye may! Strut the boards and speak your squeaky lines from your different levels of society. Here is the goal of all. Death is the great leveler of all things temporal. What matters a ten-thousand-dollar funeral or a ten-dollar pine box? Worms are no respecters of bodies. Marked with the cold dew of death, bankers and policemen, drab slatterns and society matrons, bootleggers and kings are all alike.

Who are you to puff and blow so pompously to-day? From sanctimonious Sam Kimball down to Bob, the ragged street urchin of nameless parentage! From Jersey Jim, the poetical hobo, up to Mrs. T. Wayne Gibson, the ancient and aristocratic aunt of Judge Mallory who has had her face lifted to regain a semblance of youth! To-morrow the mold of the grave will be on you—the world will have forgotten even your name, or, if remembering, will shrug indifferently. Despite your air of importance to-day you will have lived to slight avail.

Witness the faint, mocking smile about the pallid lips of this sleeper who wakes not. You, Jersey Jim, you disreputable, filthy, shiftless tramp, you are fully as great as Thurlowe Fosdick, banker of reputation! You, Thurlowe Fosdick, with your petty politics, your horrible, cold, merciless nature and thieving cant, you are even less than Jersey Jim! For the worthless tramp still lives and breathes. He is worth a thousand dead men yet, while you—you have ceased to be!

To-morrow morning you will be surrounded by sorrowing relatives, by sniveling hypocrites, by curious idlers. You will be attended by the pomp and fuss of a ten-thousand-dollar funeral. You will be eulogized by an ardent minister who keeps one eye on the billy-goat face of Sam Kimball. To-morrow—ah! To-morrow you will be well attended.

But to-night you sleep alone, surrounded only by the shadows of your iniquities. How peaceful must be death! You smile in your sleep like a happy child. The Grim Reaper has, with the assistance of Henry Greenwald, on your battered face ironed out much of the wolf's expression. You rest peacefully and smile, while a better man than you ever dreamed to be rests in the shadow of the gallows to-night.

Come! Unlock those smiling lips, open those cold piercing eyes once again. What is the secret which envelops your death? Now is no time to rest and smile at the mockery of life. A human soul is in travail because of you. Unseal the gates of death for one brief instant and speak. Only you know the secret of your murder. Speak! Speak, and in death show one act of mercy that you did not show in your life. Knowest thou aught of thy demise? Speak, and free a fellow being, or condemn him to the gibbet. That cold smile is more baffling than Mona Lisa's—than the Sphinx.

"The old codger looks pretty good, doesn't he? You should have seen his mug when they brought him in—he was a wreck."

John Hardy glanced swiftly at the downcast face of Zoe Ann Wright and then scowled warningly at the speaker.

"Can't we have a little more light in here?" he asked in a voice which radiated disapproval.

"Sure," agreed the undertaker's assistant cheerfully, unabashed at the other's attitude. "There! Take a good squint at him now. No marks of violence on his map, are there? Dermalite is the stuff that does it. That's a compound we use to fill up holes. Then we paint 'em up. We could show the beauty parlors a few tricks. You—"

Zoe Ann shuddered convulsively.

"Heavens! Can't you be quiet, man," growled Hardy roughly.

"Me?" gaped the young fellow incredulously. "Sure. But what's wrong? You said you weren't relatives, didn't you? I was just trying to explain to you how Fosdick looks so nice. Say! You sure have a beauty of a shiner yourself. Want me to paint up the old optic for you?"

"Your chatter is annoying because—this young lady is the daughter of the man accused of this deed," stated Hardy tersely. "No, I don't want my eye camouflaged."

"Oh!" exclaimed the talkative embalmer. "I didn't know it. I'm sorry if I spoke callously, miss. It's all in the day's business to us, you know. I—"

"Never mind," interrupted Zoe Ann gently, essaying a faint smile. "I know you didn't mean any offense. And we have come to learn all you can tell us about it. Please explain—to Mr. Hardy—how the body looked and—and anything he wants to ask you. Go on, John, see if you can learn anything. I won't faint, or anything. And I want to hear about it."

"Do you know Howard Wright, young man?" demanded Hardy, smiling encouragingly at the girl at this brave speech.

"Only by sight," admitted the embalmer. "Sit down. Just as well be comfortable. Fosdick won't mind. I've read his paper quite a bit. Smart man—too fast for this burg. By the way, my name's Gordon—Neal Gordon."

Hardy winced at the easy reference to the deceased banker, but he shook hands and smiled. It was hard to be angry at this garrulous apprentice.

"Let me tell you clearly where I stand before we go any further," he said. "My name is Hardy. This is Miss Wright. I am the new owner of the *Morning Blade*, and my sole purpose here to-night is to see if I can't unearth some bit of evidence which may help me to prove Mr. Wright's innocence. I am bitterly opposed to the crowd who are seeking to pin this crime on Howard Wright. In view of this admission will you aid me with all the information you can give? I ask nothing but the exact truth."

Gordon cocked his head to one side like a quizzical puppy.

"Will I? Brother, I don't know what you can learn from me except how many gallons of embalming fluid Fosdick used and how many patches I had to make in his hide, but whatever I can tell you—consider it told."

"Thank you. You are not a native son of West Fork, I take it."

"Not hardly," Gordon grinned happily. "Furthermore, I don't owe the town vultures a thing. In fact, the favors go the other way. Fosdick, there, owes me something for parting his hair so nice. Fire away. What do you want to know?"

"The banker's body was brought here some time yesterday, I think. Was it brought directly from the Country Club?"

"Yep—late yesterday afternoon after the home town sleuths got through sleuthing. I pickled—embalmed him last night. I caught myself that time, Miss Wright. Say, are you the fellow who wanted a blood test of the dead man this afternoon? The day man told me about some such request. Lucky we were able to furnish it."

"That is one of my lines of investigation," admitted Hardy gravely. "Now, about Fosdick. What became of his clothes? His family come after his effects yet? And I suppose the police hold the remains of his golf club?"

"Everything is still here—what's left of 'em."

"What do you mean?"

"The front was pretty near torn off of him," enlightened Gordon. "When the killer got through with him he looked like he'd run into the side of a speeding express train covered with barbs. He—"

For the first time confusion halted his speech, and he glanced guiltily at the white-faced girl who listened.

"Never mind me, Mr. Gordon," she declared proudly. "It was not my father. Go on. We are here to find out."

"I'll show the things to you," offered Gordon, recovering his aplomb. "Come on back here."

He sprang to his feet and started to lead the way rearward out of the mortuary chapel.

"Will there be any—er—gruesome sights?" hesitated Hardy, glancing quickly at his companion.

"Not any," beamed Gordon, carelessly pointing toward the casket of the banker. "Only stiff in the house to-night."

Hardy swung around, half exasperated. Zoe Ann quickly held out her hand to him and smiled in understanding.

"Come, John," said she. "He doesn't offend me in the least, and he's trying to be as nice as he can. Don't think of me at all, but see what you can learn. Why, if it would have helped any I'm sorry we didn't get here last night in time to see the poor lacerated body before it was touched. I can stand anything for Papa's sake—with you to lean on."

He squeezed her fingers comfortingly as they followed in the wake of the breezy and irrepressible Mr. Gordon.

The heavy white duck which had constituted Fosdick's golfing togs amply bore out the embalmer's description. The goods were badly stained with blood, and both shirt and knickers were torn and ripped unaccountably in a number of places. Hardy subjected the garments to a severe scrutiny. He found several minute slivers of hickory imbedded in the cloth. That these came from the shattered club was obvious, but why were they driven into the material?

"Were any shreds of cloth beaten into his flesh?" queried Hardy, pointing at one of the rents.

"Only in one spot in his side where I took out a good-sized splinter of wood," informed Gordon. "Otherwise he just seemed a mass of bruises."

Without comment Hardy examined the banker's golfing shoes. These were fairly new. He started slightly as he recognized the markings on the soles to be identical with the markings he had photographed in Wright's footprint in the ravine. The only difference was that the dead man's shoes were appreciably smaller.

"And this is the half of his golf club," added Gordon, holding out a leather-wrapped handle as Hardy straightened up. "The effects found in his pockets are in the safe in the office."

"How does it happen that the police didn't take charge of this?" asked Hardy, gingerly accepting the handle which the murdered man had been gripping at the instant of death.

"It was glued to the stump of his right hand with blood," Gordon replied. "I suppose you knew that the two forefingers of that hand were missing? Well, it was so apparent that no other hand had touched this handle except Fosdick's that they didn't bother to disturb it. I had to soak it loose, myself."

"Uuumm—I note that the leather, even though stiffened with blood, coils down a bit below the end of the wood grip," frowned Hardy. "In fact this leather-wrapped handle is not as long as it should be."

"Of course not," stated Gordon. "The police said that the blow which cut off those two fingers took part of the handle as a matter of course."

"That's the queer part of it," continued Hardy thoughtfully. "If the slayer sheared off two fingers and cut through the hickory handle by a particularly violent blow of his more or less sharp instrument, how does it happen that this leather grip isn't torn or cut somewhat? Can't you see that the fingers were removed and the wood was broken while the spiraled strip of leather between fingers and wood was not injured?"

Gordon whistled.

"That's mighty funny," he offered.

"There's something wrong in the theory of the blow," pursued Hardy. "Yet—I can see no way to account for the loss of the fingers by any other method, myself. Tell me how you patched up the mutilated hand. Just how did it—"

"I didn't," responded Gordon quickly. "I just washed it up and put on a silk glove with stuffed fingers. I didn't see any need of making new fingers. He'll never sign any more papers."

"Good boy!" cried Hardy. "Quick! Let's have a look at the hand."

Back in the chapel Gordon deftly removed the glove and exposed the banker's right hand. Zoe Ann, as interested as she was, could not restrain a faint quiver as Hardy bent over to examine it.

For a long moment he stared in silence at the mutilation. Some tiny cell of memory leaped into active life and waved a warning flag frantically. He had seen this very thing before, somewhere, some time. He knit his brows and strove to think what was familiar to him in the appearance of this torn flesh.

There was a difference; it had been living flesh he had examined before. This hand would never heal, because nature was forever through with this bit of clay in its present form. But somewhere in Hardy's brain was the exact knowledge of how this hand would have looked had its owner lived to see it heal. How the dickens could he know this? What elusive thought trembled on the edge of remembrance? Queer and tricky thing, the human mind.

He slowly shook his head and relinquished the cold hand. He stared uncertainly at the club handle while Gordon replaced the silken glove with its two cotton fingers. Then, at the embalmer's questioning eye and Zoe Ann's expectant silence he sighed.

"I can't quite grasp it," he said. "I guess we've seen all we can see here. Before we go, will you show us his personal things, Gordon?"

Upon his last morning on earth Fosdick had not been burdened with many of the trappings of civilization. A bunch of keys, a combination card case and billfold, a gold pencil, a clubhouse score card, an elegant watch with a belt chain, some small change, a signet ring, and a pair of monogrammed handkerchiefs were the net sum.

His companions were silent while Hardy fingered the articles delicately. There was little enough he could learn from these things. The pencil and watch were engraved with the banker's name. The pocketbook contained thirty-two dollars, a railroad pass, and membership cards to the Country Club and two fraternal orders. Loath to relinquish these inanimate witnesses to a crime, Hardy picked up the watch again.

As he stared at its face a significant little fact which he had overlooked the first time gradually forced itself upon his consciousness. The timepiece was silent. He placed it to his ear. But of course it would have run down since yesterday morning. He tested the spring. The watch was wound fairly tight. This excited his interest. He shook it vigorously and listened again. He desisted at length and looked up queerly.

"Did anyone notice that this watch has gone dead?" he asked Gordon.

"No," admitted Gordon quickly, having gathered the importance of Hardy's actions. "I didn't put these things away—Greenwald did. Beyond noting that the body hadn't been robbed I don't suppose the police paid any attention to it."

"Zoe Ann! Zoe Ann!" cried Hardy so sharply that the girl started.

"Yes, yes," she answered feverishly. "What is it, John?"

"This watch proves our case about the time limit involved in the murder," he declared with shining eyes. "Fosdick was not the man to carry a dead watch around with him, was he? And it is a foregone conclusion that nobody has wound this timepiece up since he last did so. Yet it is wound up and stopped. He wound it up early yesterday morning. And yesterday morning is when it stopped. Look! Look at the hour at which it quit working."

Both Zoe Ann and Gordon stared at the watch. It had ceased to tick off the seconds at seven thirty-six.

"Our silent witness!" exclaimed Hardy. "Seven thirty-six! Just about the time a fair golfer starting at seven would get around to the spot where Fosdick was murdered. This exonerates Howard Wright."

"Oh, it does, it does," cried Zoe Ann.

"I guess it does," agreed Gordon thoughtfully as he turned the watch over in his fingers. "I'm mighty glad if this helps your father out of a tight hole. But say, Hardy, look at this biscuit. There isn't a mark or dent on it. Why, the crystal isn't broken even. It's a cinch the murderer didn't hit Fosdick in his watch pocket and queer the timepiece. If this watch stopped at the instant Fosdick was bumped out, all right. But why did it do it? I'm not strong for psychic phenomena."

"Neither am I," agreed Hardy soberly, that same elusive memory cell playing hide-and-seek with him down through mental corridors. "I can't answer your question. All I can say is that it did so. Lock these things up in a safer place, where no one can get at them. On your life, don't surrender them until we have an expert jeweler look at the watch. I'll see that it becomes legal evidence to-morrow."

He pressed a ten-dollar bill into the young man's hand, and turned to conduct a happy girl out of the building.

CHAPTER XIV
WHO LAUGHS?

SCORCHING DAYS, but cool, comfortable nights. Up in the Ozark table-lands, at a desirable number of feet above sea level, West Fork may have sweltered during the dog days, but it cooled off delightfully at night.

John Hardy slept soundly until the chill of dawn's low temperature crept into his blood. His strenuous day, and perhaps long association with trouble, rendered him impervious to all else save slumber from the instant his head touched his pillow until the sun peeped over the rim of the world. He drew the light covers up about his form and turned on his side to resume his pursuit of Slim Brentwood through the shadowland of subconsciousness.

But his years in the cattle country had built up a habit which now played him false. Accustomed to rising at dawn to tackle another day of sweating with obdurant steers, and in days after that, obdurant well drillers, he could not go back to sleep.

He rolled over on his back and lay staring about the big, airy room. And thus he lay when the first shy shaft of sunshine launched itself athwart his bed. He heard the twittering of birds in the big maple just outside his eastern window, the whispering of the star-pointed leaves in the cool breeze of dawn.

The faint rattle of milk bottles on the side porch attested the arrival of the milkman. A shrill whistle from the street and a dull thud as a bulky newspaper caromed against the front steps announced the paper boy. West Fork was astir. The wheels of industry quivered and then, with a subdued clank of machinery, resumed

the daily grind of civilization, which halted not even for the funeral of a Fosdick.

Hardy stretched luxuriously and yawned gloriously. His eyes
fell on the braided sleeve of his pyjama coat. Almost curiously he
felt of the fine texture of the cloth. A far cry from the rough garments of Texas. He glanced toward the chair which held the damaged suit he had worn the day before. He had outfitted himself
rather lavishly in Kansas City, a sort of reaction against the lean
years in Texas. Now he was worse off than before, unless his trunk
was waiting his pleasure at the railway station.

As he had told Howard Wright, his plans had been hazy, his
reasons for coming home vague. There had been little of enmity
against a living being in West Fork. Even his remark about thrashing Fosdick had been more or less in the nature of conversation.
But he had been unsettled in plans for the future.

He was entirely too young a man to be turned, idle, upon a world
with twenty million dollars ready at his hand. The calm of two or
three months which had followed his triumph in the oil fields of
his ranch had become irksome. His descent upon unsuspecting
West Fork had been somewhat in the nature of an experiment.

He sighed deeply and grinned in remembrance of an exceed-
ingly busy Saturday. His homecoming had been all that he could
have wished. In trouble up to his neck and with unlimited ways in
which to put his money to work. While he was a big enough man to
exert his wealth and ability wisely, it is to be admitted that he rev-
eled in the joy of opposition. There was plenty of work to do in
West Fork. John Hardy was satisfied.

He opened his suitcase and began going through his papers,
counting his cash reserve, and laying plans for the bringing of part
of his main capital to the city. There was so much to do and so many
details of all kinds to handle that he began to jot down ideas and re-
solves. It was borne in on him that the first thing he had to do was to
find a permanent place of residence and then establish a regular business office. That he couldn't carry on various activities in an office
of the *Blade* was obvious. He made a memorandum to take a suite
of offices to-morrow in the most modern building in town.

Then he needed more lieutenants. Presley was one. Callahan was another of a different type. He needed a real estate man, a factory man, an organizer, a secretary, and a minister. This he entered in his notes.

In the case of Howard Wright he might yet need the service of detectives; this would come later. For a lawyer he was satisfied for the present with Barbington, who seemed to possess more than the average intelligence. When he got ready to attack the political machine, he would enlarge his plans accordingly. He glanced over the list of the names Callahan had made out for him and checked several that he found promising.

He was whistling softly as he laid out fresh undergarments, a clean shirt, collar, and socks. He felt tenderly of his bruised eye and studied it in the mirror. It was much better this morning. While swollen and still somewhat discolored, it had improved. Zoe Ann had spent enough time on it last night to all but cure it. Brentwood would be much longer obliterating the marks of that fray than John Hardy.

He shaved and bathed. Clad again in fresh garments except for the trousers which he had brushed carefully, in shirt sleeves, he descended the stairs. The grand staircase was a delight to Hardy. It made the lower rooms seem so much larger and lighter. The waxed hardwood floors, the many small rugs, the massive furniture, relieved here and there by some dainty thing of Zoe Ann's purchasing, made the great house a thing of beauty and taste.

Zoe Ann was before him when he strolled out to find the paper he had heard the boy throw a couple of hours before. He met her at the steps as she came from the rose garden with a fresh bouquet of flowers for the breakfast table. Fresh and radiant, she was lovely this morning, and Hardy caught his breath in contemplation of her beauty.

"Good morning," she greeted him with a smile. "Aren't these roses beautiful? Just smell them."

Hardy obliged with a willing sniff and drew back with his nose covered with beads of dew. With a little laugh Zoe Ann reached up and wiped away the drops of water with a wisp of a lacy handkerchief.

"Excuse me," she murmured, turning aside and gently shaking the bouquet until it showered a silvery spray to the steps.

"Ah, don't do that," he begged quickly. "They are much prettier with their pearls of dew. Besides, don't you think they are entitled to their morning bath. The land of dew is a fairy land of enchantment. Have you ever seen a cactus plant in the early morning? Or a spider's web?"

She glanced up at him in astonishment.

"I thought only romantic-minded girls thought of such things."

"Not so," he defended quickly. "He who looks sees the beauty of Nature without being a sentimentalist. But I'm surprised to find you out so early."

"Why, it's nearly eight o'clock, sir. I've been up for an hour."

"And I've been awake for twice that," he smiled. "Habit is a stern mistress."

"You have? And I thought I was letting you get a well-earned sleep. Come. I think Margaret has breakfast ready for us. I must hurry so I can take a basket of things down to Papa."

A shadow crossed her face, conjuring up for Hardy the vision of a big man pacing the length of a cell with downcast eyes.

"Certainly, if you wish it," he agreed, stooping to pick up the newspaper he had come out to get. "I must see Mr. Wright this morning myself and tell him how things are going. However, except for your wish to take him something from home, you needn't worry about his meals. I made arrangements with the Tuxedo Café yesterday afternoon to send them to him for the rest of the time he is being held."

"You did? You think of everything, John Hardy. I never met a more efficient person."

"Not quite everything, Zoe Ann," he answered gravely. "But food is one thing a cowpuncher never overlooks. You needn't worry about that item. Besides, we'll have your father out on bail before to-morrow night. I have Barbington's word for it."

The girl buried her face in the flowers she carried to hide her emotion.

"I—I don't know how we can ever thank you for all you have done," she faltered. "I—"

"Don't try," he said quickly. "Let's go on through with everything without the customary reactions of emotions. Let's take everything that comes as a matter of course no matter how out of the ordinary it may really be. Do you see? That will give us a game to play, a sort of stage drama to move through. And at the same time it will provide a safety valve for our emotions."

"I don't understand—exactly."

"I'll try to explain. Take yesterday, for example. It was a most unusual day, wasn't it? I never had so much action crowded into twelve short hours before. Yet, I think I moved through it all with more or less calm. Do I flatter myself unnecessarily, or do you agree with me?"

"You are the calmest man I ever saw," she cried quickly. "I never saw any one handle situation after situation as easily as you did. You met every exigency beautifully—especially when you broke into Mr. Brentwood's office last night."

"There! That's what I mean. I stalked through the day's doings as calmly as an actor going through a play for the thousandth time. Yet I assure you that I was hard put from one minute to the next. I was never mixed up in anything which approaches the present tangle before in my life—and I've been mixed up in plenty of trouble."

"I think I see what you mean," she said. "You mean to accept everything as calmly as though it were expected. As though the whole thing were nothing but a play."

"Precisely."

"Oh—oh, I couldn't be so banal," she whispered.

"I know it's harder for you than for me, but it isn't banality. It's safety. It lets you view things in an unbiased and detached way. It keeps you from getting a warped viewpoint. Let's try it this morning. Here we are in your home, you and I, without a chaperon save Margaret, who is putting some iced grapefruit on the table, I perceive.

"This is an unusual occurrence. Very well. Let's sit down and I'll unfold this paper while you arrange your roses in the center of the table. Here, I spread open a newspaper which is loaded with dynamite and which is going to bring a storm of trouble about my ears. All this is decidedly unusual, but we'll dawdle over our coffee as though it were an everyday occurrence. And we'll glance over the various headlines in the paper as impersonally as though they merely mention a birth in Oshkosh or a society wedding in Japan.

"Here's one: 'West Fork Needs Honest Chamber of Commerce.' Here's another: 'Sim's Gang Has Collected Sufficient Tribute.' That's a wallop to the joy, isn't it? And again: 'First National Banking Methods Strangling Business Growth.' That'll start a riot. And: 'Financial Fossils'—"

"Surely nothing like *that* is in the paper?" cried Zoe Ann in horror.

For answer Hardy passed the paper across the table to her and calmly picked up his spoon to assault the grapefruit.

"There's also a smashing article proclaiming your father's innocence, an editorial on the new ownership, but merely enlarged policy of the paper, an item on the back sheet about John Hardy thrashing two—"

"Oh! Oh! Oh!" gasped Zoe Ann as her quick eyes scanned damning headline after damning headline.

"You see, you are taking it all seriously again," chided Hardy. "That won't do at all. Come, eat your breakfast and let's discuss what kind of a car I shall buy and where I shall live. I've simply got to have my trunk. My roughneck days are over."

"John Hardy, you are simply—simply incorrigible," she informed him, wide-eyed. "Haven't you assumed enough trouble to keep you busy in fighting, to prove Papa's innocence?"

"This will give them something else to think about," he assured her gravely. "You remind me—I am in honor bound to tell Brentwood about the results of Walker's analysis. Where can I locate him, do you know?"

"You might call the Kimball residence," she suggested faintly. "They spend lots of their time there—Madeline Brentwood is Mr. Kimball's daughter, you know. I imagine they'll be there to-day."

Hardy excused himself and went to the phone. He located the district attorney and got him on the wire.

"Hello, Brentwood," he said crisply; "this is John Hardy. Last night I promised to give you the results of my third analysis, which would furnish you a clew in the blood composition of the murderer. I'm sorry to report that there was no blood about the victim save his own, impossible though this sounds. What did you say?"

"I said we do not need your admission to strengthen our case. We—"

"Just a minute," chuckled Hardy interrupting. "I'll admit that I talked a little too fast last night, and I'm sorry I can give you no direct clew. But let me add that I saw the personal effects of Fosdick at the morgue last night and I want to tip you off to the fact that his watch went dead at seven thirty-six the morning of the murder.

"It stopped at the time he was killed, and I am taking steps to make that silent witness a bit of vital testimony. In making out your case, don't overlook the time limit involved. This proves that Wright couldn't have been guilty."

"Oh!" exclaimed Brentwood's voice queerly. There was a brief pause while the attorney assimilated this new fact. Then:

"Isn't that nice?" he said. "You buffaloed me last night, Hardy, with all that evidence you flashed on me. But that you talked too fast is right. At six o'clock this morning I sent out two men to check up on that footprint you found in the ravine between the second and third holes. They found it and photographed it.

"It checks up perfectly with the shoes Wright wore that morning and is still wearing. And they also found several perfect footprints of the same shoe and its mate in the woods between the spot where Fosdick was killed and that country lane which runs along the far side of the golf links. You failed to look that far back in the shrubbery, didn't you? But your industry set the detectives an example. Thanks for the footprint clew.

"Also thanks for your information about the watch. Wright just had enough time to kill Fosdick at seven thirty-six, then retreat through the woods to Bigby Lane, drive around to the club entrance and start his alibi game at eight o'clock. Now chuckle that off."

The receiver clicked as Brentwood hung up triumphantly. Slowly Hardy replaced the instrument on its stand, all the while staring vacantly at the opposite wall.

"What is it? Oh, what is it?" queried Zoe Ann anxiously, rising and coming toward him with clasped fingers.

Hardy's eyes did not rise to meet hers. His whole being throbbed with pity at this cruel blow. He couldn't think of saying the words which would destroy her happiness, cradled in the belief that the watch proved the innocence of her father. Without answering her he grasped the phone and called Brentwood again. He couldn't tell her until he had had time to cheek over this new clew with her father.

"Hello. Say, Slim," he drawled into the transmitter. "Have you seen this morning's *Blade?* No? Well, glance over it. And you laugh that off!"

He hung up the receiver and smiled faintly up at the girl.

"What is it?" he said slowly, repeating her question. "It's just that Slim Brentwood and I have passed between us some of those calm banalities we were talking about awhile ago. He told me a funny story and then I told him one. So we're both laughing on the wrong side of our faces this morning."

CHAPTER XV
WEST FORK AWAKENS

FOR TWENTY-FOUR YEARS Terry Callahan had worked for the city without missing a day's duty outside of his meager vacations. By dint of much patient labor he had patched and mended and added to his little cottage on North Third Street during his spare time until the four small rooms and scanty porch had become an enviable dwelling.

The flowers and plum trees of Mrs. Callahan, the neat fence and the rows of whitewashed brickbats along the tiny walk and around the flower beds, the carefully tended little plot of grass and the vegetable garden in the rear marked this place as the home of a thrifty and happy couple. Some folks are blessed like that; they can make everything out of nothing.

To-day, for the first time in twenty-four years, Terry did not hurry into his coat and hat, kiss Mollie and rush to work. He no longer heard the call of civic duty: For the first time in years he was a private citizen. While Mollie cleared away the breakfast things Terry sat in the worn rocker on the front porch sans shirt and shoes. Cramming his burned and strong old pipe with tobacco, he proceeded to read his copy of the *Morning Blade* at his leisure.

His attention was gripped at the first headline. His blue eyes popped wider and wider, his teeth gripped the pipe stem tighter and tighter. The glow in the bowl died a quiet death; Terry forgot that he even had the pipe in his mouth. In a sort of ecstatic horror he read the paper clear through.

Two hours later, when Mollie Callahan came into the little living room from the kitchen she found Terry cleaning and oiling his police revolver with a grim earnestness that was little short of ferocious.

"Terry Callahan," she exclaimed in apprehension at his attitude rather than at his actions. "What on earth? I thought you had quit the police department?"

"So I have," he rejoined. "But 'tis a domned good thing I haven't turned in me permit to carry a gun."

Mollie Callahan wiped her hands on her apron and seated herself quietly.

"Terry," she said gently, "you haven't gone and got into trouble, have you? There's no kind of trouble we can't weather without the aid of a firearm. What has happened, honey?"

Terry reached over and patted his wife gently.

"Shure an' there's nothin' th' matter wid me, darlin'," he grinned. "Ye know thot I've gone to work fer Johnny Hardy at double me old salary. Shure an' ye didn't expect me to earn it by doin' nothin'? Read th' paper there an' see what Johnny's done. There'll be hell poppin' before night an' he'll be needin' old Terry to keep off th' mob."

ENCOURAGEMENT WAS ALL that Presley had needed. For a harassed editor who didn't have time to change the make-up of his paper before it went to press, he succeeded admirably. The dust must have arisen in clouds from the file of facts which had heretofore been taboo. Without mentioning it to Zoe Ann that morning, Hardy had observed that Presley had started off with a great deal more than Hardy expected. Every single item was true, but Hardy offered up a silent prayer that Presley had the necessary proofs to substantiate his statements.

West Fork was not so solidly welded together that an attack on one of the leading citizens would have brought direct reprisals from all the rest. This would have been a Utopian tyranny fortunately inconsistent with human nature. Outside of their financial deals and agreements the city's arbiters handled their personal affairs to suit themselves. Disgrace, publicity, or trouble of any sort affecting Sam Kimball would have elicited nothing from his associates, save a silence in which they would have watched him struggle out of his difficulty.

But Sunday's *Blade* opened fire upon not less than eight of the leading lights of West Fork. The things said about any one of the eight were so unusual as to seem unreal, but to see in print attacks on eight prominent citizens made for the impossible. Groups and clusters of insignificant citizens gathered Sunday morning and discussed the calamity in low tones.

It excited awe, fear, laughter, joy, or indifference, according to the personality and connections of the individual. But the majority of West Fork wriggled its toes in ecstasy and pinched itself in order to be assured that this was no dream.

In the privacy of his room in a quiet, old boarding house near the high school, Professor Walker perused his copy of the *Blade* without visible change of expression. When he had finished reading the main articles he stared off into space in such a muse that he failed to hear the call for breakfast. A light grew in his eyes and a faint flush mounted to his high cheeks.

"Just what this town needs, all right," he said aloud. "A good shaking up. I hope Hardy's not too late. How Kimball, Sims, Morris, and all the rest must be quivering in anger this morning. I'm afraid they'll ruin the boy. But this is just like him. My God! Such temerity."

JOSEPH MORRIS LIVED in a rambling, old-fashioned frame house on North Seventh Street. In appearance Joseph was like a crane. Thin, long-nosed, and cadaverous, he was never seen on the street without his umbrella, and black derby. Rain or shine, summer or winter, the black derby and furled umbrella were to Morris what high beaver and baton were to a drum major. They constituted his regalia, his distinguishing hallmark, his contribution to the fashions of men.

Ordinarily Joseph was calm itself in his munching of toast and perusal of his morning paper. In fact, the astounding article about

Major Sims had not disturbed him. Neither did the deluge about the First National Bank. And then his eye unhappily fell on that which caused the eruption. Wild excitement reigned and choleric anger grew apace. Sam Kimball's telephone began ringing violently.

"Sam Kimball, you—you—" Morris spluttered wildly. "What kind of stunt you pulling in the *Blade?* What's this monkey business about new ownership? You closed down on the paper, didn't you? Who the hell is John Hardy? What d'yuh mean by that slanderous article on me and Wilson of the Farmers' National?

"What article? About how we got our start by mismanaging the Buchanan estate, that's what. I'll sue you for this. Why—why, it's criminal liabilty, you—you—you. Hey! You didn't? Eh? You don't? What! No, I hadn't heard. I was out of town yesterday. Oh! Oh! Aha! Yes, I saw that about the First National.

"So that's who he is, eh? Well—what you gonna do about it, huh? I'll put him in jail for life. It's all your fault, you old fool! Don't you dare threaten me. I know enough about you to—what do I care about the telephone girl? Sure I'll come to see you. Right now."

Slam! Up with the receiver. Thud! On with the black derby. Buff! Armed with the inevitable umbrella. Bang! The screen door slams to behind an aroused crane.

MAJOR SIMS was a beefy, red-faced individual with flintlike eyes which were mere slits of cruel granite in a fat face. His voice was a harsh whisper which never rose to the sound of normal tones and which aroused intense antagonism in the breast of each listener. Perhaps he had ruined his voice in his youth by yelling at the stock on his father's rock-ribbed farm.

This momentous Sunday morning he was adjusting a ready-tied neck scarf by hooking it over his front collar button when Charlie, collector of bridge tax, district number two, burst into the bedroom with the *Morning Blade.*

"Pa!" he shouted. "Read this!"

Pa read. Pa snatched the paper and digested the flaming article more slowly. His face grew redder and his neck swelled.

In treating of Major Sims and his hoarse voice and coarse tactics, Mr. Presley had been merciless. The fact that three big railroads did not pass through West Fork was laid at his door. A mass meeting held twenty years before was recalled to the public mind. The survey had already been made for one of the railroads and all that was needed was a station site at a reasonable price.

"Naw!" Major Sims was quoted as having grated. "Whatcha want to have a mass meeting to give the rail road anything for? Don't make a single concession. They can't miss us; they got to go through West Fork. Ain't it a logical point? Haven't they already surveyed the way? They can't miss us. Don't give 'em nothing. We'll make 'em pay for the privilege of coming through here. For one I vote to soak 'em. I ain't gonna give any of my land away."

You were vastly influential, even twenty years ago, major. Three cheers for your foresight and spunk. You succeeded in carrying your point. You didn't give away anything. And the Central & Western railroad couldn't miss West Fork, could it? Only by twenty miles! It goes through the hamlet of Birchfield in place of putting a terminal point at West Fork to-day. In your earliest days even, you robbed the city. You manufactured the first gas and lighted the street lights under contract. Who were the two boys you hired to ride behind the old street lamp lighter to turn out every other light as fast as it was kindled? You promised to furnish street lights until eleven o'clock at night, and you paid these two boys with ponies fifty cents apiece to turn them out before nine o'clock. And the taxpayers still pay tribute.

AGAIN SAM KIMBALL's phone tinkled merrily.

"Kimball, you handled that matter of closing down the *Blade*," rasped the major's voice. "Talk turkey quick or I'll kill you. What does this morning's paper mean? You didn't? You failed for a change? Well, you've made a fine mess of things. Sue? On what grounds? A hundred to one he's got the proof. We can't sue, but I'll break him so quick he won't think he ever had a paper.

"And you get busy and see that he is thrown in jail at once on some charge or I'll not answer for myself or my sons if we meet either him or you. Huh? Damn Fosdick's funeral! Do what I tell you and do it quick. You'll hear from me again this afternoon."

DR. WARD LOFTMEAD had never had the breath of scandal lifted against his immaculate self or his prosperous clinic before. He was so astounded that he could only stare through his distinguished glasses and comb his fingers through his distinguished beard. To think that, after all these years, the little arrangement between himself and the authorities during the days of the smallpox scare, when he was health officer, should see the light of day now.

Whose business was it if they bottled up the city and forced everybody to be vaccinated, by the health officer only, at five dollars per arm? What was wrong in saving and safeguarding life—while the makers of that agreement pocketed twenty thousand dollars each?

And what was this further scathing onslaught on the rotten condition of the Wilson Avenue property he owned? Who dared call his buildings firetraps and cesspools?

Whence had come this account of the plumbing inspector's delight in examining his Royle Building and the inspector's righteous indignation at its condition—until the tenant of the first floor made a hapless remark about the structure belonging to Dr. Loftmead, a man who should, above all others, desire cleanliness? At the name of the owner, the plumbing inspector had abruptly torn up his notes and grinned pityingly at the occupant. Dr. Loftmead was beyond reach of municipal law.

This was ruinous! What had come over the *Morning Blade?* Sam Kimball and Thurlowe Fosdick had been—ah—making arrangements to take over the *Blade.* Fosdick would no longer answer to his fellow citizens, having been called to a higher tribunal, but Kimball remained to explain the catastrophe. Why, Ward Loftmead, surgeon and X-ray specialist, could never hold up his head again unless these libelous statements were retracted. And the good doctor wielded enough influence as a member of the city council to see that a suitable and soothing anodyne was offered.

Again the Kimball phone buzzed violently. It no longer rang; it had been muffled.

ALL IN ALL it was a most exciting day and a tempestuous time was had by all. There were others more or less directly affected, whom Sam Kimball had the pleasure of seeing at the funeral. And this ten-thousand-dollar affair was a fizzle. Nobody had any time to consider the pomp and glory of the last rites administered to a dead man when there was so much live news about live people.

By mid-afternoon Sam Kimball was in that mental turmoil and cataclysmic state known as majestic rage. Like a caged billy goat he trotted up and down the floor of his library, giving vent to an assortment of snorts and bleats, stopping ever and anon to glare at Cyrus Brentwood across the library table, as though the latter gentleman were the author of all these ills.

Bang! Sam's fist crashed down on the table.

"Well!" he snarled savagely. "Why don't you say something? You've heard all the squeals I heard today. What do you advise?"

"I thought it was taken for granted that I tie this Hardy up with various legal actions to-morrow," responded Brentwood coldly.

Bang! Again that blow with the fist.

"To-morrow! To-morrow! What am I going to do to-day? Where's all your foxy legality now? Sitting there and staring at me isn't helping any."

"You needn't vent your spite on me," stated Brentwood. "What can I do to-day?"

Bang! Again the massive table quivered, Kimball turned abruptly, and resumed his pacing. Two trips across the floor he made and then whirled to face his son-in-law again.

"What can you do to-day?" he growled. "You can go with me to see this young villain. That's what you can do."

"That is foolish," stated Brentwood. "It wouldn't do any good. Wait until to-morrow and I'll tangle him up good and plenty. If he's got any money left after buying the *Blade*, we'll strip him penniless."

Bang! The table vibrated.

"That isn't enough," snarled the old man viciously. "He must go to the penitentiary. I'll teach him! I'm going to see him this afternoon. How can you young and spineless men stand such inactivity? Are you afraid of him?"

At the sneer in the old man's tones Brentwood stiffened and flushed.

"You're making a mistake in hunting up Hardy," he declared, "but come on then. You know damned well I'm not afraid of anybody."

"No? What are you taking that gun for then?"

Brentwood's battered features twisted into a scowl.

"You're liable to cause trouble," he growled. "And Hardy is not going to lay his hands on me again and live."

IT WAS BETWEEN five and six o'clock. The Wright gardener had started to sprinkle the lawn. The swelling chorus of dog-day cicadas in the thickets of shrubbery hailed the soft coming of dusk. John Hardy sat on the top step and rested his head against a porch pillar. In the level rays of the setting sun he lazily surveyed the picture of Zoe Ann reclining in the hammock. It had been a busy day for them also. Intriguing noises from the interior of the house indicated that Margaret was busily engaged in preparing a cold repast of dainty sandwiches and iced tea.

The click of the gate latch aroused them. Messrs. Kimball and Brentwood were calling. The swing of their walk bespoke volumes. Even the locusts seemed to falter in their plaintive chant.

The girl sat up rather apprehensively. Hardy grinned encouragement.

"Now for a display of fireworks," he smiled.

"Young man, we want to see you," announced Kimball ominously, opening the conversation with commendable abruptness.

"Come in and sit down," invited Hardy. "It is rather warm, isn't it?"

"You—you scoundrel!" choked Kimball, shaking a badly worn copy of the *Blade* at him. "You—you—"

"This is Miss Wright, gentlemen," cut in Hardy coldly. "As this is her home I would suggest ordinary courtesy at least."

Brentwood had the grace to remove his hat and mutter a greeting. Kimball merely glared.

"Bah!" he ejaculated. "You—you—"

Hardy gravely took the tattered paper from the hand of the incensed manufacturer and noted how it was folded. Taking up his own paper from a chair behind him, he folded it in similar manner and solemnly offered it to the other.

"A fresher paper, Mr. Kimball," he said in ironic courtesy. "None of the words are blurred."

"Take it easy," warned Brentwood in an undertone to his father-in-law. "Hardy, we've come to find out what you have to say about these—these unprecedented libelous statements in your newspaper. Before filing suit against you on a number of counts Mr. Kimball wants to protect you if he can. Your life has been threatened more than once to-day and—"

"My life has been threatened? And why, may I ask?"

Brentwood ignored this interruption.

"You have launched a terrible and impossible attack against the leading citizens of West Fork," he went on. "Just what your object is no one seems to know. Before to-morrow night the town will be too hot to hold you. Instead of confining you in jail, where you will be in danger of a lynching, Mr. Kimball has come to make you an offer. You sign over to him the *Morning Blade* for the sum of one dollar and we will shut our eyes and give you twelve hours to get out of town. I guarantee there will be no prosecution if you stay away from West Fork."

"What? You offer me one dollar for the *Blade?*" gasped Hardy.

"Exactly," nodded Brentwood. "You will be getting out of a bad mess mighty lightly. I was for taking legal action, myself."

"I suppose this offer comes from your goodness of heart," murmured Hardy ironically.

"Precisely," growled Kimball. "And I've been hunting for you all afternoon. That smirking fool, Presley, couldn't be found until a short while ago to tell us where you were. You—"

"I am sorry if you have been put to any inconvenience on my account. However, until further notice, you will find me here at the Wright home. Mr. Wright and his daughter have extended me the courtesy of insisting that I remain as their guest. I am opening a suite of offices downtown to-morrow. In the future, any complaints of any nature you may refer directly to me during business hours. Don't bother to quarrel with Presley; he is merely following his orders."

"Well, what about my offer?" snarled Kimball, banging his fist against a porch pillar. "D'you want to get out of this with a whole skin?"

"I am very sorry, but I wouldn't sell the *Morning Blade* for double what I paid for it. Is there anything else I can tell you, gentlemen?"

"What? You refuse?" gurgled the old man. "Why, you young fool, don't you know it would take hundreds of thousands of dollars to keep you out of the penitentiary for all that libel?"

"We'll see," replied Hardy coolly. "And, speaking of physical violence, allow me to remind you that I have a personal guard who is watching the pair of you right now. I see that you have a gun in your right-hand coat pocket, Slim. You wouldn't live to know whether you shot me or not."

"Bah!" howled Kimball. "Bluff! All bluff."

"I never bluff," said Hardy stiffly. "Oh, Terry!"

"Yes, sir," responded the voice of Callahan promptly, and the old Irishman's form appeared in the doorway.

Brentwood and his father-in-law glanced from the ex-jailer's pistol hand to the stern features of John Hardy who stood so erect before them.

"Not only that," continued Hardy in a smooth voice, "but it is possible for two men to be held in jail for murder at the same time even in West Fork. And in this case there would be no doubt about the assassin's identity."

Kimball grew apoplectic. Emotion so choked him that he could scarcely articulate. His little goatee quivered spasmodically and he banged his right fist against the pillar beside him in his speechless rage.

Brentwood turned an expressive eye in his direction.

"I told you it was useless," he said coldly.

"Come on," whispered his father-in-law. "Let's go. As for you, you scoundrel, I'll flay you alive. I'll strip you less than penniless.

I'll make a beggar out of you and then send you to prison for life. You'll find out who runs this town before this time to-morrow."

"Stop!"

Hardy's crisp voice halted the two men at the bottom of the steps.

"When you get ready, go ahead and crack your whip," he said in a level, hard voice. "I thrive on trouble. But let me warn you to read this day's paper mighty carefully for any untrue statements before you start proceedings. I can prove everything I print. I'm more than willing for you to learn how I stand. Have one of the banks wire the Industrial National Bank of Kansas City for confidential information about me. And then drop this idea of spending your money trying to break me. You'd better spend it in trying to reform. Good night."

CHAPTER XVI
FOOTPRINTS AND FINANCE

MONDAY MORNING, the grand jury found a true bill against Howard K. Wright and bound him over for trial for the murder of Thurlowe Fosdick. Barbington presented the evidence John Hardy and Callahan had unearthed in the former newspaper owner's defense. This was taken at its face value; Hardy's testimony went unquestioned. The attendant at the country club was not even summoned to corroborate his statements. Neither was Professor Walker called to add his scanty testimony. Everything moved along smoothly. But Wright was indicted.

Doubtless the footprints discovered by the detectives in the woods between the spot where the body of the banker was found and Bigby Lane were sufficiently damning to bind Wright over. Nevertheless, it was obvious to Hardy that, footprints or no footprints, the grand jury had already received its instructions from the circuit judge or Sam Kimball direct. A different Cyrus Brentwood was presented for his approval, too. The man was keen. He was smooth and cold, utterly impersonal. There was no question of his ability.

He presented his evidence to the jurors and made out his case just as if they had not already been fixed. He saw that no hitch hindered the proceedings. His dignity and calm confidence transcended his marred countenance. He was not the same Brentwood who had cut so ludicrous a figure the previous Saturday.

Hardy realized that he was up against the first real revolution of the wheels that controlled the town. He could tell it, not in the

154

verdict of the jury, but in their manner of hearing the evidence and returning a verdict. And this was just the beginning. After all, it was a titanic task for one man to revolutionize a town the size of West Fork, no matter who the man was. It wasn't just foggy ideas and a certain amount of capital that he challenged; he was fighting many men who were under the dominance of a few men.

Hardy's formidable face became harder as he watched and listened. His jaw set tighter in contemplation of the task he had set for himself. When the hearing was over he waited with Wright while Barbington made arrangements for bond. This was set at one hundred thousand dollars at first. When Wright promptly offered to put up his own bond, using the proceeds from the sale of the *Blade*, there was a furor. This acquisition of cash had been overlooked. Irregular though it was, the court doubled the amount of bond.

Silencing the indignant Wright with a gesture, a hard smile on his lips, John Hardy wrote out a check for the entire amount of the bond himself. The check was drawn against the Farmers' National Bank of West Fork. Mallory raised an objection to the check.

"Telephone the bank," suggested Hardy grimly. "I opened an account there this morning for five times the amount of that check. Or, better still, send over and get the cash while we wait."

Brentwood used the phone. He had seen enough of Hardy to heed the latter's words. He learned that John Hardy's balance was something like one million dollars, that it had been deposited in the form of a certified check, and that a wire from the Kansas City bank on which it was drawn had confirmed the deposit. The local bank could not refuse payment on the check if it wanted to, having accepted the account.

Barbington, Wright, and Hardy left the courthouse together. They proceeded directly to the offices of the *Blade*. They found Presley busy with a notary public taking affidavits from several persons, giving himself proof on which to launch further attacks through the columns of the paper. Wright felt a trifle helpless in view of the sweeping change which had taken place during his incarceration.

"What—what am I to do now?" he murmured uncertainly. "It looks like you don't need me here any more. And God knows I can't sit idle, twiddling my thumbs while I wait for my trial to come up."

"You won't," promised Hardy. "The first thing is to help me run down this new clew on footprints. When you give me a lead on this, I have plenty of work for you to do. You know this town as well as or better than I do, Mr. Wright. I want to open a suite of offices where I can plan my different steps, of which the management of the *Blade* is only one. I need a general manager, an organizer. I'm asking you to take the job. Will you do it?"

"You want me to assume control of your various activities?" frowned Wright.

"Exactly," smiled Hardy. "This is too big a job for one man. I need you and Presley and Barbington and others. I have enough to do to clear you of this murder charge. In other words, while I work for you, will you work for me?"

"Here in West Fork? With this murder charge hanging over my head?"

"Why not? You need something to occupy your mind. And why consider West Fork? It is my desires only that you need take into account—not the self-righteous inhabitants of this town."

"Where is Zoe Ann this morning?" demanded Wright irrelevantly.

"Well, it was hardly necessary for her to sit through the ordeal of seeing you granted bond," Hardy said. "Right now she is picking out a comfortable suite of offices. By the way, she applied for the position of secretary to my new manager and I gave her the job."

Wright took a deep breath and squared his shoulders.

"And you've found your manager," he announced tersely, holding forth his hand.

The compact was made.

"Now for the matter of those strange footprints," resumed Hardy. "Yesterday you told me that you were not over in those woods and you don't remember having ever been in the rough in that particular spot."

"To the best of my knowledge and belief I have never been where those footprints were found," averred Wright solemnly.

"Perhaps the prosecution planted them," suggested Presley. "I wouldn't put anything past those eggs after yesterday's *Blade*."

"I hardly think they'd dare go that far," frowned Barbington. "It has been more of ignorance than willful enmity on the part of the law, I think."

"I hope so—for their sake," commented Hardy grimly. "Where did you get these shoes, Mr. Wright?"

"From the Whalen Shoe Company about a month ago."

"They are good-looking sport shoes," approved Hardy, admiring the two-tone pigskin leather. "The calking on the bottom is a special design for golfers, I understand."

"Yes. The Alltree people make a snappy line of men's shoes. I like them."

"I see. Does anybody else in town handle that shoe?"

"I can assure you that they do not," stated Presley. "Whalen has the exclusive on them. Our ad staff men can tell you anything you want to know about the shoe."

"That won't be necessary. Tell me something about this Whalen instead. Who is he and where did he come from? I don't remember the name."

"Whalen used to make this territory for a shoe manufacturer in Wisconsin," obliged the editor. "About six years ago he opened a retail shoe store on upper Wilson Avenue. He's a wide-awake young chap, about thirty or thirty-two. And he's having an uphill tussle to get started on limited capital."

"Six years in business and still getting started?" Hardy raised his eyebrows skeptically.

"You forget the banks," smiled Presley. "Whalen is an outsider."

Hardy nodded an understanding. He turned toward Wright.

"Do you mind going home and changing shoes for me? I want this pair for an hour or so."

"Mind? My dear boy, I've got to go home and take a couple of baths," shuddered Wright. "I haven't seen a bathtub since early

Friday morning. I feel utterly filthy, despite the clean linens Zoe Ann furnished me."

The others smiled sympathetically.

"Good enough," Hardy called after the departing Wright. "I'll meet you here at noon. Mr. Barbington," he went on, turning to the lawyer, "there is a watch at Greenwald's place that I want requisitioned for evidence. Unseal the necessary legal tape so that I can get it at once. I'll take a detective with me, of course."

Barbington bowed and lifted the telephone.

"Presley," said Hardy, turning to the editor, "who is the best jeweler in town? The Hinton Jewelry Company used to be."

"It still is," affirmed Presley. "Miles Hinton is the main squeeze. His father is dead."

"So old Blake Hinton finally drank himself to death, eh? Well, the family is much better off without him. What are you doing this morning?"

"I'm letting things ride easy for a few days while I gather up some loose ends of evidence we need. It'll take 'em some time to digest yesterday's attack."

"I see. That's why this affidavit gathering to-day."

Presley smiled his little nervous smile and nodded.

"Very well. You have full charge. You can consult me on any point at our general offices. We'll be organized this week. Well, Mr. Barbington?"

"Colter will be right over to go with you. Brentwood doesn't seem to object to your establishing your point at all."

"Certainly not. But we'll see how he reacts to what we learn about those mysterious footprints. That'll hurt the prosecution."

"Is there anything further this morning?"

"Not until to-night. We'll hold a conference at the Wright home then. And I'll expect you, Presley."

The busy editor nodded and waved a hand as he was called away.

In company with Colter, armed with the proper legal writ, Hardy proceeded to the mortuary. Obtaining the watch, he led the way to the jeweler's. Here he shook hands with Miles Hinton, who seemed quite genuine in his profession of welcome. Fifteen minutes elapsed while the watchmaker Hinton called examined Fosdick's timepiece.

Colter, a more or less silent man who had learned that he got further by keeping his mouth shut, eyed the proceedings and his hard-featured companion with interest. He remembered John Hardy and, privately, he had a wholesome respect for the broad-shouldered, hard-fighting gentleman.

"The only thing wrong with this watch is that the balance staff is broken," announced Bennett, the watch repairer, at length. "It was dropped or knocked against something?"

"There is nothing the matter with the mainspring or any other part?" queried Hardy. "Be sure of what you say. Could that dropping or knocking about have moved the hands when the balance staff broke?"

Bennett glanced at the speaker from the eye which was not blinded by his glass.

"The hands could have moved by an accident, but they weren't moved by this one," he stated. "If they've been moved someone has done it since. Like this."

"Whoa!" shot out Hardy quickly. "Don't touch them! They haven't been touched and I don't want them touched. What time would you say the watch stopped?"

"If the hands haven't been touched," said Bennett, a trifle shortly, "the watch stopped at seven thirty-six."

"Thank you. Now if I assure you that the watch wasn't knocked about, can you tell me whether or not the balance staff could have been broken by being in the fob pocket of a man who fell to the ground?"

"Yes, easily. A man might fall on his watch a hundred times in that manner without injuring it, and then again he might put it out of commission the first time."

"I see. But I didn't mean that the wearer fell on his face and therefore on his watch. Suppose he fell on his back?"

Bennett frowned.

"With his body as a cushion between his watch and the sidewalk?" questioned Miles Hinton. "That would hardly be possible," he added at Hardy's nod of acquiescence.

"Nevertheless, that is what happened," stated the latter. "And it wasn't a sidewalk, either. It was more or less soft ground."

"Then he must have had an awful fall," stated Bennett positively.

"Otherwise such an accident to his watch would not be possible?" queried Hardy.

"I won't say that," decided Bennett slowly. "Watches are delicate instruments. We got a bad batch of main springs a few months ago and I had to put three in one watch before the job stayed fixed. And the wearer is a bookkeeper who doesn't take exercise. It doesn't sound reasonable, though, for such a simple fall to break the balance staff."

"All right," agreed Hardy. "However, you can state that this broken balance staff is due to a blow or a severe shock, can you not?"

"Yes."

"Good enough. Kindly put that in writing, giving the number and make of this watch. I want both of you to sign the statement, Hinton, and then tell me what I owe you."

This business concluded, Hardy sealed the watch in an envelope and handed it to his companion.

"I'll take charge of this paper, Colter," he said easily. "You take this watch to Brentwood to be preserved as evidence in the trial. That is all you can do for me for the present. And thanks."

Colter saluted and parted from him at the corner.

In the early afternoon Hardy strolled along Wilson Avenue with a small bundle under one arm. He glanced at the different signs and names of the stores as he walked along. While there had been a number of changes, he recognized more business houses than he did faces on the street. As for himself, he went unrecognized.

Very few people remembered the appearance of the youth, John Hardy, who had gone away ten years previous, and even these couldn't have recognized him now unless they had ample reason for recalling. No one associated this calm stroller with the man who had been instrumental in turning West Fork upside down almost overnight.

The Whalen Shoe Company proved to be a very neat establishment with a ten-thousand-dollar stock of shoes. There were two clerks and Mr. Whalen himself in the house. Business was quiet this Monday afternoon and Hardy found Whalen unengaged.

"Mr. Whalen," he greeted, "I see by the gold-leaf sign on your windows that this is a corporation. 'George Whalen, Incorporated.' May I ask why?"

George Whalen took the time to make a face at a passing child he recognized and then waved gayly at the little one's response before answering. He studied his visitor curiously.

"Before I answer such a question," he said mildly, "would you mind telling me who in the hell you are?"

Hardy's eyes twinkled.

"My name is John Hardy," he answered. "I'm afraid I have the reputation of a trouble maker."

"John Hardy? The *Morning Blade?*" demanded Whalen, instantly alert.

Hardy nodded.

"Shake," declared Whalen solemnly. "I'm glad to know you."

"My main reason for coming in is to ask you about a certain pair of shoes," smiled Hardy, unwrapping his package. "You sold these shoes to a certain man in West Fork recently. I understand that it is a fairly new style. I don't expect you to name the man who bought these shoes, but can you tell me how many pairs of this exact style and size you have sold this season?"

Whalen examined the interior of the shoe in an expert manner. He shot a keen glance at his customer.

"You'll be surprised at the extent of my information," he remarked. "I'd make a guess that these shoes belong to Howard

Wright, judging from last night's and this morning's papers. However, I can tell you in half a minute whose shoes these are."

Without comment Hardy followed the dealer back to his office. Here Whalen flipped through a card index and drew forth a card. He glanced at it and looked up.

"This shoe was sold to Howard K. Wright the 11th of last month, for ten dollars, by Hudson, the clerk you saw trimming the window," he announced.

"You keep a complete record?" asked Hardy in surprise.

"Yes. It is easy, because each pair of Alltree shoes is numbered. We keep a record of the date of purchase so that we can send a couple of follow-up letters inquiring as to whether the shoe is giving satisfaction. Just an advertising stunt to prove to the buyer that our interest doesn't cease with the sale of the shoe."

Hardy studied the pleasant-faced speaker.

"You seem to be conscientious, certainly," he murmured.

"We try to be. Of course, we have the selfish motive of wanting repeat business."

"Naturally. That is permissible. Is it possible to tell me how many pairs of this same shoe you have sold?"

"It is. Nine, B," said Whalen, opening a small ledger. "Would you like the names and occupations of the purchasers?"

"If you will be so kind."

After a space Hardy looked with interest at the list of names.

Howard K. Wright, editor of *Blade*.

James S. Nealson, salesman for Central Grocery Company.

Carl Sneider, engineer on Valley-Mountain Railroad.

William Beedle, real estate and building loan.

Charles Morris, idler and insurance man.

"How do you happen to have such a complete record of sizes?" he asked.

"That answers the first question you asked when you came in," replied Whalen with a wry smile. "My capital is entirely too small to carry more than one pair of shoes of each size, when I have to carry so many different styles as well as different lines to meet different priced trade. So, as fast as a pair of shoes is taken out of those fancy wall boxes and sold, the salesman enters all data on a little ticket and files it here at the office so that we can record it each night and duplicate the shoe.

"I can't get any backing here, so I have been forced to incorporate and sell stock to small investors in order to get enough money to grow on. You've heard of doing too much business for one's capital, haven't you? Well, that has been my trouble. And I can't get help from these cursed banks."

"If you make a success of your venture, the banks will be glad to lend you money," suggested Hardy.

Whalen bared his teeth.

"Yes—then. So they can squeeze me out and get the grapes. But I'm watching that."

"They don't squeeze everybody out."

"No, but they own the souls of those they leave. Look at your newspaper, for instance. You are doing the biggest thing for West Fork that has ever been done. But if you are depending on advertising to support you, you are going flatter than a pancake."

"How do you figure that? Won't small merchants and men like you line up with the *Blade?*" demanded Hardy curiously.

"I will," responded Whalen promptly. "But mighty few of the others will. They will want to mighty bad, but they can't; the banks have them sewed up."

"Then I can't expect to win the merchants of West Fork to my banner, even if they believe in what I say and do?"

"You cannot," declared Whalen positively. "It's an unbeatable game. I just hope you have enough money to carry on."

"To carry on would be foolish unless I win adherents. What good does it do to arouse a city of sleepers if they won't or can't get out of bed?"

"There's one way you can get open indorsement and solid support behind you," said Whalen thoughtfully.

"And that, in your opinion?"

"Is impossible, unless you can get the business men out of the clutches of the banks so they won't be afraid to think and act for themselves. And you can't afford to finance every business on Wilson Avenue."

Hardy looked speculative.

"No-o-o, not privately," he agreed. "You've opened my eyes to a phase of the matter I hadn't considered. You seem to be pretty firm in your thoughts and opinions. Tell me, what do you think of West Fork?"

"Well, I'll tell you," Whalen said deliberately. "It's a mighty fine town to live in, but it's a damn poor town to make a living in."

Hardy laughed.

"Then why do you stay here?" he asked.

"There could be a great future for the place," went on Whalen. "Why do I stay here? Because I'm crazy, I guess. I'm going to marry a West Fork girl—Dr. Harper's daughter. I'm afraid I'm one of the lost souls; Isobel doesn't want to leave the town. But why these local boys stay here I can't see. They can't get anywhere. If they try to float a new idea or branch out in business that requires aid from the banks, they can't get it.

"They go to one of the bankers, and he nods and smirks and listens to their story, and turns them down. 'Yes, Billy, sure, sure, you're a fine boy. I've known you all your life. You used to play with my little Rosalie. I remember when you had the measles, et cetera, et cetera, but we just can't see our way clear to putting any money in this proposition of yours. Sure, you're a good boy and honest, but we can't help you.'

"And some flashy young stranger from another town comes in and sells them a gold brick every now and then. You are not a smart man or a hero at home."

Hardy laughed heartily at Whalen's imitation of a fatherly banker turning down a local son. Suddenly he ceased and looked at Whalen with wide eyes.

"Man, you've given me the idea," he cried keenly. "By George! There is a way to free the retailers from bondage."

"How?" demanded Whalen curiously.

"Open an honest bank," replied Hardy, as calmly as though such a matter were the easiest thing in the world. "By the way, you seem to be interested in West Fork. Are you interested enough to serve where your service can do some good?"

"Show me the way," Whalen remarked promptly.

"Will you serve on the new Chamber of Commerce when we put it through?"

"I'll give you all I've got," declared the shoe man solemnly.

"And, Whalen, if you will drop in to see me the latter part of this week and tell me the details of your business, you needn't try to sell any more of your stock."

"Why not?"

"Because I want all the stock that you have for sale myself. You've found a business partner if you want one."

"I'll be up to see you," promised Whalen.

Later in the day Hardy handed a list of four names to Callahan.

"Terry," he said, "without stirring up any commotion, I want you to find out exactly where each one of these men was between the hours of six and eight last Friday morning, and what he was doing."

"Why, Johnny," queried Callahan in surprise as he noted the names given him, "how come ye to pick these men outa all th' rest o' the population o' West Fork for investigation?"

"Because they are the only men besides Mr. Wright who have shoes which exactly fit the footprints found in the woods near Bigby Lane. We may be following a blind trail, but get the information if it takes you a week or more to do it."

CHAPTER XVII
KIMBALL'S MACHINERY REVOLVES

THE WEEK THAT FOLLOWED was a very busy one for the Hardy forces. The work of organizing a machine to fight the arbiters of West Fork went forward carefully. That Sam Kimball had taken Hardy's advice about looking before he leaped was obvious in the fact that no action was taken over Sunday's paper. How Kimball pacified Major Sims and Joe Morris was not known, but that a private meeting had been held and a course decided on was apparent.

After that first vivid flash of Sunday's *Blade* nothing occurred. Presley was not ready to launch the rest of his attacks, and the opposition didn't seem inclined to take up the gauge after learning the financial worth of the man they had to fight. Things settled into the humdrum. Everybody seemed to be marking time. It was the calm which precedes the storm.

The *Evening Planet* published a statement Monday evening to the effect that the *Morning Blade* would be involved in a series of lawsuits because of Sunday's edition. Then there were two or three sly comments in the editorials. To all of which the *Morning Blade* presented the uncommunicative face of silence.

While the danger of personal violence to Hardy was an ever present possibility, it was not likely that the issue would be met in this fashion. He walked the streets with impunity, renewing old acquaintanceships and reviving old memories, occasionally running across a real friend. He studied the town and the changes ten years had wrought, striving with all of his might to get back in touch

166

with the many people and things he had known and formerly thought about.

During the week he made two social calls at night, once to dine at the home of Eva Bailey, a girl he had known in his youth. But most of the time he was at home with Wright and Zoe Ann, scheming and planning for the real betterment of West Fork.

The game had ceased to be a game to him. It had become a matter of grim earnestness. Whether or not he lived to be thanked for what he did he intended benefiting his hometown. Freak circumstances had chosen his course for him, and he intended to follow it to a finish. The peril which overhung Howard Wright but lent zest to the entire adventure; it held before his eyes the terrible cost of failure.

There was nothing Wright could do to help himself save protest his innocence. The evidence as it stood was enough to convict him, and he could add nothing. Hence, he plunged heartily into the unique and unusual task of rejuvenating a stagnant town, while Hardy divided his time between this work and the more lethal mystery.

Wright's trial was set for some time the following month. There was little he could do about unraveling the mystery, beyond going over and over the established facts, except to wait until Callahan finished his investigations. This the ex-police officer did Thursday. He came to Hardy with a concise but thorough report on the four men he had been sent to trace.

"Takin' th' names in th' order ye give 'em to me, Johnny," he reported, consulting his notes, "I'll begin wid James Nealson. He's a fat, easy-goin' sort o' duck who travels for th' Central Grocery house. He's married an' he lives here in West Fork. He was out on his territory last week an' he didn't get home until Friday afternoon, havin' drove his flivver up from Middleton. It's an all-day trip with fast drivin' to get here, ye know.

"Well, I learnt that he spent th' night at Middleton an' started for home about seven o'clock Friday mornin'. He bought them fancy shoes because he goes in for sporty clothes. He don't play golf. He bought th' shoes 'cause he liked 'em. An' he was wearin' 'em last week out on th' road."

"I see," nodded Hardy, running a line through the name on his own list. "There can be no question that that lets Mr. Nealson out. Next?"

"Th' next one is Carl Sneider. I don't reckon ye know Carl. He's a fine, big red-faced lad from th' farm. He's a bigger man than yerself. I guess he weighs all o' two hundred an' fifty pounds. He's been an engineer or motorman, whatever ye call it, on th' gasoline motor train thot runs between West Fork an' Piney Grove for five or six years. He's married, too, an' lives at Piney Grove now. He makes th' run every other day, changin' wid a lad named Henderson, who also lives in Piney Grove.

"Th' Friday o' th' murder was Sneider's day on. His train left Piney Grove at six-forty, gettin' to West Fork at twelve-thirty, noon. He didn't get here before noon, ye see. An' th' train went back at two-thirty, gettin' him home in time for supper. His golf shoes were left at home. He bought 'em because he plays golf on th' municipal links at Piney Grove."

"That lets Sneider out. And Piney Grove is two hundred miles away, isn't it? So I guess that lets his shoes out, too."

"Next comes William Beedle," went on Callahan, consulting his notes. "Ye should remember Beedle, Johnny. He's a real estate dealer thot's made himself obnoxious in West Fork for years. He plays golf, an' thot's why he bought them shoes. I had to see him direct about his movements. He said he was at home in bed. I couldn't prove or disprove it. They's no one at his house right now but him. His family's away for th' summer."

"Not so good," remarked Hardy thoughtfully. "We'll make a note of this and see if there was any connection between Beedle and Fosdick. And now Terry, how about Morris?"

"That's Charlie Morris, th' nephew o' old Joe Morris. He's a loafer, an' he lives at th' Elks' Club. He's supposed to work in th' insurance office o' his uncle, but he spends half his time gamblin'. He plays golf when he can find a good-lookin' gal to play with. He was on a drinkin' party Thursday night until three o'clock, out on th' south side. I lost track of 'im then until he showed up at th' club for breakfast at nine o'clock. I couldn't learn whether he was wearin' his sport shoes or not. Thot's all."

"Fine work, Terry," approved Hardy. "You haven't been a policeman all your life for nothing—even in West Fork. What do you think about Mr. Morris?"

"I dunno," Callahan replied dubiously. "I don't think he's got spunk enough to kill anything, but I'd investigate his gamblin' debts jes' the same."

"That's exactly what we are going to do. There are three lines of investigation to follow. Beedle and young Morris constitute one. The second, if we cannot link them up inseparably with their shoes, there is the possibility that somebody borrowed and used one of the pairs. And the third point, while beyond the bounds of probability, will, if gone into, open up a field calling for the service of a couple of detective agencies. That is that some stranger bought a pair of Alltree golf shoes in another town in the United States and wore them in the woods near Bigby Lane."

"Shure an' thot's right," agreed Callahan. "But Johnny, th' lad who committed this deed was no stranger. He had a reason an' I'm bettin' thot th' reason is right here in West Fork."

"You're right, and we'll leave that third theory until the last. I want to think of Beedle and Morris now, Terry, and tell me if they seem to you to be big enough men to have mutilated Fosdick the way he was found. I don't remember them well enough to know."

"Nayther one o' them," stated Callahan positively. "For thot matter not a one o' th' four was big enough for th' job except Carl Sneider, to my way o' thinkin'. An' not one o' them had so much as a scratch on 'em so far as I could see an' learn while investigatin'."

"That's what I thought," Hardy said. "The farther we get into this the more mysterious it becomes. And the prosecution can't see anything unusual about the case at all except its brutality. You go ahead and see if you can find out whether or not another person could have borrowed Beedle's or Morris's shoes, while I look into the personal affairs of the two gentlemen in question."

Thus matters stood Friday, when a small news item Presley pointed out in the *Planet* brought John Hardy up against the second patient, but ruthless revolution of the wheels of power in West Fork.

"I suppose you anticipated this?" commented Presley, making a circle about the article with his blue pencil and handing it to his employer.

Hardy read:

CHANGE IN SCHOOL SCIENCE
DEPARTMENT

In preparing new contracts for the teachers to sign for the coming school year, Mr. M. H. Marlowe, superintendent of schools, announced that there is to be a different head to the science department. Professor Thomas Walker, who has headed this branch of learning for the past seventeen years, will be succeeded by a younger man from one of the Eastern colleges. West Fork will be sorry to see Professor Walker go, although we wish him well in the school to which he goes.

"And this means just what?" asked Hardy, to be sure that he did not misinterpret the item.

"Just that Walker got the jug for doing that analysis work for you," shrugged Presley. "Can't you read between the lines?"

"But—but the work he did didn't hurt the case for the prosecution," protested Hardy. "And even if it had proved Wright innocent I fail to see how it should react on Walker."

"You don't know as much about your own town as you thought," Presley remarked. "Walker did some work for you—you are opposed to Sam Kimball—Kimball dominates the school board—Walker was a man they had the power to hurt. There you are."

"I don't know enough about petty dirtiness, you mean," gritted Hardy. "What a low-down, rotten way to fight. I begin to see exactly what Whalen meant when he said folks wouldn't dare take sides with us. What far-reaching villainy I have to fight."

"Friday seems to be an unlucky day in West Fork," said Presley laconically. "Shall I send a man out to interview Walker?"

"No. I'll go myself. When is the next election of the school board?"

"Next spring."

"Walker will be superintendent of schools next fall, then," promised Hardy grimly.

"Good enough," nodded Presley. "I'll unearth all the data on school affairs I can find. Shall I hold a form open for any statement of Walker's for the morning's paper?"

"Yes. If your suspicions are right Walker hasn't another job to go to. In that case he stays here in West Fork."

To his surprise Hardy found the professor calmly reading a scientific pamphlet on the porch of his boarding house. Walker's eyes widened at his visitor's identity. He invited Hardy to be seated.

"Professor Walker, the first edition of to-day's *Planet* is out," Hardy began. "Have you seen it?"

Walker politely shook his head.

"There was a brief article in it about you that I want to ask you about," pursued Hardy.

"There was?" Walker's dark eyes almost twinkled.

"Yes. About your not teaching here this fall. What can you tell me about the matter?"

"Nothing more than you read."

"Did you know it was to be in the paper?"

"I strongly suspected it," Walker commented dryly. "I was told this morning that my usual contract would not be offered me this fall."

"You take it calmly enough," said Hardy frowning. "Were you expecting such a blow?"

"No, I can't say that I was, but I wasn't surprised in the least."

"Do you know why it happened?"

"Of course."

"And you didn't try to get in touch with me to let me know?"

"Why should I? While it was on your account, it was not your fault. I do not blame you, John Hardy."

"You speak as though you have made plans already. I realize that you are too good a scientist for West Fork, all right, but I had come I to think of you as a permanent citizen."

"I have made no plans," admitted Walker. "Why?"

"Then you are not worried about finances?" Walker shrugged.

"I am not worried with finances," he corrected. "I have nothing beyond sixty or ninety days' expenses. Fifteen hundred dollars a year does not allow one to accumulate a large bank account. My sister was sick three years ago and I went in debt so heavily then that I have not had any money to spare. Otherwise I could live comfortably on my salary."

"Do you mean to tell me that, as head of the science department, you get only fifteen hundred a year?"

"Got fifteen hundred a year. One hundred and sixty dollars per month for nine months."

"Why, that's ridiculous. The taxes are high enough to support the schools, surely."

"We tried to raise the school tax to twelve mills last year. It failed. They need the money for graft," explained the professor.

"Twelve mills? When it ought to be twenty-five per cent of the total tax assessment. Well, we'll have to dig into that later. Our present affair concerns you. As you haven't made any plans, professor, I am not too late to ask you to accept a position on my staff as chemist at five thousand a year. I need you. Will you accept?"

Walker was amazed. His black eyes were piercing as he stared into the younger man's face. Slowly he got to his feet and confronted Hardy, a touch of color brushing his high cheekbones.

"You offer me a position at five thousand dollars a year?" he echoed. "No. I am not an object of pity, sir. I—"

"Pity be damned!" cut in Hardy crisply. "You are too good a man to lose from this town. I said I needed you, and I mean it. And next year we're going to need you worse. We're going to need a superintendent of schools in this town. You are the man I want. I am begging you to accept my offer."

Walker turned away and walked toward the edge of the porch. For a long space he stared across the lawn at the sunset. Otherwise he expressed no emotion. And when he turned back his face was perfectly blank.

"I hadn't intended staying in West Fork more than another week or two," he said calmly. "In fact, I didn't know just where I was going. It's rather too late to seek an opening in other schools, you know. As far as you are concerned, my boy, you may find that you have bitten off considerably more than you can chew.

"If this comes to pass, and you will promise to tell me when it does and let me go, I'll accept your position but not your price for the coming year. Fifteen hundred is all I have been receiving and therefore fifteen hundred is all I can accept."

"You'll draw five thousand a year from here on," reiterated Hardy firmly. "Just because the school board badly underpaid you is no excuse for me doing the same."

"It wasn't me alone," Walker hastened to explain. "It's every instructor in our public school system. The salary is paltry. That is why West Fork cannot keep good teachers here; they are called to other places where the remuneration is greater. That's why we see notices in the paper such as: 'Miss Wilma Thedford comes to West Fork from Greenton to teach in the high school this fall,' and 'Mr. Smith comes up from Huntingwood to take over the mathematics of West Fork.'

"Isn't that a terrible state of affairs, John Hardy? When West Fork has to recruit its teachers from the little hamlets around here instead of reaching out and drawing educated people who already know how to teach? We teach these teachers for a couple of years, and they pass on to higher jobs, while we go back to the sticks for newer lumber. What in the world can West Fork expect of its youth when it won't pay to educate them?"

"I see that I've found the right superintendent of schools," declared Hardy with pleasure. "There's hope for West Fork yet when I can find such men as you in town. If you are through with the high school and ready to turn over your key you might begin to work for me to-morrow morning. Come down to our offices in the National Building. You shall be put in charge of the tax and school investigation."

Walker's eyes were suspiciously bright as he shook hands.

CHAPTER XVIII
THE DYING OAK

MAGICAL SESAME—money! In an incredibly short time the left hand half of the top floor of the National Building facing Wilson Avenue and overlooking North Eighth Street at the juncture of the two thoroughfares had been done over. Resplendent in new wallpaper, gleaming enamel, and glistening varnish, this long suite of rooms paralleling Eighth Street had been turned over to the Hardy forces to be furnished and equipped in such a lavish manner as to make a motion picture millionaire gasp in envy.

Duly incorporated under the necessary State laws, the neat gold-leaf sign on the glass part of the main entrance door informed all and sundry that these luxurious offices housed the activities of "Hardy Enterprises, Inc."

Before giving himself heart and soul to the revolutionists, Irving Barbington had held a long conversation with John Hardy. He was satisfied with the results of that interview and firmly burned his bridges behind him. The legal and financial loss he sustained by pledging himself to John Hardy had been amply compensated. Henceforth Hardy's interests were Barbington's interests.

The hand that controlled West Fork no longer had the power to intimidate the lawyer in even the slightest fashion. While he continued with his private practice and retained the work he had been interested in before the advent of Hardy, still Barbington realized that it was only a matter of time until Kimball would see that he was cut off from everything except John Hardy. People paid for their insubordination to Sam Kimball.

174

"What, in your opinion," Hardy asked him one day, "is the meaning of the silence on Kimball's part?"

"Unless he can prove your statements in that issue of the *Blade* libelous he is powerless to touch you," Barbington smiled thinly. "So he is merely waiting until some hapless citizen lines up with you, like Walker did, and then he'll crush him like a bug."

"In other words, he's playing the spider. And every time I befriend a man or win an adherent to our cause I must be able to protect that person immediately."

"Exactly. And, in the meantime, the days are passing rapidly," added the lawyer, nodding toward the door upon which was the legend, "Howard K. Wright, Manager."

"Meaning that the trial of Wright is drawing nearer every hour? That our manager is to be the first victim if we don't provide another?"

Barbington did not see the need of replying.

"I'm working on that myself," continued Hardy. "I hope to present you with something before long."

That Howard Wright possessed an iron nerve and implicit faith in Hardy was evident in the fact that he threw himself utterly into the work of making a live city out of an overgrown town. He never mentioned the matter of his approaching trial or the sleepless hours of anxiety he must have experienced, unless Hardy brought up the subject first.

And that his interest in his work was whole-souled was obvious in the daily strides he made toward organization and control. It was the day following Hardy's talk with Barbington that Wright came to his employer in the latter's small office in the front corner of the building.

"You haven't been to church since you've been home, have you?" he asked, seating himself and leaning for ward across the desk.

Hardy pushed back the meager personal correspondence he was reading and gave his manager complete attention.

"No," he admitted. "I've been too busy to go listen to Sam Kimball's idea of Heaven."

"Then you haven't met Rev. David Harris," pursued Wright. "They are letting him out of the church on Lintel Boulevard right away. He's a little too radical for the mossbacks. He's a Christian, but he's too broad-minded. He's the sort of man they would run out of Tennessee or Arkansas."

"Yes?"

"I've talked with him. He hasn't decided which of two calls to accept. We send two representatives to the State Legislature next year," concluded Wright significantly. "I thought I should bring the matter to your notice."

"Have you felt him out?"

"And convinced him that he can do his God and his people a lot of good by forsaking the ministry for a few years"

"A godsend to this county," Hardy agreed. "Organize a campaign program and turn him loose in the rural districts with all the facts you deem it best to give him, along with his own ideas. We'll finance him and bring him to West Fork when the time is ripe for him to win votes—and be able to hold them."

"I think we can put him over."

"And I think you are a smart man."

"I am realizing a lifelong ambition, John," replied Wright, as he rose to leave, his eyes shining. "And I have you to thank for it."

Among other things, Hardy found time to study the congestion along Wilson Avenue. He enjoyed driving up and down the street in his new roadster with Zoe Ann Wright at his side. The almost constant companionship with the girl was drawing Hardy more than he knew. Her alert mind and bright, far-seeing observations were things that he was beginning to rely on.

And while the evenings at the Wright home were not altogether given to social amenities, he learned that she could play the piano and sing. That she had acquired many of the other social virtues he well understood. And that she had a level business head he saw demonstrated each day. She took to the work in which her father found delight as naturally as Hardy took to fighting.

"The trouble with traffic on Wilson Avenue, especially on Saturday," Hardy observed, "is that they have a fool ordinance of a ten-mile limit and they try to enforce it. You're in a funeral procession when you get on this street. They ought to pass an ordinance calling for bumpers on the rear of cars only. That's where they are needed. I've seen traffic congestion right here worse than that of much larger cities."

"That's because West Fork has only one main street," Zoe Ann responded. "And we are large enough to have more. I can't see why the business district doesn't spread out."

Hardy glanced at her alluring profile. The faint breeze caused by their motion fanned some loose strands of her silken hair across her delicately rouged cheek. His eyes, as he looked toward the radiator cap, approved of the graceful curves of her figure and the slender little feet planted so primly against the footboard near his own.

"There are a number of businesses on the side streets just off Wilson Avenue," went on Zoe Ann thoughtfully. "And Elm Street has a number of wholesale houses farther down. I think Elm Street on the south and Birch Street on the north side of Wilson Avenue would make good business streets. They're nice and wide, too."

"And Greedy Morris doesn't own the property, either," remarked Hardy suddenly. "Let's drive up and down those streets and plan a business section."

Zoe Ann laughed with pleasure at the new game. Losing herself in her day-dream she chatted and planned and suggested buildings and enterprises, while Hardy listened silently and watched the play of expression on her features.

And the next week a stranger came to town and began to take options on the property one hundred feet deep on both sides of Elm and Birch Streets for a matter of ten blocks.

A FEW DAYS AFTER taking up his second task of tracing the golfing shoes of Charles Morris and William Beedle, there presented himself at the offices of the Hardy Enterprises, Inc., one Terry Callahan. He asked for neither Howard Wright nor John Hardy at first. Instead he sought the office which had been fitted up for Professor Walker. He was taking a leaf from John Hardy's notebook.

He found that Walker's office consisted of a desk and two or three chairs; the rest of the sunny room was given over to laboratory equipment. This was Callahan's first visit to the sanctum of the former high school professor. He gazed around with admiring awe. The scientist himself was busy at a table with an assortment of chemicals and test tubes. He looked up and nodded cordially to his visitor.

"Shure an' it's a chemical laboratory ye have as an office, professor," greeted Callahan. "How did ye manage to fix it up so quick?"

"Part of this paraphernalia belonged to me," explained the professor. "Part of it John was able to get at the wholesale drug house. He insisted on fitting up this room as a laboratory, although I am positive it is more or less a bluff to make me think he needs my assistance as a chemist."

"Ye seem to be at some sort o' work at th' present moment," pointed out Callahan.

"You have me there," smiled Walker, placing a test tube in a rack and picking up a nearly empty. Bottle which bore the label "Permanex." He held up the phial to gauge the remainder of its contents and then toyed with it as he spoke:

"I'm just finishing up a little analysis I started two or three weeks ago at the high school. When Mr. Kimball was so kind as to see that I was let out, I had this business still to finish for young Charles Morris."

"Charlie Morris?" queried Callahan, at once interested. "An' what might be th' nature o' th' analysis, can I be askin'?"

Walker shrugged.

"Nothing important. The boy is under the impression that a dollar per ounce is too much to pay for this golf ball enamel. He wants an analysis of the stuff so he can try to make his own."

"I see," Callahan replied casually. "'Tis like his uncle thot he is in some ways. Shure an' it must be a change to be workin' wid a man like Johnny Hardy."

"It is. John Hardy is a gentleman as well as a fighter."

"He is thot," Callahan agreed heartily. "An' th' other feller had better watch out. But, Professor Walker, he's up against a tough proposition in th' matter o' Mr. Wright. 'Tis thot I've come to see you about. 'Tis one devil a matter to prove him innocent."

A faint expression of pain crossed the scientist's face like a brief shadow.

"God knows I hope not, Callahan," he murmured fervently. "Wright is innocent, I know. Why, the father of such a girl as Zoe Ann wouldn't risk his life and honor to kill his most deadly enemy. No, he's not that sort of a man."

Callahan's eyes flicked and he scratched his head to cover his silence. The tone of Walker's voice had been almost tender. Walker was old enough to be Zoe Ann's father. But he was a single man, and then he was associated with the girl every day now. This was a worrisome thought.

While John Hardy had never shown by the least act that he was in love with Wright's daughter, the old policeman had taken the answer for granted. Slowly he nodded his head in agreement with Walker. This wasn't what he had come to discuss.

"Shure an' I know thot, professor. But 'tis likely thot those footprints found between th' spot o' th' murder an' Bigby Lane will be playin' an important part, if we don't scare up th' lad who did th' job. An' before I report to Johnny Hardy, ye can help me if ye please."

"Gladly, Callahan. What can I do?"

"I have here samples o' dirt from three places thot I want ye to peek at, stir up in solution, mix wid chemicals and whatnot an' tell me how much alike or unlike they be."

Walker laid down his pencil and put a couple of paperweights on his papers. Gravely he accepted two small envelopes and a paper twist containing rich soil mixed with leaf-mold. He adjusted a pair of glasses and carried the three little packages over to the half of his fairly large room that served as a research laboratory.

Callahan seated himself and patiently awaited the chemist's results, watching the various actions of the scientist with interested but uncomprehending eyes.

"There is no question but that all three specimens are alike," stated the professor at length, turning to face the sitting man. "Of course, there are bits of oak leaves and a twig and an acorn cap in the larger package you brought that I didn't find in the envelopes. Do you want the exact composition of the soil given you?"

"Thanks, but 'tisn't necessary, professor. Shure an' I don't know whether I know more or less than I did before. I'll be takin' th' specimens wid me if ye please. An' if it hadn't been for Johnny Hardy shure an' I wouldn't of bothered ye."

Going from the office of Walker, which was the rearmost room, so that the chemist could have light from the alley windows as well as from the side, Callahan traversed the distance to the front office of Hardy.

"Johnny, shure an' I've been on th' trail o' those sport shoes all this time," he stated without preamble. "I don't know whether I've much to tell ye or not. I couldn't learn any more about th' movements o' young Morris or Beedle, but I found out thot nobody has been wearin' their shoes but themselves. It was impossible. An' jes' a minute ago Professor Walker looked over these dirt samples for me and said thot they're alike."

Callahan spread his specimens out on Hardy's desk. The latter eyed them without touching.

"And where did you get these samples?" he inquired.

"Thot in envelope number one came from Bill Beedle's golf shoes. Thot in envelope number two from Charlie Morris's golf shoes. An' thot in th' paper poke came from th' spot where Preston an' Colter found those footprints over in th' woods. Morris an' Beedle was either in them woods or on ground almost identical wid th' same. I can't find any record o' their movements. An' between th' pair o' them they could of done th' job, I'm thinkin'."

Hardy frowned.

"Perhaps so, Terry. But wouldn't it be a long stretch of coincidence for two men whose movements you cannot trace to be the wearers of the same sized shoe and to have had the same style shoe on the same morning and to have been at the same spot?"

"Shure—unless they were there for a purpose."

"But didn't the clubhouse attendant say that no one was playing golf that Friday morning save Wright and Fosdick? How would this account for the presence of Morris and Beedle?"

"How did they account for th' presence o' Mr. Wright at thot spot?" countered Terry ironically. "Understand, Johnny, I'm not sayin' thot these two men are guilty o' anything. They might be a hundred places on th' golf course where they could of picked up dirt like this, but I'm carryin' out yer instructions. Ain't ye learned anything yerself?"

"Yes, I have," admitted Hardy. "I know that Fosdick and Kimball disagreed not so long ago over insurance matters—you know that the First National Bank writes insurance, Terry, as one of the side lines. And since then young Morris has been writing insurance for and getting thick with Kimball.

"I also learned that there is no love between the Fosdicks and young Morris. Fosdick objected to Morris's attentions to his daughter. I learned that Beedle and Fosdick have been speculating in real estate together and that there was some hard feeling between them. When you let two crooks associate too closely, Terry, there's bound to be friction.

"And with all this I've gathered here and there about town, I'm not satisfied that Morris and Beedle had anything to do with the matter. You know what gossip is like in towns like this. There might be a lot in it and then there probably is nothing in it. And I can't get away from the mystery of how the assassin killed Fosdick in such a bloody affair without getting a scratch himself. There's something queer about the whole damned business, Terry, and it's worrying me."

"Shure an' I'm doin' th' best I can," declared Callahan gloomily.

Hardy arose and gripped the older man's shoulder encouragingly.

"I know that you are, Terry," he smiled. "You're doing exactly what I ask you to do. Nobody can do more than that."

"An' what will ye be wantin' me to do now?"

"Morris and Beedle are a long way from being cleared of suspicion. In fact, it is just my private idea that the murderer must have had a club six feet long and have been a physical giant that keeps me from jumping to the conclusion that we have found the culprits. What I want you to do is to keep on digging after the details of their movements that fateful morning and also learn if there is a bond of any sort between the two of them."

Callahan departed and Hardy continued to frown and turn the matter over and over in his mind. The more he thought about it the more eager he was to have a look at the golf course again. Of course, there would be nothing to discover now. Doubtless the turf had long since been replaced and the spot trampled over by numerous players since that morning many days ago. Nevertheless, he felt like refreshing his mind on the matter.

Taking out the chart that Jenkins, the club attendant, had given him, he studied it.

"As I remember it, that is an open expanse along there, which is visible from the road, paralleling the course from hole six to seven," he mused. "True, Bigby Lane turns off of that road. But what a glaringly open spot for a murder. There are fifty better places where a victim could have been attacked."

He closed his desk abruptly and sought Zoe Ann.

This efficient young person, looking cool and intensely desirable in her simple linen dress, was dictating a letter to a nimble-fingered stenographer. She smiled up at him as he paused at her desk.

"Just a moment," she said, and he nodded.

He turned to stare out upon the sweltering street below. He was almost startled to feel a soft touch on his shoulder and to find her at his elbow.

"You are worried, John," she said, looking frankly into his eyes. "You want to talk with me about something. What is it?"

"It's about your father's case," he admitted. "Terry and I are making some headway I think, but I'll swear there is a mystery about it that puzzles me. I just can't put it into words, but first one thing and then another nags at my mind until I have a hunch that the answer isn't as simple as any of us think. I want to go out there and look over the spot again. Maybe I'll have a fresher viewpoint. Will you go with me?"

Zoe Ann's eyes widened and as Hardy looked into them they darkened with apprehension.

"Certainly I'll go," she said. "Right now?"

"Yes," he almost growled.

On the way out to the grounds Hardy explained his new idea about it being such an open spot for a murderer to select, even

though it was close to the shrubbery and trees that intervened before one came to Bigby Lane.

"And then Fosdick was found on his back in the shrubbery and
there were no indications that he had been dragged there or turned
over," he concluded. "Why did his watch stop then? And why didn't
they look carefully for footprints as soon as they found the body?

"Jenkins told me that the ground was as torn up when they
found the body as it was when I looked over the spot more than a
day later, but you know that's impossible. They just botched up
matters."

"But what difference does it make now that they have found
footprints farther in the woods?" Zoe Ann pointed out.

"I don't know," admitted Hardy.

They tramped out across the links in silence, the beauty of the
surrounding scenery lost on them in the contemplation of the mystery which clouded Howard Wright's life. When they reached the
spot Hardy briefly outlined the details for her. The turf had been
fixed, but the dangling and withered branches of the shrubbery
still showed the place where the banker's body had crashed through
to the earth.

"The actual fight took place some fifteen or twenty feet out from
the tree line," explained Hardy, indicating a rough circle. "You can
note how open and visible this spot is. Isn't that the road over there?"

Zoe Ann nodded.

"Why didn't they decoy him back into the woods or drag him
down into the ravine? Why this particular spot?" continued Hardy.

"That's queer," said the girl suddenly, glancing up and down
the fairway.

"What is?"

"I've often watched Mr. Fosdick play, as we met on the course
more than once," she explained. "He used to have a penchant for
dropping his ball into the ravine in driving off from the tee at the
fifth hole. He had a bad hook to his ball."

"Whatever that means," commented Hardy.

"He over-reached his ball and drove it in a bad left curve," she
said, making a motion with her hands, as though swinging a golf

club. "I've heard him say that this particular hole was his Water-loo. The way he corrected his drive here was to drive toward the woods on the other side. He generally drove from one hundred and fifty to two hundred yards from the tee."

"I see," said Hardy as patiently as possible. "And what has all that to do with his death?"

"I don't know. But he got into the habit of driving right to the edge of the rough, in his anxiety to stay away from the ravine. *And right along here is where his ball always came to rest.*"

"You mean that he would have walked here from the tee to make his second shot?" questioned the man in interest.

"Yes, invariably."

"Well, that explains how he happened to be slain here. They must have known his game and waited in concealment until he came this close to the woods. But what became of his golf ball then?"

"They must have struck him just after he drove it on toward the sixth hole," shuddered Zoe Ann. "Doubtless it was found by a caddy afterward."

"Let's scour the bushes along here again then," suggested Hardy. "We may find something overlooked before."

They turned to enter the shrubbery near the spot where the murdered man had been found, and both of them stopped at the same instant. They stared.

A young oak tree stood within a foot of the spot where the banker's head had rested. The bole was hardly four inches in diameter at the base. However, it was not the youth of the tree which was unusual; it was the condition of the leaves.

While every other tree and bush within sight was still green with summer life, every bit of the foliage of this oak had turned a sickly brown. From the topmost twig to the branch near John Hardy's hand, every single leaf drooped like lifeless hands dangling toward the ground. The contrast between this young tree and the others was startling. The tree was dying.

"Oh!" whispered Zoe Ann to John as she glanced at the tree. Her face whitened and one slim hand clutched at her throat. She stared at her companion out of startled eyes. "Oh!" she whispered again.

Hardy could only gaze in wonder. Then his eyes fastened on the trunk of the tree at a point approximately waist-high. The bark was stained a tan color here, a stain which ran down the bole for some distance. He stepped forward and touched the place.

Zoe Ann uttered a little cry, and then took a firmer grip on her emotions.

"I'm so silly," she tried to smile. "But I couldn't help thinking of that old superstition about the tree upon which a man is hanged always dying. And—and this frightened me for a moment."

"There's a natural explanation for this tree's death," said Hardy in a queer voice. "It has been bleeding. See here? And there is a hole in it like someone has driven a shingling hatchet into its heart."

Zoe Ann came nearer and studied the wound. Hardy attempted to probe in the two-inch wide slit with his penknife.

"Are you afraid to stay here while I run up to the clubhouse and borrow an ax?" he asked her.

"No," she smiled at him. "Besides I see a threesome coming over the hill."

Hardy ran all the way to the clubhouse. He was back, accompanied by the man Jenkins, in a short space of time. At his direction the attendant felled the tree, cutting it down just above the discovered wound.

Several curious golfers gathered about them as Hardy took the hand ax and began digging cautiously down to the place where the tree had bled its life away. At length he was rewarded by the slithering of metal on metal. After another breathless moment he dug out of the heart of the tree stump a large lump of metal. Nestling close to this queer find was a two-inch trapezium of brass perhaps a quarter of an inch thick. Ignoring the inquisitive golfers, Hardy and Zoe Ann bent so closely over this bit of metal that their heads touched.

The strip of brass was slightly corroded from the action of the sap of the tree and there were six holes pierced through it. It was

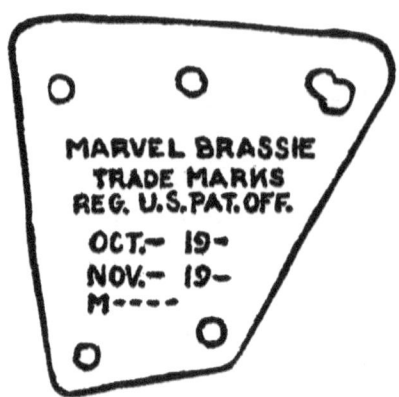

scarred and scratched, but fairly flat. Hardy rubbed it with his pocket handkerchief and certain letters became legible.

"Queer, isn't it?" murmured Hardy under his breath. "Is this one hole or two holes together? What do you make of it, Zoe Ann?"

"Make of it? It's the sole of a golf club—the metal bottom of a brassie. That double hole is where one screw pierced the end of the shaft of hickory and held it firmly in the head of the club. The other four holes are where brass screws held this plate on the bottom of the club head."

"That's it, Miss Wright," put in Jenkins keenly. "And this slug you dug out first, sir, must be the weight from the side of the club. Here you are. Like this, sir," he added, snatching a wooden club from the hands of one of the gaping spectators. "Look at the sole of this club and you can see the comparison."

Hardy compared the strip of brass he held with the metal bottom of the club Jenkins had confiscated in his excitement. While dented and battered, the strip of brass was easily recognizable. He took both pieces of metal and went back to the stump.

"This lump was farthest in," he mused. "Then the brass strip lay next to it, almost flat. The slug went in first. If any one swung a golf club against this tree he either held it upside down—which wouldn't have permitted such a blow as the handle would have been so long as to dig into the ground—or the club was swung by a left-handed man. Judging from the angle at which this strip lay in the tree heart, the blow was ascending from the ground. It would have taken a giant to swing a club against a tree waist-high *and be striking upward.*"

"It would have taken more than a giant to drive two pieces of metal into the heart of an oak tree like this," amended Zoe Ann. "Brass is malleable, too. This sole would have been battered into a shapeless wad."

"Somebody planted it there, mebbe," offered Jenkins.

"No," vetoed Hardy. "They were too firmly imbedded. You saw me dig them out."

"Where on earth could they have come from?" wondered Zoe Ann. "Could they have been part of Mr. Fosdick's missing club head?"

John Hardy jerked erect and stared sightlessly into the girl's flushed and anxious face. That elusive memory cell which had so tormented him that Saturday night at the mortuary, upon sight of the dead banker's mutilated hand, stood on tiptoe and shouted into his mental ear.

CHAPTER XIX
THE MISSING GOLF BALL

"Jenkins," said Hardy, turning to the attendant, "has any one given any thought to the golf ball Fosdick was chasing over this society pasture the morning he was murdered? I do not recall the mention of a golf ball in my presence by a single person. I didn't think of it because I don't play the game."

"Why, no," replied Jenkins in mild astonishment. "Now that you speak of it I don't think the ball was mentioned. The detectives said nothing about it to me, sir."

"And yet, as a clew, the missing golf ball might have proven invaluable, don't you think?"

"Perhaps so, sir," assented Jenkins dubiously. "Although I fail to see how," he added honestly.

"Principally because it is—missing."

"There might be a dozen explanations for that, Mr. Hardy. It seems to me that these bits of metal are more important."

"They may be," agreed Hardy. "We will find out. What kind of a ball did the banker use? Do you know?"

"Yes, sir. He used the Longflite and he bought them by the dozen. I know that because he always brought them to me in the original box to be stamped with his name."

"You have a name marker at the club then?"

"Yes, sir. About fifty or sixty of the members have name plates which I use to stamp their balls with."

"Then Fosdick's golf balls can all be identified by his name? How were they marked?"

"T. C. Fosdick," Jenkins replied. "Black lettering."

Hardy spoke to the murmuring and curious golfers about the stump of the felled tree:

"Of course, you men realize that we are investigating the murder of Thurlowe Fosdick still. Would you like to help?"

At their quick assent, Hardy turned toward Zoe Ann.

"You have seen Fosdick play his ball from here many times," he said. "How far and about where would he have driven it on the next shot, do you think?"

Zoe Ann wrinkled her brow prettily.

"That would depend on the wind and his game," she answered dubiously. "I should say anywhere in the fairway between one and two hundred yards from here."

He was not in the least disheartened by this vague information.

"You men go about seventy or eighty yards down the course and search every inch of the ground from the ravine to the woods on this side all the way to the sixth green. I will give fifty dollars for that Longflite ball with Fosdick's name on it."

The young men began their search, fifty dollars lending zest to the game for them. Hardy turned back to his two companions with a queer smile.

"They won't find it," he said.

"Why not?" Zoe Ann demanded.

"Because the murderer carried it away with him in his pocket. With your help I will prove it. Jenkins, run up to the clubhouse and get a measuring tape and a long piece of cord. Also, bring a club something like the one Fosdick was using, back with you. Wasn't it a brassie that was missing from his golf bag? And you might question every caddy on the course and see if a ball of Fosdick's has been found in this neighbor hood since the murder and let me know later."

The attendant hurried off and returned shortly with the required articles. He found that Hardy had fitted the two pieces of metal back in the heart of the oak stump as he had found them. The private investigator now took the length of cord and staked out a straight line from the pieces of metal along the angle at which the brass sole lay. This line met the ground about fifteen feet out from the shrubbery and in the fairway. Here a stub trimmed from one of the oak tree's limbs was driven.

Jenkins watched in silent bewilderment, while the girl took the brassie he had brought and addressed herself in a left-hand position toward the tree. She made a number of varying slow-motion swings, while Hardy, with his eyes close to the stump, watched every move.

"You see, Zoe Ann," Hardy said at length, "if it had been possible to drive that metal into the tree from the club itself they wouldn't have gone in at the angle at which we found them. My theory is proving itself. Now, let's try the other position."

"Oh, it's horrible," the girl shuddered.

Then she walked out to the stub and addressed this innocent stake with her club in a right-handed manner, as though she were going to drive it toward the sixth green. Jenkins wiped his puzzled brow with a handkerchief, but forbore asking questions.

At her first slow swing Hardy gave an exclamation of delight. Quickly he adjusted the cord around the tree stump and tautened it at the stake. The girl swung again. Hardy nodded and took the club. Standing as near like the girl had stood as possible, he made the same sort of slow swing, the bottom of his club touching the end of the cord and being practically parallel with it when the face of the club was meeting an imaginary golf ball.

"Just what are you doing, Mr. Hardy?" Jenkins could contain his curiosity no longer.

"I am proving how Fosdick met his death, Jenkins. When it is all figured out, you shall be told all about it. There is one thing more you can do to help us this evening. Do you know that you didn't relate all that you heard or saw that eventful morning when the banker was killed?"

The attendant paled slightly.

"My God, sir," he gasped. "What could I have left out?"

"Nothing intentionally. Don't be alarmed," smiled Hardy. "Tell me, what kind of hunting could be done in these woods and fields at this time of the year?"

"N-not any that I know of, sir," stammered Jenkins uncertainly. "Besides, the farmers around here have their fields posted."

"Then why," asked Hardy keenly, studying the man's face, "why didn't you think it queer when you heard the bellow of a shotgun that Friday morning?"

Jenkins frowned.

"A shotgun? I didn't hear any shooting. I was working inside the clubhouse that morning part of the time. You—"

His voice fell away as he noted that Hardy's hard blue eyes were boring into his with a burning force, a fierce command to remember something he hadn't heard. It frightened him.

"A shotgun?" he repeated timidly. Then he knit his brows in painful thought. "A shotgun? A—that's right! I did hear a shot. I didn't give it a thought because the farmer boys around here shoot at crows sometimes and—great Heavens! How did you know I heard a shotgun?"

The eyes of Hardy met those of the girl. A look of relief and understanding passed between them.

"Calm yourself, Jenkins," he said gently. "There is nothing supernatural about my knowledge. I just have a few more facts gathered than you have. You are a jewel and you will be one of the first persons to whom I explain the mystery."

They left the uneasy fellow with a crisp bill in his hand and following them with troubled and amazed "eyes as they drove away. Poor Jenkins would have been more puzzled than ever had he known that they spent the rest of the afternoon in search of the farmer's lad who fired off the shotgun. Fosdick wasn't killed with a shotgun.

CYRUS BRENTWOOD hung up the receiver to his telephone and frowned at his wife. Every time he heard from John Hardy it spelled trouble. He was very thoughtful as he reseated himself at the dinner table and toyed with his dessert. When his wife sought to interrogate him, he silenced her with a gesture. Why Hardy requested his presence at a conference to-night he couldn't understand.

He had no reason for presenting himself at the offices of the Hardy enterprises to view the various lieutenants to this *de luxe* prodigal son. It made his gorge rise—it spoiled his after-dinner coffee—to think of Presley, of Walker, of Callahan, of Wright—of Hardy himself. Nevertheless, Brentwood went. John Hardy had been very urgent.

The prosecuting attorney found all of his aforementioned friends present in the main office, including Barbington and a farmer with his half-grown son who seemed to be afflicted with the itch, so nervous was he. Be it said to the credit of his courage he entered without faltering and seated himself to hear what Hardy had to offer.

"I have asked all of you people here to-night," Hardy said gravely, "to hear how Thurlowe Fosdick met his death. Presley, you are here as a newspaper representative. Mr. Brentwood, you have been asked here, not as a member of the moneyed faction to which we are opposed, but as an avenging arm of the law. Laying aside any personal differences there may be between us, Brentwood, I am addressing myself to you as the prosecuting attorney and not as the son-in-law of Sam Kimball. Are you willing to hear me on this ground?"

"Perfectly willing," Brentwood agreed. "Did I understand you to say you intend disclosing the manner of Fosdick's death?"

"Exactly, sir."

"Continue. Rest assured that you have my strict attention."

These were the last words the prosecuting attorney uttered until Hardy had completely laid out his case.

"We must go back to the morning of the banker's death," Hardy resumed, smiling encouragement into the strained face of Zoe Ann who was staring from him to her father and Brentwood and back again. "The fact has been established that Fosdick started to play around the course at seven o'clock. I will not take up the discussion of Mr. Wright's game here, my purpose being to prove that Fosdick did not meet his death in the manner supposed and to offer this new evidence as the starting point from which Mr. Brentwood can search for the actual murderer.

"At approximately seven thirty Mr. Fosdick drove his ball off the tee at the fifth hole. He always hooked his ball on this shot, and to correct this tendency he addressed himself so far to the side of the ball as to drive it to the edge of the woods away from the ravine. To be exact, a fair shot always dropped his ball within twenty yards of the spot where his body was found. He could see this spot from the tee. Hence, he knew exactly where his ball landed.

But he could not see this spot in walking toward it, as he had to pass down a faint rise from the tee and over a small hill—hardly more than a rolling mound, but sufficient to cause him to lose sight of his ball for a minute or two. This fact and his peculiar game can be established by any number of witnesses.

"While he was out of sight of the golf ball, an unknown person crept out of the woods and picked up the ball. This unknown, who left the footprints that Colter and Preston found later, substituted another ball for that of the banker, and retired to the woods again.

"When the victim arrived at the spot he was unaware of the change. To all intents and purposes this was a Longflite ball with his name stamped on it—the ball he had been playing with all morning. He selected his brassie, dropped his golf bag where it was found later, and approached the little white sphere. Perhaps he removed a twig or two from the way. Maybe he glanced about at the green life around him and drew a deep breath before he took his stance. Then, at exactly seven thirty-six he swung at the ball."

Zoe Ann shuddered at the graphic manner in which Hardy told his story. Everyone else in the room was leaning forward breathlessly at the dramatic nature of the recital.

"Fosdick swung at the ball," repeated Hardy impressively. "He was too good a player to miss it. And any man who can drive a ball two hundred yards puts a lot of swing into his stroke. From the instant that his club started downward I am confident that Fosdick remembered nothing. He didn't have time.

"There was a flash as the head of his club connected with the ball, a bellowing explosion, a rush of air—and Fosdick's body lay some ten feet away, just in the underbrush. The unknown assassin didn't have to come back to learn if his job was well done; his ears told him that. And that was how Fosdick was found—just as he died."

"My God!" whispered Barbington. "What happened?"

"What happened? That was not a golf ball he struck. It was the outer shell of a golf ball. The inside was filled with nitroglycerin or that more powerful explosive known as TNT."

Wright shivered like he had the ague.

"Horrible," he said hoarsely. "What a devilish way to kill a man."

"Yes," nodded Hardy. "And yet, in a way, it was clever. While it doesn't come under the head of suicide, he made Fosdick kill himself. Doubtless he made his way off toward Bigby Lane, grinning to think of the fitness of his revenge. I've never seen Fosdick play golf, but, knowing the man as I did, I imagine he took an almost vicious pleasure in socking a golf ball and listening to the resultant click and whish of his club. Perhaps the assassin thought of all that and laughed to himself, for there is no doubt that he knew how his victim played."

"And now for your proof," said the grave voice of Professor Walker. "Brentwood will need convincing, John. What have you got to show that you are right in your theory?"

"Listen while I read the items off. First, the condition of the body and the condition of the ground point toward an explosion. The reason Fosdick got the brunt of the shock instead of the earth was due to the fact that nitroglycerin explodes toward the point of greatest resistance.

"That explains the shattered golf club and the missing fingers. These were torn off. The rest of the club wasn't found because it was shivered into a myriad fragments. One piece, however, was buried in the side of the body.

"My next point is the very fact that the two fingers were blown off. I couldn't recall it until this afternoon, but I saw that very same thing happen at an oil well in Texas. It was a cool morning and a helper was getting ready to lower a quart of nitroglycerin down so they could shoot this well. The quart container was on the ground beside him. The chain he was making ready to use was kinked. It was used for this purpose all the time, and thus a drop or two of nitro-glycerin had dried or congealed at the very place where it was kinked.

"Carelessly the fellow knocked the two links together in his hands. There was a quick flash, a faint report, and he was minus two fingers. All he could do was to stand there and stare dumbly at the stump of his hand. Strangely enough the quart can of stuff which was within five feet of the other flash did not go off. Anyway, that was where I got my first clew that something was oddly familiar in the appearance of the dead man's hand.

"My next point is the stopped watch. I have here a statement from the jeweler that it was stopped at seven thirty-six by a severe shock. Mr. Brentwood has the watch itself. My next proof is the condition of the victim's clothes. This was first pointed out to me by Gordon, the undertaker.

"And last, but not least, I present the matter of the dying oak tree. Here in my hand I hold two pieces of metal which came from the sole of Fosdick's golf club. By a strange freak these two bits of iron and brass were driven with a velocity greater than that of a bullet on a straight line back in the direction they had come as part of the golf club. They were buried in the heart of the tree which was almost at the murdered man's head.

"There remains but the matter of how such an explosion went unheard. Jenkins, the club attendant, recalled the sound of a gun shot at my prompting. I wasn't satisfied with this, because I feared that the prosecution would not be. Zoe Ann and I called at the nearby farmhouses to learn if there was corroboration to the attendant's story. We were very fortunate.

"We found another man who mistook the sound of that explosion for a shotgun. Let me introduce Mr. Castell, a farmer whose place adjoins the grounds of the golf club. He had threatened his son, Clyde, here, if he caught him playing with his shotgun. Mr. Castell, and Clyde, will now testify to the fact that there was a painful session in the woodshed on that fateful Friday morning, when Clyde received a whipping for firing a gun he did not fire."

The farmer and his bashful son gave their testimony to Barbington. While the lawyer took their affidavits to this effect and identified the farmer's mistake as being the sound of an explosion over near the golf course the others entered into a babble of talk, discussing this peculiar turn to the case. Brentwood did not utter a word. He merely sat and stared at first one and then the other. Appealed to for an opinion, he did not answer. Silence gradually fell as it was seen that the prosecuting attorney did not display any emotion.

"I failed to add," said Hardy to Brentwood earnestly, "that I still have samples of the ground in which no blood was found save that of the victim. If you are unconvinced, Professor Walker can analyze the soil, or your city chemist can, to see if there aren't evidences of an explosion of nitroglycerin. Also, you might exhume the body and demand a thorough autopsy which I know will establish the fact that Fosdick died, not of the apparent wounds he sustained, but of the terrific shock."

"There is no need to delve into the matter further," Brentwood replied in a level voice. "You are a very clever man, Hardy, and I will concede that you have established the manner of Fosdick's death beyond questionable doubt. The very unusualness of the deed called for knowledge outside the general understanding of our local authorities. Fortunately, you happened to be a man who could supply the necessary knowledge, and you came home at the right moment."

"And now that we have established the fact that it did not take a giant to do the deed without receiving a scratch in return," said Hardy, "Terry Callahan, here, has two suspects who wear the same shoes as those of the murderer for you to investigate. When you find the man who has now a golf ball marked with the name of Fosdick, or who has recently rid himself of it, you will have found the murderer of the president of the First National Bank."

"I don't need Callahan's assistance," replied the prosecuting attorney coldly. "Your testimony this night has riveted my case. Just one week before the murder of Thurlowe Fosdick the accused,

Howard Wright, received a book he had ordered on the manufacture of deadly explosives."

Hardy could only stare at the lean, triumphant face of the attorney. Slowly, in the stunned silence that followed this damning statement of Brentwood's, he heard a girlish sob. He knew Zoe Ann was weeping. He felt that every eye was on him at this moment. Gradually he controlled himself sufficiently to turn about, and then it was that he saw every eye was fastened on the accused Wright. And Wright was staring at Hardy with an intensity of gaze that was pitiful.

"Mr. Wright," Hardy scarcely recognized his own voice. "Mr. Wright," he repeated, "is Brentwood's accusation true? Have I worked hard just for this just to put your neck further into the noose?"

Wright continued to stare up into the standing man's face as if he would find his answer written there. The only sound was the soft sobbing of the girl. Even young Clyde Castell ceased to scratch himself. Out on Wilson Avenue folks were going to picture shows or riding around in search of pleasure. The drug stores would doubtless be filled with hot and thirsty drinkers who besieged the fountains. While up here above the street a tragedy was being enacted.

Slowly Wright sagged down in his chair. All the spirit, the life seemed to have gone out of him. When he spoke it was like the sighing of the wind through the trees on Elm Street.

"God," he mumbled. "God, who on earth would have thought of circumstances arising like this. Yes," he added heavily. "Yes, Brentwood speaks the truth."

And John Hardy wanted to sob with Zoe Ann.

CHAPTER XX
"WE'VE JUST BEGUN TO FIGHT"

CURIOUSLY ENOUGH, it was Wright, himself, who first recovered from the crushing blow of Brentwood's unanticipated statement. After the coldly polite withdrawal of the prosecuting attorney, and the departure of the taciturn Castell and son, the accused man pulled himself together and gazed about the glum circle around him.

Presley sat at the desk he had used for writing down the points of Hardy's statements. He was staring at his notes as though he feared to look up, thinking he might meet some one's glance. His nervous little smile was missing, but his slender fingers toyed with his pencil and made queer little marks and tracks on the margin of the paper before him. Wright was fascinated by the odd monogram on his signet ring. Odd, too, how bald Presley was getting. And he was a young man—only in his thirties.

Barbington was tilted back in a swivel chair, his eyes fixed on the emptiness of space, one hand stroking his imperial and the other tapping a tattoo on the arm of his chair. The lawyer was growing old.

Queer that Wright had never noticed the network of lines and wrinkles on his attorney's face. Doubtless the crisp whiskered ornamentation had served as a sort of shield by furnishing a counter attraction.

Callahan sat in a straight chair, his hat on the floor between his feet. He was leaning forward with his elbows on his knees, his eyes glued to his head covering. At intervals the ex-officer shook his head slightly and scratched one ear reflectively. At his right hip, under his dark coat, Wright noticed the telltale bulge which attested the presence of a gun.

He turned from these three men who studiously avoided one another's eyes and glanced toward Professor Walker. The scientist was looking at him. Their gazes met and locked. With an odd feeling Wright noted that the other was contemplating him with a profound sort of pity or sympathy. Walker was not wearing his glasses. Wright couldn't remember having ever looked into his face without them before. He marveled at the professor's fine, intelligent, dark eyes.

Wright turned farther and looked toward his daughter. She and John Hardy were standing near a window, conversing together in low tones. Wright's eyes lit up in pride and admiration. He knew Zoe Ann was beautiful and as stanch as she was pretty. And, in profile, Hardy's face was handsome.

Now that he thought of it, either he had become accustomed through daily association to the hard expression on the younger man's countenance, or else Hardy's features were somehow softening. They made an admirable couple as they stood there and, without analyzing his exact reaction to their picture, Wright realized the fact.

Yet, of the entire group, not a one had met his eyes except Walker, whose gaze had expressed sorrow and pity. It was not, however, that these friends believed with Brentwood that he was guilty of the crime, after all. He and Hardy had come to a complete understanding between themselves that Saturday weeks before, when they had been confined in adjoining cells in the county jail. It was the apparent hopelessness of his case in the face of the evidence as interpreted by the relentless prosecuting attorney; it was the fact that Brentwood was accepting all the evidence Hardy was unearthing, but, instead of using it to seek further for a criminal, he was building up his case against the defendant already indicted.

The matter of the text-book on explosives Wright had been able to explain. A month before the murder which had rocked West Fork to its foundations, a tank car of molasses had exploded mysteriously while on a siding at the sorghum factory in South West Fork.

An altercation had arisen with the insurance company. The adjuster had refused to make a settlement, claiming that the explosion had been spontaneous. He brought an expert to town who investigated the matter and then made the statement that the explosion had been caused by internal heat and ferment within the product. The insurance company disclaimed all responsibility.

This had caused the sorghum manufacturers to take up the matter of the condition of the tank car with the railroad. Immediately the railroad company filed a counterclaim, demanding an adjustment for the loss of this unit of their rolling stock. The three-sided wrangle dragged on until all West Fork had become interested in the "Molasses Car Case."

The city chemist was called in to make a statement. Major Sims and Sam Kimball being stockholders in the sorghum plant, the chemist's statement flatly contradicted the insurance company's claim that the product itself had been at fault. In a roundabout way it was learned that Professor Walker's opinion coincided with that of the insurance company's expert. He was not asked to make a statement.

The newspapers became interested in the case to the extent of taking up the subject of explosives and explosive materials in general. Having no technical man on his staff, Howard Wright had ordered a treatise on the subject from a publishing house. Presley had corroborated his story in every detail.

But this explanation fell on deaf ears. The coincidence was too striking for the prosecutor to swallow.

As far as Brentwood was concerned, Wright's doom was sealed.

"Presley."

The editor started slightly at the sound of Wright's voice.

"Yes, sir."

"You will publish Hardy's discoveries in detail."

Presley essayed his nervous smile.

"I was considering the matter," he said. "In view of Brentwood's knowledge of that text-book and the interpretation the *Planet* will lay upon it, I rather think it best to kill the news for the present."

"There is no doubt in your mind regarding the truth of the facts Hardy has established, is there?"

"No, but—"

"If you don't publish them the *Planet* will," Wright remarked crisply. "Brentwood said nothing before he left about keeping silent."

"No, but he will if we do."

Hardy and Zoe Ann approached to take part in the discussion. The girl slid a comforting arm about her father's neck, giving him an affectionate little pat.

"Dear old Dad," she murmured softly.

Wright stroked her head gently, as though she were in the greater trouble and he were the comforter.

"I demand that you print the facts, Presley," Wright spoke in a firm voice. "You can expose the matter of that text-book on explosives and explain it before the *Planet* puts a nasty interpretation to it. We've got to play fair or the people won't believe anything they read about me in the *Blade*."

Presley appealed to Hardy for advice.

"I haven't told you folks the lines of investigation that Terry and I are following," said the latter slowly. "And Brentwood refused to hear my theories further than the reconstructed crime. But I will say that we have found two men of West Fork whose shoes and footprints correspond with those of yours, Mr. Wright. And the movements of these two men that Friday morning are a matter of question."

"Shure, an' I've just learnt from Professor Walker thot one o' them has been interested in golf ball enamel," put in Callahan suddenly. "Now that Johnny has been talkin' golf ball bombs they might be somethin' in th' matter."

Professor Walker jerked around and stared at Callahan.

"You refer to Charles Morris?" he asked. At the ex-officer's emphatic nod the scientist turned toward Hardy. "And you say that those mysterious footprints could have been made by young Morris?"

"Exactly. What is this matter that you and Terry seem to know about him?" demanded Hardy keenly.

"Uuumm—I wonder," mused Walker half to himself. "Of all queer things! Yet, how could that young idler be involved?"

"But what is it, Professor Walker?" cried Zoe Ann anxiously.

The scientist bestowed a gentle smile upon her. He explained about the little bottle of golf ball enamel, Permanex.

"But don't be too quick to draw conclusions," he advised quietly. "Remember the unjust suspicion against your father."

A general discussion arose. Presley seized the opportunity to speak to Wright.

"At least you will wait a day or so until Hardy looks into this matter?" he pleaded. "It will probably lead to something promising."

Wright shook his head.

"No!" he said. "I think the public is entitled to know all the facts as we find them to be facts. And I want the *Blade* to tell them first."

"All right," agreed the editor savagely. "I'll do it and get the damned business over with. Anyway, it's a whale of a story."

"That's the idea," said Wright, and he managed to smile.

"What do you think about the matter, Professor?" Barbington asked the scientist.

"I think," Walker weighed his words deliberately, "I think that John Hardy has solved the mystery concerning the manner of the banker's death beyond question. His undoubted ability to build up much out of so little is astounding. Of course, I will be glad to check over the chemical problems in the case with him, but I am sure that Presley will not have to retract a single statement."

"And what do you make of this Morris clew?" continued the lawyer, turning to Hardy. It was obvious that Barbington was trying to probe the bottom of every angle which presented itself.

"I don't know," admitted Hardy frankly. "In a way it looks like everything I do turns out backwards. I think I have established a point that is of material aid in lifting the cloud from Howard Wright, and it proves a boomerang every time. Look at the matter of that footprint I found in the ravine. When I called Brentwood's attention to it, thinking to prove Wright's alibi, the prosecuting attorney discovers a number of the same kind of footprints over in the woods near the scene of the murder.

"Then to-night—the manner of Fosdick's death. All I am doing is to involve Wright more deeply at every turn. I think—I think Professor Walker is right. We don't want to jump at conclusions regarding this Morris even if he is an idler, and was forbidden the freedom of the Fosdick home by the banker.

"Let's look at the matter from the angle which a keen detective would take. We have the given problem of a murdered man and very few clews. If you will assist me by questioning me, Mr. Barbington, I believe we can get a clearer grasp—vision, rather, of the mystery."

"Just how would you have me question you?" frowned Barbington.

"Say, as if I were on the stand."

"Very well," the lawyer agreed. "We have the problem of a rich man who has been killed. The only thing we have to work on is the unusual manner of his death and a few footprints. Is that right?"

"Precisely," nodded Hardy. "The first question is motive."

"Very good. In your opinion, is or was robbery the motive?"

"No; for two reasons."

"Which are?"

"His valuables and money were left untouched. Second, the unusual method used in killing the victim argues forethought, knowledge of the victim's habits, and preparation."

"Then comes the question of benefit," said Barbington, falling into the spirit of the argument. "Who would have been benefited by the death?"

"If he carried heavy life insurance his family would profit," stated Hardy. "As he was already a rich man it is improbable that he would have been killed by relatives for money. However, that opens up an avenue for speculation that I hadn't thought of before. Suppose you investigate Fosdick's affairs and the matter of his will thoroughly, Mr. Barbington!"

"I shall do so at once," agreed the lawyer, making a note of the matter. "However, if this proves to be a blind alley, we must fall back on the motives of vengeance. Speaking broadly, there are only two motives for premeditated murder—gain and vengeance. Could this have been a murder for revenge?"

"It could. Howard Wright is the first logical suspect. The two men, Morris and Beedle, form the second and third possibilities."

"Waiving the matter of footprint evidence, can you suggest a field which can be narrowed to a limited number of persons?"

"I can. It is obvious that the assassin knew explosives well enough to work with them. This narrows the field considerably. And that he knew the victim's personal habits limits the field to West Fork and its environs. Professor Walker can aid us here by compiling a list of the residents of West Fork that he thinks know enough about explosives to employ them.

"That he will miss a number of people out of thirty thousand is highly probable, but we have a vital clew to consider against this fact. The murderer, besides understanding explosives, knew the game of golf and exactly how his victim played it. He planned his deed on an eccentricity in Fosdick's style of playing."

"That leaves Mr. Wright and the other two suspects still to be considered."

"Plus a few others we have not yet discovered."

"How would you go about uncovering these others if the present three men prove innocent?"

"First, by investigating Fosdick's estate through you."

"And second?"

"By investigating the murdered man's past life to find a man—or woman, with a powerful enough incentive to plan revenge."

"And how will you go about such an immense task?"

"I shall wire to-night for the best private investigators in the United States," declared Hardy. "I am afraid to meddle in the affair any further myself; I am too much of an amateur."

"Wright's trial comes up within the next three weeks," pointed out Barbington.

"And you are to drag it out as long as you can. Within thirty days I hope to have the banker's life bared of its most intimate details. Within sixty I hope to have the real murderer behind the bars unless—"

"Unless what?" prompted Zoe Ann breathlessly.

"Unless Terry hangs it onto one of his suspects in the meantime," Hardy rejoined. "We're going to show Kimball and his outfit that we've just begun to fight."

Without warning, acting on an irresistible impulse, Zoe Ann flung her arms about his neck and kissed him squarely on the mouth. It was a tingling shock to both of them. And Callahan noticed that Professor Walker quickly turned aside his head.

"But these astounding revelations concerning the golf ball clew and the way Fosdick was killed will put the murderer on his guard," Presley observed. "He'll know we are hot on his trail. Do you think, Hardy, that it is advisable to run the story?"

"Go ahead," Callahan answered for the almost confused Hardy. "Stick it in an' I'll be watchin' for reactions to it."

And thus it was that the front page of the *Morning Blade* presented news of such startling import that all West Fork sat bolt upright to gasp. Thus the Fosdick murder case leaped into renewed prominence in the dailies of the larger cities and caused the spotlight of publicity to focus again on Hardy's hometown.

The hotels became crowded with newspapermen, detectives and curiosity seekers. Purists and preachers talked and lectured on the affair. Criminologists, alienists and psycho-analysts discussed the complex of the defendant. While John Hardy fled from importunate reporters like a hunted thing.

CHAPTER XXI
NOCTURNAL GARDENING

JUST ONE BLOCK up the street from the building which furnished offices to Hardy Enterprises, Inc., on the corner of Seventh Street and Wilson Avenue, stood a solid but ancient two-storied structure. The first floor now housed an Italian fruit store; it had once been a pool hall, once a grocery, once a shooting gallery, once a saloon.

And at one time it had served as a motion picture house until two of the lesser members of the financial circle had seen fit to erect a couple of buildings designed for picture theaters at the outset. Prior to all this, other retail enterprises had flourished or languished here throughout the years of changes wrought by the hand of time.

But the upper floor of the place had not been subjected to anything more drastic than an occasional renovation. A weather-beaten, creaky sign which was repainted every two years and replaced every six was suspended just above the middle window of the second story. This artistic effect in red and black proclaimed the fact that William Beedle's real estate office occupied the front half of the upstairs.

This sign, and its predecessors, had swung there in the wind and sun and rain for years too numerous to contemplate. While the first floor had housed many different merchants and had undergone various vicissitudes, the upstairs continued to house Mr. William Beedle, unaltered and impervious to the inroads of time and the winds of fortune.

206

To the younger generation he was a landmark; it seemed that he had always been there and had always trafficked in real estate. As a child John Hardy's eyes had been attracted by the glitter of that red and black sign which proclaimed the name and business of the upstairs occupant.

As a barefoot boy when the hot pavement burned the soles of his feet, he had seen it swinging nonchalantly above the twenty-foot height prescribed by city ordinance. It had been there the day he left home to conquer more fruitful worlds. It was there when he returned.

However, Beedle had not always been a resident of West Fork. An examination of the birth records of the county would have revealed the fact that he first saw the light of day at Charleswood some fifty-six years previous. It would not have surprised Hardy to learn this.

In the days of his formative period he had come to the conclusion that half the population of West Fork had come originally from Charleswood, Huntingwood, or Greenton. Before the advent of the present generation, in these three little villages which surrounded the larger town, parents who did not know each other now, had once been next door neighbors in humbler days.

Thus, despite the present change, surprising and intimate bits of the family connections, disgraces, vices and virtues of others could be heard at the supper table at home. John Hardy had lived through a small town boyhood. He knew.

But he could not recall anything about William Beedle, save that the man had been a real estate dealer since the beginning of time with an upstairs office at Seventh and Wilson. The matter of investigation rested with Terry Callahan.

In appearance William Beedle was not extraordinary. True, closely observed, his head narrowed distressingly at the top, as though his nurse had molded and shaped the infant's skull to conform to a tapering candle. As his jaw was heavy, his neck short, his shoulders narrow, and his waistline extended with the paunchiness of maturity, he had more or less the look of a cone from his hips to the crown of his head.

His hair was colorless and brushed up like a rooster's comb. His eyes and lips were pale. Taken *ensemble* by a cruel caricaturist who would discount his legs, he was a cylindrical wedge.

The wits of Mr. Beedle cannot be said to dwindle to the same dull point as his cranium. Rather, they came to a sharper point. However, Mr. Beedle was very quiet in demeanor and generally soft-spoken. He was a deacon in the church and a favorite committee man for the Chamber of Commerce. He was the father of a grown son who was in a law office in New York and of two daughters of indifferent pulchritude yet marriageable age who lived at home.

Every summer Mrs. Beedle and the two girls moved to a colony of idle rich folks up in the mountains, while Papa Beedle remained in West Fork and bravely carried on the ceaseless work of filling the family exchequer which emptied automatically.

This summer was no exception. Beedle closed up his house, dismissed the cook for the summer and ate his meals downtown. He passed his evenings at his office or at the Elks' Club, occasionally accepting an invitation to dine out. He used his home for sleeping purposes only.

Mr. Beedle was not a member of the first social set of West Fork; he swung about in his orbit of the second circle. This he did not mind. In the first place he had not been born in West Fork, although his wife came from the ranks of the town's middle class. Thus, Mr. Beedle figured that he had climbed far from his lowly origin, and perhaps he had.

The pastime of the real estate dealer had formerly been gardening; now it was golf. For some time after he took up the Scottish game, there was nothing to distinguish one hobby from the other. Nevertheless, he preserved and gradually his golf became less like landscape gardening and his garden became more like a landscape.

Yearly his garden occupied less and less space in his back yard, while his golfing paraphernalia encroached more and more on the other things in the spare back bedroom closet. The glowing accounts of the size of his tomatoes and the tenderness of his sweet corn gave way to tales of the length of his drives and the accuracy of his putting.

At last his assortment of gardening tools fell into utter disuse. Rust ate deeply into the once shining blade of his hoe, while he polished the heads of his golf clubs. A small strip of garden was now planted by the man who came weekly to mow the grass and Beedle erected a practice driving net near the house to improve his game.

The tools of which he had once been so proud, now were forgotten. What the neighbors had not despoiled lay neglected in the little tool-house which was built against the garage.

How much wealth William Beedle possessed was not known; it was a matter for speculation. And the good housewives whose husbands could not afford to send them on vacations dissected his affairs with the liveliest interest.

The fact that his wife before her marriage had been a milliner at Rosenbaum and Brady's, was an item of vast importance which called for tart sniffs, although what bearing this had on Mr. Beedle's financial ability to send her away for the summer, must be left to the ladies; a mere man is not capable of reading the significance therein.

Whatever had been his standing in past years, in the privacy of his soul Mr. Beedle knew that his affairs were not going so well. Behind his quiet exterior the real estate man was like a squirrel in a wheel. Disaster grinned at him with ghastly familiarity and harrowing care bestrode his brow.

Misfortune had had its roots in the new addition he had invested in heavily. His attempted boom had proved a failure a year before. Then, with Thurlowe Fosdick's sanction, he had played the cotton market without hedging, the bank carrying him. Cotton dropped and dropped, until the First National Bank lost twenty thousand dollars on him. And this was not the worst.

Beedle was the secretary and treasurer of the Mutual Home Savings and Loan Company, a local institution of which Fosdick was the president. The First National Bank wasn't the only loser in the cotton disaster; Mr. Beedle had placed too much faith in his judgment of the cotton market and there was now an alarming condition of the accounts of the building and loan company.

There were various details involving insurance, real estate mortgages, promises unfulfilled, the Mutual Home, the bank, Beedle's private affairs, and other items of consideration that would have taken an astute accountant, a detective and a squad of efficiency experts to unravel. In plain words, the summer John Hardy came home Mr. Beedle was badly involved in a financial morass, out of which he could not clearly see his way.

His colorless hair was fading another shade or two toward the hue of bleached straw and the sergeant of worry recruited line after line of wrinkles about his eyes, while he racked his brain and his ingenuity for a solution short of suicide. Despite all broken promises, despite his loss of credit and standing at the bank, if he could worry and bluff his way along until fall, he expected to win clear of his difficulties in the cotton which had ruined him the preceding year.

Beedle cherished his smug standing and his position too highly to abscond, default or embezzle. While admitting to himself that he was going in far deeper when the cotton market opened, he realized that he was going to recoup and pay back every penny, including the bank, or go to his grave. This thought became an obsession which transcended all else.

He was glad to sacrifice enough to send his family away so their chatter wouldn't annoy and distract him. What mattered a few hundred or a thousand dollars to a man involved for more than fifty thousand?

All might have worked out according to Beedle's expectations and hopes if Fosdick hadn't privately discovered the shortage on the loan company's books. Beedle found him going over the books one night when he had been forced to leave the banker in his office while going out for a time on other business.

This discovery was fraught with embarrassment for both of them. Fosdick smiled thinly, but he did not speak the words which would precipitate the secretary-treasurer's doom. For three days Beedle existed in a trembling anxiety while he awaited the falling of the blow.

He hadn't forced the question with Fosdick because there was the remote possibility that the banker had not seen the discrepancy. True, it wasn't like Wolf-face Fosdick to overlook anything like that, and why had he taken the notion to examine the Mutual Home books, anyhow?

Yet it wasn't like the cold-blooded banker to remain silent either. After the third day of anxiety which slowly ate out his moral fiber, Beedle succumbed to the strain. He sent an urgent message to a man to come to his office. Behind closed doors he faced Thomas Kimball.

"Well," demanded the younger man, "what's on your mind? Why send down to the factory for me?"

"Fosdick has found out about the Mutual Home accounts," replied Beedle hopelessly. "The blow-up has come."

"I haven't heard my father explode yet," commented Thomas cynically. "When did Fosdick learn of it? This morning?"

"Three days ago," groaned Beedle in despair.

"You're dreaming," replied Kimball promptly. "It doesn't take Fosdick that long to take up the matter with Sam Kimball."

"I don't know what's his idea, but I know he knows."

"All right," shrugged the other. "Suppose he does. Why call me up here to tell me about it?"

Beedle's expression was indecipherable. He fixed his pale eyes on the face of the other with as much contempt as he dared feel in his pleading anxiety.

"Because I want you to get for me thirty thousand dollars at once. I've got to have that balance of ten thousand you still owe on your losses with me and I want your share of this fall's investment to cover up the shortage in the Mutual Home. After this danger is past, you won't have to put up anything this fall for our cotton pool. I'll draw it all out of the loan company to—"

"You talk like a fish," interrupted Kimball. "Where do I get the thirty thousand? Where do I get the ten thousand, even? You lost the ten thousand I put up. I haven't a cent left. You don't know how hard it is to get money out of Sam Kimball."

"But, my God, I've got to have it or I'm ruined," cried Beedle feverishly. "You pledged me twenty thousand for last year's speculation, and you knew the risk we were taking in playing the market. I trusted you for the second ten thousand and carried your share with money borrowed from the Mutual Home. You've got to get that much to me before night. I haven't bothered you. I've been patient. But I've got to have the money now. I can't let you break any more promises."

"Where in hell am I going to get ten thousand dollars, you fool?" snarled the younger man uglily.

"Where?" Beedle's lip curled. "Don't spring that hard luck story about the tight fist of Stingy Sam on me. Get it where you got that first ten thousand you didn't dare invest yourself."

Tom Kimball recoiled and paled a trifle. He eyed the real estate man appraisingly.

"So," he responded coolly, "so you are threatening me?"

"I want my money," declared Beedle flatly. "Perhaps I can spread ten thousand over enough space to hide things for a time."

"I haven't got it, and I'm not going to falsify the books of my factory to furnish it to you."

"Then I'll take you with me in the smash," Beedle promised grimly.

Kimball sneered.

"How? What proof have you got that I didn't come by that money honestly?"

"I know that you stole it from your father out of the factory you are the head of," stated Beedle flatly.

"Prove it," snapped Kimball, smiling thinly.

Beedle collapsed. He ran his finger around the limp collar which was choking him. The faint rat-tat of a typewriter in the outer office sounded through the silence.

"Don't let's quarrel, Tom," he pleaded. "You'll inherit your father's money some day. I know how tight he is, and that you are not to blame for increasing your salary. But I'm facing the end. I've told you before how sorry I am that I misjudged the cotton market. But I'm going to make everything back this fall. I'm going to pay back the First National. I'm not a thief. My God! Aren't you going to help me?"

Kimball softened visibly.

"You're not a bad sort, Beedle," he said slowly. "And I'm damned sorry to hear of this fix. I never intended to beat you out of that ten thousand dollars—although you deserve to lose it for poor judgment. You should have been more careful with that damned nosy Fosdick. I'll see what I can do to help you, but it is impossible to do anything for several days."

"I can't wait," whispered Beedle hoarsely. "I'm done for if I don't cover things up. There's a meeting of the board of directors Friday afternoon—to-morrow, and Fosdick is going to demand an examination of my books."

"I can't help it. Stall off the accountants until next week. I *can't* do anything before then."

"Not even if your wife learned about the interest you have been showing in your stenographer?" Kimball's eyes narrowed.

"What do you mean?" he shot out.

"You know what I mean," replied Beedle deliberately. "I am not figuring on turning on you, but I know a few things that nobody else knows. I sold that place on Park Drive to—a certain young woman who works in your private office. I know that she couldn't have had enough money to buy it. And her father's a mechanic at the roundhouse. He couldn't have done it. And there are a few other items which I took pains to look into after making that unusual sale."

Kimball gripped the speaker by his fat neck. He shook him roughly but silently.

"If you dare breathe one word of what you think, Bill Beedle," he choked, "I'll kill you—understand? Kill you! There's a lot between that girl and me which goes back a long time before you stuck your thick nose into my business—before I even met my wife, and I'll not have you dragging it into public."

Beedle gurgled faintly. He wrenched the frenzied man's hands free.

"I have no intention of starting a public stink," he said, not without some dignity. "But you have betrayed me to the extent of ten thousand dollars and I've got to have help—now. I want you to comprehend the fact that I have acted a gentleman to you. It won't hurt you to know it."

Kimball drew back and bit his lip. A faint flush stained his face at the other's words. He clenched and unclenched his fists.

"I'm sorry, Beedle," he said haltingly. "But, God, I can't do anything right now. You don't know the state of my affairs. Stall off Fosdick and the board for a few days until we can think of some scheme."

Beedle slumped into his chair. He watched the other depart with dulled eyes. He had exhausted his only hope of succor. His name and reputation were facing annihilation. In this hour he knew the desperation of despair.

And the next morning had come the sudden death of Thurlowe Fosdick. It was an unbelievable respite, and Beedle, after recovering from the shock of the fact, breathed easily for the first time in days. All he needed now was time to recuperate his various losses. The only man who could have exposed him was dead. Mr. Beedle began to sleep again at night and to take more than a perfunctory interest in what he ate. The clouds of catastrophe began to lighten along the horizon of the future.

Until the *Morning Blade* came out with the peculiar facts John Hardy had unearthed surrounding the murder of the banker.

This occurred after weeks of comparative quietude, during which the guilt of Howard Wright was an accepted surmise despite the activities of the returned prodigal of turbulent character.

But now, William Beedle knew, everybody remotely connected with Fosdick would be examined for a possible motive. Now would the books of the Mutual Home Savings and Loan Company be gone over for a surety. This time there would be no respite. The danger, while not so imminent, was inadvertible.

Still in the grip of a hundred emotions, William Beedle went back over the front page article from headlines to conclusion and read it very carefully, anxious to absorb it all. And then, unbidden, a single statement stood out with such vividness as to blot out all his other worries. He read this simple little phrase over and over, while fear permeated his entire being:

Mr. Hardy concluded his dramatic and astounding
revelations to the prosecuting attorney with the

simple statement: "When you find the man who now has a golf ball marked with the name of Fosdick, or who has recently rid himself of it, you will have found the murderer of the president of the First National Bank."

A cold sweat broke out all over Beedle's pudgy body. The very walls of his office became suspecting eyes which stared at him suggestively. Why hadn't he taken the time to open this morning's paper at home instead of waiting until reaching his office? Now he didn't dare go back home until his regular time in the evening. If he did so, he knew a thousand eyes would follow him, everybody would wonder at his unusual behavior.

And while he stayed downtown and tried to carry on his business, his house stood alone and empty, an open invitation to the police to ransack it at will. Of course, he had locked the door and the windows were all kept locked while the family was away, but what was a broken lock or window to the police?

The day was one of agony to the real estate man. He had a vital reason for going home, but he didn't dare make a single step in that direction. Every time the phone rang he jumped and paled. He knew it was the chief of police calling him. Every time the office door opened he knew it was an officer with a warrant for his arrest. How he existed until six o'clock without collapsing Beedle never knew. His stenographer and bookkeeper both commented on his appearance and told him he was sick. They tried to get him to go home.

Sick! He was sick, sicker than he had ever been in his life. And go home? Good God! That's what he wanted to do more than anything else in the world. But he didn't dare. He didn't dare.

He couldn't eat supper at the restaurant; it choked him. He went to a picture show; he was too nervous to sit still. He was afraid to go home earlier than usual; that would excite comment. Yet, every minute was an eon of agony; he was impressing more people with his peculiar actions than he would have by going home. At nine o'clock he was unlocking his front door.

Locking it behind him, he raced toward the back bedroom closet where his golfing togs were kept. Like a starving dog that has been tossed a bone, he flung himself into the dark closet and clutched at a certain corner. He sobbed in relief as his fingers closed on the handle of his golf bag. Thank Heaven it was still here!

His relief was short lived. He remembered the interrogations of Terry Callahan concerning his movements that terrible Friday morning. That grim ex-policeman could never be shaken off the trail. His breath wheezed noisily through his nostrils as he hastily jerked down the window shades and then turned on the light. With fingers that could scarcely obey his will he unstrapped the golf ball pocket on the side of the bag and shook the contents out on the bed. Among half a dozen other balls rolled a Longflite.

Giving vent to a wordless exclamation he dropped the golf bag and snatched up the ball. As he turned it over the name "T. C. Fosdick" was revealed to him. He wilted from the relief. Flinging himself across the bed, he sobbed and groveled in delight. He was safe. He was safe!

After a space came a sobering thought. Now that this ball had not yet been found in his possession, how was he to get rid of the accursed thing? This renewed his fright. There was no place in the house where he dared hide the thing. He didn't know how to destroy it successfully. He knew that he would not dare carry the thing away with him in the morning and try to dispose of it. To go outside and throw it away was utterly out of the question. He couldn't toss it far enough to rid himself of suspicion, as none of his neighbors played golf.

He could go out to the back yard and drive it a hundred yards or so. He shuddered at the idea. That was how Fosdick met his death—driving the substitute for this very ball. He couldn't do it. Besides, some of the neighbors might see him.

Still this idea invoked another. He could go out into the yard in the dark. And in the dark he could bury this ball so deep that neither himself nor another would ever unearth it. The feasibility of this plan grew the longer he contemplated it. This was far better than trying to destroy this tough-skinned bit of gutta-percha or whatever the thing was made of.

Shrinking in terror from the dark he made his way down the stairs and let himself out the back door without lighting so much as a match, the damning golf ball in one pocket. Luckily he knew the exact contour of his back yard and the position of every tree and obstacle. He felt his way carefully to the little shed which contained his long-forgotten tools. He didn't remember whether the place was locked up or not. Every little sound he made was magnified by his terror.

He cursed himself now for not driving his car into the garage as usual, instead of leaving it out in front of the house. He wasn't disguising the fact that he was at home; in fact, he was calling particular attention to it. Had he driven into the garage he would have had an excuse to leave the car lights on for a moment while he searched for a spade. He failed to remember that this burial idea had come to him after he had found the golf ball safe.

He felt about in the dark for the spade he had used in former days to dig potatoes and to dig around the rosebushes. What if it were no longer here? His flesh crawled at this horrible thought just as his groping fingers encountered a familiar handle. He drew it forth and felt of the other end.

With a groan of disappointment he realized that it was a fork instead of the spade. He started to look further and then suddenly decided to use the implement he had without wasting more time. The garden spot was soft yet from the work of spring gardening; he could dig down for three or four feet without much effort.

He felt his way over to the plot of ground which dwindled in size each year and began digging vigorously. For a time no sound was heard save the soft click of the fork prongs as they met a fragment of glass or rock and the occasional grunt a particularly heavy forkful of dirt wrung from him. The sky was overcast. There was scarcely any light from the thin crescent of the new moon and the angry clouds blotted out the stars.

At last the hole was ready. With a sob of thankfulness he took the golf ball from his pocket and knelt to drop it into its grave.

There was a soft click, and Beedle found himself bathed in the round beam from a flash light. He cringed into a rigid pose, his face a mask of terror as a heavy hand fell upon his shoulder.

"I'll be takin' thot golf ball, if ye please," spoke the voice of Terry Callahan. "An' ye'll be comin' wid me."

CHAPTER XXII
A FUDGE RECIPE

LOVE, LIKE TAXES, being no respecter of time or person, struck John Hardy a stunning blow squarely over the heart when he least expected it and when he had the least time to devote to it. While there was little doubt in his mind from the first moment he had seen Zoe Ann in her little runabout besieged by two attorneys, that the future held something for him besides fighting to rejuvenate West Fork, he had expected it to await a sane and sober moment when other vital matters did not press.

He was astounded at its swiftness. One moment he and Zoe Ann were standing safely on that unromantic, prosaic plane he had taken pains to establish. The next minute—chaos. That's how it often happens. Like lightning.

Curled up like a lithe kitten in one corner of the big divan, Zoe Ann was opening the fussy package of candy Hardy had brought home. While lending an ear to the speech of Mr. Wright the younger man kept his eyes on the girl, delighting in the grace of her slender figure, in the play of expression on her features, in the clustering, wavy hair about her shapely head. Aware of a sudden silence, he spoke aloud:

"I never cared for the style of bobbed hair," he said, "but it is most becoming to Zoe Ann."

"I wasn't speaking of hair," commented Wright dryly. "I said that we have put the Henley Phord project over without a hitch. The Kimball forces are still under the impression that their Chamber of Commerce has choked it off."

Zoe Ann looked up and flashed a smile at Hardy for his compliment.

"You mean that assembling plant deal, papa?" she asked.

Wright chuckled. He nodded.

"Yes, my dear. We've been communicating privately with the Phord people ever since Presley got wind of their offer to the Chamber of Commerce here. We simply couldn't let that project get away from West Fork. And you know how quickly Kimball would have throttled the idea because of the much higher wage scale Phord would cause. Well, your man, Fabryne, who is acquiring that Elm and Birch Street property for your enlarged business district, has done a little work for me. He secured an option on that factory site across the tracks from the Bed and Bedding Company, and one of Phord's big men arrives to-morrow to conclude the deal with us. It is costing us about fifty thousand all told, John."

"It is worth it," Hardy replied. "We'll get it back."

Wright selected a fresh cigar, declining any of the opened box of candy his daughter proffered.

"Yes," he said, "we will. Presley told me to-day that his attack against the Kimball gang is renewed the first of next week."

"I'm ready for the fireworks," commented Hardy, accepting a bit of confection. "Are you? Thank you, Zoe Ann."

"And waiting," Wright replied. "Have you heard anything from Callahan since that story came out this morning?"

"Not a word," admitted Hardy. "He—ouch! That nearly broke my tooth. I hope you like hard centers, Zoe Ann. That's the only kind of candy that one can buy in the summer time and be safe. I hate 'em myself."

"You do? I never would have suspected you of being a softy," she said mischievously.

"You wouldn't?" he scowled ferociously. "Don't I look it?"

She shivered deliciously.

"Don't look at me like that. That's how you looked the first time I saw you. I was almost frightened to death."

"I took him for a ruffian at first myself," remarked her father.

Hardy laughed as he dropped the remainder of his candy into the ash-tray.

"And now I've gone and ruined my reputation with one little piece of candy," he lamented.

"No, you haven't," the girl responded, rising to her feet. "I'll confide a secret to you too. I like creamy chocolates the best myself. Come on, let's go make some fudge. I have the dearest recipe."

"Not on my account, please," protested Hardy. "I am sorry about that box of candy. I'll do better this winter, really. In fact we'll order an express shipment right away if you like."

"No, indeed. And I do appreciate this box. But fudge is better in hot weather. Come on," she urged.

"Will you excuse us, Mr. Wright? I see I'm to take a lesson in candy-making."

In the spick-and-span kitchen Zoe Ann tied a neat little apron about her waist and rummaged around for a larger one of Margaret's for her companion. This starched linen badge of the kitchen Hardy slipped clumsily over his head and stood docilely, while she reached around his waist to tie the strings in the back.

"Now what do we do?" he demanded helplessly.

"As I measure out four cups of sugar and four big tablespoon-fuls of cocoa in this stew pan, you mix them together," she commanded, bringing the utensils and supplies into sight from nowhere. "And be sure to get all the lumps out of the cocoa," she admonished severely.

Obediently he set to work with a big spoon, watching her with his eyes as she deftly opened a can of condensed milk and mixed it with the same amount of water.

"Are you ready?" she smiled. "Two cups of milk."

He looked down at the stew pan and stirred furiously.

"All set," he announced.

"Stir carefully," she said as she added the liquid. "And a pinch of salt. I nearly forgot that."

This item she added with that supremely careless gesture of the cook who is sure of herself, and then lighted the fire on the stove.

"You keep all kinds of recipes in your head?" he marveled.

"Of course, silly," she laughed.

"And you never get 'em mixed up?"

"Certainly not. Come here and place that vessel on the fire. And continue to stir it slowly without stopping an instant until it begins to boil."

"Good gracious!" he groaned nervously. "How will I know just when to quit?"

"When I tell you," she answered, wrinkling her nose at his comically dismal face. "I shall stand right here and watch. Did you think I was going to desert you?"

He sighed in relief and proceeded to stir.

"A stove is mighty hot in the summer time, isn't it?" he offered as he began to feel the heat.

"A woman has to stand it even in the heat of the day," she reminded him, bringing him a stool to sit on.

Men, thanks to centuries of training in other fields, are generally helpless in the kitchen. John Hardy seemed especially so. He was completely under her dominance, not at all like the crisp, hard-fighting man she had known heretofore, and Zoe Ann thrilled at the thought that, here, she was master and he was humble apprentice. For the first time since she had known him he appeared like a big, helpless boy, and she loved him for it.

Her natural pride at his awe and her truly feminine emotion were of brief duration.

"It's beginning to bubble around the edges," he exclaimed suddenly.

She halted the spoon by laying her fingers on his wrist. Without releasing him she leaned over under his nose and peered through the rising spirals of steam at the dark mass below, a dainty flower that swayed lightly before him. A shock swept through Hardy. He almost trembled at her nearness, at her beauty, and the clustered ringlets of saucy but beautiful hair.

"All right," she said, drawing back. "It is beginning to boil. You may stop stirring. If you kept on you would probably turn it back into sugar. While it is boiling you can crack some pecans to go into it. One cupful of the meats. Here, I'll show you."

The nut cracker was properly fastened to the kitchen table and with two pans before him, one full of pecans and the other empty, Hardy set to his new task. After dropping a bit of the boiling candy into a cup of water to test its consistency, Zoe Ann sat at the side of the table with a measuring cup and began picking out the meats of the nuts.

Their fingers touched more than once at this work, affecting them both strangely. Zoe Ann, being one of those rare girls who could lapse into silence and yet increase her charm, became speechless. There was no noise in the room save for the crack-crack of pecan shells and the faint bubbling from the stove. The silence and her closeness troubled Hardy. He endured it as long as he could and then spoke.

"So you remember all kinds of recipes for candies and salads and other things? And I suppose you like to make them?"

"Yes, I do," she said, still conscious of her superiority.

"Well, that's mighty nice. And I know that women love delicate, dainty things to eat. But let me tell you something, young lady—don't make a practice of serving such foods to your husband. He'll enjoy it once in a great while, but not often. Imagine a hungry man coming home to supper to find a lettuce or a cucumber sandwich of tiny proportions and a slice of pineapple with a bit of grated cheese on it. Ugh!"

This was a let-down. She almost gasped at the fervor of his words. Engaged in the surer occupation of cracking pecans he had ceased to be so helpless. She was almost sorry she had put him at this task.

"I'll have you understand that I can prepare other foods, sir," she returned loftily.

"So can I," he came back easily. "One doesn't live on a ranch without a cook unless he learns how to feed himself."

This was interesting. Zoe Ann forgot her pique. "What can you cook?" she challenged.

"Biscuits, pancakes, potatoes in any fashion, eggs, vegetables, meats—and I have made pies."

"Well!" she gasped. "You are accomplished; aren't you? And I thought you were so helpless you couldn't break an egg in a skillet."

"I am helpless in a spotless kitchen," he admitted. "I'd be scared to death here."

She sprang up to test the contents of the stew pan again.

"It's ready to take off the fire," she announced, turning out the flame.

"How can you tell?"

"When it will form a soft ball in the water that you can pick up in one mass without it sticking to your fingers," she replied, filling a dish pan with water and setting the stew pan therein to cool. "Now, a teaspoonful of vanilla flavoring and a heaping tablespoon of butter, and then we wait until it cools."

She added these two items and then came back to help him with the pecans.

"Tell me about your ranch life," she said.

"There's little to tell that is of interest," he replied. "The romance of the old cattle days can be found now only in the novels of Zane Grey, Mulford, Friend, and such romancers of the old West. To-day cow-punchers go to work in flivvers. Everything is fenced, sheep have crowded cattle, and settlers have crowded them both.

"The cattle are migrating to old Mexico. And recently they started a drive in Montana to round up and slaughter the bands of wild horses, the beloved mustangs of the range rider, because they graze on pasturage which can be used to feed sheep. Think of it! Sheep!"

"Oh, that's awful to think about, isn't it?" she shuddered. "Isn't there some way to prevent it?"

"How? Why? The cayuse, the horse has outlived his usefulness. He must pass on like the Indian, the buffalo, the frontiersman."

Tears filled the girl's eyes at the thought. The cup of pecan meats was filled and forgotten, the cooling chocolate might as well have been at the North Pole.

"But there a few glories of the rangeland that we won't live to see effaced," Hardy hastened on comfortingly. "We won't live to see civilization conquer the mountains. There was one point on my ranch where I could stand and count seven ranges of hills, one beyond the other in varying hues of blue. And the vast stretches of desert upon which lays the purple haze, which hovers and seems to rise and fall like a soft blanket lifted from the ground by the wind. One can peer off into the purple mysteries of such painted deserts and see images, pictures, and mirages which let the imagination run riot."

Zoe Ann had clasped her hands on the table, careless of the fragments of nutshells which pressed a network of designs in her soft flesh. She was leaning across the corner of the table, lips faintly parted, eyes fixed on the man's face, literally drinking in the description he was offering.

"And the nights," Hardy went on. "The nights, Zoe Ann. Out on the silvery desert under the stars you are alone and yet how much closer to the Infinite. The mournful howl of a dog or perhaps a coyote, the bawl of an uneasy or lost yearling, the creeping chill of the night—for it gets cold at night on the desert. And the stars are not the faint, twinkling, uncertain little things you see in the sky here. They are bright and scintillating bodies which shine like great jewels strewn by a lavish hand upon the sable robe of the heavens. They give you something to think about. And the thoughts one has! I have lain out there, rolled up in my blanket, and stared up into the limitless space begemmed with those far-flung suns and—"

He happened to look into her eyes. What he saw startled him so that he could not go on. She was gazing at him with her very soul in her wide, dark eyes. The faint mist of fancy veiled and yet revealed the depths of her heart. Hardy fancied he was looking into the fathomless spaces of the sky he was describing. He was drawn completely out of himself. An indefinable wave of tenderness engulfed him. Before he realized fully his action his lips were pressed against hers.

There was a delicious instant before she drew back and tried to look at him. The vision was still in her eyes. They both rose to their feet. Hardy was trembling in actuality now. He extended one hand in a groping, half-blinded manner. Whether it was a gesture of apology or an appeal neither of them ever knew. They lost contact with their surroundings and with time.

At length she stirred in his arms and laughed tremulously. There were tears of happiness on her long lashes.

"I knew that love would come," she whispered. "But I didn't know when."

"Love," he murmured uncertainly, striving to regain his seat of calm reasoning. "I reckon I've loved you from the minute I first saw you and didn't have sense enough to know it."

"I—I was sure that night when you burst into Mr. Brentwood's office," she said.

"Love," he said. "What a trite, hackneyed word to express the wonderful emotion I am experiencing. Little girl, I—I feel like lying on the floor and letting you walk all over me with your slim little feet."

"How ridiculous!" she smiled. "I'd rather kiss you— Oh! The fudge!" she exclaimed in dismay.

"Ah, yes, the fudge," he sighed, relaxing his embrace.

They examined the contents of the stew pan.

"Quick!" Zoe Ann directed. "It's cool. Take your spoon and beat it for dear life."

"Beat it? Do I have to do more work on that stuff? I thought it was finished."

"Beating it and whipping air into it is what makes it luscious and creamy," she replied. "Hurry, while I grease a big pan to pour it in."

Hardy bent himself to the task of beating the candy. Gradually it changed from dark to lighter brown, becoming heavier with each turn of the spoon. Zoe Ann poured in the cup of pecan meats. As she leaned toward him Hardy bent forward for a kiss. She granted him a quick little peck of the mouth.

"Out with it into the pan," she cried. "It's turning. Hurry, because it sets almost instantly when it starts to harden."

Hardy obligingly upended the stew pan and raked out the thickened contents while Zoe Ann spread it deftly over the buttered surface of the flat pan with a knife. Hardy discovered that she knew whereof she spoke, and he had to work in frenzied haste to get the candy out of the stewer. At length it was safely accomplished, He stood by and watched her tenderly while she moistened her knife and cut the confection into symmetrical squares.

"Now," she said at last.

"Now," he murmured, slipping an arm about her.

Again time was not. The world stood still while two hearts thrilled and yet ached in that fierce yearning tenderness which comes but once, and then only in the heyday of youth.

"Ahem!" coughed Howard Wright from the doorway.

Slowly the lovers turned to face him.

"Fudge!" said John regretfully.

"Fudge, papa?" said Zoe Ann, reaching for the pan of the finished product.

Her father shook his head with a smile.

John Hardy took his courage in both hands.

"Mr. Wright," said he, "I never was good at making speeches, but I'll be wanting to talk to you after we've taken the kinks out of West Fork. Then I'll want to ask you something."

"About fudge?" inquired the other, lifting a quizzical eyebrow.

"Er—exactly," nodded John Hardy.

"I'll listen," promised Wright. "Now, if I might interrupt this fudge business for a moment, I'd like to say that Terry Callahan is waiting in the library with a prisoner for us to examine."

CHAPTER XXIII
A PRIVATE THIRD DEGREE

FOR A MAN CAUGHT RED-HANDED disposing of criminal evidence, William Beedle proved a most docile prisoner. He submitted to Callahan and accompanied him to the Wright home without a word of explanation or protest. Callahan desisted in his questioning, thinking the other's silence to be the stubbornness of a trapped criminal. However, this was not the case; it was the sheer paralysis of terror.

The terrible blow had fallen. The shaft of horror which he had been dodging all day long had at last transfixed him. Beedle was no longer a thinking entity. His thought processes had congealed at their source. He was a mere shell of a man.

Without being aware of the fact, he had walked all the way from his home to the Wright dwelling in company with his captor. He had been ushered in by the head of the house himself and led to the library. He had collapsed leadenly into a big armchair without hearing the murmured words between Callahan and Wright.

While the latter withdrew in search of John Hardy and Callahan seated himself on the long divan opposite Beedle, the real estate man's mind dumbly revolved about the one fact that he was standing in the shadow of the scaffold.

Callahan almost started when he broke his silence.

"Where are we?" he asked huskily.

"At th' Wright home," responded Callahan in surprise.

"Why have you brought me here instead of the jail?"

"So ye can explain yer actions to John Hardy," was the grim response.

"John Hardy? Then this is not an arrest? John Hardy has nothing to do with the law here."

"Don't kid yerself, my b'y. I've thot which even Brentwood can't twist onto Mr. Wright now. I'm givin' ye th' chance to talk first to one who'll listen—if ye have anythin' to say."

Beedle shuddered convulsively and passed one soiled hand across his wet forehead, leaving a streak of dirt from his garden there. He lapsed again into a sort of coma before the others came in. Terry Callahan arose and stood at attention. When Hardy spoke he was the only one to answer; Beedle did not stir.

Hardy contemplated the seated man with attention. It was more or less like the phantasmagoria of a nightmare for him to have a prominent citizen of West Fork crushed and broken before him in the home of Howard Wright, to realize the deadly seriousness of the situation, and yet to have just come from the paradise he had found in the kitchen and which, as he glanced at Zoe Ann, seemed hardly more than a dream. It was all unreal. He frowned at Callahan as he tried to rid himself of this feeling. Now was no time for love; he must return to that practical plane of hard, keen thinking.

Callahan had brought this man here because it was a matter of the greatest importance that he be interrogated. As it probably meant life or death to Howard Wright it was perfectly obvious that neither father nor daughter was calm enough to take charge of the interview. So Hardy frowned at Callahan while he strove to collect himself.

"Well, Terry," he asked at length, "why have you brought Mr. Beedle here?"

Callahan produced the damning golf ball from his pocket and extended it. He dropped it into Hardy's outstretched palm.

"Shure an' I've brought him here to explain where he got this golf ball an' why he was tryin' to bury it to-night in his garden."

One glance at the golf ball was enough to clear Hardy's head of the mist. As Wright sprang forward he held up a restraining hand.

"Just a minute," he said softly. "This might mean much and then it might mean very little. Do you feel strong enough to stand the disclosure either way?"

"Yes, yes," snorted Wright impatiently. "What was that ball Callahan gave you?"

"I think," said Hardy, "that is the missing golf ball of the murdered banker."

The girl's face went white and she stared at the real estate man in horror, while her father put his arm about her, reaching forth his other hand for the tiny sphere.

"Tell us about it, Terry," Hardy said, turning back to Callahan.

"I've had me hands full watchin' both suspects today, since th' facts about thot golf ball came out in this morning's paper. I've had Jake Bowles helpin' me wid th' pair o' them. We been switchin' men off an on all day so they wouldn't get suspicious o' seein' th' same man every time they happened to see us. But it became apparent thot Beedle was th' most nervous o' the two, so I shadowed him from supper on. An' just awhile ago he went home an' tried to bury thot ball in his garden. I was waitin' for him, so I just brought him on over here for a little talk before I take him to jail."

Beedle's dulled eyes lifted to Callahan's face as the latter made his explanation. The dull expression slowly gave way before the sharper look of reawakened fear. He started when Hardy spoke to him.

"Mr. Beedle," Hardy said in a hard, level voice, "I guess you realize fully what this means."

Beedle did not answer. He dropped his eyes to the carpet.

"And because it took the hint that possession of such a golf ball would prove dangerous, to frighten you into trying to rid yourself of it, there is no question of your criminal complicity. Have you anything to say? Are you guilty alone? Or do you wish to make a statement against your confederate?"

"Oh, my God!" burst forth from the agonized man's lips. "I am not guilty of murder. I swear it, I swear it."

"But you knew of it," pursued Hardy. "You are guilty of being an accessory—"

"No, no, no," declared Beedle wildly. "Tom Kimball had nothing to do with it, either. I know that he wouldn't have done it—for me."

"*Tom Kimball?*" ejaculated Wright in stark amazement.

"Callahan said he'd been shadowing both of us," replied Beedle wearily. "He couldn't have found anything on Kimball. We—"

"Why, Callahan," cried Wright, "what's all this? I thought it was young Morris you—"

"Hush!" silenced Hardy crisply. "What do you mean, Mr. Beedle, that Kimball wouldn't do it for you?"

"I guess you'll find out everything you don't know already," responded the real estate dealer dully. "Kimball wouldn't have done it after I appealed to him for help, because no one would have been ruined if Fosdick exposed the book accounts of the Mutual Home Company except me."

"Why did you appeal to him for help?" demanded Hardy. "I knew that you were involved."

"Why? Because he owed me money on a cotton speculation we had made together," replied Beedle petulantly, never realizing the fact that he had given them an entirely unknown clew in his mention of Thomas Kimball.

"You say he owed you money? If you do not think him guilty explain how you come to feel so guilty yourself."

"That—that golf ball," Beedle managed to gurgle. "I was afraid to have it found in my possession."

"Doubtless," agreed Hardy dryly. "Yet, how did it come to be in your possession?"

"I was playing golf with Charles Morris the Thursday afternoon before the murder," the man gasped out. "We lost Morris's ball somewhere in the woods between the fifth and sixth holes and we tramped around there looking for it. We couldn't find it, but I found this ball Fosdick probably lost a day or so before that. He sometimes drove over into the rough."

"You claim to have found this ball in the woods near the spot of the murder the day before Fosdick was killed?"

"I did, I did," chattered Beedle. "Of course, I kept it—every one keeps the balls they find on the course. I put it in my golf bag and forgot all about it until I read that story in the *Blade* this morning. Then I knew I was in terrible danger, as this ball would be taken for the one the murderer picked up the next morning. I knew I would be the logical suspect if Wright were not guilty, because my affairs have become tangled up and Fosdick was the only man who could have exposed me. And then Callahan had already been around to ask me about my movements that Friday morning. So I tried to bury the ball to get rid of it."

"Do you know why Callahan inquired about your movements?" Hardy asked keenly, peering into the tortured man's face.

Beedle dumbly shook his head.

"Because your golfing shoes are exactly the size and shape to fit those footprints found by Brentwood's detectives in the woods, those footprints laid by the prosecution on the murderer."

Beedle actually groveled in his chair.

"Oh, my God!" he groaned in anguish. "And those footprints are really mine. I didn't know that. I guess I'm done for."

Hardy straightened up, satisfied with the reaction the other had shown in response to his statement.

"If you make a clean breast of it, you may not be done for. Those footprints also fit Charlie Morris. Don't you know that you two have the same kind of golfing shoes, and that they are the same size?"

"I didn't know they were the same size," denied Beedle, shaking his head. "I— But you can't lay this deed on Charlie. He was out there with me Thursday afternoon. He made his share of the footprints then the same as I did."

"Shure, an' I've th' proof thot ye was there by th' bits of soil from off yer shoes," remarked Callahan. "But we're wantin' to know was ye there Thursday afternoon or Friday morning?"

The real estate man's eyes were growing bloodshot from the strain and pressure.

"If you know all that you are telling me about my movements," he cried, "you know that I am telling the truth, that I was there Thursday and not Friday. I told you some time ago that I was at home and in bed Friday morning until eight o'clock. I was, I was, God knows I was. Go ask Charlie. He'll tell you the truth. He'll tell you that we were out there Friday—I mean Thursday morning—Thursday afternoon—*Thursday afternoon*," he shouted wildly.

"Before God I am innocent. I don't know anything about the murder at all. Howard Wright is the guilty man if anybody is. Oh, God—"

"Here! Control yourself," commanded Hardy, gripping the man's shoulders and shaking him roughly. "Come out of the hysteria. You are not yet convicted of the murder. If you are really innocent, you must retain your grip on yourself and help us. Come, tell me exactly the state of your affairs."

With an effort Beedle composed himself and flung himself back in his chair exhausted. In a calmer voice he went into the details of his business and, under the skillful questioning of Hardy, laid bare the facts around his connection with Thomas Kimball.

"As God is my judge," he finished earnestly, "I don't know who is guilty. I swear that I truly believed Howard Wright the man."

"Believed?" interposed Wright himself at this point. "And that being the case, what has caused you to change your mind now?"

Beedle looked up, his face a mixture of fear and pity.

"Because of my own predicament now," he answered huskily. "I guess I look guilty in the eyes of every one of you because of the evidence you have against me, but I am innocent. I can see how it is to be possibly innocent and yet be condemned."

"You spoke of Thomas Kimball's affairs," went on Hardy. "You say you threatened to take him to ruin with you if he did not protect you with money?"

"That was just talk. I was desperate," Beedle replied.

"All that may be," admitted Hardy, "but if you succeeded in frightening him enough, he may have done the deed."

"How could I frighten him with the threat that I would tell he had stolen money from his father? I couldn't prove it."

"No, but you would have caused old man Kimball to investigate. Are you sure you don't know something more damaging to Kimball than the suspicion that he is robbing his father? What was that you started to tell about a real estate deal on Park Drive?"

Into Beedle's eyes came a look of such profound question that the others were surprised. He opened his mouth to speak and then closed it, shaking his head.

"There was nothing to that," he declared firmly. "If that had really worried Tom to the point of committing murder, it would have been me and not Fosdick he would have killed."

"Nevertheless, let's have that story, if you please," commanded Hardy.

Beedle obstinately shook his head.

"Very well," commented Hardy. "You needn't tell us that which might throw light on a dark mystery; you can just go ahead and stand trial for the murder."

The real estate man broke down again at this purposely callous reminder. He glanced from one to the other like a trapped wild thing. Zoe Ann couldn't stand to watch; she turned her head aside and bit her lips.

"Don't torture him, John," she whispered to Hardy. "Please, dear."

"It's his life, or his knowledge against your father's life," responded her lover harshly. "I have no mercy for him."

Tears filled the girl's eyes. It was hard to believe this was the same man who had professed his love for her in the kitchen. And yet, she desisted. She knew he was right.

In the end Beedle told everything he knew. When John Hardy had squeezed him dry of all information he possessed about Thomas Kimball's expensive amours and Charlie Morris's expensive liquor parties, the man was limp and completely exhausted, although still feebly protesting his own innocence.

"Now then, Mr. Beedle," stated the inquisitor, "you have by no means cleared your skirts of this crime, but I'm going to be kinder to you than the law was to Mr. Wright. I'm going to release you without arrest, while we investigate the other men in this case. Before you go, you will sit at this table and write out the statement that Callahan caught you attempting to bury this golf ball which you will designate by accurate description.

"Sign the statement and then swear to keep what has passed here to-night a complete secret. I don't think there is any danger of you talking, but you might. And if you do say anything to either Morris or Tom Kimball, you will find yourself in a very unenviable position. Is this clear?"

Beedle nodded hesitatingly.

"You mean that you will let me go free on my own recognizance?" he asked unbelievingly.

"Exactly—because I believe your story. However, if you make one move to leave West Fork, you will be immediately arrested for the murder of Thurlowe Fosdick."

The real estate man's gratitude was pitiful. He cried like a woman and begged them to keep the condition of his affairs quiet for the present.

"If you are innocent of any complicity in this Fosdick affair," Hardy promised, "I may find a way to help you get your business straight."

After they finally got rid of Beedle, they paused to consider this latest strange development.

"D'ye think ye was wise in this move, Johnny?" questioned Callahan doubtfully. "I'd have been afraid to let thot lad Beedle go."

"It was the only thing we could do under the circumstances, Terry," Hardy hastened to explain. "I think the fellow is innocent of the crime, don't you?"

"Oh, I'm sure of that," Zoe Ann was the first to say. "I just knew he was telling the truth. Didn't you, Papa? Oh, it was awful to watch him break like that—a well-known citizen like him. Besides, his hysteria was to real to be feigned, and he got mixed up once on Thursday and Friday like an innocent man probably would."

"I reached the same conclusion," stated Hardy thoughtfully. "And that's exactly why I took the chance of letting him go. If Terry had taken him to jail, they would have turned him loose in the morning, anyhow. And because we didn't send him there, we have the advantage of knowing a few things and suspecting a few more that Brentwood doesn't even dream about."

"John, John," cried Wright, his eyes shining, "I see what you are doing. Without letting Brentwood learn of it so he might be able to spoil things, you have Beedle as an unsuspected witness to prove that I didn't make those footprints in the woods. I know that."

Hardy nodded.

"At last, thanks to Terry, we'll spike that gun of the prosecution and convert the footprint clews to our advantage after all."

"And you suspect?" asked Zoe Ann earnestly.

"That Beedle being innocent, the roots of this mystery strike closer to home than Brentwood dreams. And to-morrow morning we'll have two keen detectives here who will investigate Thomas Kimball among others."

CHAPTER XXIV
MR. KIMBALL'S BAD DAY

THE THOUGHT PROCESSES which lit up, or, rather, darkened, the gloomy caverns of Sam Kimball's mind were open to the analysis of no one. What impulses moved him were unknown, if impulses played any part in his hard life. His business deals, his secrets, his mind were his own. In effect, he was a combination steam roller and spider.

Those persons and circumstances he could not bend to his wishes he ruthlessly crushed; those unfortunates he could control he sucked as dry of all that was valuable to him, as a spider would a fly. Down through the years he had left many a dried and shriveled victim dangling in his web exactly as the said araneidan leaves the husk of the hapless insect.

What philosophy he had evolved out of his seventy-odd years of life, what joy he found in living, what real purpose he had accomplished were matters of mystery. Without doubt his own children's estimate of his negligible worth came perilously close to the truth. And yet, mentally, he was so weirdly accoutered that he actually believed his sanctimonious mien entitled him to the mantle of high immortality.

Seventy years of past and present misendeavor set aside and discounted by the smug complacency of thought. Strange thing the conscience of man! Simple and yet ponderous the ego of Sam Kimball!

It was the Monday morning just two days before the beginning of the trial of Howard Wright for murder that he seated himself, the original autocrat of the breakfast table, and glanced at the faces of his two sons at right and left and the timid countenance of his daughter-in-law at the foot of the table. He granted them a frosty good morning smile and bowed his head.

The three subjects of this domestic sovereignty silently did likewise. While the butler stood motionless at the buffet with downcast head the voice of Sam Kimball rose and fell in musical cadences as he murmured a lengthy grace calculated to propitiate his God for the sins of the forthcoming twelve hours and to please the ears of Mr. Kimball himself.

"Thomas has informed me that you would like to go to the mountains for a month, Ruth," he spoke to the young woman opposite him as the servant began serving the cantaloupe. "In view of the hot weather and the recent sad bereavement in our family I think it a very good suggestion, providing you remain more or less in the proper seclusion. Why don't you go?"

Another day was started in the Kimball ménage and it bade fair to prove good weather. The tempo of his majesty being established, the younger people relaxed in thankful relief and small talk ensued, which was more or less general, until Sam Kimball unfolded the morning paper the butler brought him with his second cup of coffee.

Sam Kimball had continued to take the *Morning Blade* for the very good reason of keeping an eye on the activities of his enemies. Aside from the agitated conference held with his maligned associates that unforgettable Sunday when Hardy had refused to relinquish his newly-acquired paper, Kimball had set some of his favorite machinery in motion. Among the thousands of factory workers, laborers, small merchants, and house tenants, he had been able to lop off a cool five thousand in circulation for the *Blade*.

Five thousand subscribers at seven dollars a year hit the morning paper for thirty-five thousand dollars, not to mention its greatly reduced value as an advertising medium for local and foreign firms. Thus, the lone subscription of Sam Kimball would not help the *Blade* one whit. Furthermore, forbidding a certain thing to one's employees and denying oneself were two distinct propositions.

This enormous drop in circulation had certainly had a sobering effect on the *Morning Blade*. Combined with his anxiety over the predicament of Howard Wright, it was apparent that young Hardy would think mighty seriously before making another move against Sam Kimball.

True, the *Blade* had developed into a daily paper which put the *Planet* to shame. There was no doubt that Presley was a good news-paperman. But why should Hardy's opponents fight the *Blade* with a heavy expense to themselves, owners of the *Planet?* Let Hardy go broke pouring his money into the morning paper; nobody un-der the control of Sam Kimball dared buy it. To keep up with the news of the day they had to take the *Planet*. It was the perfect little waiting game of the spider and the fly.

These pleasing ruminations filtered through Mr. Kimball's mind this morning as he unfolded his copy of the *Blade*. He knew the game with all of its ramifications; the role of the spider fitted him ide-ally. But Mr. Kimball had never before enmeshed a gilded gadfly.

He could hardly believe his eyes as he read the first headline. After several weeks of quiescence—this! Inarticulate gurglings bubbled up into his throat, the black distillation of vicious rage which lusts to injure and destroy rose in his heart. The paper be-gan to tremble in his hands. The wind had changed; storm clouds were gathering fast.

The *Blade* had burst forth in a recrudescence of vitriol which was appalling. This time the attack was concentrated; it was the beginning of a direct, smashing campaign. This was not an ordi-nary taunt or a deluge of nasty mud-slinging. The seriousness, the very tone of the articles cried aloud that it was an appeal to the people to rebel against the crooked manipulations of the men who throttled the town.

On the front page was a four-column cut, a picture of the can-celed notes the First National Bank had held against Howard Wright. Below was a full explanation of the bank's attempt to steal the paper. It was a clear, scathing account which spared nothing. It was called the first of a series of articles promised long ago. An article a day was to be the program. To-morrow's paper would give the details of the ruin of David Hardy, former contractor. The truth was to be told.

Parallel with this was a two-column cut, the photograph of Major Sims. It was a fine likeness of the gentleman in question. In fact it was the only fine thing Kimball could see about the matter. This was headed: "Lives of West Fork Leaders." The story accompanying the cut bared the major's life of a number of intimate details which would have put an ordinary footpad to blush. It was an exposé of the principal frauds Major Sims had perpetrated in and on West Fork, giving cold, hard facts and figures.

The subject of to-morrow's story was to be Frederick Clinton, the present mayor of West Fork and faithful satellite of Samuel Kimball.

These were no veiled insinuations, no ordinary innuendoes which could be torn apart or waved aside. They were accounts from the pen of a writer who knew he had the proofs. And Mr. Kimball knew that the proofs could be produced in court. He found his own name in both articles linked with private details which no one in the world, aside from the principals, was supposed to know. This spelled disaster unless Hardy was stopped and stopped immediately.

Bang! At last the explosion came. Sam's horny fist crashed down on the table with such a harsh suddenness that his relatives jumped. He was not looking when he smote the spread before him with the hard gavel nature had given him, and his heavy fist descended upon the unoffending second cup of coffee. The china shivered into fragments and, fortunately, did not injure his hand. But the warm liquid splashed over every one and ran onto Kimball's lap. This did not tend toward soothing his temper.

He snarled furiously as he sprang up, overturning his chair. He ripped the newspaper in two with a violent gesture. Bang! He smote the table a mightier blow, this time selecting the spot where he struck with more care.

"Get Brentwood on the phone!" he roared at the semicircle of startled faces before him.

"What's up?" queried Robert, wiping drops of coffee from his hand.

"What is wrong, Father?" asked Ruth Kimball timidly. "Has something—somebody—"

"Call Brentwood!" reiterated Sam madly. "Tell him to meet me at the main offices right away. Move! Don't sit there and stare at me when I speak."

Thomas flashed a glance at the torn newspaper and hurried to the phone.

"But what—" began Robert, rising to his feet.

"Shut up and get your hat," growled his father as he stamped out of the room in high passion.

Robert picked up the discarded paper and pieced it together to solve the mystery. He whistled softly and glanced at his sister-in-law. He caught a glimpse of an item at the bottom of the page.

"Great guns!" he muttered. "This fellow Hardy and Presley are at it again. No wonder the old man went up in the air. Read this."

"Come on!" bellowed the raucous voice of his father. And Robert fled, leaving Ruth Kimball and the butler facing each other uneasily in the dining room.

As the Kimball car sped down the length of Wilson Avenue with a fine disregard for traffic regulations a huge canvas sign before a building undergoing remodeling caught the old man's eye.

"What's that?" he said sharply. "West Fork National Bank to occupy that building?"

"There was an item at the bottom of the front page of the paper," replied Robert mildly, turning to speak to his father, after glancing at the face of his furiously driving brother. "I guess you missed it in reading that other dope."

Thomas swung off Wilson Avenue to Birch Street, at the foot of which lay a network of railroad tracks and the main offices of the five factories Sam Kimball owned outright. They passed a cleared piece of ground where plans for deep excavation were already under way.

"Who's going to build there?" grunted Sam Kimball aloud.

The younger men shook their heads.

They found Cyrus Brentwood awaiting them at the offices of his father-in-law. The old man plunged into the matter which obsessed him without preamble.

"Have you seen this morning's paper?" he shouted before they could crowd into his private office.

"Yes, sir," nodded Brentwood, motioning to Robert to close the door. "I was on the verge of calling you when Tom rang up. That First National Bank article, of course, is designed to build up public sentiment in favor of Wright, whose trial begins day after to-morrow."

"Public sentiment be damned!" howled Kimball, banging his desk viciously. "Your job is to get the circuit judge, the Federal judge, the Municipal judge, the City attorney, and every other official and lawyer you need to tie Hardy up right now. D'ye hear?"

"I hear you, sir, but not so loud. Your office force will be listening. Now, you want—"

"Damn the office force!" Sam roared lustily. "They work for me, don't they? You get busy! You've loafed on this matter long enough."

Brentwood's lean jaws tightened.

"You are hardly just to me this morning, Mr. Kimball," he stated succinctly. "Nevertheless, I will do as you say. You want suit instituted for libel and—"

"I do not," thundered the old man. "That takes time to prove or disprove. I want that paper stopped—put out of business. And I want it done quick."

"I don't quite see how we can do such a thing at once," confessed Brentwood thoughtfully. "I was in favor of starting legal action some time ago and you held off. Such things can't be handled in a minute. Now—"

"That's your worry," ripped out his father-in-law. "I don't care a damn how you do it, but stop his press if you have to blow up his plant. Silence him, understand? Now get out and do it!"

Brentwood departed without a word more. Kimball glared at his sons.

"Go to work," he bellowed at them. "Whose idea was it for you to come trailing into my office?"

"Yours," responded Robert calmly.

"Get out! Go to your own factory divisions. I don't pay you to sit around this office."

The two brothers departed in company. Kimball viciously punched a button at his desk. A white-faced secretary came into the room at a run.

"Yes, sir? You rang, Mr. Kimball?"

"I did. What's this business about a new bank opening in West Fork? How does it happen that I haven't heard a word about it?"

"It seems to be true, sir. I found out as soon as I saw the morning paper, sir. John Hardy has been granted a charter by the comptroller at Washington. The bank is organized and has the required number of stockholders, although Hardy practically owns the bank."

"What else?" demanded Kimball ominously.

"As soon as a new ten-story building goes up on Elm Street the bank will move into it. The Harlan Building on Eighth and Wilson is to be temporary quarters only. He says that his savings accounts will pay six per cent interest, and he will lend money at seven per cent to merchants and businessmen. I under stand that there is to be a unique department in connection which is to finance West Fork boys who want to go to college."

"Go on," grated Kimball heavily.

"Well, the rest is hearsay, sir," replied the secretary hesitantly. "Hardy is reputed to have said that he will create opportunities here in West Fork for these same boys if they will come back home from school. He says the town needs more college men. Rev. Harris is stumping the rural districts for the State Legislature, and he is preaching this same thing and praising Hardy."

"Is that all you know?" inquired Kimball ironically.

"Yes, sir," faltered the secretary uneasily.

"Hamilton, I hired you for a private secretary, didn't I?"

"Yes, sir."

"And I assigned you to the task of seeing what Hardy Enterprises were up to, didn't I? So I could prevent any activities I might not like?"

"You did, sir."

"You were to come to me before Hardy did anything, not after. You're fired! Get out!"

"But, Mr. Kimball," cried the abashed Hamilton. "I tried to learn what they were doing, but they are a close-mouthed bunch. Nobody learned anything until this morning. They've been working secretly. I know that I've learned more this morning than anyone else could have. I got it from one of the stenographers I planted in their offices. But they don't let their clerks and assistants in on important business until it is concluded.

"Mr. Wright's daughter writes all important letters for them. I—I have been doing my best. But their letter files are of steel, and they keep them locked. I've tried, Mr. Kimball. I'll swear it isn't my fault. Please, please—"

"Shut up," interrupted his employer savagely. "Get out and go to work."

Hamilton hurried out of the room before his angry employer could again change his mind. He collided at the door with the person of Mr. Morris, who was bent on entering the lion's den.

Mr. Morris, the gentleman of the derby hat and furled umbrella, had run all the way from his office on Wilson Avenue, his linen coat-tails flapping behind his gaunt form for all the world like the wings of a less noble genus. Highly agitated, he slammed the door in Mr. Hamilton's astonished face and whirled to confront the only man who could help him.

"Sam," he burst out, "have you seen this morning's paper?"

Kimball merely glared his contempt of such a question.

"The new bank—Hardy's new bank," Morris hurried on. "He's attacking the First National. He's going to ruin me."

"How?"

"I just found out that this fellow, Fabryn, has been buying up options on property all along Elm and Birch Streets for John Hardy. Hardy's going to erect better and taller buildings on those two streets than I own on Wilson Avenue. Excavation has already started on both streets. The building permits were given the first thing this morning. Out of town contractors have come to build skyscrapers. And Hardy's got a crew of men calling on the business men on the avenue this morning and selling them on the idea of an enlarged business district.

"They're giving leases on buildings which haven't gone up yet. I'll lose my tenants. They'll get out of my buildings, and I can't force them to do business with your bank. They'll bank with Hardy and rent from Hardy. You can stand it, but it'll ruin me. I tell you, it'll ruin me."

"How sure are you of this information?" rasped Kimball quickly.

"How sure? Didn't I sell that Fabryn my vacant lot on Ninth and Birch for a fancy figure? Didn't I see that squad of men working the avenue? Didn't I verify the building permits on three structures? Didn't I find out that Fabryn has secured options on ten blocks of property on both sides of Elm and Birch Streets, where business houses are not already erected? I'll be ruined!" Morris wailed, whacking his umbrella across the desk.

Kimball punched the bell on his desk again and again. He still had his finger on it when Hamilton came scurrying in.

"Check up on the real estate along Birch and Elm Streets at once," commanded Kimball. "See if Hardy or Fabryn have options on much of it. Quick!"

He turned back to Morris.

"You're a fool, Morris," he thundered wrathfully. "Why weren't you watching your real estate better than that? How did they get away with such a big deal?"

Hamilton was able to answer this question some time later. He came in to make his report. Confirming all that Morris had said, he explained the mystery.

"Hardy bought Woods, who is in the recorder's office, and the various deeds have been recorded under blind names. It seems that everything has been sewed up tight, Mr. Kimball. I'm sorry, but that was none of my duties. I—"

"Get out!" roared Kimball. "Woods, eh? He'll be fired to-morrow. I'll have that whole office cleaned out. I still control the law."

"I told Woods that," put in Mr. Hamilton, who had not fled. "He admitted that he helped Hardy—said he went to school with him. He said he'd be back in an elective office at the next election."

Mr. Kimball's rage transcended that attributed to royalty. His private secretary saw fit to retire. Mr. Morris was left to bear the brunt of the old man's rage. At last his spirit flared up in resentment.

"Don't jump on me, you old goat," he snarled. "You don't stand to lose much, but I'm ruined, I tell you. One thing is certain, though. When Hardy gets through with you in the *Blade*, and gets his bank and buildings going, you won't control the vote here any more. The women will all support him. I heard a lot of talk about Sims this morning. Do you know what that means?"

"It means that I've got to put the thumbscrews on our lavish prodigal son," commented Kimball grimly. "Get out! Go home! You annoy me. I'll do what I can for you."

Hard on the heels of the departure of Mr. Morris came a frightened Hamilton.

"Mr. Kimball," he gasped faintly, "the secretary of the Chamber of Commerce just phoned that he had received a letter from the Henley Phord people telling him to drop the matter of their project, as John Hardy had already donated a site for their assembling plant and closed the deal with their field man last week."

"What?" Kimball thundered.

Bang! Bang! Bang! His fist bombarded the desk in a fit of rage.

"Hardy again? He got wind of that through Presley, I'll bet. And he took up the matter privately while Layton was choking it off. Layton! Lay—" he choked over the secretary's name and glared at the cringing Hamilton with a growing flame in his eye.

"Layton may have bungled the affair," he stated, "but it was your job to watch the Hardy Enterprises. You are the one who has failed. You—"

"Honest to God, Mr. Kimball, I couldn't help it," quavered the stricken private secretary. "I did all I could. I told you how tight that office is."

With a suddenness that was gravely ominous, Sam Kimball quieted down. He turned from his secretary and sat down at his desk to think. This was not a time for hot words or explosions which terrified his subordinates into a palsied fright. This last disclosure struck home with a vengeance. With the coming of the Phord plant to West Fork would come a new era. Outside capital would force its way into the town now that an opening wedge had been driven. Sam Kimball would no longer control the destinies of West Fork.

Worse than that, the coming of Phord meant a higher wage scale. A dollar or two a day out of Kimball's pocket for five thousand employees meant from five to ten thousand dollars per diem. The workers would become more independent, too.

Too late Kimball realized that he should have been guarding every approach against this de luxe prodigal as soon as he had learned the extent of his net worth. He should have watched like a hawk the turbulent Hardy, who was eight or ten times as wealthy as himself. But who would have dreamed that the hard-headed young fighter would have had time to plunge the financial ring of West Fork into chaos and disruption at the same time that he was pushing a newspaper campaign against those who controlled the city, and striving also to clear Howard Wright of the consequences of murder?

The thoughts of the old man were bitter. When he was hit in the pocketbook he was mortally wounded. If he could not stand the strain, conscience went by the board. His religion stood still and marked time while he recouped monetary losses. His hatred for John Hardy mounted as the outward manifestations of his rage cooled. Every proof of Hardy's activities showed, not the lavish hand of a foolish prodigal, but the forethought which bespoke permanence.

He must remain calm while he rallied all his resources and learned the exact extent of Hardy's damage to his personal, his own little universe. While Hardy had had the advantage of a surprise attack, all the fighting would be out in the open henceforth. Hardy had the most money, but Kimball still controlled the town.

"If it will do any good, sir," ventured Hamilton, who stood neglected and forgotten in the middle of the floor, "I can tell you that Hardy has fallen in love with Zoe Ann Wright. My stenographer told me that they are both hard hit."

"Eh?" Kimball looked up vacantly. Then, as the meaning of the secretary's words penetrated, he nodded. He reached for the telephone and began calling to locate the prosecuting attorney.

"Hello," he said at length. "Hello. Yes, that's the place I want. Is Brentwood there? Hello, Cyrus? Cyrus, drop that work on the

Morning Blade and hurry down here as quick as you can get here. No, don't give it up—just hold it where it is indefinitely. I want to see you."

CHAPTER XXV
THE REFUSED OFFER

JOHN HARDY RAISED HIS HEAD and listened to the sounds coming from the general office. He frowned and glanced at the companion who was sharing his little private office.

"What do you make of that noise, Zoe Ann?" he queried.

Zoe Ann looked up from the blue print she had been studying. She smiled at him and sought to listen. She waved one hand toward the open window through which floated noises from the street without.

"I can't tell because of the street noise," she said. "It sounds like a dog fight, though."

Hardy went to the door and opened it. The nature of the disturbance became apparent. Sam Kimball was attempting to force his way through the main office, the prosecuting attorney in tow. A brawny guard recruited by Callahan was opposing the factory owner.

"That's all right, Reynolds," Hardy called out. "Let the two gentlemen pass."

Kimball glared at everybody in general. Wright, attracted by the disturbance, came to the door of his office as the incensed Kimball strode forward. The latter waved him back and pointed at Hardy.

"That's the man I want to see," he said.

Wright looked a question at his employer. Hardy nodded and spoke to his visitor.

"I am sorry if you have been inconvenienced, Mr. Kimball," he said apologetically, "but I have been so pestered with newspaper reporters that the guard has positive instructions not to let any one in without appointment. If I had known when to expect you—"

"I'm here now. Can you spare us a few minutes privately."

"Come right in," Hardy invited, standing aside. "My personal quarters are rather small, but I guess we can manage."

Brentwood drew back at sight of the girl within. "Mr. Kimball said we wanted to speak to you privately," he said coldly.

"You haven't given me time to ask Miss Wright to withdraw," Hardy responded, his tone equally chilling.

"Never mind, Cyrus," decided Kimball. "I'm glad the girl's here."

"I shall be glad to leave, Mr. Hardy," Zoe Ann spoke coolly, impersonally, ignoring the two men who had ignored her one Sunday evening on her own front porch.

She was suiting her action to the word when Kimball barred the way.

"No, no," he vetoed testily. "You stay right here, Zoe Ann. This matter concerns you most nearly. I want you to hear it."

He attempted a conciliatory smile, the effect of which, being so at variance with his usual nature, was little short of ghastly.

The girl turned her face away. She went and stood at the window gazing out on the street below—a street where the asphalt still simmered under the late afternoon rays of the sun.

In seating himself, Kimball observed the outspread blue print. His keen old eyes told him at once what it was.

"I see you are at work on your plans for an enlarged business district," he grinned through his set teeth. "A great improvement, but it takes time—and favorable legislation."

"I am not worried over adverse legislation," replied Hardy calmly.

"You have not had the experience of running against it," returned the factory owner significantly. "It can break a capitalist."

"I'm always ready for trouble," Hardy said grimly. "Is this what you wish to see me about?"

"Not exactly, not exactly," Kimball hastened to say.

"Then I suppose it is about this morning's *Blade?* Let me tell you before you start, that it is useless to say anything. The *Blade* is carrying that fight through to a finish. We're ready to fight in the courts, also. The only way you can stop it is to dynamite the plant."

The two men started faintly and glanced swiftly at each other. Hardy smiled thinly.

"I see that the idea has already occurred to you," he went on in a hard voice. "I suppose you realize that I, knowing the extent of the trouble I am making, have also considered such a thing. I will be frank enough to inform you that the *Blade* is now heavily guarded, *day and night*. And the guards have positive instructions to shoot the first person in or about the place who acts suspiciously."

"That's not what I've come to see you about, either," said Kimball, choking down the wrath which threatened to engulf him.

"Then what do you want?"

"I'll be as frank as you are," barked the old man. "I'll lay my cards on the table. I have spent to-day investigating things my assistants should have discovered before. I know exactly where you stand, what you have done, and how much money you have invested in West Fork. You have accomplished a whole lot, young man—a lot that would raise you above your generation if you had given the same interest and thought to the salvation of your soul. You—"

"If you please," Hardy raised a wearied hand, "I do not care to discuss or listen to your idea of conscience and religion."

"Well, listen to this, then," snarled Kimball, almost forgetting himself and banging his fist down on the other man's desk. "If you want to fight, I can give you all the fight you want. You have money, but I control the law here. If, on the other—"

"At present you control the law," corrected Hardy.

"At present," agreed Kimball, looking toward the figure of Zoe Ann. "And the present is all I need. With all your energy and money, you haven't proved that any one else is guilty of the murder of Thurlowe Fosdick. You haven't proved that Wright isn't guilty. While you are playing in the world of finance, I shall be sending

Howard Wright to the electric chair—and I've got the power to do so."

"Ahhh!" It was a soft sigh of anguish from the girl at the window.

"You are overlooking that fact," sneered Kimball. "Wright cannot escape that fate. Shall I tell you why? Because he is guilty."

"Oh, he is not, he is not!" cried out Zoe Ann fiercely.

Hardy rose to his feet and put a comforting arm about her shaking shoulders.

Kimball looked triumphantly at Brentwood

"Prove his innocence," he challenged. "You can't. Brentwood has a complete case out of gathered evidence which can't be shattered except by a signed confession of another murderer. And you can't get that because there is no other."

Hardy pointed at the door.

"If this is what you came here for," he said fiercely, "get out quickly before I throw you out this window."

Kimball looked startled.

"That is not why I came," he protested. "I just wanted to show you that phase of the case. If you doubt me, wait for the trial. This is what I am here to offer." He lowered his voice and spoke straight at Hardy. "If you will drop everything you have meddled with in West Fork at once; if you will leave town and promise not to come back, in return I promise you the acquittal and freedom of Howard Wright for the murder of Fosdick. There! That's my offer. If you want to fight, we'll fight—and Wright will die. If you'll drop all this trouble you're brewing, Wright shall be acquitted. Remember, I control the law."

Hardy stared at Kimball, completely stunned. This was the last thing in the world he had expected Kimball to say. He could hardly credit his ears. Gradually he became aware that Zoe Ann was gazing from him to his visitors and back again. He swallowed hard, and found his voice.

"You—you mean that if I will quit, you offer the life of Wright in exchange? You would prostitute the law to the extent of freeing a man you think to be a murderer of a member of your family?"

"A man that I know to be a murderer," snapped Kimball. "And you know it, too. It's a steep price to pay, but I'll bargain with you. Take it or leave it. But you must decide to-day. If another issue of that yellow sheet of yours comes out, I'll kill you instead of bargaining with you."

Bang! This time the fist descended squarely on the blueprint. A pencil beneath it poked through the tough paper. Hardy regarded it thoughtfully, studying the little brass cap which held the eraser, the crown of the pencil. And just like that Kimball had crowned his offer. It might have been an omen, this tearing a hole through the plans of Hardy.

He waved aside the threat of violence, although he fully understood that it was not an idle one. He looked at Brentwood.

"And you, Brentwood, hearing this plain bribe, countenance this offer?"

Brentwood dropped his eyes to the floor.

"It is a bitter blow to me," he replied, "for I expected to secure a conviction. But Mr. Kimball has the power to do what he says."

Hardy turned to his fiancée.

"What do you think of this, Zoe Ann?" he inquired.

"Oh, I—I cannot advise you, dearest," she whispered.

But Hardy knew that her heart had already surrendered. He looked at the man who had made such an offer.

"This—this is too momentous a matter to decide offhand either way," he said uncertainly. "Besides, it is really beyond me alone. I have others to consider now. If I were to accept your proposition and leave West Fork, what would become of Walker, of Callahan, of Barbington, of all the others who have thrown in their lot with mine? I can't desert them, now."

"I—yes, I'll leave them alone," promised Kimball reluctantly. "I'll hold no grudge against them—any of them."

"You have already fired Professor Walker."

"He shall be reinstated."

"Come with me," decided Hardy. "Mr. Wright himself is entitled to know about this."

They walked through the main office and sought admission to the quarters of the manager. They found Professor Walker in consultation with Wright. Brentwood demurred at his presence, but Hardy disagreed.

"Your treachery to your oath is safe with us," he said. "Walker has the right to hear this amazing offer. Next to Wright, he has been hit the hardest. Explain your whole proposition again, Mr. Kimball."

While the manufacturer did so, Hardy noticed that Walker gazed upon the speaker with inscrutable eyes. On the other hand, Wright's face was a study in conflicting emotions as he listened. It was a most amazing situation. There was silence for a space after Kimball ceased talking. Wright studied the tips of his fingers. Then he glanced at Hardy.

"Well, John," he said softly, "what is your decision?"

"I haven't made any, Mr. Wright." Hardy was deeply troubled. "That's why I had these two men state their case again before you. I thought you ought to hear it."

"Thank you," Wright murmured quietly. "Now that I have heard it, suppose you give your answer?"

"But—but, Mr. Wright," cried Hardy. "Can't you see that it is probably your very life that you are asking me to pass judgment on? Must I assume this responsibility?"

"However you decide," spoke the big man softly, "I will be no worse off than I was the day you found me."

Hardy glanced at each face in perplexity. Walker, he observed, was now studying his face with an intensity that was startling. Kimball and Brentwood waited, grimly expectant. He turned to the girl.

"Zoe Ann!" he cried in real anguish. "Zoe Ann, what must I say?"

Her heart was in her eyes, but she drew herself up proudly.

"It is yours, and yours alone, to make this decision, John Hardy," she declared firmly.

Hardy ran a worried hand through his hair. He began striding back and forth, avoiding the faces of his audience. Where he had sought to lighten his load of responsibility, he seemed to have made the burden heavier. He lost a precious five minutes in being unable to think at all. His brain simply refused to function properly. Little, insignificant things crowded through his mind. The fly buzzing futilely against the upper window pane, the intent expression on Professor Walker's face, the scratch on the nearer of Sam Kimball's square-toed shoes, the shout of a newsboy in the street selling the *Evening Planet*, the design in the lace of Zoe Ann's handkerchief.

Queer how the little figures stood out, and yet nine out of ten people never knew they were there. Lace making was an intricate art. He remembered a picture he had seen of an old French woman at work with a vast bundle of little shuttles under her hands. Of course, this kind of lace had been made on a machine and—he aroused himself with a start.

Yes, yes, this question about Wright and Kimball. Involving a man's life. What should he decide?

He could refuse. Wright had spoken the truth when he said that Hardy's decision would leave him no worse off than before. But freedom was offered as an assured thing in exchange for withdrawal. On the other hand, this task of rejuvenating his hometown had grown on Hardy like a mania. It was no longer a jest of any sort; it was a wonderful mission to perform.

If he quit now he stood to lose nearly a million dollars, and just when he was on the verge of victory. Of course, the battle was by no means over, but he had topped the hill, he had the other side on the defensive, Kimball's declaration of war to the contrary notwithstanding.

To refuse did not mean that Wright would die. Weren't they fighting every inch of the way to prove his innocence? Weren't they hoping to unearth much, now that two brilliant minds were delving into the affair? The admission of William Beedle anent the footprints in the woods would tear a gap in the circumstantial evidence of the prosecution. But it wouldn't destroy it. Unless something else developed in the favor of the defendant, Wright undoubtedly would be lost.

Now that an avenue of escape was offered, dared he take the risk of refusal? To condemn Zoe Ann's father to the chair! What was a mere million dollars? In the person of Zoe Ann Wright he had found all the treasure he wanted in the world.

He groaned aloud and turned swiftly to face the waiting group. A twisted smile parted his lips.

"This is the first time in my life I was ever forced into a corner and made to quit cold in a fight," he said hoarsely. "I feel like a traitor to West Fork, but—but I accept your terms, Sam Kimball. The price is too high to refuse."

With an inarticulate little cry Zoe Ann was in his arms, sobbing on his broad chest.

"Oh, thank God!" she murmured brokenly. "Thank you, John. Oh, my dear, I was afraid you'd be too hard to give in. And I couldn't—couldn't beg you. We'll go away—far away and forget that West Fork exists—just you and Papa and I. We know he is innocent and God knows we are doing right."

"Dearest, dearest," he murmured brokenly, "if you think I have done right, I have nothing to regret. But I must see that no harm befalls our friends. We cannot forsake Professor Walker, Presley and the others."

"Oh, we won't, we won't," she cried. "We'll—"

"I promised to leave them alone," Kimball's triumphant voice broke in harshly. "You have chosen wisely, young man. God will reward you for saving all this strife."

"Don't talk to me of God," responded Hardy coldly. "I'll stop all my financial activities, but I stay right here and hold my fort until the day Howard Wright walks out of your courthouse a free man."

"Without explaining to anyone outside of those now present why you are giving up your various plans," added Brentwood carefully.

"I agree," replied Hardy. "Zoe Ann, telephone Presley to come up here at once to see me."

Then: "Wait!"

The voice of a man who had been forgotten for the nonce, the voice of the principal about whom all this turmoil swirled, rapped out that command.

Howard Wright rose to his feet, the flame of the zealot lighting his eyes. He seemed to tower above even the tall form of John Hardy. All eyes turned on him as he flung out one hand toward the man who had decided in favor of his life.

"That is your decision, John," he declared. "But it isn't mine. Sam Kimball, you travesty on honest men, you shall not succeed in your intention of refastening your hooks in the throat of West Fork. I refuse your terms. Do you comprehend? I refuse!"

This rather, dramatic but wholly earnest statement caused an uproar. Everybody seemed to be talking at once, everybody except Professor Walker, who now turned his inscrutable black eyes on the manager of the Hardy Enterprises. Kimball slowly recovered from his stark amazement and began to bellow reasons at Wright why the latter was a fool and an idiot.

Brentwood began to look frightened to think that he had been committed to a bribing offer which had been refused. He had a wholesome fear of the *Morning Blade*. He attempted to reason with Wright. Zoe Ann and John Hardy began to plead with him. And Wright stood serene against the onslaught and waved them back.

"No, no, no," he declared, "my refusal is final. I love you, John, for the sacrifice you would have made for my sake, but I refuse to accept it."

"But, Mr. Wright," cried Hardy, "think what you are giving up. Of course, we've hoped to clear you, but that is problematical and this is positive."

"There is always hope for an innocent man," smiled Wright.

"You refer to the detectives and to the footprints of William Beedle?" Hardy forgot that Brentwood and Kimball were present.

"Partly," assented Wright.

"But that hasn't cleared you. And what if nothing else turns up?"

"In that case I shall die," agreed Wright studiedly. Then he went on, his face lighting up with the force of his ardor: "I hope to prove my innocence, but if I fail I am willing to die as a sacrifice to save thirty thousand people from falling back into the clutches of Sam Kimball. It has been the dream of my life to do something for this unfortunate town, and I am on the threshold of seeing West Fork freed from bondage.

"Do you think that I will accept my one little life which is more than half spent, in exchange for the chances John Hardy is opening to thirty thousand people to own their own souls and to enjoy life as God originally intended? No, I say. A thousand times, no! Get out of here, Kimball, you sanctimonious hypocrite. You have lost.

"You sought to beat John Hardy because of his love for my daughter and his regard for me. But you have pledged your soul to the Devil in vain. Thinking me guilty of murder, you come offering me freedom to spare your petty tyranny and your fat pocketbook and your whitewashed name. Get out of here before I soil my hands in reality by wringing your dirty neck."

Kimball backed away before the blazing eyes of the speaker. His goatlike features worked spasmodically. Any instant Hardy expected him to give vent to a mad cry. When he did speak his voice was shriller with emotion than it had ever been in his life.

"All right, Howard Wright," he shouted viciously. "I'll go. And you shall go to the electric chair as sure as there is a God in Heaven."

The door closed behind the precious pair. Zoe Ann collapsed in the arms of her father.

"Oh, Papa, Papa," she sobbed, "why did you do it? Why did you do it? You mean more to us than all of West Fork."

"The fat is in the fire now, for a fact," commented Hardy rue-fully. "And wouldn't Presley give his right arm to learn of this offer of bribery? I can see how he'd spread it across the front page now."

"Aren't you going to give it to him?" demanded Wright, em-bracing his daughter tightly.

Hardy solemnly shook his head.

"I cannot," he uttered. "Of course, it was a crooked offer, but I knew it was the wrong thing for them to do when I accepted. There-fore, I am as guilty as they."

For the first time Professor Walker broke his silence. His fine eyes were clouded with pain from the memory of the tender scene between Hardy and Zoe Ann. He sighed heavily and spoke:

"John Hardy," he said, "do you mean to say that you were actually going to give up all this work you have started just to be sure that Howard Wright would go free?"

"I was," Hardy smiled. "But I would never have forsaken you, my friend, to the mercies of Sam Kimball."

"And now you are too honorable to give these facts to Presley?" pursued the chemist in profound surprise.

"I shall never reveal them," declared Hardy gravely. "We shall whip the Kimball outfit without that."

Professor Walker shook his head to himself as he turned toward the other man.

"And you, Mr. Wright, are you really willing to give up your life rather than have John Hardy cease this work? Or was it just the fervor of the moment? Tell me, if you are convicted and you stand in the shadow of the chair, will you still want Hardy to carry this on rather than redeem your life, if it proves possible?"

"As God is my judge, I shall never waver," avowed Wright. And then his voice broke a trifle as he continued: "You'll be good to my little girl, John, if—if I don't come through?"

Hardy held out his hand. And as they gripped hands, they felt the clasp of Professor Walker's on theirs. He said:

"Gentlemen, let me thank you for restoring my shattered faith in the nobility of human nature. I never expected to witness such a day as this."

They were puzzled by his remark.

"Why, Professor Walker," declared Zoe Ann, "how queer of you. I didn't know that you had lost faith in human nature. What do you mean?"

Walker smiled sadly.

"Nothing," he said gently. "God bless you, my dear. You deserve happiness if any creature ever did. It is long after closing time and I must see about locking up the offices. I am sure the office force is gone. Good night, my friends."

CHAPTER XXVI
BEFORE DAWN

Brr-rr-rr! Brr-rr-rr! The sharp, insistent ringing of a telephone in the dead of night. Compelling! Imperative! The unreal sensation, the loss of time sense, the thrill of annoyance, of uneasiness during the struggle back across the borderland of dreams to the realm of the actual. And all the while, interlarded with impatient little pauses, that urgent calling of the bells, those two small nickel-plated shells brought to life by the electric vibration of a metal baton. *Brr-rr-rr! Brr-rr-rr!*

His life, and the peril of his life, on his Texas ranch had sharpened John Hardy's resistance to deep, unconscious slumber. He was the first to respond to the summons. In the dark he groped his way from his room and found the instrument in the upper hall. He had already lifted the receiver and was awaiting the cessation of the buzzing when the two thin lines of light which sprang respectively into being under the doors across the hallway, announced the awakening of father and daughter. They both came out into the gloom of the landing as Hardy listened in horror to the message being poured into his ear.

"Mr. Hardy? This is Detective Cutler. An awful thing has happened. Old man Kimball and Professor Walker have been killed in an explosion at the Kimball residence. No one else has been injured. Miss Morgan called me at once, and I've been here ever since, going over the grounds with the local police. The two bodies have just been taken from the ruins of the library and are on the way to the Greenwald morgue.

"I examined them and found nothing to indicate other than accidental death. Pretty badly battered and bruised and Kimball's right forearm is missing. Blown off! First chance I've had to call you. I would have waited until morning, but in view of discoveries Miss Morgan and I made to-day, I think it best that you come at once."

"I'll be there in fifteen minutes," promised Hardy crisply.

He replaced the instrument on its stand and ran toward his room.

"Sam Kimball and Professor Walker are dead," he flung over his shoulder at the two questioning faces. "Explosion of some sort at Kimball home—no one else injured."

"But—but—" Wright cried after him. "What caused it? Did you learn?"

"No. I'll get the details. Cutler has something to report. I'll probably be busy the rest of the night," Hardy called through the door as he hurried into his clothes. "You two had best go back to bed. I'll meet you at the office in the morning and tell you what I find out."

"Professor Walker?" murmured the stunned girl, looking at her father. "Dead? What could the professor have been doing at Kimball's?"

Wright shrugged his shoulders helplessly. Zoe Ann shuddered.

"How horrible," she said. "And they were both alive and well this afternoon." Then, as Hardy was going rapidly down the stairs: "We can't go back to sleep, John. Please call us as soon as you can."

Hardy waved a hand and shouted an assent. An instant later the back door slammed behind him, as he sought the garage.

The grounds of the Kimball estate were heavily guarded and a small crowd recruited from the neighboring estates and the all-night restaurants, where the news had spread, was clustered about the gate. Hardy glanced at the clock in his instrument board as he swung in and sounded his horn. It was now two o'clock.

The besiegers of the grilled iron gates scattered like chaff before the glare of his headlamps, and he rolled up until the front bumper nosed the barrier. Again he sounded his horn authoritatively. The pair of gates swung inward as a corpulent blue-coated figure opened the way. The figure of a man in dark clothes came running down the driveway as Hardy eased into second gear and pulled in.

The corpulent policeman stepped into the glare of the lights and held up a hand as unseen assistants clanged the gates shut behind the car. Hardy, perforce, stopped again. The officer stepped to the side of the roadster.

"Who are you?" he demanded. "I thought you were the chief when I opened the gate."

"My name is John Hardy, officer. Thanks for your promptness. Please step aside as I'm in a hurry."

"You can't go any farther," snapped the policeman aggressively. "These grounds are under police surveillance. Nobody admitted. You'll have to get out."

"Sorry," snapped Hardy, equally as curt. "I have more business here than the chief of police you're expecting."

"Open the gates!" the policeman responded by shouting to the men behind the car.

Hardy replied by starting forward. The officer leaped upon the running board and shoved a gun against his neck.

"If you don't back out at once, I'll bore you," he snarled grimly. "I've orders from the prosecuting attorney to keep everybody out."

"Here!" yelled the man in dark clothes as he came up. "What's the row here?"

"This man is trying to force an entrance, Mr. Colter," responded the policeman respectfully.

"Who is it?" demanded the plainclothes man.

"John Hardy," replied the aggressor himself. "And as soon as this cop takes his gun out of my neck, I'm going on."

"John Hardy?" exclaimed the detective. "I've been waiting for you. Your detective told me you were coming."

"Well, he ain't," stated the policeman harshly. "I got orders to keep everybody out. And he goes out."

"Get off that car, you fool!" ripped out Colter. "Hardy goes with me. Why, he's a better detective than the whole force put together. I'll be responsible for him. Get out of the way!"

The policeman responded grumblingly. A mocking voice spoke from the darkness behind the car.

"'*Le roi est mort, vive le roi!*' Colter knows what side to turn to, now that Kimball's dead."

The detective climbed into the car with Hardy. "That isn't true, Mr. Hardy," he said to his companion. "I want you to believe that."

"I believe you, Colter. And I thank you. I won't forget this, however."

They alighted under the portico. Another policeman guarded the front door.

"You wish to go right in?" asked Colter. "No part of the house is damaged except the wing where the library is. Brentwood has taken charge of everything. The servants are all held in their quarters on the third floor."

"Can we get into the library from the main hall?"

"No, sir. The door is jammed. Besides, it would be too dangerous. The bodies were taken out through the windowed side of the library. Half the wall was blown out on that side."

"Let's walk around there first, then," suggested Hardy. "I'd like to get a glimpse of the damage."

The library was the front room in the right wing of the structure as one approached the house. A wide, roofless veranda curved around that side of the house and French doors opened from the chamber onto the porch with its ornate stone balustrade. All of the windows of the library were shattered and, as the two men rounded the corner of the building, the full force of the havoc became apparent.

Stones, broken laths, dust and plaster strewed the terrace. A gaping hole in the side of the house showed where the French doors had once been. A section of the balustrade was missing. And in a semi-circle about the wrecked area were a number of lanterns. An officer stood guard here with a flashlight. And scattered here and there through the trees danced the beams of half a dozen others.

"All those men policemen?" queried Hardy, gesturing toward the distant lights.

"No, sir. But they are trusted men who helped take care of the mess here."

"You know them, then?"

"Yes, sir."

"All right. Where's Cutler?"

"He's in the dining room talking to Brentwood and Robert Kimball."

"What did Brentwood say at his presence here?"

"Nothing, sir. He was here when we came. In fact, he had taken charge and was the person who called the police and the prosecuting attorney. He's a smart man, Mr. Hardy. I think he knows something about this matter already."

"Perhaps. Borrow this officer's flashlight and let's look in the library."

Colter did so. They picked their way to the gaping hole and the detective played the beam about on the interior. The place was a wreck. Bookcases were shattered, furniture splintered, books all over the floor, plaster and debris everywhere. Queerly enough, with every globe shattered and at a crooked angle, the chandelier was still suspended from the ceiling.

"I wouldn't go in," cautioned Colter at Hardy's advance. "The ceiling sags quite badly. It may give way any minute, sir."

Hardy glanced up.

"What rooms are above this?" he inquired.

"The suite of Thomas Kimball and his wife."

"Where are they? Were they not injured at all?"

"They weren't here, sir. They left hurriedly some time before the explosion, for the mountains."

"I see," murmured Hardy. "I'll take a chance on the ceiling. Lend me the light a moment. And Colter!"

"Yes, sir?"

"Didn't we go through grade school together?"

"We did, sir."

"Suppose you drop that 'sir' business with me?"

"Thanks," rejoined the detective, his features registering a friendly smile. "It has become more or less a habit with me in my work. I see you are the same old Johnny Hardy."

"You haven't been all this time coming to that conclusion?"

"You can never tell about rich men," commented the detective.

"Nor any other," said Hardy. "How were the bodies found? Can you tell me?"

"The professor was lying nearer the corner. Kimball was nearer the center of the room. From all appearances the library table was between them at the moment of the explosion," Colter obliged, indicating fragments of the article of furniture.

"His right arm was blown off? Then he must have been nearer the source of the explosion?"

"So we believe."

"What could have caused an explosion in the library? Did you discover any evidence of any kind?" went on Hardy, playing his light about the floor.

"We have found nothing important as yet," responded Colter. "But with the coming of daylight we expect to find traces of the same sort of thing you discovered about Fosdick's golf ball."

"A bomb of some sort?"

"Yes, sir. A time bomb."

"U-um—hello! What's this?"

Hardy stooped and picked up a flat jagged black object. It was part of the leather-covered back of a book. In letters of gold under the dust he distinguished the words *Holy Bible*. He frowned and was about to seek farther when an ominous crackling overhead sent him leaping for the terrace. The sound ceased, but he did not go back.

"Let's interview Cutler now," he decided.

They found the detective in the dining room as Colter had said. Brentwood stared at the form of Hardy and rose to his feet.

"You!" he said harshly. "What are you doing here? Is no place safe from you? Colter, what do you mean—"

"Lay off of Colter," stated Hardy crisply. "I'm here on the trail of a murderer and I haven't time to quarrel with you or any of your ilk."

"We can handle this matter without your assistance," Brentwood glowered. "You get out!"

"Where is Miss Morgan, Cutler?" said Hardy, ignoring the attorney and turning to the private detective.

"Upstairs, under custody with the servants," replied Cutler. "That was Mr. Brentwood's first order when he came—to keep the help in their quarters pending examination. I thought it best to agree. I had already compared notes with her."

"Go after her, Colter," commanded Hardy. "Miss Morgan is the new housemaid here."

"What do you mean by sending for Kimball servants in such a high-handed manner?" snarled Brentwood angrily. "I—"

"Miss Morgan is not a servant," stated Hardy. "She is one of the best detectives in the country. She has been assuming the role of housemaid in following the case of the Fosdick murder."

"The Fosdick murder?" repeated Brentwood in amazement. "And working on that in the Kimball home? Why, why—you dared to suspect any one here of that crime? In the face of the evidence I have gathered against Howard Wright?"

"Didn't Wright's refusal of your proposition yesterday evening in my offices convince you of his real innocence?" Hardy demanded.

This question went unanswered. Brentwood turned a shade paler at mention of the offered bribe, but his eyes blazed with anger at the horrible reflection Hardy was throwing on the Kimball family. He clenched one fist and half raised it.

"You—you dirty scoundrel!" he gasped. "You dare to presume that far? You would seek to involve the Kimball relatives of the murdered man? You—"

"Has the Kimball family ever shown itself to be above criminal actions," cut in Hardy contemptuously.

Brentwood swayed in the excess of his emotion. Then the reaction from the entire tragedy at hand set in. His face became gray and drawn. He lowered his arm and wiped his brow with a trembling hand. With a faint groan he dropped back into his chair at the table.

Robert Kimball was on his feet.

"Oh, come now, Hardy," he protested angrily. "That was a raw thing to say even if Cy insulted you."

"It was," admitted Hardy instantly. "I apologize. I am sorry for you men at this hour. I know that you are horror-stricken and I guess that Mrs. Brentwood is almost crazy. But you are men—one of you the prosecuting attorney. You'll have to stand it. Murder has been done a second time, and I am positive that the assassin is the same. Cutler, you know something. What have you to say?"

"After Miss Morgan," said Cutler, a sharp-eyed man with a wide, humorous mouth.

The woman operative was being ushered into the lining room by Colter.

"Miss Morgan," greeted Hardy, "as time may be everything, will you proceed to give us what information you possess at once?"

The woman in maid costume bowed and produced a notebook from a pocket in her dress. She was a pleasant featured person of probably thirty years of age, but the square angle of her jaw and the level gaze of her eye bespoke efficiency. And her tones when she spoke were firm, her words concise and to the point.

"I have been interrogating the butler," she began crisply. "At nine o'clock he admitted Professor Walker to see Mr. Kimball and showed him into the library. So far as he could see the professor had nothing about him except a Bible, which he carried under one arm. Howell—the butler—was told that he might retire, by Mr. Kimball. Thus, no one was on the first floor except the two men in the library. I was upstairs assisting Mrs. Thomas Kimball to pack her things. She and her husband left at nine thirty for a summer resort called Dona Vista.

"After their departure I retired to my room to arrange my notes on an interesting conversation that had taken place an hour or two previously between Thomas and his brother, Robert, in the latter's room."

Robert Kimball started to his feet. Then, as he became the cynosure of all eyes, he subsided wordlessly.

Miss Morgan went on. Young Kimball fastened his eyes on her in horrified fascination.

"It was some time after ten that the house rocked with the concussion of the explosion. I glanced at my wristwatch and noted that it was ten forty-three. I was the first person to reach the lower floor. I couldn't get into the library because the door was jammed. I smelled

the fumes and rushed out the front door to the side entrance. Seeing that a bad accident had occurred, I came back into the house,
without attempting to enter the library, and called Mr. Cutler.

"Upon his arrival he called Mr. Brentwood and the police. We
compared notes and what I am now about to read out of my notebook, had I reported it sooner, might have averted this tragedy.
But the departure of Thomas Kimball disarmed me.

"Immediately after dinner to-night Robert Kimball came upstairs
to his room. Very shortly afterward I saw his brother enter it, laboring
under nervous excitement. I went to the door and listened, copying
down the gist of the conversation in shorthand. It was obvious that
Sam Kimball spoke at the dinner table of a visit to the Hardy offices
and a refusal of bribery by Mr. Wright. The matter of certain footprints made by a William Beedle had excited Thomas. I will now read:

> "Thomas said: 'My God, Bob, Beedle is the man who
> murdered Fosdick. I didn't suspect him before—I
> thought it was Howard Wright. But those footprints
> in the woods were Beedle's. The fool lost his head
> when I couldn't promise him quick money, and he
> killed Fosdick to prevent his exposure.'
>
> "Robert said: 'Perhaps so. I never more than half
> suspected Wright, anyhow. What about it? Why all
> the excitement?'
>
> "Thomas said: 'Why? Can't you see? I still owe
> him ten thousand dollars. I've got to give it to him
> at once—I've got to give him more than that so he
> can cover up all his crooked bookkeeping and de-
> stroy any evidence of a motive. I've got to get him
> out of his difficulty.'
>
> "Robert said: 'I fail to see how you are obligated.'
>
> "Thomas said: 'My God, if I don't help him,
> they'll grab him. And when they do, he'll expose all
> he knows about that—that affair between Opal and
> me. It'll ruin me in West Fork, and Ruth will divorce
> me. I've got to help him. I've got to.'

"Robert said: 'Ah! I see. Well, you'd better see him and do it then.'

"Thomas said: 'But that's it, Bob, I can't. I haven't any ready money. You know that.'

"Robert said: 'And so you've come to me. Well, I haven't anything but a few hundred. You know how Sam pinches me down.'

"Thomas said: 'Yes, yes, I know. But I've got to have it and I don't dare ask him for it. If I only had my share of the estate, I'd be safe. I've tried time and time again to get the old devil to divide it now, so as to cut down the inheritance tax.'

"Robert said: 'Too bad the old boy can't kick off and oblige you.'

"Thomas said: 'The old goat ought to have been dead a long time ago, but that doesn't help me now. What can I do? What can I do?'

"Robert said: 'If it is really as bad as you think, you'd better leave at once for the mountains with Ruth until the big scandal blows over. I'll tell the old man you are gone.'

"Thomas said: 'I will not let Beedle drag that girl's name through the mud. By God, I'll kill him first! Oh, if I only had money now.'

"Robert said: 'I am sorry for you, Tom. I can't help you out. The only way you can command big money right away is for Sam to pass out. I wouldn't hinder you from digging into the estate to cover up family skeletons before the administrator got to it. There's nothing for you to do unless—'

"Thomas said: 'That is it. Unless—'

"Robert said: 'Bad thoughts, Tom, bad thoughts. All you can do is to hit for the mountains for awhile.'

"Thomas said: 'I will. Ruth and I will go tonight, but—'"

"He approached the door and placed his hand on the knob," went on Miss Morgan, closing her notebook and looking up. "I had to withdraw quickly to escape discovery. That is all."

Robert was on his feet. This time he spoke.

"This is horrible!" he cried passionately. "I admit that dialogue—we have talked disrespectfully of the old man for years. There was no love between us. He was always hard and cold. But he was our father, after all. I know that Thomas had nothing to do with his death. Oh, I can see the conclusions this woman spy is drawing, but she is wrong. She's wrong. Cyrus, you've heard us talk about the governor. My God, you must believe me."

"We are not accusing Thomas Kimball of murder," Detective Cutler said. "Neither are we accusing you. But I have reason to believe that a time bomb was placed in the library to kill Sam Kimball. You have seen the evidences of explosion. It was not common knowledge that your father invariably spent every evening in his library; some person who knew his habits planned his destruction.

"That it was a time bomb is indicated by the fact that an unexpected visitor came in after it had been set and also met his death. Then, a time bomb would give the murderer time to get away before the explosion. However, I shall be able to state positively what caused the disaster after I have gone over the room in daylight.

"In the meantime, Thomas Kimball, a possible suspect, is speeding away every minute while we sit here. He couldn't be guilty of his father's death unless he already had the materials on hand. Yet, if he is the person who murdered Fosdick he could have had the necessary items ready. In fact, both deeds could have been planned a long time and but wanted execution, despite his remarks concerning the possible guilt of Beedle or Wright.

"If he is guilty, he will be expecting a wire informing him of the tragedy. If this was a carefully planned and premeditated crime, he will be sure to return, as he has an alibi. If it was done under the impulse of emotion, he may keep on going for a long time.

"There is quite a chance that he is innocent, as I have another suspect to name. However, a wire must be sent to Thomas Kimball, and my advice is to send a man an hour or two before the wire with the power to bring him back if he doesn't want to come.

"Now for the other. You knew from my last report, Mr. Hardy, that I have been making friends with that German girl, Hilda Frieling, who was the cook in the Fosdick family for a number of years, and who is now working for Major Sims. Among other things, I have been learning from her a number of Fosdick failings, friends, enemies, and troubles.

"To-night—last night, rather—I took her to a picture show. A little amusement goes a long way with a girl of simple tastes. In leading her around to the discussion of Fosdick affairs I somehow got her on the subject of Major Sims and that defaming article in this morning's paper. She told me enough to make me forget the Fosdick case for the time being.

"In short, Major Sims nearly went mad at the breakfast table. He was worse than Hilda had ever seen him before. The whole family was in a turmoil. The major already had threatened the life of Sam Kimball once before. He did so again, and in no uncertain terms. It was a trying day. He refused to leave the house and face the public, staying indoors and ranting and raving wildly.

"Hilda, in going into his room later in the morning to make the bed, came upon him cleaning a pair of pistols he had carried in the Spanish-American War. He frightened the poor girl nearly to death and shouted her out of the chamber.

"Later, in the afternoon, he telephoned one of his sons to get him a ticket for New Orleans at once. He packed a suitcase and fumed until dark. Without having eaten a bite since breakfast, he took the railroad ticket and left the house under cover of darkness, leaving his two pistols on the sideboard in the dining room— doubtless as proof to Hilda that he was not going to kill Kimball in reality. But his train didn't leave until ten o'clock; and he left his home before eight.

"Although it was after nine o'clock when Hilda told me this, I got rid of her rather abruptly and hunted for the trail of the wrathful major. I didn't catch up with him until ten minutes after his train left for the South. That was at ten three, and I ascertained that, beyond question, he was on the train. But his movements for more than two hours previous to his departure were a blank.

"I finally returned to my hotel. I had not yet retired when Miss Morgan called me shortly before eleven o'clock. I came right out here. I've been here ever since. It was all this that I thought you should know at once, Mr. Hardy."

"It is certainly plenty," said Hardy grimly. "Do you see the duty of the law, Brentwood?"

The prosecuting attorney raised haggard eyes. "This is terrible," he groaned. "I can't believe any of it. It—it is beyond belief."

"It isn't a question of either your belief or my belief," snapped Hardy. "We don't know yet who is guilty, but these two men have got to come back to stand investigation. Are you going to set the proper machinery in motion, or must I do it?"

Brentwood raised his eyes heavenward. He shuddered throughout his gaunt frame. Like an old man he rose to his feet.

"I'll do it," he replied hoarsely. "And may God help the guilty man!"

CHAPTER XXVII
THE LETTER

IT WAS NINE O'CLOCK IN THE MORNING. The *Morning Blade* fairly screamed with an account of this second and double disaster which overshadowed the scathing article on Mayor Clinton and the promised exposé of Dr. Ward Loftmead on the morrow. Even the *Planet* had come out with an extra on the dual murder. The city was wild with excitement and speculation was rife.

This was West Fork's supreme moment, the climax of a number of successive shocks which had rocked the town. Business was more or less suspended while groups of men gathered on street corners and in cigar stores, and women hung over back yard fences and gathered on front porches to talk about the tragedy born of the night.

In the office of Howard Wright, fortified by several cups of strong coffee, John Hardy discussed the details with Zoe Ann and her father while he awaited reports from various points.

"Colter went after Thomas Kimball at once," he concluded. "Terry Callahan was deputized to bring Major Sims back from New Orleans. He left before daylight. Brentwood has buckled under the strain, leaving me to cooperate with the police department. Robert Kimball, Beedle, and Charles Morris are under close surveillance. Miss Morgan has taken charge of things at the Kimball home.

"Under her direction they are searching the place for chemicals or any evidence at all which will free Thomas or condemn him. And then there are the Sims premises yet to be searched and the connections between Sims and Fosdick now to be analyzed. I've been to the morgue and, with the coroner, verified the manner of death the two victims met. Right now I'm waiting for a positive report from Cutler, who is examining the ruins in the Kimball library. That is all we can do for the present—wait."

There was a knock at the door. One of the stenographers appeared in the opening, a small rectangular package and a red card in her hands.

"A registered, first class parcel for you, Mr. Hardy," she murmured. "If you are too busy, I can sign for it."

"I'll take it, Miss Matthews," he replied, extending his hand.

He signed the receipt card, and the girl returned to the postman in the outer office. As the door closed behind her, Hardy examined the manila-wrapped package. He experienced a queer feeling as he recognized the precise, angular chirography of the address.

"It is from Professor Walker," murmured Zoe Ann in an awed voice. "I recognize his handwriting."

Hardy nodded as he opened the package. He exposed to view a bulky envelope which was marked with the simple name "John Hardy." Beneath the envelope was a pair of serviceable moccasins which showed signs of wear. A small, spherical object of white lay half embedded in the pliable leather of the uppermost slipper. It was a Longflite golf ball which had seen enough service to have removed the pearly glisten of white enamel. In black lettering upon its surface was the name "T. C. Fosdick."

Not one of them spoke as Hardy opened the envelope and unfolded the closely written pages of the letter. He spread them flat on the desk. In profound silence they read the contents together.

The letter ran:

Monday, August 24.
Seven o'clock, P.M.

Dear John Hardy:
What caprice of fate brought you back home to West Fork just when you came, God only knows. In fact, were it not for the hand of Providence, which I have

seen time after time throughout this affair, I would be tempted to say to you as I have said in the past: "This was my show. If you wanted to run one, you should have gotten a tent of your own."

For I killed Thurlowe Fosdick.

I wonder if you shudder as you read this simple statement, if your mind revolts against the unruffled serenity with which I make this admission? Do you find amazement that I can be so calm and so re-morseless, as though I had but stepped upon an in-sect? Ah, my friend, it was a venomous little serpent that I trod upon.

It is a long story, and I will spare you all but the briefest of details, which you can enlarge upon by investigation. I must hurry so that I can register this package for you at the postal sub-station in the neighborhood pharmacy. Aside from that, I have much to do within the next few hours.

Five years ago I perfected a formula for an elas-tic paint which has nearly the same expansion and contraction as iron. From your knowledge of chem-istry you can see that this discovery can revolution-ize the paint industry and save millions of dollars a year. Instead of having to paint bridges, battleships, and all metal structures every year because of flak-ing paint, my product would last four or five years. It should have been worth a fortune to me.

However, without funds or business experience I knew not what to do. I went to the president of the First National Bank for advice. At first he was skep-tical of my claims, but I was so insistent that he con-sulted Sam Kimball. With my consent the two of them decided to test out the paint in Kimball's metal furniture factory before doing anything else. If it proved a success under test conditions, a company was to be organized to manufacture my product.

To-day my paint formula is being used by Sam Kimball.

Matters drifted along for several months until I became uneasy. There were a number of meetings between the three of us at night in Fosdick's home, where we discussed plans.

They put me off with one excuse and another, until one night I delivered an ultimatum. I told them they would have to organize a company at once to put my paint on the market, or I would be forced to offer my formula for sale to paint manufacturers in the East. It was then that I made a horrible discovery. They had stolen my formula. It was patented or copyrighted in the name of Sam Kimball.

Too late I learned that I had put myself in the lion's mouth. I could not sell my own formula. I threatened suit, and they laughed at me. How was I, a poor high school professor, to fight against their wealth, when they already had possession of my discovery?

My disillusionment was complete. I became bitter and vowed revenge. This was the end of my hopes and dreams. I left the Fosdick home for the last time, so I thought. Doubtless my threats would have come to naught. I would have taken no steps after the edge of my anger had worn smooth, if another complication had not entered into the affair.

About a year after this my only sister became desperately ill. She rallied a bit, but she never got up again. She gradually went downhill, dying for the want of money to treat her case, to send her away. I could have saved her life or at least have eased her last days, had I had the money rightfully mine. I swallowed my bitterness.

I went to the two men who had robbed me and begged for enough money to care for my sister. Imagine that! Begging money from the men who owed me.

Alas! I humbled myself in vain. In place of hearts these cold brutes had nothing but money bags with tightly drawn strings.

The poor woman died while those two fiends fattened their pocketbooks on the fruit of my time and brain. I went heavily into debt during her last days; I am paying off the last debts this summer. Can you wonder that I became soured against human nature in general? Is it surprising that I contemplated murder?

Murder! It is queer how calmly I can write that ugly word, how callously I can contemplate the deed I have done and the deed I am about to do. Why? Because it is not murder; it is justice.

I began to plan revenge the day my poor sister was buried. From that day forth I steadily shaped everything to that end. I began by studying the personal habits of Fosdick and Kimball, while I cast about for a method which would leave me at liberty to laugh over my revenge. It was nothing for me to lie for hours in the shrubbery of the Kimball grounds and listen to the snarling of that family and learn their characteristics and failings.

It was nothing for me to do the same at Fosdick's home. It was nothing for me to hide out along the golf course and study the game of the banker day after day without being observed. And all the while I thought and planned the blow which should fall.

I learned every inch of the golf course and the woods and fields thereabout without ever being seen. I studied text-books on the game and watched Fosdick's style of play until I knew exactly what he did. I did this secretly, for this was to be my best alibi—my entire ignorance of golf.

What was time to me? It had ceased to exist. I matured my plans with the infinite patience of an Indian. Ah! Do you remember a discussion we once had in the classroom years ago, you and I? Wherein you objected strenuously to the idea of an amalgamation of the white man and the Indian? You did not know it then, and you are probably still unaware of the fact, but I have Indian blood in my veins. Why shouldn't I have had the patience of an Indian?

Your reconstruction of the exact manner of Fosdick's death was perfect. And your description of his vicious joy in striking a golf ball was so apt that it chilled me with horror at your insight. There is Scotch blood in your veins; you almost possess the gift of second sight.

I can add nothing to what you have said, except to remark that the cover to my little bomb was from one of Fosdick's own golf balls. I found more than one in the woods. He scattered golf balls as he never distributed seeds of kindness. I am inclosing the golf ball I took when I substituted mine. And, also, the moccasins I wore when skulking about, the footprints of which no civilized eye was sharp enough to see.

The matter of the little bottle of Permanex which I found at the eleventh hour I had to have, is easily explained. It was a simple matter to talk young Morris into bringing me a bottle for analysis and let him think it was his own idea. Thus, I was protected there. The other items I needed, and which a chemist or a high school teacher does not ask for, I procured by mail at long intervals from different cities. If you will examine the contents of my trunk here at the boarding house, you will find ample evidence, chemicals, invoices, and such like, to corroborate my statement that I, and I alone, am responsible for the death of Thurlowe Fosdick.

And this brings me to the matter of coincidence or Providence. Who would have dreamed that

Howard Wright had just had trouble with the First National Bank and that he would choose the fateful morning to play golf that I chose for the banker's death? Who could have foreseen that his footprints matched those of young Morris and William Beedle and that the latter two men would make imprints for him in the woods where I had to be in order to carry out my purpose?

Rest assured that I would never have allowed Wright to go to his death or to imprisonment for my deed. It was my intention to kill Sam Kimball while Wright was still being held in jail. I was arranging this plan Saturday on the grounds of the Kimball home at the same moment you called on me at the boarding house and left samples of soil from the golf grounds to be analyzed.

Imagine my tumult at this second evidence of the pranks of fate. I dropped my plan for awhile, deeming it best to await developments. A few days more meant nothing to me; I had already waited three years. And Sam Kimball proved his gratitude by having me fired from the high school faculty for doing that bit of work for you. Can you wonder that I laughed? Yet, you are the man who heaped coals of fire on my head by employing me at once upon your staff. Against my will, you have drawn me to your side and you have made me love you.

That interview this afternoon with Kimball and Brentwood warned me that my procrastination must end. Your agreement to quit fighting for the first time in your life and your subsequent honor in refusing to give the facts of that bribe to the *Blade* because you had accepted it, completely shook me.

Then the surprising refusal of Howard Wright to accept this sacrifice was little short of sublime. I thrilled to his nobility and courage. And, alas, when the brave spirit of Zoe Ann faltered at that moment, she turned, not to her father or to me, but to you. It was the blindness of an old bachelor which had led me to hope otherwise.

However, it was without a trace of bitterness that I observed this. My association with you three has been the best period of my life. From the bottom of my heart I thank you for showing me that man can rise above his meaner passions, that all humanity is not dross. All life is not vain, and I am happier for having known you.

And yet the irony of life! How well exemplified! In the hour that I found you, I realized that I must lose you. It was hard, hard to bid you good-by there in the office, knowing that I was bidding you good-by forever.

And yet there was no other way. You have woefully tangled my carefully laid plans, John Hardy. Do not think that I chide you for it, dear boy. It was not you; it was the hand of Fate. I realized days ago that I was lost. The coming of your detectives to investigate the past life of Fosdick meant my eventual downfall. I knew that the time was short when Cutler got onto the trail of the woman, Hilda Frieling. This simple soul saw and heard enough while she was in the Fosdick home to be able to give much information under skillful questioning.

If you can find it in your hearts to pity me, do not mourn my loss. My revenge is completed in my death. My sister is gone, I am alone in the world, there is nothing for me to live for.

I set down these facts, not as a plea for sympathy, not as a justification, but as an explanation only. There is little more for me to write.

I go from here to mail this letter and package along with two copies explaining my deed, one to the prosecuting attorney and the other to the chief of police. Then I must make a last call upon Sam Kimball in his library—and accompany him where he is going.

For the information of the detectives I will add that I am taking eight ounces of nitroglycerin concealed within a Bible. I shall place it conveniently on the library table which Kimball delights in striking with his fist. Then I shall bring up the past to him and arouse his anger. We shall sit close together. And when he strikes I will see that he smites this Bible.

At last he will give vent to his anger once too often, he will strike a symbolic blow with his hard fist one time too many. A flash—a heavy detonation—a billow of fumes and smoke—and Sam Kimball will have fleeced his last victim.

And what more fitting end for this fiend than that he should bring about his own death by striking the Holy Scriptures? What could be more just than for this hard, soulless blasphemer who has prated about religion and stood upon the Bible while he perpetrated some outrage, to die by the Bible?

It is queer, John Hardy, how the threads of our lives are interwoven. As I write down the method of my crime, if crime it be, I again see the hand of God in our destinies. It was that foolhardy exploit of yours when you manufactured a bit of nitroglycerin and blew up the wall of the school laboratory that came back to me and gave me the idea for the destruction of my enemies.

Try to think of me as a friend, and entreat Zoe Ann not to remember me too harshly. And if she would do something for this old man, ask her to pray for me. God grant that I may be atoning in part to you and to West Fork, by what I am about to do, for the pain and suffering I have unintentionally caused.

Farewell, my friend, and God bless you.

Thomas Walker.

CHAPTER XXVIII
THE KEY TO THE CITY

LATE SEPTEMBER! The upsetting of autumn's paint pot. The vast army of nature's growing things were beginning to rally to the colors, lining up for the inspection of the recruiting sergeant Jack Frost. The mornings were beginning to carry a tang and the sale of meats began to increase. Anxious troops of school children awaited the first kiss of frost to lend the finishing touch to ripening persimmons. It was the season of the year for nutting parties and chicken roasts.

The nights were becoming clear and the stars cold. The air became sharper and radio improved. Picture shows, card parties, and dancing began to take on a charm wholly lacking during the hot weather. Sitting in the moonlight in porch swings had not lost its appeal, but the chilliness of fall began to make wraps comfortable to girlish shoulders and a woolly sweater something to snuggle deliciously into—or against.

The small fire in the Wright drawing-room grate crackled a merry song in the evenings now. It was cheery, pleasant. After a good hot dinner such as only Zoe Ann knew how to superintend and Margaret to cook, the fireplace was an irresistible attraction. A comfortable armchair and the luxury of stretching one's legs toward the blaze! To relax with the consciousness of a good day's work done!

To-night there were three easy-chairs facing the fire, three pairs of legs stretched toward the blaze, and from three cigars three delicate spirals of smoke were ascending into the darkness above the mellow light of the floor lamp and the glowing coals.

Said Presley: "I am almost at a loss for news for the *Blade*, now that our sensational campaign against capitalists and politicians has run its course."

He flicked the ash from his cigar and went on lazily: "I suppose I'll have to settle to the humdrum existence of a country editor."

"You'd better not let John Hardy hear you insinuate that this is a country town," drawled Barbington. "If you want something new, why don't you go talk with Whalen, the new secretary of the Chamber of Commerce? He can give you a lot of ideas on civic improvement to take the place of the lurid stuff you've been running. You'll have everybody in West Fork sleeping uneasily, if you don't change your tactics."

"We've changed this week," said Presley, closing his eyes contentedly and smiling his nervous little smile. "Mayor Clinton resigned his office this week. And Major Sims is retiring from the thankless job of saving the politics of the town. He is going into voluntary retirement back on his farm."

"So?" said Wright, raising his eyebrows. "I hadn't heard that. I've been so busy with our enterprises. And then, so much is happening now that I can't keep up with it. I suppose you know that the Kimball heirs have approached John, with the idea of closing out their interests to him as soon as the estate is straightened out? We're going to deal with them. Yes, they want to move away from West Fork."

Silence fell for a space, while the three men gazed into the flames and the three spirals of cigar smoke resumed their simultaneous journey ceilingward.

"What happened to Beedle's affairs?" inquired Presley at length.

"Beedle?" responded Wright. "Oh, John helped him get straightened out. You never saw a more grateful man."

"There's the doorbell," remarked Barbington regretfully. "Is there any one to answer it? Where's Hardy and Zoe Ann?"

A maid answered the door and the sounds of several men entering the hall floated into the big living room which did duty as a reception chamber also. Reluctantly the three men arose and

turned to greet William Beedle and two other men whom they recognized as city commissioners.

"Good evening, gentlemen," smiled Beedle cordially, as he surrendered his light topcoat to the maid. "Er— where is Mr. Hardy
this evening? We have called to see him in particular."

"He and Miss Wright went out together," replied Presley. "He'll
be back shortly."

"Be seated, gentlemen," offered the host cordially. "Join our
circle here at the fire. Cigars on the table in that humidor."

The three visitors seated themselves, accepting the further
invitation concerning the tobacco. Conversation was general for a
few moments. Then:

"John Hardy has done more for this town than any other man
who ever lived here," declared Beedle. "Personally, he has befriended me as no man ever has."

A chorus of assents.

"And he's rejuvenated the city in the face of one hundred per
cent opposition," went on Beedle firmly. "Don't you think it is about
time for the city of West Fork to show its appreciation?"

"It will," remarked Presley.

"In what way do you mean?" demanded Barbington, mildly surprised.

"I mean that Mayor Clinton has resigned his office this week.
Mr. Maledon and Mr. Bruton here, the commissioners, have ap-
pointed me chairman of a committee composed of themselves to
ask John Hardy to accept the office of mayor of West Fork. An election will unanimously confirm their choice. In brief, we wish to
give the key to the city to John Hardy, as well as offer him the
highest honor within our power. Do you think he will accept?"

Howard Wright had arisen and was looking out the window
across the dead flower garden. Now he chuckled.

"Come here," he said without turning his head. The others clustered about him and followed his pointing finger.

On a stone bench in the center of a sward of swiftly turning grass
sat John Hardy and Zoe Ann very close together in the moonlight.

Hardy was in his shirt sleeves, his sweater wrapped about the shoulders of his companion. And as the men at the window watched, he proceeded to embrace his sweater tenderly.

"Bruton," chuckled Howard Wright, "you and Maledon had better reconsider your offer. You'll have West Fork like Texas and Wyoming. I can foresee petticoat rule in this town."

Unaware of their audience, oblivious to the presence of any other living soul on the same planet with them, John and Zoe Ann walked slowly about the dead garden, his arm around her waist. The rustle of drying leaves, the rattle of dried pods which had fulfilled the mission of the plant's life by coming to the fruition of seeds for renewed life the following spring, the cooling kiss of the night wind, all impressed one with thoughtful solemnity.

"Autumn," murmured Zoe Ann. "The saddest and yet the most beautiful time of the year. I love it, don't you, John?"

"I love all the seasons," John replied simply. "All weather is good weather to me. Autumn is the most beautiful, sweetheart. And its wonderful coloring reminds me of you."

She smiled up at him wistfully.

"I can't forget poor Professor Walker," she said. "Somehow, I can't think of him as something to be abhorred."

"Why should you? That letter threw light upon his very soul. It is queer how close we can live to our neighbor, see him every day, laugh and talk with him, study him, and yet how little we know about the real soul that inhabits the body we see. If I had only known! If Walker had only told me of his troubles, I'd have fought for his rights and we'd have won for him in the end."

"But he couldn't tell you, dearest. Don't you remember that he had already taken an irretrievable step in the death of Mr. Fosdick before you came home?"

"I shall never forget him," said Hardy. "I have learned something about life from him. I understand more. I—I think I shall have more tolerance for other people in the future. I shall understand more of their weaknesses—their strength. And to think that he, too, loved you, Zoe Ann. I—I understand much."

"That is what love is, don't you think?" she whispered. "It isn't just the thrill of attraction. It's the knowledge of character and the joy of loving it for its weakness and glorying in its strength."

They halted and turned to face each other. Zoe Ann raised her face to his under the moonlight.

"Aren't you cold without your coat, dear?" she asked affectionately.

"Not when I'm in your heart," he answered as he kissed her.

What cared they for the honor awaiting them at the hands of West Fork? What cared they for the key to a mere city? They had found the key to happiness and understanding.

COACHWHIP PUBLICATIONS

COACHWHIPBOOKS.COM

BLOOD ON HER SHOE

MEDORA FIELD

ISBN 978-1-61646-275-8

COACHWHIP PUBLICATIONS
COACHWHIPBOOKS.COM

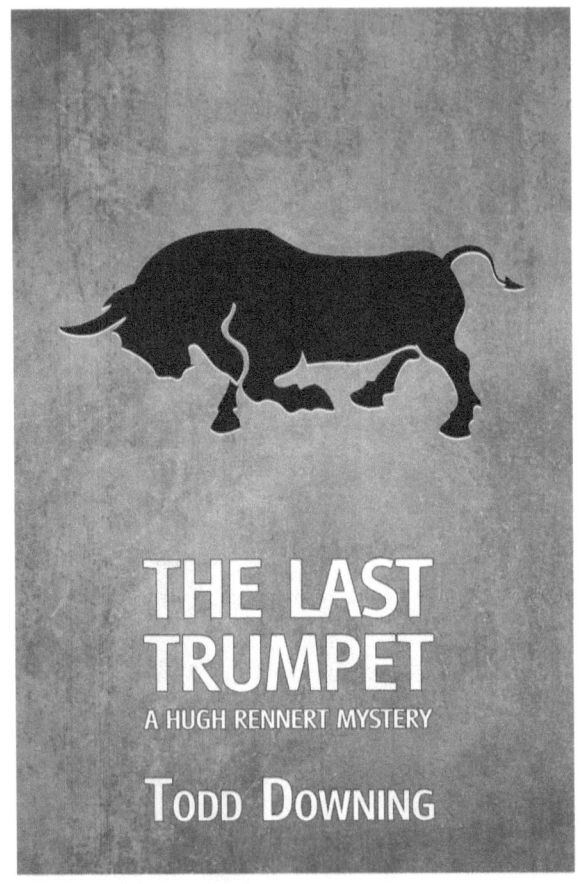

THE LAST
TRUMPET
A HUGH RENNERT MYSTERY

TODD DOWNING

ISBN 978-1-61646-152-2

THE QUINNY HITE
MYSTERIES
CHINESE RED · HERE LIES THE BODY

RICHARD BURKE

ISBN 978-1-61646-247-5

COACHWHIP PUBLICATIONS

COACHWHIPBOOKS.COM

THE MUMMY
CASE MYSTERY

DERMOT
MORRAH

ISBN 978-1-61646-250-5

THE
MUSEUM
MURDER

JOHN T. McINTYRE

ISBN 978-1-61646-252-9

COACHWHIP PUBLICATIONS

COACHWHIPBOOKS.COM

THE
DEATH
OF A
CELEBRITY

HULBERT
FOOTNER

AN AMOS LEE MAPPIN MYSTERY

ISBN 978-1-61646-263-5

COACHWHIP PUBLICATIONS

COACHWHIPBOOKS.COM

ISBN 978-1-61646-253-6